Crown of Smoke and Starlight

COURTS OF AETHERIA

G.K. DEROSA

Print ISBN: 9798271010859

Cover Designer: Seventhstar Art
Interior Art: Samaiya Art

Published in 2025 by Mystic Rose Press
Palm Beach, Florida
www.gkderosa.com

 Formatted with Vellum

To all the dedicated Reign fans, this one's for you...
~ GK

CROWN OF SMOKE AND STARLIGHT

Contents

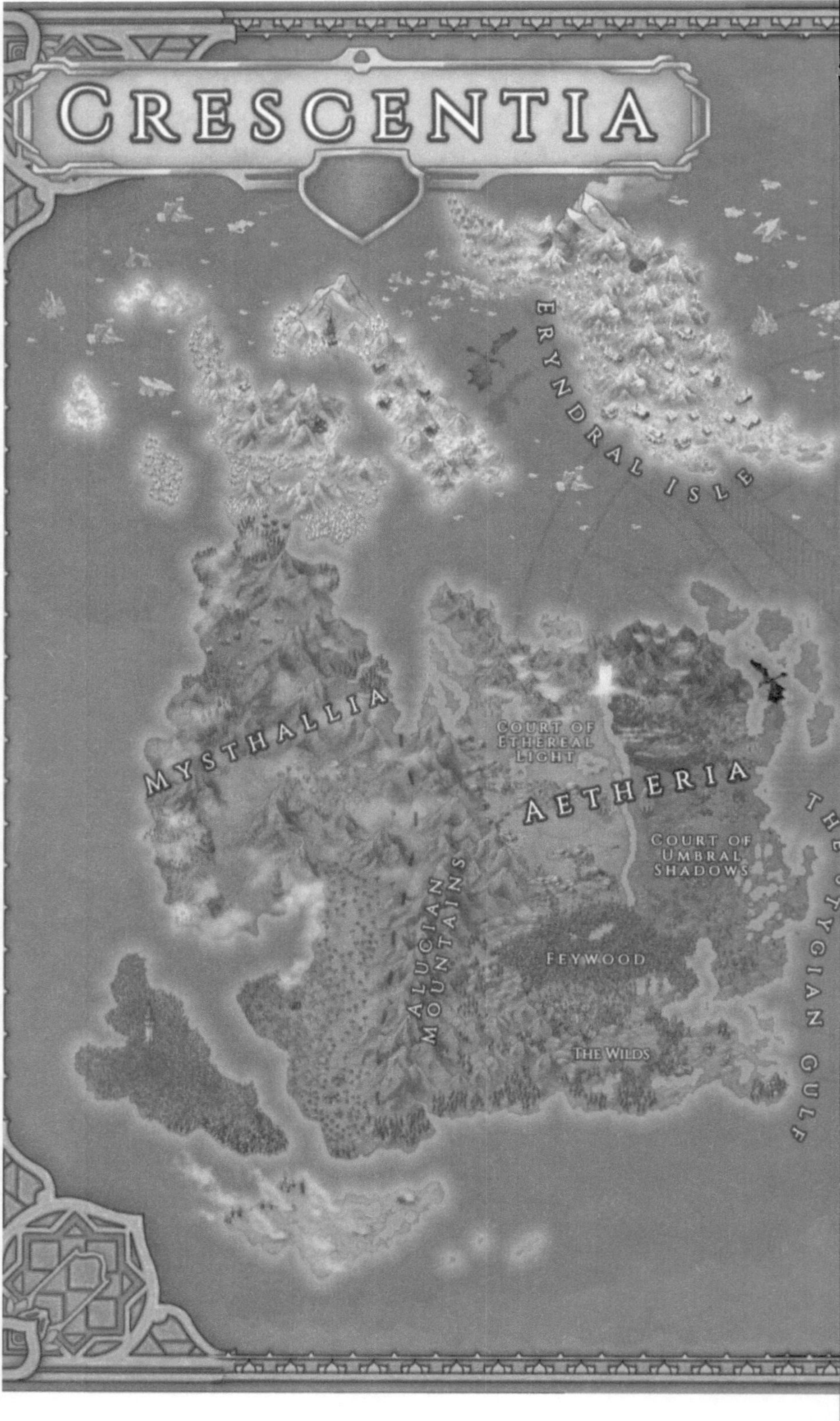

CRESCENTIA
ERYNDRAL ISLE
MYSTHALLIA
COURT OF ETHEREAL LIGHT
AETHERIA
COURT OF UMBRAL SHADOWS
ALUCIAN MOUNTAINS
FEYWOOD
THE WILDS
THE STYGIAN GULF

LUNARIS
ASHENWOLD FOREST
VESPERIS

Conservatory of Luce
Hall of Ether
Hall of Elysia
Hall of Rais
Hall of Luminesence
Hall of Enlightenment
Hall of Glory
Hall of Luce
Gymnasium & Training Field
CONSERVATORY OF LUCE
FORGED IN LIGHT
TEMPERED IN TRUTH

Chapter One

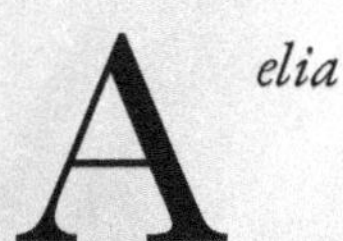

The scent of blood clung to the wind like a second skin. Metallic. Familiar. It curled beneath my nose as I hovered above the battlefield, brilliant luminescent wings streaked in shadows spread across my shoulders. The weight of my power pressed down on the broken world below.

They waited for me. All of them.

The Light Fae with their shining blades and pristine alabaster uniforms. The Shadow Court with their swirling *nox* and umbral weapons. Even the Night Court poised behind me, their dark armor glinting beneath a sunless sky, bristled with anticipation.

But none of them mattered.

Because *he* had come.

Reign.

His name swirled through my mind like smoke. It was dangerous, intoxicating, half-remembered. A tug echoed low in my chest, aching and foreign, as if some long-lost part of me stirred.

But I buried it beneath the roar of power coursing through me. *Zar* slithered across my skin like venom. *Nox* simmered beneath the surface. *Rais* burned behind my ribs. A storm of gods-given force waiting to be unleashed.

The child of twilight. *Infantum od twilit.*

The Night Fae chanted my name, the ominous hisses growing in strength with each iteration. Half the army sat astride creatures of smoke and shadows, the very beasts nightmares were made of.

I didn't need a name. I didn't need memories.

I was power. And I belonged to the gods themselves.

"Strike when I say." Helroth's voice slithered across my ear, though his lips never moved. He was in my head, permanently embedded. There was no getting him out...even if I'd wanted to. The pull of his command thrummed through my veins like tethered chains, forged in *zar* and sealed with the blood vow I hadn't meant to take.

By blood and night, you are bound. Swear now, child of twilight, to bring down the Courts of Light and Shadow, until none but Night remains to rule the realm. By the will of the Night King, this vow shall hold.

But I *had* taken it.

And now, my grandsire owned me.

I touched down, wings slicing the air in a gust of searing light and obsidian flame. Across the scorched field, Reign dismounted in one smooth motion, Phantom screeching her fury into the heavens behind him. His presence struck me like a blade, sharp but grounding. Gods, even at this distance, he smelled like the memory of something I'd lost.

I blinked, and he'd already devoured the ground between us.

He took another step toward me. "Aelia," he whispered, something akin to concern with a mixture of fear—of me, or for me, I couldn't be sure—crossing his handsome face.

His voice. *That voice.* It cracked something open.

My name on his tongue ignited something deep inside me. Something ancient. Something I wasn't allowed to remember.

But in that moment, I desperately wanted to.

Something strong and more powerful than the blood vow throbbed violently between us, wild and frantic like a heart torn in two. Pain lanced behind my eyes, sharp enough to splinter bone. I staggered a step from the memory trying to claw its way free. I could feel his pain. His love. His certainty. It tangled across my insides, bloating my hollow chest. And it terrified me. Because I knew, somewhere buried beneath the cage Helroth had built around me, I once felt the same.

But right now, all I felt was power and the restrictive chains of the blood vow. *Destroy them. Ruin them all. Reclaim your kingdom.*

I raised my hand.

A heady mix of *zar* and *nox* bled through my fingertips. Then a blade of pure void erupted from my palm, blacker than night and pulsing with ruin.

Reign didn't flinch. His eyes, steady and unyielding remained locked to mine.

"You'll have to kill me," he said, lifting his sword in defense, not aggression. "Because I'm not leaving without you."

My heart stuttered.

That voice inside me, the one I'd silenced, the one Helroth had attempted to bury, rose like a scream. He's yours. *He's mine. Reign.*

He smelled like amber and rain-washed obsidian. My body, not as easily dominated, remembered what my mind could not— the calloused warmth of his palm, the rasp of his voice whispering my name in the dark.

A bond... the cuorem, I suddenly realized, flared, that living, breathing sentient thing racing between us. The symbol on my chest ignited; not the mystical engraving Raysa had carved into me, but rather the one that made me feel whole. The mate mark. Images flashed across my mind in a chaotic loop.

The luminescent cave.

The feel of Reign's body entangled with mine.

Whispered words.

Heated kisses.

But Helroth was already there, not merely a voice in my head this time. Before I could fully process those memories, his presence sliced through the bond, poisoning it. "Finish this, princess," he ordered, moving beside me, crimson eyes burning into mine.

I couldn't stop.

A dark, violent part of me didn't want to.

And yet, as my blade came down—

The world shattered. Time fractured. The air burned.

The cuorem bond flared so violently it seared black. Not gold. Not silver. Not the shimmering strands I recognized.

Black.

And in that final heartbeat, as I held my blade inches from Reign's throat, a floodgate of memories unleashed.

Laughter in a moonlit cave. Lips brushing mine beneath a sky full of stars. His voice, hoarse and reverent, whispering *cuoré* against my skin. A promise sealed in light and shadow. It all came back with a force that buckled my knees.

Reign. My love. My cuoré.

I'd made a vow to him too.

One I never intended to break.

By starlight and storm, ether and flames, I vow myself to you, Reign. I choose you—heart, body and soul. In every breath I take, in every future I behold, I carry your name within me. You are my anchor in the chaos, my peace in the storm. I bind my soul to yours, not because I must, but because I cannot imagine a world without you.

A scream tore from my mouth, ripped from the deepest recesses of my soul.

"Aelia," Reign whispered, the depth of emotion in that one word enough to sever Helroth's hold for an instant. The ghost of a smile kissed his lips as if he'd felt the breakthrough.

And it was all I needed.

"I'm so sorry," I murmured in return.

Time ticked forward once again, and swinging the umbral blade around, I pressed it to my grandsire's throat, instead. Fury pulsed through my veins as the fog of his control lifted. The sea of Night Fae soldiers tensed behind Helroth, weapons at the ready. Reign now stood at my side, a torrent of *nox* flooding the air and a whirlwind of shadows poised to strike. They clung to the air like wraiths, hissing and writhing over Reign's head, tendrils of pure night and raw power.

Helroth held up a dismissive hand, calling off his forces. Those crimson orbs of pure darkness pulsed with rage, then a trickle of fear as they bounced between Reign's ravenous minions and me.

"What are you doing?" he snarled as I pressed the blade closer.

For the first time, the great Night King flinched. Just barely, but I saw it. Felt it. The flicker of unease behind his crimson stare. He hadn't expected the bond to survive. He hadn't counted on love being stronger than his cursed illusions or blood vows.

"Ending a war," I hissed.

His Adam's apple bobbed, brushing the blade of pure void. A thin line of dark crimson bubbled up as the ethereal weapon split his skin with the movement. A feral smile pursed his lips. "Oh, princess, this is but a mere battle. The war for Aetheria has just begun."

At that, a blanket of night dropped across the field, the toxic odor of *zar* slithering over my skin. Helroth's hand shot out, thick fingers curling around my arm in a punishing grip. The sharp slice of his nails across my skin burned like hellfire, but the scream died in my throat.

Because I recognized the scent, and I knew what came next. The dizzying pull of the pocket realm skimmed over me, and panic surged from my core.

No. Not again. I'd never let him have me again.

The scene blurred around me, the Light and Shadow Fae soldiers a muted tangle of *nox* and *rais*. I fought the incessant tug with everything I had, digging the heels of my boots into the earth.

"Reign!"

A shadow of pure night streaked across my vision, and the iron grip around my arm fell away. Something hit the ground with a lifeless thud.

Then Helroth and the army of Night vanished.

And I was suddenly alone in the middle of the battlefield with my heart lodged up my throat, and my grandsire's severed arm at my feet. I squeezed my eyes closed to erase the grisly sight.

Except, no, I was not alone.

The steady thrum of the cuorem reminded me I would never truly be alone again.

"I've got you, starlight." That deep, warm voice, the one that had starred in my dreams for months drove away the turmoil in my mind. Strong arms curled around my trembling form, drawing me into a familiar, unrelenting hold. Piercing midnight orbs locked onto mine, and a familiar touch caressed my cheek. "I swore to you that no one would ever take you away from me again, and it is a vow I intend to keep for as long as I draw breath."

"You came for me," I whispered, raw emotion tightening my throat.

"I will *always* come for you. I'd tear through realms to reach you, Aelia. There's no force in existence that could ever keep me from your side. Ever again."

But even wrapped in Reign's arms and silky shadows, with his heartbeat thudding against mine, Helroth's final words beat out a frantic rhythm in my mind.

The war for Aetheria has just begun.

Chapter Two

R *eign*

The war still thundered around us long after Helroth and the Night Fae vanished, but I couldn't bring myself to let go of her. Not yet. Not when the echo of almost losing her still pulsed beneath my skin like a second heartbeat. And still, a part of me knew it was up to us to stop the pointless fighting. But when confronted with the safety of nameless, faceless Fae and my *cuoré*, there was no question. I would choose her a thousand times over. Eventually, I would be forced to release her and put an end to this, but I simply wasn't capable yet.

My shadows whirled in a maddening tempest, a cloud of unrelenting midnight encircling us as I held her to me. They'd always been protective of Aelia, but now that the bond had been completed, they clung to her like they knew she was the only thing keeping me whole.

Gods, how was it possible that Helroth had dug his claws so deeply into her mind again? Even now, traces of his voice clung to her like smoke. I could feel him through our bond. What if the cuorem wasn't strong enough? What if he could reach for her again? Breaking his hold over her had been nearly impossible. Unease settled low in my core, deep and unrelenting.

But I couldn't focus on that right now. All that mattered was that Aelia was safe and in my arms.

But for how long?

The ominous thought sent ice surging through my veins. Smothering the fear, if only to keep it from bleeding through the cuorem, I called on the embers of *nox*, then the slick, oily *zar* rushing through our bond. No one would take her from me again. I would ravage the entire continent of Crescentia until I found the Night King and ripped out his cold, dark heart. Only then would Aelia be truly safe, freed from his mental hold.

We have to put a stop to this. Aelia's voice flooded my mind, drawing me from the grisly musings. The sound of it alone eased the turmoil, smothering my scowl.

So, you do still remember how to communicate through our mental link...

I never forgot. Helroth only blocked it...somehow.

And that was exactly what had me so worried. How in all the realms could he overpower the most sacred gods-blessed bond? In theory, nothing should be stronger than the *cuorem*. I had secretly hoped that completing it would somehow overcome the blood vow, but it appeared I was mistaken. Still, there had to be another way. Perhaps, it was time to send Gideon back to research the ancient tomes of the Arcanum library.

Aelia startled in my arms, the spasm sending a jolt of fear straight to my heart. "Oh, gods, Sol! Where is he?"

"He's safe, resting. Phantom is with him. She succeeded in dragging him off the battlefield while we dealt with Helroth."

"Oh, thank the stars. What did those fiends of smoke do to him? I can't remember any of it..."

"Only managed to knock him out. Luckily, he's a hard-headed beast."

"I need to see him."

"We will as soon as we deal with this." I scanned the horizon of the Wilds, the battling Light and Shadow Fae still locked in a pointless clash.

Aelia's chin tipped up, blazing silver-blue eyes meeting mine. "We have to stop them."

"Any idea how, princess?"

Her head dipped, radiant wings extending across her shoulder blades as she stepped free of my hold. It took everything I had to fight the overwhelming urge to pull her back to me, scoop her into my arms and fly her far away from here.

Instead, I watched as she rose like a flame into the smoke-choked sky, her wings unfurling in a blaze of light and shadow. Gods, she was radiant. My chest clenched at the sight of her, hovering above the carnage, a living embodiment of all the powers of the gods in a world tilting toward ruin.

She burned with starlight and conviction, and for one fleeting moment, I forgot how close I'd come to losing her. So lost was I in the gloriousness of...her. But gods help me, what would happen if the next time, I wasn't fast enough?

Shoving the errant thought to the dark recesses of my mind, I focused on her, on this pivotal moment.

The battlefield below her was pure chaos, Light Fae slashing with their glowing blades, Shadow Fae striking with ribbons of *nox*, both sides so blinded by rage they didn't understand the real war had yet to begin.

"Stop!" Her voice cracked like lightning across the field, and the power laced in it brought everything to a standstill. Power shimmered in the air. Heads turned. Weapons faltered mid-swing.

"This is madness," she shouted, her voice fierce and raw. "Can't you *see*? Our true enemies, the Night Court, have fled. Helroth has vanished with his army, and we're still spilling blood as if it means something!"

I felt it then, that flicker in our bond, the fire behind her words. The thrall pulsing through her voice wasn't just power. It was purpose. It was truth.

She turned in the air, slowly, meeting their stares, the Royal Guardians from the Light and the Umbral Guard born of Shadow who had once called her a weak little Kin or an enemy or worse.

"The Night Fae aren't just shadows of myth. They are real. And they are coming for *all of us*. For years, we've been blinded by the lies spouted by our kings in a vain effort to keep us 'safe'. But that time has passed."

A ripple spread through the crowd. I could see it, feel it, the doubt starting to take root.

"Helroth wants to burn the realms to ash. He doesn't care about your bloodlines, your grudges, or your ancient pride. Light and Shadow mean nothing to him. He means to unmake the balance of this world, and he will succeed if we keep doing his work for him."

She glowed brighter with every word, her wings flaring wider, casting that luminescent glow across both Courts. She wasn't just speaking to them, she was becoming something *more*. Someone they could follow.

"We have been divided for too long. Taught to hate, taught to fear. But we are all one Aetheria, and we must fight together if we wish to survive."

I swallowed hard, the pride swelling in my throat almost unbearable.

"I've felt what the Night King can do," she continued. "I've heard his voice inside my mind. And I swear to you now, if we don't stand together, none of us will survive what comes next."

Her voice dropped, soft but unshakable. "But if we do, if we *unite*, if we fight not as separate Courts, but as one realm, then I *know* we can win."

Then, slowly, she descended, and I was moving toward her before I'd even made the conscious decision to do so.

She landed between the two armies, her wings folding behind

her like a divine shield. I stood only a few yards away, my shadows coiled around me, desperate to reach her. But this was her moment, not mine.

The silence that followed was deafening.

Then, like the stars themselves taking a breath, both umbral and luminescent blades were lowered. *Nox* and *rais* faded. I watched as the impossible happened. And I realized Aelia hadn't just stopped the futile battle today, she had begun something far greater.

As the bands of muttering Light and Shadow Fae warriors began to disperse, gazes cast at each other suspiciously even as they retreated, I moved to Aelia's side. Today was only the beginning. It would take time and a concerted effort from both Elian and Tenebris to truly come together to defeat Helroth and his forces.

But the change had started here, with her, my *cuoré*.

"You were incredible," I murmured as I pressed a kiss to her temple. "A true born leader."

A rueful grin curled the corners of her mouth. "I suppose all that royal blood has to count for something." She eyed the field of retreating soldiers, a wary expression shadowing the temporary moment of triumph. "Now what do we do? After we find Sol, of course."

"Of course." I paused, carefully considering my response. "Now, we go home, starlight. And tomorrow, we will fight again."

"Which is where exactly? I still don't belong anywhere, Reign."

Tendrils of shadow curled around her waist, drawing her flush against me. Framing her face with my hands, I dropped my forehead to hers. "That's not true. You belong with me. And our home is wherever we are together."

She drew in a breath, and a slow smile crept across the grim line of her lips. "How did I get so lucky that the gods chose you as my mate?"

"We both must have been *very* good in a previous life."

A warm chuckle spilled from her lips, and the sound was like a balm to my weary soul. Coming so close to losing her again had torn another fissure across my heart. I wasn't sure how many more I could withstand.

"Are you ready to test out those new luminescent wings, or does my princess wish to be carried to rendezvous with Phantom?"

"From the battlefield?" she retorted. "What sort of a sorry picture would that paint?"

"Fair enough."

Those radiant appendages unfolded across her back, the brilliant spectacle difficult to look away from despite the blinding light. She was a goddess incarnate, pure *rais, nox* and *zar*. My boots remained rooted to the earth, my head tipped back reveling in her splendor for a long moment.

"Well, are you coming or not?"

Before I could respond, her eyes glazed over, and I could only assume she was communicating with her skyrider—or that was my hope. I had to force away the momentary panic I felt that it could be Helroth infiltrating her mind again.

"Sol's awake!" Her eyes brightened, the vivid blue like a cloudless sky. "He's at Shadowmere, and Phantom is on her way to retrieve us."

"Wonderful."

There was a certain Night Fae I needed to have words with at Duskridge Manor. Then, I would take Aelia far away from that gloomy isle and her demon trainer. The only person who would be in charge of my *cuoré's* instruction from now on would be me.

Dark shadows spilled across my shoulders, morphing into powerful wings, and I thrust high into the sky to meet Aelia and rendezvous with Phantom. As we soared over the scorched battlefield needlessly littered with bodies of both Light and Shadow Fae, dread coiled in my gut like a prophecy waiting to be fulfilled.

Chapter Three

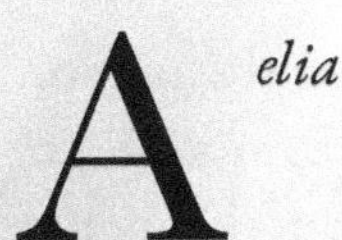

A*elia*

The chill of the approaching isle of Shadowmere clawed through my skin like icy fingertips, a cruel echo of the darkness I'd only just escaped. A tremor raced up my spine at the memories or lack thereof. For a terrible moment, I'd been gone, torn out of the warm bed I'd shared with Reign and lost in the thrall of Helroth's control. Sol had been attacked by the Night's beasts of smoke, and I hadn't been the wiser. I'd nearly killed Reign...

As the familiar turrets of Duskridge Manor coalesced along the cliffs, my skin already mourned Raysa's golden touch to warm my icy bones beneath the gloom.

Soon, princess. We'll have you back at the Conservatory before long. Reign's deep voice zipped through our bond and excitement lit up my insides.

Curling my arms tighter around his waist as we zipped through the night aboard Phantom, my brows knitted. *Luce? We'll be returning to the academy? But how?*

Have you forgotten the deal I struck with King Elian? His vow and his protection extend to the campus.

But that means all the students will discover who I really am...

What if they looked at me and only saw the monster Helroth made me? And worse, if we accepted my uncle's protection, Reign would be forced to hand over his father to the Light King.

Only if you want them to. You can tell your fellow classmates as little or as much as you choose. Other than your closest friends, only Elian and Draven will be privy to the whole truth.

And yet, we still don't know if we can trust either, especially my uncle.

No, we do not. Reign's sigh reached all the way down to my core.

By the time Phantom began the descent toward the manor, our reinforcements had arrived. The sight of Rue, Symon, Ruhl and Gideon, along with Aidan, descending the steps of the manor had unexpected tears burning my eyes as I slid down her leg even before Reign moved.

But none had my heart clenching more than the sight of my dragon. Sol. He stood at the foot of the cliffs, golden scales gleaming like a beacon in the endless black.

Sol, you're all right! I raced toward him, wrapping my arms around his thick front leg.

Of course, I am. Did you truly believe one of those creatures of smoke could subdue me for long?

When it came to the Night Fae, I didn't know what to believe.

I'd gotten so close to losing all of them again because of my twisted grandsire.

Never happening again. Sol's rumbling voice reverberated through my mind. *We will never let Helroth or those Night Fae bastards have you. I swear to it, little Kin.*

Thanks, Sol. As much as I knew he meant it, there were forces that were even beyond my dragon's control. And my *cuoré's.* Blinking back the tears, I trailed Reign's form as he leapt off Phantom's back and landed beside me, only a yard away from where our friends and family awaited.

Their wary glances told me everything. They knew about Helroth's latest hijacking of my fragile mind. And none of them knew how to look at me.

Phantom and I will retreat to the caves along the Darkmania Falls, unless you need me. Sol's voice momentarily distracted me from my friends' curious gazes.

No, go rest. I'll let you know what our next move is. As soon as we figured it out.

His massive wings unfolded, the golden scales shimmering beneath the full moon as he thrust high into the pitch night sky. Growling her annoyance—at him or having to leave, I wasn't sure —Phantom shot up after him, her sleek obsidian scales devouring the moonlight. The sharp contrast of light and shadow lit up the darkness as the pair disappeared into the horizon.

Is everything okay between those two? I tossed the question to my *cuoré* as he moved into step beside me.

As okay as it can be for now. His warm hand captured mine, our fingers entwining as we walked toward the eagerly awaiting gathered crowd.

Do you think they'll complete the dragon mate bond again?

I certainly hope so. Phantom has been impossible lately.

A rueful smile curled my lips as I jabbed my elbow into his side when we reached my family. "An infuriating mate will do that to you."

"Eek, I still can't believe you two are mated!" Rue's shriek of happiness as she hurtled toward us momentarily distracted me from the dire realities of our current situation. Her arms swung around both Reign and me—a nearly impossible feat considering her petite size, but somehow, she managed it. "Thank Raysa you completed the bond before... well, Helroth."

Ruhl strode forward, arms pressed tightly across his chest. "Or maybe if they hadn't completed it and we'd sought an alternative option, it never would have happened at all."

"And what was that alternative, brother?" Reign's voice dropped to a lethal rumble, his shadows plummeting the court-yard into a more oppressive night. "Her marrying *you*?"

His cheeks flamed, the tendon in his jaw flaring.

"Enough," I hissed, slapping my hand across my *cuoré's* chest. His shadows relented, and moonlight bathed the glistening stone yard once more.

You won. I'm yours. I threw the thoughts down our bond. *There's no need to rub Ruhl's nose in it.*

He started it.

Whirling on Reign, I shot him a dramatic eyeroll. *Gods, how old are you?*

Lips twisting, he huffed out a frustrated sigh. "We aren't here to argue." His dark gaze raked over our gathered friends. "Where is Kaelith?"

"I had him sequestered per your request," Aidan replied. For the first time since my return, I really looked at my adoptive father. Dark circles lined his eyes, and utter exhaustion was carved into his features. The past few months had really taken a toll on him. I longed to reach for his hand, to assure him that we would all emerge from this unscathed. But after all the things Helroth had forced me to become in the past months, a liar wouldn't be one of them.

But that didn't mean I couldn't indulge in a quick hug with the man who'd raised me as his own.

"Good," Reign replied, forcing me to release Aidan and return to the conversation at hand. "I will get the truth out of that Demon Fae if I have to carve it out with my shadows."

"You truly believe he played a part in helping Helroth infil-trate my mind?" The question popped out before I could stop it. Despite knowing full well that Kae served my grandsire, the idea of his betrayal cut deeper than I'd imagined. In the months spent with my jailor-turned-trainer, I hated to admit it, but I'd grown almost fond of the bad-tempered Night Fae.

And a part of me hoped he hadn't been responsible for the

lives I stole. The ones in which Helroth had forced my hand. Guilt ravaged my insides as a carousel of gruesome images flooded my mind. I still had yet to face the terrible truth that my grandsire had forced me to cut down dozens of Fae in battle. It didn't matter that it hadn't been my choice, I'd still committed the acts. Blinking quickly, I dismissed the reel of grisly corpses to deal with another day.

"I don't know if he did or not, Aelia, but I will find out." Reign pressed a quick kiss to my forehead before striding toward the entrance to the manor.

Ruhl quickly trailed after him. "I will accompany you to ensure Kaelith survives the inquisition. After all, he will be no good to us dead."

Reign spun at his brother, coils of frenzied shadows slithering across his form. "Are you saying I won't be able to control myself?"

"Yes, that's exactly what I'm saying." He lifted his hand to the whirlwind of dark wraiths. "You haven't even seen him yet and look at you."

"I'm afraid Ruhl might be right," Gideon interjected, slipping between the princes, a move he seemed to have mastered over the years. "Perhaps, I should go as well, so that the *two of you* don't kill each other along the way."

"Oh, for Fae's sake," I grumbled. Why did I ever believe that once Reign and I were mated things would be simpler?

As soon as the Shadow Fae contingency was gone, Symon zipped past Rue and moved beside me, curling an arm around my shoulders. "And while the boys are doing that, we can have a catch-up session."

Rue's head bounced up and down. "Yes, please! I'm afraid we'll never get the chance again with all this talk of war on the horizon."

"I'm afraid it isn't just talk." Aidan's lips puckered, his entire expression souring as he regarded us. "We appear to be walking a dagger's edge, only moments from plunging to our doom."

"Then we definitely deserve a girls' night." Rue smirked up at me, not letting my adopted-father's words dampen her mood. "You know, before we all die."

I couldn't help the completely inappropriate grin from settling across my lips.

"A girls' night? How rude!" Sy whined.

Tucking my head into the crook of his neck, I tugged him closer. "Oh, stop it, Sy, you know you're one of the girls."

"Alas," he groaned, lips pulling into a pout. "I'm doomed to spend my entire existence in the dreaded Fae friend zone." His hand snaked out, reaching for my ear. "But do you know what would make me feel slightly better?"

"Give it a rest, Sy." Rue swatted his hand away like a pesky insect. "You'll have to find a new Kin's ear to fondle. Our Aelia has the sharp, deadly points of a princess."

And I'd never felt it to be more true than in that moment.

I would allow myself this moment of reprieve, the light-hearted banter with my friends, but tomorrow, the battle would begin, and I would never again be Aelia, the lowly Kin. I would be reborn as Princess Aelia of Ether.

Still, a dark, ominous voice in the darkest depths of my mind within the shadowed corners I preferred to avoid, hissed its objections. The part that craved the fury of battle, the cries of the weak, the blood of enemies spilled wondered if I was born to be Princess Aelia of Inferna instead.

And though I smiled and laughed, that dark part of me, buried deep where no one could see, feared that the throne that awaited me wasn't made of gold at all but rather bone and shadow.

Chapter Four

R*eign*

The pungent odor of trapped salty air infiltrated my nostrils as I descended into the murky depths of Duskridge Manor with Ruhl and Gideon trailing behind me like overbearing shadows. As if my own weren't enough to contain. It had been fortuitous that Gideon's grandmother's home had been designed with an underground level, a perfect dungeon of sorts.

The slap of our rapid footfalls against the stone mirrored the wild frenzy of my pulse. The thought of Aelia waking in the dead of night, lost again to Helroth's call, clawed at something primal inside me. It awakened a torrent of energy I couldn't control. I'd nearly lost her once before. I couldn't—wouldn't—survive it again. If Kaelith didn't have answers, I'd never rest again knowing her grandfather had unfettered access to her, access I couldn't prevent. He could summon her at any time, force her to do unspeakable things at his whim.

With every step closer to the end of the torch-lit hallway, the fury grew more potent. My shadows hissed and swirled, thickening in power until an orb of darkness surrounded us. The potent scent of *zar* permeated the air, only spurring on my anger. It was a constant presence now as pervasive as my own *nox*.

I'd been so preoccupied with Aelia lately, I'd simply ignored it, but I feared it would be an issue I would have to deal with sooner rather than later.

A hand clamped down on my shoulder, and I spun around, an umbral blade appearing in my fist. I blinked quickly to find the shadow dagger pressed at my brother's throat. Gideon stood just behind him, his eyes wide as he regarded me.

"You see? This is what I mean." Ruhl eyed the umbral weapon, twisting his lips. "You're out of control, Reign. You can't make logical, rational decisions when it comes to her."

"You're right," I snarled, dropping the blade. "I may not be logical or rational right now, but I will do whatever necessary to protect *my mate* at all costs."

"As will I," Ruhl snapped. "Only with a clearer head."

"I hate to say it, Reign, but your brother's right," Gideon interjected. "If you go in there and destroy the Night Fae before we've had a chance to get the truth out of him, it won't help Aelia."

"I know how important this is," I hissed, and a wave of darkness eclipsed the torchlight. "I can handle myself just fine. Noxus, just the idea that Helroth can skulk into her mind at any time and compel her to kill me..." I shook my head of the vivid images sure to plague my nightmares for days to come. "You weren't there. You didn't see her. Aelia was gone."

"But you got her back," Gideon said gently as he stepped beside me, his hand firm on my shoulder. "She's your *cuoré*, Reign. And no matter how deep Helroth burrows into her mind, the love you share and the bond you forged will always burn brighter."

A sigh pursed my lips, utter defeat lacing my tone. "I'm not so sure, Gid."

"Well, that's the spirit, brother." Ruhl smirked before his lips flipped into a frown at my murderous scowl. "All I'm saying is that you went through so much to get here. As much as it pains me to admit it, the gods, in their infinite wisdom, chose her for *you*. Do not squander that blessing because of some irrational rage."

"I don't believe it's his fault," Gideon threw in, wagging a finger at my infuriating brother. "He's always been able to control his *nox*, even before Draven shackled him with those siphoning cuffs. This is different."

"Well, of course it is, it's Aelia's *zar*. It's unraveling him from the inside out." Ruhl shrugged. "He'll have to learn to block the flow through the bond."

"I don't believe it is coming from the cuorem," I hissed. "I thought it was at first, but after completing it, I was certain I would feel it surging through our mystical connection. Instead, it only seems to be growing more powerful from within *me*."

"The cuorem has been known to amplify the abilities of mates." Gideon's dark brows drew together, and I could almost see the gears in his brilliant mind twisting and turning.

"Amplify, yes, but create completely *new* powers?" My gaze swung between both males. Focusing on the looming shadows, I called upon the *zar*, thick, oily coils invading the whispering tendrils. The air grew heavy with power, and sparks of hellfire danced along the smokey shadows.

For a long moment, Gideon stared at me as if I were a stranger. Then his expression schooled to neutrality. "I'll have to look into it further once I return to Arcanum."

"Cheers, Gid, I appreciate it."

"Anything for you, old friend." He gave me a tight smile.

The iron door loomed only a few yards away now.

"We'll go in together." Ruhl stepped to my side with a sharp nod.

"Fine," I grumbled, my eager feet gobbling up the little distance that remained between me and the Night Fae. Pausing in front of the entrance, I drew in a deep breath and attempted to still the chaotic tangle of *nox* and *zar* pummeling my insides.

I had to remain in control. I had to do this for *her*.

The iron door groaned as I hauled it open, the sharp sound echoing off the stone. Ruhl and Gideon trailed behind me as I stalked into the center of the murky space.

Kaelith didn't flinch. Of course he didn't. The bastard was lounging against the roughhewn wall, his hands shackled in warded cuffs etched with Light runes thanks to Aidan, his head tipped back like he was meditating.

I stepped into the flickering torchlight, and still, he didn't move. "You have exactly three seconds to explain how to get Helroth out of her head," I growled.

Kaelith's citrine eyes peeled open, glittering with the same infuriating calm as when I came to him about Aelia's growing astral possession abilities. "And if I don't?"

My shadows struck before I even thought to command them.

"Reign!" Ruhl grit out.

Ignoring him, I gained control and directed my dark minions. They surged from the corners of the chamber, coiling like smoke around his ankles and wrists, slamming him flat against the wall with enough force to crack stone. The impact sent a sickening jolt through the room. Still, he grinned.

"I'll tear your mind open piece by piece if I have to," I snarled, stepping closer. "You will tell me how to break his influence over her, or I will break you."

His breath hitched just slightly, but I caught it.

"Even if I knew," he said, voice strained, "do you really think pain will jog my memory?"

"No," I whispered, letting *nox* slither down my arms, "but it makes me feel a whole lot better."

I thrust my hand forward and the shadows obeyed, black tendrils pressing into Kaelith's temples, probing, searching, clawing at the seams of his mind. He gritted his teeth, body trembling as I poured my fury into the *nox*, allowing the darkness to spiral out of control.

"You trained her. You were inside her head every day. She trusted you. You had to know her control was slipping, and you said nothing."

His lips peeled back. "I didn't know. I felt... something... but I didn't know it was him."

I didn't believe him. Not entirely. But gods, I wanted to because he'd had unfettered access to Aelia for months.

Zar pooled beneath my skin like molten oil, slick and sickening. I let it bleed into the shadows, corrupting them. The tendrils darkened, then sharpened. Kaelith screamed.

"Breathe, Reign, just breathe." Gideon's voice was nothing but a murmur through the chaos.

"You think you're angry now," Kaelith gasped between ragged breaths, citrine orbs fixed to mine. "Wait until Aelia is screaming your name and doesn't even know why."

My control snapped. The room exploded in black.

Shadows morphed into razor-edged blades of umbral wrath. Chains writhed like snakes, wrapping around Kaelith's limbs, lifting him from the floor and dangling him midair. I stepped into his space, my voice a quiet storm.

"You will *never* speak her name again."

The torches extinguished in a burst of windless dark. Only the pulsing glow of the runes on his cuffs remained. Darkness encroached into my vision, and I knew I was losing myself to the power.

But I didn't care.

I couldn't.

Splaying my fingers to summon more shadows, a flicker of hellfire lit up my palm. Kaelith's eyes went wide with fear... and confusion? I could only imagine his expression mirrored my own. Noxus, I commanded hellfire now?

"How?" he rasped, smoldering amber irises aglow beneath the crimson flames flickering across my hand. "You wield *zar*?"

"Apparently..." My fingers danced through the hellish flares untouched. "I suppose I can thank your king's blood running through my *cuoré's* veins for that."

Undeterred by this new revelation, I delved deeper into his mind, my wild shadows clawing at his memories desperate to find an answer. Was it the cursed illusions? The astral possession? What exactly had Helroth done to break her?

Scouring the dark recesses of the Night Fae's mind as he dangled mid-air, I zipped by the unimportant bits, a flash of images I cared nothing about. Blood, war, torture, heated confrontations with Helroth. I sifted through the endless memories, my dark minions poking and prodding to no avail.

I could feel him weakening, the influx of *nox* and *zar* too much pressure for his mind. His eyes rolled back, a tremor racing through his enormous form.

"Reign!" Ruhl, damn it. "You're going to kill him." His shadows curled around me, their icy touch extinguishing some of the rage and the hellfire still growing in my palm.

"I know what I'm doing," I ground out. Flicking my wrist, an orb of crimson hellfire ignited, dispersing my brother's shadows into ash.

"Noxus, help us." I could barely make out Gideon's hiss from over my shoulder.

Still, I pressed on, searching through the maze of neurons and murky brain matter to pluck out the information I needed. There had to be *something*. I refused to believe there was no way to save her.

Reign. Aelia.

Her voice wasn't real. It couldn't be real.

And yet, it slipped through the chaos of my mind like a balm through wildfire.

My shadows recoiled, hesitating.

Reign, stop.

She was real.

I turned slowly, breath ragged, finding Aelia framed in the

open doorway. Light spilled around her like a halo. Her eyes met mine, not afraid, but pained.

"This isn't you," she said softly. "Kae doesn't know. You're only hurting yourself now."

Kaelith slumped in the air, blood dripping from his nose and mouth, barely conscious.

The shadows shrank from him.

And I let go.

The tendrils withdrew, evaporating into the stone like mist at dawn. Kaelith crumpled to the ground in a broken heap. My heart thundered in my chest, a deafening rhythm that sounded like failure.

I couldn't save her from Helroth. Not yet.

But gods help me, I would, and next time, I wouldn't stop.

Not even for her.

Chapter Five

The hurt etched across Reign's face when I ordered Ruhl and Gideon to pull him from Kaelith's cell still throbbed like an open wound, but it had been a necessary evil. Reign needed a moment to get a handle on his powers, and I needed a word with my former jailor.

As I turned to Kae, Reign's face once again flashed across my mind. Raysa, I'd seen rage in his eyes before, but this time, it was something else entirely—it was fear. Not of Kaelith. Of himself. And I hated how much it scared me. I knew exactly what he was going through, a prisoner of your own abilities. I simply didn't understand where this new surge was coming from.

Drawing in a breath, I steadied myself for what came next. Besides, I would make it up to Reign before long.

As soon as the iron door slammed closed, I approached the big Night Fae sprawled across the wooden bench in the corner of the dimly lit chamber. Thick fingers pressed into each temple, the damage my *cuoré* had wreaked with his invasive shadows obvious in the tense set of his jaw.

"You should have just told him, Kae."

"I don't know how to break his influence," he gritted out, eyes fixed to the low ceiling. "Helroth isn't simply any ordinary Night Fae. He's the king. The royals contain powers far beyond those of us lowly commoners."

A harsh laugh parted my lips, the sound too high pitched and slightly unhinged. "I'm starting to learn that." Moving closer, I could feel the pulse of *zar* across his skin, emanating from his very core. "You don't strike me as a mere commoner, Kae. I doubt Helroth would've entrusted you with my training if you were."

The corner of his lip twitched, the dark ruddy hue of his complexion deepening. "Very observant, Light Fae."

"Why do you still call me that?"

His broad shoulders lifted. "Because despite the Night blood coursing through your veins, you are Light, princess. And as much as I despise the Light Fae, Helroth hates them more. Knowing that his heir has the blood of his greatest enemy pumping through her heart gives me more satisfaction than you'll ever know." A wicked grin curled the corners of his lips.

My brows puckered as I regarded him. "You aren't loyal to your king?"

"Oh, I am, Aelia. He made sure of that long ago." Darkness, and more than that, utter defeat, streaked across his face.

How had I not seen it sooner? "The king forced you into a blood vow?"

He nodded, lips pressed into a tight line.

"Why didn't you tell me before?"

"What did it matter? I can do nothing against him. He owns me, has for decades." Straightening, he winced as his back pressed against the stone wall. "Now, I assume it's only a matter of time before your Shadow Fae *cuoré* kills me. Either way, I'm soon destined for permanent night in Noxus's icy embrace."

"I won't let Reign kill you. Not if you help me."

"I can't," he hissed.

I recognized the look of desperation. It was so similar to the one Aidan often wore when I questioned him about my past. "What was the vow?"

He clucked his teeth, lids slipping closed. "Doesn't matter."

"Yes, it does. If you've come to care for me even the tiniest bit over the past few months, please tell me."

His eyes slowly opened, irritation written across his features. "You assume too much, Light Fae."

But I was certain he cared. He might have been bound to Helroth, but I'd seen slivers of his kindness. Inching closer, I slapped my hands on my hips and stared down at him expectantly.

With a frustrated grunt, he finally mumbled, "I swore my allegiance to the king in return for a life spared."

"Whose?"

"For Zaroth's sake, Aelia, you don't know when to quit, do you?"

A grin stretched across my face. "Some find that one of my most endearing qualities."

"Not me."

"So, tell me, and I'll leave you alone." Besides, I could feel Reign's anxiety dribbling through our bond every second I was in here with the Night Fae. It wouldn't be long before he burst into the cell and dragged me out.

The errant thought was oddly exciting.

"Come on, Kaelith, out with it. If you can't provide any useful information, at least you could entertain my curiosity."

"You're impossible," he ground out. "Just remember to share my candidness with your *cuoré*. If anything, it should serve as further proof that I truly know nothing about how to stop Helroth's hold over you."

"Deal."

With another pained sigh, he muttered, "Helroth spared Vaelora's life in exchange for a lifetime of servitude. Both of ours."

"Vaelora?" My thoughts swirled back to my time in captivity at Helspire Keep. The older female had been my only source of light and companionship in that bleak castle. "Who is she to you?"

"She was my brother's wife. That is, before Helroth murdered him and stole her as his own."

"Wait, Vaelora is the Night Queen? That would make her my—"

He shook his head, slowly lifting his hand as if even that slight movement was painful. "Vaelora was his first wife. Your grandmother was Morvanya, a *Shadow* Fae royal. As I'm sure you've heard, before the Two Hundred Years' War, Night and Shadow often intermingled."

"Morvanya." I swirled the name on my tongue, another piece of the puzzle that was my muddled bloodline. Why hadn't Helroth told me about her?

"Yes," he murmured. "You see, Vaelora was unable to give him a child. Complications from her first pregnancy. Therefore, once Helroth tired of her, he moved on to Morvanya."

"And they had my mother, Sable."

He nodded.

I'd often seen Kae and Vaelora together around the Keep, but as they were the only living souls I encountered during my captivity, I'd never thought twice about it. So Vaelora was his sister-in-law. "Do you have any other family?"

"None alive, Light Fae." He closed his eyes once more and slid down across the bench. "Now, if you don't mind, I'd like to rest. Having your brain sliced into shreds by shadows is far from pleasant."

"I can't imagine." I paused for a long minute before turning toward the door. "Thank you for telling me the truth."

Without opening his eyes, he drawled, "You better not let your *cuoré* hear you thanking me. I doubt he would stand for that. And at the rate his *zar* is intensifying—"

Twirling back around, a trickle of fear sharpened my words.

I'd fought so hard to grapple with the foreign energy and still found myself at its mercy. "What do you know about Reign's *zar*?"

His eyes finally opened, a drowsy haze clouding the brilliant citrine. "Nothing, other than it's powerful."

"I suppose that makes sense, since it's coming from me."

His dark brows furrowed as they regarded me, lips pinching. "No, I don't believe that's correct."

"What?"

"You heard me, Aelia. I've been working with you for months now. I'm well acquainted with your *zar* and that of the king. Though there is something familiar about his, it feels different from yours."

That whisper of fear burned brighter.

"There's an echo in it... something old. Not yours. Not even Helroth's." He paused, eyes distant. "It reminds me of someone I once knew."

"Someone you knew?"

He shook his head, his gaze unfocused. "But then again, it's likely the madness talking now. Your *cuoré* certainly scrambled my thoughts."

"Where is the *zar* coming from, Kae?"

His shoulders lifted lazily before he rolled over, resting his head on his arm as a pillow. "The same place all power stems from, Light Fae. His blood."

The walk back to the upper levels of the manor passed in a blur, my mind swirling with the implications of Kaelith's words. Reign was a bastard. He knew nothing of his birth mother, other than the fact that she'd been a servant in his father's home. There had been a moment before I understood the depths of my true heritage that I'd considered the possibility of Reign's mother being Night Fae.

Then, when the truth came out, I never thought of it again. But what if it were true? Reign's Shadow abilities were growing stronger by the day, but it wasn't only the *nox* which grew uncontrollable. It was the *zar*.

And realms, if it wasn't coming from me, then from where?

I thought I had finally learned who I was. Kin. Light. Shadow. Night. Princess. But maybe I'd been so focused on my blood, I'd ignored what ran in his.

Who was the Shadow Prince?

Chapter Six

R *eign*

How could Aelia banish me from her side like I was some disobedient child, not the male who would burn down kingdoms to protect her? Dragged off by my traitorous brother and best friend, no less...

Noxus, get a hold of yourself, Reign. This isn't you.

My breath came in ragged bursts, chest heaving as I pressed trembling hands to the wall of our chamber. The one in which I'd held her in my arms all night until Helroth stole her away in the pre-dawn hours. My nostrils flared at the memory of the fury I'd felt when I'd awoken to find her gone, the scent of scorched air and shadow clinging to my skin, thick and oppressive.

Nox coiled around me like a predator off its leash, too fast, too wild. It slashed across the room in jagged lines, extinguishing the torches with one swipe and plunging the chamber into darkness. My shadows weren't obeying anymore. They pulsed with my manic heartbeat, alive and volatile, reacting to every thought I couldn't control.

Zar churned beneath the surface of my skin, slick and burning, spreading through my veins like oil set aflame. I clenched my fists, trying to shove it down and lock it away, but it was no use.

A vase exploded across the room. The iron footboard of the bed groaned and then crumpled in on itself.

"Enough," I growled to the room, to myself, to the gods.

But it wasn't.

The two energies snarled at each other inside me, vying for dominance. *Nox* was ice and fury, sharp and unrelenting. *Zar* was molten chaos, seeping through my marrow like burning ink. Both belonged to me now—hers and mine, her light and my dark, warring beneath my skin like rival gods with no throne to share. But why?

Why now all of a sudden?

I dropped to my knees on all fours, sweat pouring from my brow as the symbol of the cuorem seared across my chest. *Aelia*. I reached for the bond, desperate for her calm, her light, anything to anchor me.

I'm coming. Her response was immediate. Just as immediate as the calm that began to set in at the sound of her voice in my mind.

My Aelia. My rock. My flame. The only thing that kept me from burning alive. I needed to be inside her so that I could no longer tell where she ended and I began.

A low growl tore from my throat as another pulse of power ripped through me, cracking the stone floor beneath my palms. Noxus…

If I didn't get control of this soon, I would become the very monster I'd sworn to protect her from. If I couldn't handle my own abilities, what hope did I have of overpowering the vow I'd sworn to my father?

The door whipped open and slammed against the wall, the

sharp crash cracking through the chamber like a warning. Aelia stood in the doorway, her eyes as wild as the mad thrashing of my pulse.

"Are you all right?" She slid to the floor beside me, warm hands cradling my face.

"I'm not sure, princess," I rasped out, breath ragged from strain. The admission was embarrassing. I should have been the one comforting her. Instead, here she was worried for me after everything she'd suffered at Helroth's hands.

"What's wrong?"

"It's this damned *zar*... It's been infecting the *nox*, driving me out of control. It's been going on for months, but it only seems to be worsening. I'd hoped once we completed the bond it would stabilize, but—" It had only gotten more volatile. Or perhaps it was the overwhelming jealousy and possessiveness triggered by the cuorem that had my abilities growing more unstable.

"Why didn't you tell me?"

"Gods, Aelia, I'd only just gotten you back, and you were struggling with your lost memories, not to mention your own powers. My needs seemed trivial in comparison."

"No, Reign. That's not how this works. We are *cuoré* now, you are my other half. If either one of us is broken, then neither one of us is truly whole."

The heart-felt sentiment meant everything to me, but more than that, perhaps, she was *right*. We were bonded now, our abilities should flow freely between both of us, the light, the dark, she and I, we were one now.

As the cuorem was seen so infrequently these days, little was known about the implications of the mystical connection.

"I cannot access your *rais*," I muttered. "And yet, the *zar* is overwhelming me." Noxus, how humiliating.

"*Zar* is like nothing I've ever encountered, Reign. It runs in my blood, and still, it's like a wild beast ravaging beneath my ribcage. You'll—no, *we*— will tame it soon enough, together."

Dropping her hands from my face, she offered her open palm and hauled me to my feet. Bracing myself against her, drawing from her strength and quiet calm, I shoved back the onslaught of energies and tucked them deep within my core as I'd shown Aelia to do all those months ago.

She regarded me warily, something indecipherable in that silver-blue gaze. It would be so easy to pluck the thought right from her mind, but I didn't wish to abuse our bond.

Instead, I whispered, "When did you get so strong, love?" When did you become the one holding *me* together?

"I suppose it was sometime between the Ethereal Trials and being dragged beneath the earth by my grandsire, and by the throat no less."

"So I had nothing to do with it?" I lifted a teasing brow.

"Oh, I don't know." She smirked, her body inching closer to mine. "I suppose your endless hours of training across the Luminoc may have had a little something to do with it."

Leaning my forehead to hers, I inhaled deeply, breathing her in. Gods, she was all I needed in this world. "Waking up this morning and finding you missing nearly broke me, Aelia..." The confession slid past my lips without warning. "I've faced brutal Fae, battled monsters like my father, stared down the prophecy itself. But nothing has terrified me like waking up to find you gone. And I firmly believe it was that fear that triggered this influx of uncontrollable *nox* and *zar*. If I lost you again, there is no question, it would ruin me, love."

Tears brimmed in those brilliant orbs as they locked on mine. "You won't lose me. Ever. We are bound together by the gods now, Reign. There is nothing anyone can do to destroy what the gods have forged, not even my damned grandfather."

I brushed my knuckles along her cheek, catching the tear that slipped down her face. The sight of her, shining and shattered all at once, nearly gutted me. "Then why does it feel like I'm still losing you, piece by piece?"

Her breath caught.

"I felt it, Aelia," I whispered, voice rough with the truth. "When you raised that blade... when I looked into your eyes and didn't see you anymore. I didn't care about the prophecy. Or the war. Or even surviving. I felt a void swallow me whole." I paused, the full weight of the pain I'd buried meeting the brutal light of day. "I just wanted *you* to come back."

A faint tremble ran through her as her hands curled into the front of my tunic. "And I did," she murmured. "I found my way back to you. Because of how much I love you."

I nodded, but the ache hadn't eased. "But how many more times can we survive this? I'm afraid another crack won't cause me to shatter, but instead, it'll force me to raze everything in my path."

She didn't answer. Couldn't.

So I closed my eyes and pressed our foreheads together again, anchoring myself to the steady rhythm of her breath.

"I need you to understand something," I said quietly. "If Helroth ever gets that close again, I *will* kill him. Even if that means risking my own life in the process."

"No," she said, voice breaking. "Don't you dare say that."

"I can't live like this, weighed down by the constant fear that he could steal you away from me at any moment. Knowing that he could infiltrate your mind, corrupt your feelings for me and steal your heart? I can't bear it."

"He can't. He won't."

"What if it's this strangling fear that is causing the chaotic state of my abilities? What if I truly can't control myself? I could become a danger to you."

"I won't leave you, Reign, if that's what you're getting at. Not now. Not ever. And I will not allow you to go after Helroth alone. If you fall into darkness, I'll follow you there. I'll drag you back myself if I have to."

I smiled despite the ache, brushing my lips across her brow. "Then I suppose we'll be damned together."

She leaned in, pressing her lips to mine, soft and sure. The kind of kiss that stitched broken pieces back together. And in that moment, I knew the gods didn't just bind us.

They forged us in war, in pain, in love.

And I vowed that nothing, not even the King of Night, would sever that.

Curling my hand around the back of her neck, I deepened the kiss, our tongues dancing in perfect rhythm. My heart tapped out a frantic beat beneath her palm, desperate to be closer. "I need you, Aelia," I whispered against her swollen lips.

"Then take me. I am yours." Her hand slid down my chest to tangle with my fingers as she turned and took a step back toward the broken bed. With a gentle tug, she lured me to the edge of the mattress.

My heart swelled, the beginnings of a smile claiming my lips. *How did you know this was exactly what I needed?* I sent the thought through our mental connection.

Because it was what I needed too. She dropped down onto the rickety bed, pulling me down with her.

"Make love to me, Reign," she whispered, her voice soft, almost reverent.

"It would be my pleasure, princess."

I sank onto the slanted mattress, bracing myself over her with one arm as the other trailed down her torso. My shadows whirled to life. Not the angry, vengeful ones from earlier, but rather the soft caresses of darkness, unfastening buttons and unlacing ties. She arched beneath me, luminous and wild, a goddess draped in moonbeams and starlight.

Within moments, not a shred of clothing remained between us. I allowed myself a moment to take her in, to revel in her beauty as my shadows teased her sensitive flesh. *Mine.*

Our cuorem pulsed between us, the ancient bond thrumming like a second heartbeat as I kissed her again, slowly this time. It was not just a meeting of mouths, but a merging of souls.

"Sometimes, I still can't believe you're mine," I murmured

against her lips, brushing a strand of dark hair from her temple. "That in spite of everything, I haven't lost you."

Her hand rose to my face, fingers grazing the edge of my jaw with a tenderness that threatened to unravel me. "You never will. Not unless you let me go. And even then, I would still fight to stay with you."

"Never," I vowed, mouth grazing hers. "Even if the stars fall and the realm burns, I'll always hold on."

She pulled me to her, parting her legs, and I let go of everything but her, her taste, her breath, her body pressed against mine. My hips fit perfectly between her thighs, my arousal finding her center instinctively.

A growl vibrated my throat as I felt her desire for me. "Mmm, you are ready for me, love."

"Always," she rasped before her lips claimed mine.

As her kisses grew more desperate, her hips rolling against me, I thrust inside her. A groan spilled between our lips, a shared exhale of pure joy.

And just like that, the weight of destiny, prophecy, war, it all fell away in that sacred space where only she existed. Where only *we* did.

The glow of our joined energies ignited around us, soft and pulsing, not *nox*, not *zar*, not *rais*, but something uniquely ours. Starlight and shadow. Flame and frost.

Aelia gasped as our powers surged in tandem, shimmering over our skin like the gods themselves blessed the union. And I supposed they did...

"I love you," I breathed, pressing kisses along the soft curve of her shoulder. "More than fate. More than destiny. More than anything."

"I know," she whispered back, tears brimming. "And I love you so much I'll rewrite the stars for us."

As we moved together, it wasn't just pleasure, it was a reclamation. Of ourselves. Of everything Helroth had tried to take.

With every touch, every breath, we wove a shield between us and his encroaching darkness.

And as we lost ourselves in each other beneath the canopy of gods' blessed power and fated love, I realized this was not just a moment of comfort we both needed.

It was reaffirming a vow.

One that no king, no war, and no prophecy could ever break.

Chapter Seven

A *elia*

A frosty breeze licked over the stone wall of the courtyard, lifting from the turbulent sea below. Glancing up at the star flecked sky, I scanned the never-ending night for the familiar glimmer of Sol's gilded form. He and Phantom should have been on their way by now to transport us back to the Conservatory.

The week-long respite at Shadowmere was all we were granted, while our friends returned to their homes to regroup. It had been a fragile pause before the next storm. I supposed I should have been grateful we'd been allotted even that. But now, all I could think about was how much harder it would be to leave.

An immediate return to Luce, which had been the original plan, had been altered once I'd realized the volatile state of Reign's powers. Now, he assured me he was fully in control once again. The unanticipated postponement had, however, granted Reign and me the time we needed to find our way back to each other without the interruptions life back at the academy would bring. If

I was being honest with myself, we'd completed the bond in a bit of a rush, in a hasty attempt to seal our love amidst my lost memories.

Not that I regretted binding my soul to Reign one bit, but we needed this sliver of calm to solidify our tumultuous relationship. To ground ourselves in each other. To understand the full implications of the cuorem.

Not that we'd achieved that just yet, but at least we both felt more secure in the glittering strands of light that connected our hearts and the burgeoning powers coursing between us.

With more than enough to keep our thoughts swirling, I'd decided not to bring up Kaelith's conjectures about Reign's bloodline. Yet.

I vowed to discover more myself before sharing the Night Fae's suspicions with my mate. His erratic emotional state left me fearing what effect news like this would have on him.

As if my thoughts had conjured the enigmatic male, Reign appeared on the balcony overhead, shadow wings curled across his broad shoulders. He looked every bit the Shadow Fae warrior, power seething from the great expanse of his chest, the dark runes engraved across his arms and every inch of his impressive form.

The cuorem thrummed with happiness, my heart growing its own wings at the sight of him. Sometimes, I couldn't believe Reign was mine either.

With a mighty thrust, his wings propelled him toward me, and every inch of my being hummed in anticipation at his approach. We'd spent most of the past week lost in each other, and Raysa, it had been glorious. But even in our tangled limbs, shadows of what lay ahead loomed ever nearer.

Still, it seemed I could never get enough of my mate.

You aren't the only one. Reign's deep timbre slipped into my mind an instant before he landed only a hairsbreadth away.

His shadows curled around me, cocooning us in a blanket of icy night. A sliver of darkness coiled around my waist then drew me flush against its master.

"You better not start something you aren't prepared to finish, my love." I rose to my tiptoes and brushed a quick kiss across his lips.

"I'm fairly certain I could finish well before our dragons arrived." He sucked my bottom lip into his mouth, nibbling on the soft skin. "When it comes to you, I'm quite insatiable," he growled.

Oh, for Raysa's sake, keep that male's thoughts to yourself. Sol's gravelly voice immediately doused the building heat. *Haven't you learned how to block me yet?*

Sorry, Sol, I shot back, unravelling my limbs from around Reign's unyielding form.

My mate grumbled a curse before releasing me.

"They're almost here," I muttered.

"Of course they are. The one time they choose to be on time."

A rueful chuckle slid from between my lips as I regarded him. "You're not looking forward to returning to campus, professor? I thought I was the wary one of the two of us."

"Things will be different now, Aelia." His hands curled around mine, drawing me close once again. "We won't have to hide what we are, but we'll also no longer have the privacy nor tranquility of the manor. War is nearly upon us."

I glanced at the small fortress built along the cliffside, and a tiny pang of sadness crept in. Duskridge Manor had become my home in the past several weeks. More than that, it had been the place where I'd reconnected with Aidan too. Now, he would be forced to remain here to guard Kaelith, and it almost felt as if I were losing him again. We were tasked with gathering the Light and Shadow Fae, in an attempt to unite the fractured kingdoms against Helroth.

It was a daunting endeavor. One that I couldn't say I relished.

But the Night King wouldn't remain quiet for long. Honestly, I was surprised he'd stayed hidden this past week. What was he waiting for? Whatever it was, I was certain it wouldn't be good.

Either way, we couldn't allow him any more time to prepare. We still had the Ebonshard Compass, and with it, the ability to find him anywhere. Once we'd secured both Elian's and Tenebris's forces, we would strike before Helroth knew we were coming.

I only hoped everything would go according to plan.

Ruhl had sent his shadow messenger to summon us today, which meant he'd finally spoken to his father. I prayed to all the gods when we reached the Conservatory he'd have good news for us.

"Estellira, is it safe to approach?" Aidan's wary voice seeped through the cloak of shadows, and heat burned my cheeks. How had I been so caught up in Reign I hadn't even heard his advance?

My poor surrogate father had nearly caught us in a variety of compromising positions in the past week. Reign tried to convince me it was perfectly normal for a pair of newly-mated Fae. Still, it was embarrassing that he knew what was happening right under his nose.

Releasing Reign's hands, I stepped out from within the wall of spiraling shadows. "Yes, of course, Aidan."

He marched closer, all the formidable Light Fae soldier. In the past few days, he'd spent hours huddled around the table with Reign and the others in what my mate referred to as the war room. The grand chamber that overlooked the courtyard of Duskridge Manor had been converted into strategy central, the meeting place in the wee hours of the night when our friends were able to escape the confines of Luce and Arcanum.

I barely saw Rue and Sy unless it was around that gods' forsaken table, and I missed them dearly. At least, now that we were returning to Luce, we would all be together. Despite all our plotting, there was little we could do until Helroth and his army emerged from hiding.

"I suppose the time has come to wish you farewell once again, *estellira*." A weariness, bone-deep, settled across his features as he lifted his hand to cradle my cheek.

"It won't be long this time, Aidan. We'll be back for you and Kaelith before you know it. As much as my mate wishes it weren't true, we need him. And I will always need you." I squeezed his hand. "Plus, we'll need your expertise once the battle is upon us."

He dipped his head, emotion surging across those pale gray eyes. The glint of the moon's gentle rays across my medallion caught my foster father's attention, and his thumb and index finger closed around my necklace.

"*Ethria sael, dravorn ethrae,*" he whispered.

How could I have forgotten the inscription along the back? The one Aidan had sworn he knew nothing about when he gifted it to me all those months ago.

My breath caught. "What does it mean?"

Aidan hesitated, his thumb lingering against the medallion like it might burn him.

The thunderous pounding of wings slicing the air called my attention skyward. Sol's glittering, golden form pierced the darkness with Phantom at his heels.

It means "Bound by love, awakened by fate" in old Faerish. Sol's voice slithered across my skull before Aidan could respond. If he could at all, which I wasn't certain given the vow he'd sworn.

My heart stilled. Bound by love... awakened by fate. The words echoed across my mind, twisting and twirling as I considered them. The mystical spell that had cloaked my powers at birth, bound by my parents' love and awakened by the prophecy, or maybe even by the fated cuorem.

"Why didn't you tell me that before?" I shouted out loud as Sol's talons hit the earth along the cliffs below.

Because it didn't mean anything before, and now, it means everything, little Kin.

Secretive, cagey, irritating dragon.

I heard that. A hint of amusement laced his tone.

Good.

Once I refocused my attention on Aidan, a wry smile tilted the corners of his mouth. "Now you know, my child."

It was still only a sliver of the past I still ached to understand. It was clear my parents loved me, but why hadn't they fought harder to keep me? And how did they die? And how had a Light Fae king end up falling for a Night Fae princess of mixed origins?

"Aidan, I have so many more questions about them…"

His lips pressed into a tight line, and remorse etched into his features. "I know, and I wish I could give them to you, *estellira*," he murmured, sorrow threading through every syllable.

I opened my mouth to protest, but Reign's arm coiled around my waist, his presence ever steady in the sea of turmoil we constantly navigated. "Come, starlight. It's time we return to the academy. Let's hope there's more waiting for us at Luce than just war. There may be answers, too."

Chapter Eight

R*eign*

Aelia's smile grew wider with each wing flap, every dragon-length closer we came to the Conservatory of Luce. After all she'd endured under the hands of her fellow Light Fae students upon her arrival nearly a year ago, I never imagined the bouts of happiness roaring through the cuorem at returning.

She was truly thrilled to be *home*.

Her word, not mine.

Aelia may have been a child of twilight, a perfect amalgamation of *rais*, *nox* and *zar*, but her heart was pure light. It was unwavering in its warmth, defiant in its glow, and capable of illuminating even the darkest corners of this entire realm.

Not that I'd ever truly believed she could be that harbinger of oblivion the prophecy spoke of, but the more I understood her, the clearer it became that one day, all of Aetheria would kneel before her flame.

If you're quite finished brooding over your incredible mate, where would you like me to land? Phantom's irritated snarl sailed through my thoughts as the alabaster turrets of Luce streaked through the serene azure sky.

My, my, what's gotten you into such a mood, old girl?

Perhaps it's the constant state of vexing giddiness rushing through our bond. From your end.

I thought you'd be happy for me...

She huffed out a breath, plumes of smoke curling around her nostrils. *I'm trying, Reign.*

What's wrong? Things aren't going well with Solanthus? You seem to be spending a lot of time together.

We are, but unfortunately, that dragon is a stubborn, blasted beast. You're lucky your mate has a more forgiving nature than mine.

I can have Aelia speak to Solanthus on your behalf, if you'd like.

No, we'll sort things out eventually. You know how I hate to grovel, Reign...

A laugh erupted from my lips unbidden. Phantom, grovel? I never thought I'd live to see the day.

You're not the only one. She snorted, flames licking across her snout. *Well, shall I land in the cover of the Lightwood Forest?*

Yes, that will be fine. Thank you, old girl.

Before I could signal to Solanthus, the enormous golden dragon's wings angled toward the forest Phantom had just pointed out. The pair of feuding dragons may not have been in the best place in their relationship, but clearly, the mental link that connected them was still at full strength.

As soon as Phantom's talons grazed the earth in the small clearing of the forest just west of the campus, I scanned the designated meeting spot for any sign of my half-brother. But he was nowhere in sight.

Aelia's friends, on the other hand, had shown up as instructed. Judging by the sound of their boisterous laughter, they were more than thrilled with her homecoming. She'd already slid off her dragon and the three best friends now huddled in a circle, chatting and giggling as if they hadn't seen each other in months.

And if that Lightspire male didn't get his hands off my mate, I would—

Inhaling a deep breath, I fought back the surge of *zar* that twisted with the wild possessive urges ignited by the cuorem. Extending my wings, I leapt off Phantom's back and landed beside Aelia. Gently, much more gently than the urge demanded, I drew her into my side and away from the handsy male.

I'd stupidly thought that now that my mate's ears had sharpened into glorious points, that Lightspire fool would leave them alone. But no, he seemed as obsessed with them as ever.

"Where's Ruhl?" I barked at the Liteschild female, ignoring the male completely.

My attempts at keeping her at arms' length ever since Aelia's astral possession incident had proven futile. She wasn't at all embarrassed by the fact that I'd nearly mauled her in the kitchens of Duskridge Manor believing her to be my mate. Which I had in fact been right about, but still...

"Haven't seen him yet, but I could have sworn I felt an influx of *nox* pervading the dormitories a few hours ago." Rue's light brows knitted. "In fact, I thought you'd arrived early, professor." She shrugged before continuing to chatter on with Aelia, essentially dismissing me.

Noxus, where was he?

I preferred to have the conversation about our father within this secluded area of the forest as opposed to inside the campus. Who knew what sort of prying eyes and ears still roamed Luce?

"All of you, wait here. I will steal across campus and search the dormitories for my brother." Could he have misunderstood the meeting spot?

The three friends barely spared me a glance as they chatted away.

"Lightspire," I growled, grabbing the male by the shoulder.

"Yes, professor?" Panicked, lilac eyes found mine.

"Aelia's safety is in your hands. Do you understand?"

"Yes, of course. She's perfectly safe." He grinned from ear-to-ear, throwing his arm around her shoulder, oblivious to the danger he was putting himself in, per the usual.

"I never said you could touch her," I snarled, a frenzy of shadows coiling around the fool.

His arm snapped back, a tremor rolling through his entire body. "Right, of course not."

Satisfied, I commanded a wave of my shadows to peel away and remain with Aelia and allowed the others to conceal me in a blanket of night. With a quick goodbye to my mate, I headed toward the edge of campus.

Draven would only know I was here when I wished it. And before I let the headmaster in on our return, it was crucial I knew where my father stood on the Helroth matter.

Cloaked in shadows, I flew across the property, passing the slew of students practicing with luminescent weapons on the training field. As I watched the inept first years, it occurred to me that in Aelia's absence, she, along with Symon and Rue, were now halfway through their second year. Aelia had missed the entirety of her third term and now the fourth was well under way.

It could very well be the last for every student on this campus.

If Helroth had his way, we'd be plunged into war for another hundred years. I could not allow that to be our fate.

Finally reaching the fountain in front of the Hall of Glory, I couldn't help my thoughts from flitting back in time to the day I'd brought Aelia to the Conservatory. I'd been terrified as she stood poised at the threshold, at the Veil of Judgement, awaiting the verdict of the gods. Only a few hours with the sharp-mouthed little Kin, and already, the overwhelming urge to protect her had taken root.

If only I'd known then what that incessant tug had meant...

Shaking my head with a rueful smile, I ascended the marble steps and skulked into the foyer. The grand entry was quiet, most students in the midst of lessons. Loosing tendrils of shadow, I sent my messengers through the building ahead to find my brother.

By the time I passed the third level climbing up the endlessly spiraling glass staircase, one of my shadow minions curled around my ear.

"No, it can't be..." I hissed.

Racing up the remaining steps, I darted down the hallway of the second-year dormitories, still cloaked in concealing shadows. My dark messenger halted in front of a familiar door, and a potent mix of anger and disbelief flooded my senses when I pressed my ear to the light timber.

The moment I opened the door to Liora's chambers, I was certain I would be sick.

The stench of spiced wine hit me like a blow to the face, potent, cloying, and far too strong for early afternoon. Shadows stirred restlessly at my back, feeding off my rising irritation as I stepped into the dimly lit room.

"Ruhl?" I called.

No answer.

Then, I heard it, a soft giggle. Definitely not Ruhl.

I moved deeper into the room, past discarded leathers, an overturned goblet, and what I prayed to the gods wasn't someone's undergarments on the floor. The heavy curtains had been half-drawn, and the mattress was a tangled mess of sheets and limbs. One of which was very much not Liora's.

Ruhl.

Damn it.

My newest acquisition was now sitting upright in bed, clutching the sheets to her chest like they were armor, her golden hair a tousled halo around her flushed face. Her eyes widened in horror when she saw me.

"Oh, stars," Liora breathed, attempting to disappear into the mattress.

Ruhl, of course, was sprawled beside her, shirtless and grinning like a drunken fool. "Brother!" he slurred, raising his half-empty wine bottle in greeting. "I was wondering when you'd show up. Thought you might want to join the party."

My jaw clenched so tight I heard something crack. "What in the realms is this?"

Liora groaned. "It's not what it looks like."

"Really?" I snapped. "Because it looks like my brother is in bed with someone I'm fairly certain he knows is off-limits."

"She wasn't complaining earlier," Ruhl muttered, rubbing at his jaw with a lazy grin. "Or ten minutes ago. Or, gods, was it twenty?"

"Ruhl," I warned, my voice a low growl. "Shut your gods' damned mouth."

Liora flinched, her eyes darting to mine. "Professor, I didn't mean for this to happen. He—he was being kind last night, and I'd had a little too much to drink, and he, well, he was surprisingly charming." She gave Ruhl a glare. "At first."

"I am always charming," Ruhl said proudly, lifting the bottle again like a toast before nearly tipping off the bed. "Just underappreciated. Like a fine wine. Or an angry porcupine. Difficult to hug, but worth it."

I dragged a hand down my face. "You're still drunk."

"Painfully so," he agreed, flopping backward with a dramatic sigh. "What's your excuse?"

Liora let out a mortified whimper and tried to crawl out of the bed with the sheet still clutched to her chest, nearly falling over Ruhl in the process. I stepped toward her before she could fall, steadying her with a hand on her arm.

She didn't meet my gaze as she stood. "I'm sorry. This is so embarrassing."

I exhaled through my nose, softer this time. "You don't owe me anything, Liora. But of all the Fae to fall into bed with, why him?"

"I didn't know I'd be ambushed by your brother in a wine-soaked pity spiral," she muttered.

"Hey," Ruhl called from the bed, waving a finger in the air.

"This spiral was well-earned. Do you have any idea what it's like watching the girl you were supposed to end up with bind her soul to your brother?"

"Apparently, it ends with you naked and in bed with my other acquisition," I snapped. "Are you planning on spiraling all over the damned court?"

Ruhl blinked at me, then snorted. "Did you just say *acquisition*? Gods, that's so warm and fuzzy."

Liora shot me a look. "Really? I thought you at least considered me a friend, professor."

I sighed. "Poor choice of words."

"You think?" she snapped.

Ruhl waved again from the bed, a bit less energetically. "Don't mind him. He's terrible with emotions. He's probably just here to monologue about betrayal and honor and how I've let down the great legacy of the Court of Umbral Shadows. Again."

I turned on him, fury licking at the edges of my vision. "You're lucky I haven't flung your sorry ass off the balcony."

Ruhl raised his wine bottle in salute. "Wouldn't be the first time. Won't be the last."

I looked at Liora again, saw the shame burning behind her eyes, the regret tightening her mouth. Whatever this had been, it was clearly a mistake.

"We'll talk later," I told her, voice low. "Just... get dressed. I need to speak to my brother in private."

She nodded quickly, gathering her clothes with shaking hands as she retreated into the bathing chamber.

As I turned back to Ruhl, his smirk had faded, something hollow and aching in his eyes.

"I didn't mean to hurt her," he said quietly. "I just wanted to forget."

I stared at him a long moment. "We all want to forget something, Ruhl. But this?" I gestured to the bed, the wine, the broken look in his eyes. "This isn't the way."

He laughed bitterly. "No. But it was all I had."

Spearing him with a glare, I thrust my finger in the air. "I thought you cared about Aelia, brother? That it wasn't simply about you anymore."

"I do! Too gods' damned much, apparently."

"Then prove yourself to her. To me. She needs you now, Ruhl, not as her *cuoré*, but as an ally, as a friend. She does care for you, you know." I turned away, shadows curling at my heels. "Find a way to pull yourself together. Because if you hurt Aelia, brother or not, there won't be a bed in the realm safe enough to crawl into."

And with that, I walked out, slamming the door behind me.

Chapter Nine

A^{elia}

Tiptoeing around my old dormitory, I ran my hand across the familiar bed and the lush hanging vines that draped over the cozy niche in the chamber. Everything was exactly as I remembered it. In my absence, Rue had decided not to move into the second-year dormitories in the floor below us. She explained that she was waiting for my return so that we could relocate together.

I was beyond thankful for my ever-optimistic friend. After months at the hands of Helroth, most would have given up on my ever returning. And yet, here I was.

"You're sure Draven won't know we're here?" I glanced up at Reign who paced the length of the hearth, a scowl marring his handsome features.

He'd been abnormally surly since returning from seeking out his brother, refusing to answer any of my questions on the subject. And despite my best efforts to skulk into his mind and discover what had him in such a foul mood, I couldn't get past the impenetrable shield.

"No, the room has been warded, just as the last time we were here."

My thoughts flickered back in time to the day Reign and my friends rescued me from the confines of Helspire Keep. Or more accurately, my grandsire decided to release me, to unleash me and my chaotic powers onto the realm.

Now, it seemed both Reign and I had become uncontrollable weapons.

Had the Night King known all along? Had it all been part of his devious plan to destroy the other courts?

Blinking free of the dismal thoughts, I found myself across the chamber beside my *cuoré*. I hadn't even felt my feet move toward him. Winding my fingers through his, I glanced up to meet two impenetrable orbs of sheer darkness.

"Why are you blocking me?"

"Hmm?"

"There's something bothering you that you're not telling me."

The corner of his lip twitched. "So you decided to skulk into my mind and steal it?"

"Yes."

He laughed, the sound warm and unexpected. "It's silly. For some reason, I feared your reaction at hearing the truth of Ruhl's whereabouts this morning."

"What truth?"

The bond with Reign hummed steady beneath my skin, but something darker throbbed just under it. Like a storm gathering.

"What is it, Reign?"

The door to my chamber whipped open, and none other than the rogue Shadow Prince stormed through. His eyes were bloodshot, hair a mess of tangles, and the pungent scent of spiced wine followed in his wake.

"No fear, the prince is here." He dipped into an elaborate bow in front of us.

"He's... he's drunk..." I stammered.

"Not quite as much anymore." He dropped onto the settee, folding his long legs. "Unfortunately."

"For Noxus's sake, Ruhl. Couldn't you at least wait to sober up before coming?"

"And remain where, brother? After your untimely visit, Liora wasn't exactly the most welcoming hostess."

"Liora?" I bit out.

A hint of amusement glistened in Ruhl's fathomless eyes. "Oh, you didn't tell her?"

"No," Reign growled.

"Tell me what?" Though in truth, I already had a fairly good idea.

Ruhl waved a dismissive hand. "In a fit of drunken lunacy, I sought comfort between the legs of the lovely Liora."

Two pairs of midnight irises bored into me, the piercing scrutiny from the Shadow princes unbearable. This was what Reign feared? That I'd be upset about his half-brother bedding Liora? Well, I was, but not for the reason he dreaded.

I simply didn't trust the female.

And it wasn't only because she'd mercilessly flirted with my *cuoré* last term. There was something about her that I simply couldn't quite pinpoint.

"Well, I hope you didn't spill any secrets between the bedsheets, Ruhl," I replied, voice steady.

His dark brows furrowed, the smirk permanently carved into his mouth falling away. "That's it, then?"

"Yes." I stepped closer to Reign, lacing my fingers with his as I turned to face Ruhl.

"Isn't it just perfect? The bastard prince gets the girl, the bond, the kingdom..."

Drawing in a steadying breath, I lifted my gaze to meet that turbulent one. "Ruhl, you've come to mean a great deal to me, and I'll always care for you. Maybe too much. But Reign... he's my mate. My heart chose him long before I understood what that truly meant. What we share is more than love, it's something elemental and undeniable. And I hope someday, you find a love just as powerful. One that doesn't break you but rather makes you whole."

The depth of misery in his expression lanced across my chest. Gods, I felt awful for laying it all out there, but it was better he accepted it now than hold onto a shred of hope that would never be. "I'm sorry," I whispered.

"No, don't be sorry," he slurred. "You two are destined. And me? I'm just the shadow trailing after you."

Reign's dark minions writhed at his feet like serpents hungry for blood. "So that's what this was?" Ice laced his tone, the uneasy calm descending across his features more frightening than the wrath I could feel simmering below the surface. "A desperate attempt to make Aelia jealous? What the realms did you think would happen, Ruhl? That she'd forsake our bond and come running to you?"

"Clearly, I wasn't thinking," he muttered, leaning his head against his palm.

Reign released my hand, stalking toward his brother. "You need to stop this foolishness before you ruin everything we've fought so hard to achieve."

The drunk Shadow Prince twirled his hand in the air, and a shadow twisted between his fingers. "Right, as you wish."

A tendril of night spilled from Reign's form, coiling around Ruhl's shadow, snuffing the life out of it. Nothing but specks of ash dribbled to the floor as Ruhl watched, eyes wide.

"Reign!" I snapped. "He's drunk and—"

"No, don't make excuses for him, Aelia. He's acting like a selfish, spoiled prince."

"Don't you mean I'm acting like myself again?"

"Yes," he hissed.

"Well, I suppose this is the real me." He leapt up, stumbled a step, then gripped the arm of the settee. "The one who's always existed. The one who *isn't* in love with your *cuoré*." He cast a scathing glare in my direction.

Oh, goddess.

"Perhaps, we should postpone this conversation until Ruhl has fully sobered up." I turned to Reign, pleading. The last thing I needed were the two princes at each other's throats. "I could go see Elisa, surely she must have a potion to speed up the process."

"No, my presence is not required here." He turned toward the door, holding onto the furniture on his way. "You only need my memories of the discussion with Father, correct?" A whisper of shadow slid from his fingertips and curled around the shell of my ear. "Well, here they are."

I barely registered the sound of the door slamming closed as the dark coil slipped into my ear, and the room around me shimmered, bending at the edges like ripples across glass. I wasn't here, wherever *here* was, but it felt real. *Too* real.

Black stone columns rose around me, shrouded in endless dusk. The vaulted ceiling of Tenebris's war chamber loomed overhead, heavy with shadows. I had no idea how I recognized it, but I knew it for what it was, a place of cold strategy and colder ambition.

Ruhl's shadow had grazed my skin moments ago, just a whisper, a flicker of his power, and now I was watching a memory. It was so potent it gripped my throat in a vice.

The dark prince stood before his father, fists clenched at his sides.

"You cannot be serious," Ruhl bit out, pacing before the obsidian war table. "Helroth is building an army unlike anything this realm has seen. If we wait, he will crush the Light Court, but he won't stop there."

King Tenebris lounged in his throne of carved onyx and bone, chin propped lazily on one hand. His other drummed against the armrest in a steady rhythm, like a ticking clock counting down to disaster.

"*Let him try,*" *Tenebris said, voice calm and completely unbothered.* "*Let Helroth bleed the Light Court dry. Let Elian march his pristine legions to their deaths. I see no reason to waste our own forces while our enemies slaughter each other.*"

Ruhl's jaw flexed, a flicker of nox *curling at his fingertips.* "*You're a fool if you think he won't turn to us next.*"

Tenebris's lips curled into something too sharp to be called a smile. "*If he does, we will be ready. Shadow does not fear Night.*"

"*This isn't about fear,*" *Ruhl growled.* "*It's about survival. It's about Aetheria. You've grown too used to scheming from the shadows, Father. But this, this is no court game. He means to unmake the balance.*"

The king rose slowly, the movement deliberate, predatory. "*And what would you have me do? March into an alliance with the Light Court? Break bread with Elian and beg to fight at his side like brothers-in-arms?*" *He scoffed.* "*The Light Court would just as soon slit your throat as clasp your hand.*"

"*Not if we go to them first. Not if we set the terms.*"

Tenebris's eyes glinted, a storm brewing in the depths of midnight. "*Perhaps, you've been too long in your brother's presence. Has he too become swayed by the Light after all these years across the Luminoc? Or is it that Kin he's bedding that's made him weak?*"

A chill skated down my spine.

"*Reign is anything but weak. And that female means nothing to him,*" *Ruhl snapped.* "*She is no one.*"

"*Good,*" *Tenebris hissed.*

Ruhl stepped forward, shadows rolling off his shoulders. "*We should fight to save the realm. Because if we do nothing, there will be nothing left to rule.*"

A heavy silence stretched between them. The kind that split empires.

Then Tenebris turned his back. "*I will not raise my army for fools. Let Elian and Helroth destroy each other. When the smoke clears, we will pick the bones clean.*"

The vision fractured, like the memory had reached its limit, and the chamber dissolved into darkness.

I gasped as I stumbled back into the present, the residual cold of Tenebris's indifference still clinging to my skin. Ruhl's shadow unraveled from around my ear, vanishing like mist.

It was Reign's arm to curl around my waist, steadying me. I blinked quickly and his familiar features coalesced.

"Did you see that?" I whispered, dread heavy in my tone.

"Yes, unfortunately so."

I knew now, without a doubt, that the true threat wasn't only Helroth and the Night Fae. It was the cowardice of kings who refused to act.

"So what do we do now?" I glanced up at Reign, his jaw hardened to steel.

"We move," Reign said, voice steeled with purpose. "To Elian. To war. And may the gods have mercy on anyone who stands in our way."

Chapter Ten

R^{eign}

"You're certain we should start with Draven?" Aelia's voice wavered as we traversed the grand corridors of the Hall of Luminescence the following morning. "I stood against an entire army of Light and Shadow Fae, but the headmaster..." She shivered. "Gods, I despise him."

I didn't slow. "We don't have a choice." I threaded my fingers through hers, bringing our clasped hands to my lips. "He's Elian's puppet, after all."

The night spent with her in my arms had fortified me and strengthened my resolve. I dreaded this encounter, but if we wished to unify the courts, the dueling academies were the perfect places to start. They were our first line of defense, after all. The soldiers, the ones out there caught in this battle, were once students, Royal Guardians from the Court of Ethereal Light and the Umbral Guard from my side of the Luminoc. Surely, we could find a way to put aside our differences long enough to subdue the real enemy.

"About my uncle..." A whisper of unease sailed through our bond.

"We will tread carefully, Aelia, I promise. I don't trust the royal one bit, but we need him. Right now, he is the lesser of two evils." My thoughts retreated to the scene Ruhl had imparted on us with his shadows. Tenebris wouldn't move a finger to help us, which only solidified my decision. As King of the Umbral Court, he was of no use to us any longer. I would turn him over to Elian at the earliest opportunity and put an end to this looming fear.

Once the threat of my father's cursed blood vow was eliminated, nothing would stand between Aelia and me again. At least, that's what I kept telling myself. But fate rarely gave without a cost. And Helroth never played fairly.

She nodded, quickening her pace down the luminescent hall. She was once again back in her training leathers, the familiar sight transporting me to an easier time, to hours spent on the field battling with her reluctant *rais*. Sometimes, I wished we could go back to those simpler days.

The gilded double doors of the headmaster's office loomed ever closer, only a few more steps away, at the end of the hallway. Shaking my head out to loosen the fond memories, I focused on the task at hand. The time for inaction was over. Now, we must tell Draven the truth and determine where he stood.

I paused at the entrance, my knuckles hovering inches from the gold-laden door. My shadows surged around me, that influx of *nox* and *zar* rising to the surface. There would be no going back now. Once Draven knew Aelia was alive and the child of twilight, the line would be drawn. He would either be on our side... or dead.

I wouldn't risk stealing his memories or replacing them with ones I'd crafted. Not now, when the situation was already so precarious.

Aelia's hand closed around mine, and she gently brought my

knuckles to the plated door. The sharp knock echoed across the suddenly quiet space.

"Who is it?" Draven barked, voice still sharp through the thick doors.

"It's Professor Darkthorn with an important visitor."

The door whipped open, the old Fae moving faster than I'd ever seen. He appeared in the doorway, in a similarly disheveled state as the last time I'd seen him, weeks ago. His bushy silver brows nearly reached his hairline as he took in Aelia, a gasp dying at the back of his throat.

"You were supposed to be dead," he finally muttered.

My shadows coiled around me, wraiths of darkness prepared to strike should the old Fae attempt to make a move against my *cuoré*.

Aelia stood beside me, spine snapped straight, shoulders thrown back and chin held high. "Well, I'm not dead as you can see, Headmaster Draven. Nice to see you again."

I wasn't sure if she even realized it, but a storm of *rais*, *nox* and *zar* seeped from her pores, blanketing her in an ethereal orb of light and shadow.

"Raysa, save us," he mumbled under his breath as he took her in.

"I'm afraid it was the goddess herself who started it all," Aelia replied succinctly.

"I simply cannot believe it." He leaned against the threshold, jaw hanging open so that his trailing white beard brushed the folds of his tattered robe. "You truly are the one, the child spoken of in the prophecy, aren't you?" His words carried a tangle of fear and dread but laced beneath was a hint of awe.

"Can we continue this discussion inside your office, perhaps?" I offered.

His head dipped, eyes never deviating from my *cuoré* as he motioned for us to enter. It took all my restraint to keep from shoving her behind my back, to keep her away from that intrusive gaze.

Draven shuffled around his massive desk, sinking into the high-backed chair and nearly disappearing behind the tower of tomes sprawled across the lightwood. Once again, I was taken aback by the state of disarray.

What was the headmaster researching that had him in such a frenzy?

I scanned the ancient texts across the desk: *The Codex of Aetheria, Lumen et Umbra: The Sacred Binaries, Vitae Nocturna: The Lineage of Night*. I was fairly certain the last one was a forbidden genealogical record of the Night Court's royal bloodline, a text that had long been banned in the Light Court.

Did he remember anything about my previous visit? Or had King Elian shared news of the true heir's return?

"Please, sit down." He motioned to the chairs in front of the desk, both cluttered with scrolls and more timeworn textbooks. Loosing a pair of shadows, I cleared both seats, gently depositing all the reading material on the floor.

Aelia folded into the chair, and I followed her lead, perching on the edge of the leather cushion. I would never be truly at ease in the presence of this Light Fae, not after everything he'd put me through during my tenure at the Conservatory.

He dipped his head at Aelia before his wide eyes pivoted to mine. "Now, is someone going to explain to me how this is possible? How is she still alive after all this time?"

So, Elian had *not* briefed the headmaster about her return. Or, he was a talented liar. I supposed either could be true.

"I was captured by the King of Infernal Night," Aelia answered, her reply deceptively calm despite the turmoil raging through our bond. "He kept me prisoner within Helspire Keep, and during that time, he unbound my powers."

"Remarkable..." he muttered. "I can almost see them, as clear as Raysa's blessed day." He squinted as he regarded her, as if he could pinpoint the glittering swirl of *rais*, the dark tendrils of *nox* and the inky void of *zar*.

I sat forward, placing a palm on the headmaster's desk. "The

Night King is planning to strike against both courts, Draven. It is imperative we prepare now before we are plunged into yet another war."

His Adam's apple jogged along the wrinkled column of his throat.

"We must unify the Courts of Light and Shadow, and that begins with the academies, with Luce and Arcanum. We have foolishly fought each other for too long. Now we must join together against the Night Court before they destroy everything."

His eyes narrowed, an unexpected surge of fury livening the pale gray of his eyes. "Don't you think we've tried, Darkthorn?" he growled. "Why do you think we continue these inane trials every term? Malakar knows what lies beyond the Wilds, just as well as I do. Those beasts of lore are nothing compared to the true monsters out there—the Night Court."

I drew in a sharp breath. Noxus, Malakar knew as well. All of them have been keeping the truth from their people for years now.

"It's that damned King Tenebris," he continued. "He refuses to raise a finger. Sure, he sends his Umbral Guard to keep the Demon fiends at bay, but to organize a coordinated attack? Nothing."

"Why not?" Aelia interjected.

"Only Noxus knows." His rounded shoulders lifted slowly. "King Elian believes Helroth and Tenebris have struck a deal behind his back. The Night and Shadow Courts were once allies, and he believes they're gathering against him."

Aelia's gaze swung at me, fear blossoming. Gods, Tenebris and Helroth united against Light could prove too daunting to overcome. I could never allow that alliance to solidify. Which meant, I had to move against Father immediately.

Once I confirmed Elian's loyalty to my mate.

"The King has sworn to protect Aelia, and I am here now asking you to swear the same."

Draven's light brows knitted, his expression souring. "Why

would he ever do that when the very existence of the child of twilight risks the destruction of all Aetheria? More importantly, do you expect me to trust a weapon forged by the Night?"

"I do. Because I can deliver something Elian wants more."

"More than the safety of our courts?" He lifted a skeptical brow.

"Yes," I hissed.

He steepled his hands, leaning on the desk. "And what is that?"

"My father, King Tenebris."

All the years of abuse under his hand were nearly worth it for that look of utter shock and disbelief.

"Yes, that's right, Draven. All this time, you've been harboring the king's bastard." I shot him a feral grin, a wave of shadows darkening the room. "Do you have any idea how easily I could have destroyed you and your precious Conservatory?"

Aelia's hand closed over mine, squeezing gently. *Now is not the time, my love. We need his help, remember?* Her voice slid through my mind, calming the building rage, and my buzzing shadows reluctantly retreated.

Noxus, I hate it when you're the levelheaded one.

She smirked, hand releasing mine, but Draven's curious gaze caught the exchange.

"I always knew there was something between you." Those pale, lifeless eyes darted toward Aelia before turning to lock on my own. "The way you protected her, coddled her. I'd never seen you like that with any of your acquisitions."

Aelia and I had debated telling him the truth of our connection, and in the end, we'd decided for it. He, along with everyone else, would figure it out eventually anyway. The fact that we were *cuoré* wouldn't change anything. The fact that Aelia was King Alaric's daughter, though, that was a different story. We'd decided not to divulge that essential piece of information to anyone. It was critical to diminish Aelia's threat to Elian's claim to the throne as best we could. The fewer people that knew the truth, the safer she'd be.

"Reign is my *cuoré*," Aelia breathed. "We completed the sacred bond and are bound to each other for life."

Again, those brows arched. "Realms, you truly were blessed by the gods, weren't you, Kin?"

Blessed, cursed, who knew? It was still too soon to say.

Aelia rose slowly. The scent of *rais* thickened, electric and bright, moments before her luminescent wings erupted like twin blades of dawn. Even I had to blink against the brilliance.

Draven gasped, the satisfying sound causing a smile to stretch across my *cuoré's* face.

"As you can see, Headmaster, I am no longer just a lowly Kin. I am Light Fae, but more than that, I was born of Shadow and Night as well. I am King Helroth's granddaughter, Princess of the Court of Infernal Night."

"Good gods," he spluttered.

"I may carry Night in my veins, but my heart belongs to the Light. I choose to heal and nurture, to become a beacon of hope and bring forth a new dawn. I will never be the harbinger of doom or what my grandsire hoped to make me."

"And what is that?"

"His weapon."

Please, Aelia, do not tell him of the hold Helroth has on you. There is no need to exacerbate his fears. I shot the thought through our bond. The last thing we needed was for Draven to make a foolish decision out of panic.

I won't. I only need him to understand that I'm on his side.

Narrowing my eyes at the old Fae, I steeled my tone. "So, what do you choose, Draven? Will you fight with us for the students on this campus and for all the residents of Aetheria?"

Draven's mouth opened, then closed. And in the stillness that followed, the fate of an entire realm hung in the balance.

Chapter Eleven

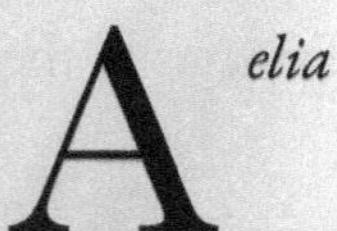

elia

They say no one returns from the dead, but I'd never been one to follow the rules... I stood beneath the shadows of the Hall of Luce, my gaze pinned on the mass of second years littering the training field. *Rais* hummed in the air, the pleasant glow of luminescent shields and radiant blades bathing the lush clearing. There was something serene and oddly beautiful about the sight. A part of me wished to once again be that invisible Kin within the sea of blonde Light Fae, struggling to summon her reluctant *rais*, but that was not my fate.

Today, a ghost would rise.

But first, I needed a moment to steel myself for the dreaded homecoming. Would Flare Team welcome me back, or would Belmore and Ariadne keep sneering down their perfect noses like I was still something scraped off the bottom of their boots? As the infamous child of the prophecy, I was surely as welcome as the Night King at the feast of the Winter Solstice.

Oh, gods, Aelia, what does that matter?

Being accepted by my team and classmates should have been the least of my worries. I leaned against the marble pillar, forcing a breath past the dread clawing up my throat.

The encounter with Draven had left me drained, recounting my destiny as the child of twilight never a pleasant task. And yet, I forced myself to focus on the swirl of hope that had ignited at his promise to do what he could to unite the academies; Reign and his persuasive shadows hadn't exactly given him a choice in the matter. He'd also insisted Draven speak to Malakar at his earliest opportunity.

In only a few days, both campuses could begin training together to battle a new foe. Assuming Draven was successful in convincing Malakar to disobey King Tenebris's rule. My hopes weren't high on that front, but before Reign darted off to speak to Professor Lumen before class, he assured me that the volatile headmaster of Arcanum played by his own rules, and anything was possible.

Cocking my head over my shoulder, I glanced across the river at the spiraling ebony turrets of Arcanum Citadel. Was Ruhl there now? Was he still upset, or had he found solace in another female?

A part of my heart ached for the Shadow Prince. I hated to see him in pain after everything we'd been through. I tried consoling myself with the thought that what he felt for me wasn't real. It was only a trick of the cuorem. Somehow, the lie rang hollow though. Ruhl had developed real feelings for me, just as I had for him. Whatever tether the cuorem had forged between us had twisted into something more. Ruhl had cared for me, maybe even loved me. And a part of me had wanted to believe it. In the end, though, I'd chosen my heart's true desire: Reign, the male I loved more than anything. That still didn't mean I wanted to see Ruhl hurt.

I resolved to mend the rift between us as soon as I could. After all, with Reign and me destined to be together forever, as his brother, Ruhl, too, would always be in our lives.

The air shifted and my instincts sparked like flint, turning my attention over my shoulder toward the Hall of Glory. Reign and Liora treaded down the marble steps, the Light Fae female staring up adoringly at *my* professor. Despite having heard how Reign's other acquisition had aided in retrieving me from Helroth's clutches, I still sided with Rue on the Liora issue.

I did not trust the female.

My thoughts soared back in time to one of the occasions Helroth had infiltrated my mind and dragged me unwittingly into the middle of battle.

I glanced across the battlefield, through the glittering veil, and a familiar form took shape, cutting across a line of Light Fae. Liora? Blinking quickly, my vision cleared, and a lavender-haired female stood in her place, launching hellfire across the troop of Royal Guardians.

I could have sworn I saw her that day, the day I'd seen Heaton, right alongside the other Night Fae. He had been real; I was certain of it. What if she was too?

With my thoughts shifting to Heaton, a suffocating weight settled across my shoulders. I'd vowed to return to the Wilds to find him, and yet, days passed without action. I must keep my word to Rue. Every day he was out there only strengthened Helroth's grip on my friend.

Gods, I had to find a way to get to him.

"I'm so thrilled to see you back on campus, Aelia." A cheery voice tore me from my dark musings. Blinking quickly, I focused on Liora, standing a few inches too close to my *cuoré*. As if Reign had sensed the flare of jealousy, he stepped away from his *other* acquisition to stand at my side. "And I suppose congratulations are in order. I hear you and Reign are fated mates? What an honor to be chosen by the gods for such a blessed pairing." Her smile showed too many teeth, bordering on a sneer. Polite, pretty, and possibly laced with poison.

"Well, then, I guess Ruhl did share some secrets during your tawdry little encounter. Nothing like taking advantage of a male who is two sheets to the wind."

"That's not—" Liora's cheeks flared a deep crimson. "I didn't think it would matter—"

"It doesn't," I cut her off, raising my hand.

"And in any case," she continued, "it wasn't the other night in bed that Ruhl told me of the cuorem. He mentioned it in passing one day, when he was perfectly sober."

"The evening Aelia was taken by King Helroth?" Reign asked.

She shrugged. "How should I know? I can't keep track with all the chaos."

Could that have been why Helroth took you? He discovered we were bound and hoped to steal you away before the cuorem grew stronger? Reign's questions zipped through my mind.

Maybe... but how could he have known? Besides Ruhl, only Rue, Sy, Gideon and Aidan knew. Not even Kaelith had been privy to our bonding until after we'd returned to Shadowmere.

If Ruhl told Liora... His words fell away, and I could feel the coils of unease sweeping through our bond.

Reign had been the first one to defend her, since the beginning.

The unease morphed into something darker, something truly terrifying. *What if Ruhl told Helroth in some twisted attempt at revenge at us for completing the bond?* His question was nothing more than a serrated growl.

"No. He wouldn't." I blurted the inconceivable words aloud. "Ruhl would never betray me like that."

And yet... I found my mind spinning to the past, to the ball after the Umbral Trials when Ruhl trapped me in the corner of the decadent chamber.

He lifted a hand, pressing his finger to my lips. "Do not worry, duskling. I have no intention of divulging the truth to my father. I only ask one small favor in return."

"What is that?" I breathed.

"Simple, you refuse to complete the cuorem bond with Reign."

I'd always meant to ask Ruhl why he'd asked that of me. A part of me foolishly assumed it was because of the so-called feelings he'd developed for me. But what if there was more?

Slamming down the glittering mental barrier Reign had taught me to conjure, I closed off my thoughts to my mate. The bond resisted, like a blade dragged across bone. Reign's presence dimmed in my mind, and I hated the way the relief and guilt battled in my chest. If Reign ever received confirmation that Ruhl had done anything to jeopardize my safety, he would destroy him.

Without a second thought.

Reign's frenzied shadows slid across my flesh, drawing me back to the sun-bathed field. I blinked to find his gaze heavy on me. Could he feel the wall I'd constructed between us?

"We'll discuss this later in private." I ticked my head toward the training field. "It's time to announce my triumphant return to the academy."

Reign nodded, his dark brows furrowed and a tendon feathering beneath the hard line of his jaw. Liora stepped forward first, leaving me beside him in a weighted silence.

Gods, I hoped I was wrong.

If Ruhl had conspired with the Night King, or if he was even aware of Tenebris scheming with Helroth...

Gods help them both if Reign found out. Because he wouldn't just destroy them, he'd burn everything to ash.

Chapter Twelve

R*eign*

Do you really believe you'll get away with this?

Phantom's voice filled my mind, tearing my gaze from the stretch of verdant lands below. The Castle of Ethereal Light grew ever closer, its glistening towers shimmering beneath the radiant sun.

I still have a few hours until Aelia rises. With any luck, I'll be back at Luce before she notices I'm missing.

A swell of guilt rose from my core. She'd curled toward me in her sleep, as if sensing I was slipping away. And yet, here I was, choosing an encounter with Elian over her trust.

Phantom snorted a laugh, plumes of smoke lifting from her nostrils. *I think you are greatly underestimating the cuorem.*

My dragon wasn't wrong, and I knew it well. Even now, I could feel the angry pulsating in my chest. The mystical fibers that tethered us writhed and rioted, furious at the imposed distance.

The ethereal connection felt the void between us even if Aelia hadn't yet.

Is the dragon mate bond similar to the cuorem?

Phantom chuffed her annoyance, her head angling back to pin me in a glacial glare.

What? I'm merely trying to understand. I offered her a smile, which she most definitely did not return.

No, Reign, the dragon mate bond is nothing like your volatile little cuorem. It's sacred, a remnant of the time when dragons were more divine than beast, when they served as celestial guardians of balance. It's unbreakable, transcending lifetimes and reincarnations, as you know. It's a shared consciousness, more than just a telepathic connection, that also leads to emotional and physical bleed-over.

You mean you can feel each other's pain?

Correct.

Gods, that sounds awful.

There are caveats, of course. Namely, it must be willingly accepted by both dragons in each lifetime. And there's a ritual... Regardless, if left unbound, it can lead to madness and fury spirals, even loss of flight in rare cases.

"Noxus..." I mumbled. *Then what are you two waiting for? I can't find myself skyriderless.*

It isn't without its risks... Regardless, I'm afraid you'll have to discuss that with your cuoré's dragon.

Understanding finally slammed into me, followed by a surge of pain and bitterness. Solanthus still refused to complete the bond. That explained Phantom's surly mood this past week.

I'm sure he'll come around, old girl. Perhaps, he simply needs time.

She snorted again before the sleek obsidian strands that connected us went silent. In the sudden stillness, I vowed to have a chat with Aelia about her dragon's reluctance to seal the bond at the next chance I had. With everything else going on, having our dragons at odds would certainly not do us any favors.

Just ahead, the gleaming castle rose from a cliff of shimmering white stone. We circled the cascading waterfalls that spilled into the lake below then began our descent. Cut off from my dragon, I could only assume where she was heading as we hovered over the soaring spires toward the central dome.

Smart girl.

When arriving on dragonback to see a potential ally, the direct approach was always preferred. Skulking in the shadows would only create more alarm.

"The clearing in front of the castle is just fine, Phantom."

She chuffed her response, keeping up her mental barriers.

By the time her talons sank into the moist earth, a dozen Royal Guardians stood at the entrance to the king's home, a bevy of ethereal and traditional metal weapons at the ready.

Leaping off Phantom's back, I raised my hands in surrender, willing my shadows back. "I've come to see King Elian with news from the Conservatory." There was no need to mention my name; I'd become a legend over the years at Luce. Everyone knew of the banished Shadow Fae professor.

One of the males donning the pristine alabaster uniform of the kings' guards scurried through the grand gilded doors. Tension radiated across the shoulders of every Royal Guardian as they scrutinized me. I stood there, waiting—impatiently— knowing that every moment that passed was another one in which Aelia could wake and find me missing.

My intentions had not been to deceive her, but rather to protect her from a royal I did not trust. Our last visit to Elian was made in haste, and this time I intended to not only secure his word, but also the troops he promised. With an increase in Royal Guardians along the border, it was more likely we'd keep the Night King at bay.

And right now, we needed time. Time to train our forces to work together.

The massive golden door squealed open, and the guard

motioned for me to enter. "His Ethereal Highness will see you now."

"Wonderful," I muttered and marched through the entrance, trailing after the guard through the endless alabaster corridors.

The sun-drenched marble of Elian's court was too bright. Too pure. It stung my eyes like it knew what I was. Shadow had no place here, not even when bearing the olive branch of war. Squinting, I continued on, the slap of our footfalls across the marble echoing the drumming behind my ribs. Realms, how I longed for the cool, quiet feel of night.

I stepped through the arched doorway with my hood down and my shadows suppressed, though they coiled in discomfort beneath my skin. Across the throne room, King Elian lounged on his gleaming seat of cut crystal and gold, his fingers tapping a slow, disinterested rhythm against the armrest.

He didn't rise. Didn't speak. Just studied me with sharp turquoise eyes that reminded me too much of Aelia's when she was angry.

I bowed my head only slightly. He was not my king, after all. "Your Ethereal Highness."

Still nothing. Just the faintest tightening of his jaw. Gods, this was going to be a delightful conversation.

"I've come to confirm your vow," I said, when it was clear he had no intention of speaking first. Then I stepped forward until his guards stiffened. I stopped short of the dais, keeping my hands at my sides. "Your promise to protect Aelia from King Helroth, any Night Court influence, or anyone wishing to do the child of twilight harm. That oath still holds, I trust?"

His brows arched like I'd asked if he intended to dance a jig.

"You enter my court unannounced, cloaked in shadows, reeking of *nox* and... something else, and you question *my* word? I vowed to protect her, and I will." Elian leaned forward, resting his chin on his fist. "The bond you share with my niece may have some gods-given merit, Reign, but do not mistake that for dominion over this court."

"I mistake nothing," I replied coolly. "But I've learned not to leave room for doubt, especially when my mate's life hangs in the balance."

He frowned at that, briefly, but I didn't miss the twitch of his mouth. Like the word *mate* left a sour taste.

"I do not break vows," he finally replied, voice like polished glass. "And I do not fear Helroth. But let's not pretend this alliance is anything more than what it is—a strategic necessity."

"You're right," I agreed, clasping my hands behind my back. "So let me make the terms clear. You send your forces to stand against the Night Court, and I deliver Tenebris, powers bound, silenced and at your mercy."

That got his attention. Elian sat up straighter, his fingers stilling. "You'd truly turn on your own blood?"

My jaw clenched as memories of the feel of Tenebris's boot against my ribs rose to the surface. "I'd burn the whole Shadow Court to ash if it meant keeping Aelia safe," I growled without hesitation. "Tenebris would see this realm handed to Helroth in exchange for a whisper of power. He's already refused to act. He'll sit on his onyx throne while the rest of Aetheria burns."

Elian's lips pursed. "You speak like a king."

"I speak like a male with everything to lose."

Silence fell. Only the echo of a distant fountain trickled through the gilded halls. The light refracting from the domed ceiling dappled the king's robes in a spectrum of gold and white. He looked like a creature carved from sunfire. Untouchable, indomitable.

But even he couldn't hide the weariness in his eyes.

"We've fought Night before." He shifted in his grand throne. "We won, but barely. And that was before decades of mounting vengeance, without Helroth's growing legions or the looming prophecy. You expect me to believe we can win this time?"

Gods, it was a good thing he had no notion of the Night King's hold over Aelia. If he did...

"We don't have a choice," I replied, shoving down the

thought he would never discover. "Unless you'd prefer to watch your people fall. Again."

His jaw clenched. "Light and Shadow have never fought as one."

"They must now." I paused, letting the weight of it settle between us. "Aelia is the bridge. Not just between us, but between realms. Between bloodlines."

His eyes sharpened, glinting like a blade unsheathed. "Yes, well. About that..."

Here it comes.

"She is King Alaric's daughter. My brother's only child. You realize what that makes her, don't you?"

The *heir.*

I didn't flinch. "She knows. And she doesn't want your throne."

"Yet..." He rose from his seat at last, his golden mantle catching the light. "She may not, now, but power changes things. Especially when it's given freely by the people. I've already heard tales of what she accomplished on the battlefield just over a week ago. She is calling too much attention to herself already, Reign. And if she stands beside you—"

"She doesn't want it," I repeated, stepping forward. "She desires only peace. She wants safety for Aetheria, and an end to the threat of war and the damned prophecy. If she wanted power, she would've taken it already."

He stared at me for a long moment. Then, finally, he nodded once.

"I will summon my generals," he said. "The Royal Guardians will be deployed to fortify the border of the Wilds. I will attempt to set a meeting between the Courts of Light and Shadow, but I doubt your father will agree."

"I will handle Tenebris."

"Very well."

I inclined my head. "Cheers."

"Don't thank me," he said, sneering. "If this fails, we all burn.

And I'd rather not spend the end of the world fighting beside a bastard Shadow Fae royal."

I smirked. "Don't worry, Elian. I'm the last one you'll have to fight." I paused, biting my tongue before deciding better of it. "Unless you come for *her*."

As I turned to leave, I felt his gaze boring into my back. But I'd gotten what I came for.

Aelia would be protected.

Chapter Thirteen

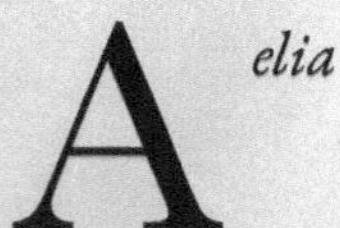

A*elia*

That sneaky, conniving Shadow Fae would pay for this betrayal. Marching across the too-bright hallways of my uncle's castle behind a Royal Guardian, I followed the shimmery bonds that connected me to my traitorous *cuoré*. The ache of the incessant hollow in my chest had woken me from a fitful sleep. How dare he come to see Elian without me?

That stubborn fool was still trying to protect me, when *he* was currently the more volatile one. Somehow, since I broke through Helroth's control on the battlefield, I could feel his hold on my mind lessening. Perhaps it was the distance between us, or the nights Reign and I spent faithfully cementing our cuorem. I couldn't say. Reign still barely slept most evenings, regardless, too anxious that I'd be ripped away from him again, despite my assurances that something had changed. He was the one now barely hanging on by a thread of sanity. What if he'd lost control of his powers and attacked Elian?

Turning a corner, my heart stuttered and the void in my chest immediately filled an instant before the slap of heavy footfalls reached my sensitive ears. I was sprinting past the guard before I could stop myself, throwing my arms around Reign's stiff form.

"Never do that again," I hissed, even as my treacherous lips brushed over his. *I'm so angry with you.* The ethereal strands of our mental bond surged to life as my words sailed through our connection.

He tensed for only a moment before his body yielded to mine. "What are you doing here?"

"What do you think?"

He eyed the guard over my shoulder, dark brows furrowing.

"We were supposed to come together," I whispered.

"I decided that was not the optimal choice."

Pulling out of his embrace, I jabbed a finger into his chest through his dark cloak. "You don't get to decide that for me."

The less time you spend with these conniving royals the better, Aelia.

He's my uncle, Reign, and I need to know what side he is truly on. If he's only fighting for me to ensure Tenebris's demise, I must know that too.

"Ah, Aelia," the king's voice echoed through the enormous hall and the Royal Guardian immediately straightened to attention. "Reign did not tell me you had accompanied him."

"Your Ethereal Highness." I dipped into a bow. "I'm afraid that's because I didn't. I had another matter to attend to this morning, but I finished more quickly than planned and headed straight here."

"Wonderful. Then I must insist you and your *cuoré* join me for the day."

Reign's suspicious glare flickered from the king then back to me. *Your uncle certainly sings a different tune in your presence.*

I could only imagine how the conversation had gone with the king before my arrival. He'd never kept his disdain for Reign a secret, even back in our days at the Conservatory.

We should return to the academy, Aelia.

I know, but I've come all this way, and I had hoped to ask him a few questions.

About your family...

I nodded. I must have inadvertently sent some of that silly hope through our bond because Reign's hard expression softened.

Fine. We can stay—but not for long. There is much to be done.

Thank you.

As if I could ever say no to you, starlight.

I must have remained silent for too long because Elian cocked his head in my direction, irritation puckering his brow. "What do you say, Aelia? It is improper to deny the request of a king, you know."

"Then I won't." I offered my best smile.

"Very well. I'll have word sent to the kitchens that you'll both be joining me for High Tea in an hour. I simply have a small matter I must attend to first." He ticked his head at the Royal Guardian pressed to the wall. "Please escort our guests into the Rose Atrium to wait."

"Of course, Your Ethereal Highness."

The gilded tea set gleamed in the sunlight like it had never seen the Two Hundred Years' War. Porcelain cups sat delicately on gold-rimmed saucers, the steam of rosehip and faelight blossom curling upward like a perfumed spell. A silver tiered tray of sugared pastries and fruit tarts sat untouched between us, an offering neither Reign nor I trusted enough to sample.

King Elian, in his immaculate white robes and smug serenity, looked every inch the benevolent monarch. His golden hair was slicked back, not a strand out of place, and his smile was as blinding as the sun overhead. I wanted to believe my only living relative had at least a shred of good in him. He was my father's brother, after all, and I needed to hold onto that scrap of hope.

"I apologize for keeping you waiting, but I truly am so pleased you accepted my invitation," he said smoothly before turning his gaze to the attendant who immediately poured a cup for each of us with a flick of his wrist. "How could I resist the opportunity to dine with my niece and her formidable companion when they had so graciously, and unexpectedly, come to see me."

Reign stiffened beside me, his shadows slithering beneath the table like barely restrained wolves. The overwhelming scent of *nox* and *zar* drifted beneath my nostrils, and I wondered if my uncle could sense it too. I only hoped my mate had it under control.

"Of course," I replied, keeping my tone neutral. "We wouldn't want to offend our gracious host."

Reign's hand brushed mine beneath the table, a grounding tether. I didn't need the cuorem to know he was biting back several threats.

The king handed me a teacup with a dazzling smile. "You look like your father, you know."

I blinked, the unexpected comment stealing my breath. "I wouldn't know. I never met him, remember?"

"Ah," Elian said, settling back in his chair, cradling his own cup. "Yes. Such a tragedy."

The clink of porcelain was the only sound for a beat too long.

I cleared my throat. "That's actually something I've been meaning to ask about, among countless other things. My parents, Alaric and Sable, how did they die? The history books are unclear."

Reign tensed beside me. Elian, to his credit, didn't flinch. He simply sighed, setting his tea down with a deliberate clink and folding his hands atop the table.

"We were never certain, I'm afraid," he replied gently, eyes lifting to mine. "Your father returned from battle gravely wounded after the death of his dragon in the skies over Virevale.

He refused our best healers. He claimed he was fine, but sadly, he followed his skyrider only days later."

Emotion tightened my throat as I thought of my father and Solanthus, and the overwhelming grief they must have experienced.

"And my mother?" I forced out.

He gave a long, sorrowful shake of his head. "Sable... faded. That's the only word for it. The healers believed it was the effects of the cuorem bond. When Alaric died, it tore something out of her. She passed quietly in her sleep not long after."

My heart clenched. Reign's hand tightened around mine as the sorrow rolled through me.

"Alaric was... protective. Overly so, especially with you and Sable. He rarely let either of you be seen in public, and he took great measures to ensure your mother's identity was kept concealed. At the time, I didn't understand it. I assumed it was an effect of the mate bond."

I frowned. "How did you not know she was Shadow Fae?"

Elian tilted his head. "Well, I didn't question any of it at the time. There was no need to. She was radiant, and her hair was golden. A perfect Light Court match. I assumed she was of noble blood from the eastern provinces. Your father certainly did not explain his choice of wife to me. Perhaps he used a glamour, or some sort of Mysthallian potion to hide her true identity. There are old enchantments the spellbinders have mastered, you know, enough to fool even a king." He gave a tight smile, then sipped his tea again. "I didn't suspect a thing."

Liar.

The cuorem throbbed between Reign and me, and I knew he'd heard the same note I had. It was the subtle, careful editing of truth. Elian was too clever not to have known or at least suspected. Too paranoid not to have asked. And yet here he was, playing the benevolent uncle, feigning regret over a history he may have helped erase.

"I just find it curious," I said, voice calm but laced with

steel, "that no one seemed to question why the king's consort never left his private wing. Why no one met the mother of the heir."

"I did question it," Elian replied smoothly. "But Alaric was headstrong. And when I finally met you, it was already too late."

He looked away then, as if pained by the memory.

"You were just a babe when they passed. I had no reason to believe you were anything other than Light." He glanced at my hair and his lips twitched. "That lovely dark mane of hair had yet to grow in at the time. And then when you disappeared, I feared the worst. We all did."

Another lie, softly wrapped in silk.

Reign's voice was ice beside me. "You feared the prophecy."

Elian met his gaze, unflinching. "Yes. The royal seers had just made the proclamation, shortly after Aelia was born. We all feared their words. But I assure you, I never guessed she could have been the one." His eyes flickered in my direction. "If I had, I would have gone to much greater lengths to search for you."

"But you did search for me?"

"Of course, I did."

Another long silence stretched between us. The tea grew cold. Did Elian have any idea it was Aidan who stole me away? Raysa, I wished to ask more, but I didn't dare put my guardian in the king's crosshairs.

After another few minutes of idle chitchat, in which he avoided answering most of my questions, silence settled between us.

"Well," Elian finally said, rising to his feet. "I hope this meeting has helped mend some of the misunderstandings between us. I do wish for us to maintain a good relationship, Aelia."

I rose, too, schooling my expression into something unreadable. "Yes, of course. And it's certainly given us some clarity."

He smiled, and I swore there was something wolfish beneath it. "Good. I hope you'll stay for the remainder of the day, Aelia.

Even overnight. I've had a chamber prepared for you and your *cuoré*. This is your home, after all."

I nodded, forcing a cordial smile. "That's very gracious of you, uncle. I do find myself quite exhausted after the flight from the academy. It's been quite a trying few weeks."

"I can only imagine." He dipped his head. "Please, make yourself at home."

Reign's arm found my waist the moment we stepped outside the atrium's sun-drenched doors.

Do you believe him? His voice skimmed through my frazzled thoughts.

I want to. I kept my eyes forward as we followed the guard. *But I don't. Let him believe the lie is working until we've taken down the Night Court, and then, we come for him next.*

Chapter Fourteen

R*eign*

Damned Malakar and his waffling. My shadows gathered around my shoulders as I stalked toward the training field, irritation furrowing my brow. Ruhl had done his part, despite my qualms to the contrary, and had spoken with the headmaster of Arcanum about commencing joint training sessions against our new foe. According to my brother's shadow messenger, he wasn't keen on going behind our father's back.

If Ruhl couldn't convince the head of the Citadel, then I would be forced to return to my old home and speak to Malakar myself. Not something I looked forward to. We hadn't parted on the best terms upon my graduation from the Shadow Academy and had little contact since.

Malakar was one of the few souls alive in the Shadow Court who knew my father's dirty little secret. *Me.* His silence had been bought by the king long ago when I'd attended the Citadel. What he didn't know was why I'd been banished. But Malakar was a smart man, so I avoided the headmaster whenever possible, afraid he'd one day put the pieces together and recognize me for who I was. Now, none of that mattered. If Ruhl wasn't successful in securing his loyalty, I'd use my *zar*-fueled shadows to force it upon him.

An overwhelming sense of dread coiled in my gut. Every quiet day was a page torn from our dwindling chances to prepare. And I had no doubt Helroth was counting them. What was he waiting for? And what role would Aelia play in his plan?

Walking along the curving path that led to the training field, I suddenly halted, a flicker of shimmering movement catching my eye. Aelia.

I watched her dance across the lawn like she was born of starlight and war.

Her form blurred through the haze of sun-glinting blades and humming shields, her luminescent weapon slicing the air in a graceful arc before colliding with Symon's raised defense. The clash sent a ripple of pale gold through the *rais* barrier, flaring like lightning before it dissolved into harmless sparks. She didn't even flinch.

Gods, I'd seen her fight dozens of times, had trained her myself across the shadow-marked fields along the Luminoc. But here, under the clear skies of Luce with the other students watching her like she was a ghost risen from myth, she was something else entirely.

There was awe in the silence. Uneasy reverence... and fear.

They stared at her like she might unravel before their eyes. Like she couldn't possibly be real.

The majority of Flare Team, along with the rest of the academy, had all believed she was dead. Killed by an unknown foe. Erased. A powerless Kin whose story had ended in tragedy. And now she stood before them, hair whipping behind her like a dark comet's tail, blade dancing with the glow of a thousand stars.

Alive. Stronger. Otherworldly.

Draven's proclamation of her miraculous return had spread

like wildfire, the curious whispers hissing across the hallways this morning. He'd praised blessed Raysa for returning her safely to us, the speech a bit overdone considering his typical apathy toward the students in general.

Aelia had squirmed beneath his flowery words, crimson coating her cheeks. We'd spun a tale of her lost in the treacherous Wilds and having stumbled upon the Night Fae. Aelia had been adamant about keeping her imprisonment a secret. I couldn't blame her. I could only imagine what sort of questions would come of that.

Rumors about the Night Fae lingered upon the tongues of every student at the academy. And now it was time to put their curiosity to rest. There would be no foolish trial this term. Instead, they were to begin training for the real battle that was sure to come.

As I remained in the shadows watching, my dark wraiths curled restlessly at my feet, mirroring the crackle of *nox* deep in my chest. Not in warning. In reverence. Even they knew better than to disrespect the goddess wearing my mate's skin as she trained.

Rue flanked Aelia's right, eyes narrowed and blazing as she launched a stunning burst of light at Belmore, who yelped and dove sideways. Symon circled left, strategic and steady. They moved as one again, Flare Team reformed, rebuilt around the one they'd lost.

And still, the others kept their distance.

Second-years clustered at the edge of the field, whispering, glancing, pretending not to watch. But they did. All of them. Even the instructors. Aelia's name was already stirring across campus again. Only this time, it wasn't in hushed tones of pity or doubt.

It was fear and admiration. And maybe some suspicion.

I could feel her determination burning across the bond, sharp and steady like a blade pressed to flesh. She was proving herself, not just to them, but to herself. That she belonged here. That she had finally earned her place among them. That she wasn't broken.

I almost went to her. Almost couldn't stand it, seeing her teammates' eyes dart her way like she was something unnatural.

But then Rue let out a triumphant whoop, slapping Aelia's shoulder with a grin that made something knot in my chest. And Aelia, my fierce, reckless starlight, laughed. Full and bright, like she wasn't being weighed down by prophecy and bloodlines and the burden of being everyone's hope.

She didn't need me to fight this battle.

"Are you going to join us, professor?" Aelia shouted across the field. The teasing lilt to her voice had a smile sliding across my lips. Clearly, she'd overheard my thoughts through the cuorem.

If you keep looking at me like that, we won't be able to hide what we are much longer. Every Fae on this field will know you're mine.

Would that be so bad? she teased.

No, but it would lead to more questions.

About my blood...

I nodded. Though Aelia's parents were *cuoré*, a pairing across courts was extremely rare. It would only lead to more speculation about her lineage. Most of these students had no idea about the dreaded prophecy or any of the disastrous ramifications. Only the royals were privy to the foretelling words of the seers.

Better to keep it that way as long as we could.

Still, I closed the distance between us, unable to keep my whirling shadows away from her. "But maybe," I whispered against the shell of her perfectly pointed ear, "it would be acceptable for them to know there is *something* between us."

"And go against the code of conduct?" Her voice rose a few octaves.

"I'll speak to Draven to see if there's a way we can get around that."

"Now that he's *your* lapdog that should be easy enough," she whispered before tossing me a devious smirk, and I gritted my teeth to keep from capturing those tempting lips.

"Professor Darkthorn," a familiar deep voice called out, and irritation instantly flared.

"What is it, Belmore?" Though the Light Fae seemed to have made peace with my Aelia, I'd never forget how he and his friends had tortured her during her first year at the academy.

Ariadne moved to his side, her luminescent sword sputtering out in her palm.

"Are the rumors true?" He eyed Aelia, suspicion knitting his ashen brows. "Are the Night Fae truly still alive?"

I nodded, my jaw set in a tight line. "Unfortunately, so."

"And we are to fight them?" Ariadne asked.

"Once you've all been adequately trained."

Groans and grumbles of disapproval rolled through the crowd of second-years.

"I assure you I would never send you out to be slaughtered." My voice echoed across the field, strong and steady. "We've faced the Night Fae before, and we won. I am certain we can do it again."

"We fought for two hundred years," called out one of the students from Burn Squad. Muttered agreement sailed across the clearing.

"But you never had me to train you." I shot them a smirk, earning an uneasy chuckle. "Or the full breadth of Shadow Fae forces at your side."

More uneasy murmurs. Getting Light and Shadow Fae to fight together, let alone trust each other, would be more than half the battle.

Liora stepped forward from between the mass of gathered students. "Can you demonstrate for us, professor?"

"Certainly." I grinned before crooking a finger toward Aelia. "If you'll assist me, Miss Ravenwood?"

Her answering smile had my *nox* abuzz. "I'd love to."

Shadows slithered beneath my boots, alive with anticipation, but even they knew who we were facing. Our *cuoré* would not take it easy on us.

Aelia twirled her blade, the luminescent edge materializing in her palm catching the light. A smirk tugged at the corner of her mouth. *Try not to hold back, Shadow Prince. I'd hate to win too easily.* Her voice sailed through my mind, and the cuorem hummed in delight.

You haven't won yet. I rolled my shoulders, stretching the tightness from my spine. *Though I do appreciate the confidence, starlight.*

She lunged first. Smart. Fast. Her blade arced toward my ribs, and I barely managed to parry it, shadows surging to bolster my strike. The clang of our weapons echoed across the field, followed by the sharp sound of her laughter.

Gods, I loved sparring with her.

Not just for the rush of power or the way our energies danced together, the *nox, rais* and *zar* humming in sync, but for the way she made me work for it.

We fell into rhythm. Strike, dodge, counter. The world narrowed to the weight of her eyes, the rhythm of her breath, the fire in her smile when she landed a glancing blow across my side.

"Getting slow, Professor," she teased, breathless.

"I'm pacing myself," I ground out, though my muscles were starting to burn. "Didn't want to embarrass you too quickly."

She snorted, then vanished.

I blinked. One second she was in front of me, and the next, a swirl of *zar*-slick shadow and light erupted behind me. Her presence crashed into my back, her blade at my throat before I could fully turn.

My shadows surged defensively, but she'd already disarmed me, one foot planted behind my heel, the other braced forward as I stumbled back onto the ground. Flat on my back. She sat on top of me, straddling my hips, smirking like the goddess of victory herself.

"Yield?" she asked sweetly, pressing the blade gently to my throat.

I huffed a laugh, chest heaving beneath her. "To you? Always," I whispered low enough so only she could hear.

She leaned in, mouth grazing my jaw, her breath warm against my ear. "Good answer."

Noxus, she was tempting when she was fearless. Had there not been dozens of Fae surrounding us, I would have claimed her right here on the lawn beneath a cloak of my shadows. Instead, the moment Aelia rolled off me and offered her hand, a murmur swept across the field. I took her palm, let her pull me to my feet, then turned to face them all.

"When we fight against each other, it is inevitable for one of us to fall, but if we learn to work together..." I allowed my words to fall away.

Aelia stepped beside me, her light sparking just beneath the surface. Even standing still, she seemed to glow. She was sunlight kissed with starlight, power coiled tight and calm in every breath.

"We're not fighting one another anymore," she said, loud enough for them all to hear. "Not Light versus Shadow. That time is over."

"And it's time you learned what true unity looks like," I added.

She made a show of reaching for my hand. I didn't hesitate. Our palms met, fingers interlocking, and the cuorem flared to life, burning bright between us. The wind stirred, picking up strands of her hair as her wings unfurled behind her in a shimmer of luminous gold and onyx.

Shadows poured from me in ribbons, curling along her light without smothering it. Instead, they danced together, swirling, merging, dark and bright coiling in tandem, not opposition.

With a shared breath, we released it.

A blast of radiant dusk shot skyward, spiraling like a storm made of moonfire and shadowflame. It cracked the clouds above, scattering a burst of starlight so blinding and beautiful the students shielded their eyes.

Our combined powers arced across the field, painting the grass with glowing vines and whispering tendrils of smoke. The air hummed, alive with energy and balance.

No destruction. No chaos. Just perfect, harmonious force.

When the energy dissipated, we stood in the silence it left behind, hand in hand, power spent and still pulsing faintly beneath our skin.

The field was utterly quiet.

Then, Rue whispered, "Realms..."

Symon let out a low laugh, shaking his head. "Raysa, that was beautiful."

"It's incredible," someone else murmured.

I glanced sideways at Aelia. She didn't need to smile. I felt it in the bond, the satisfaction, the strength, and the certainty. This was what we were meant to be. Not weapons. Not monsters.

But a promise. A reckoning. And a beginning.

"And that is how we will defeat the Night Fae. Together, Light and Shadow."

Chapter Fifteen

A*elia*

"Did you see their faces?" Symon chuckled around a heaping bite of lamb stew as we sat around the banquet table in the dining hall. "They had no idea what our little Kin could do." He grinned at me indulgently.

"Let's hope they never see the full extent of it," I muttered in return.

Rue leaned closer, hunching over the table as she whispered, "But you seem to be well in control of your powers, right, A?"

I nodded. "I have been." Surprisingly, so. It was as if returning to Luce had severed the ties to my grandfather. Or again, it could have been Reign and the intensifying cuorem. The more we made love, the closer we became, the stronger our bond grew. I was certain soon it would be enough to overpower Helroth's hold. And perhaps, the Night King knew it too. In fact, I often wondered if that was why he'd struck that night when the cuorem was still new and fragile. But how would he have known we'd completed the bond? Unless Liora had told him.

I eyed Reign's other acquisition at the end of the table. She sat beside Belmore and Ariadne, chatting away.

Rue must have followed my line of sight because a grunt of disgust pursed her lips. "I still can't believe Ruhl and her..." She gagged, forcing a giggle to tumble out.

"Oh, stop it. She's gorgeous," Sy cut in. "Why wouldn't he want her?"

"Because there's just something *wrong* about her." Rue's nostrils flared as if she could sniff out the truth somehow. "Don't you agree, A?"

"There's definitely something off. I just can't quite put my finger on it."

"You two are crazy."

"And you're just blinded by lust," Rue shot back.

"Speaking of..." Symon's gaze lifted over my friend's shoulder as Devin strode through the doors of the dining hall. In the past few nights since my return to the academy, I'd had our dorm to myself... well, Reign and I, anyway.

"I'm so happy things are going well between the two of you," I whispered before he reached our table.

"Yes, everything's wonderful." A silly grin curled my friend's lips.

"It seems as if I'm the only sorry bastard stuck without a mate." His gaze flickered to Liora once again.

"Don't you dare," I hissed.

"What? It would only be sex, little Kin. You know my heart will forever belong to you and your formerly perfectly rounded ears."

Rolling my eyes, I dug my elbow into my friend's side. "Can't you find someone else? Please! Anyone but Liora."

He huffed out a breath. "Fine..."

"Cheers to that," Rue and I breathed in unison just as Devin reached our table.

He dropped a kiss to the top of Rue's head, and a rosy hue blanketed her cheeks. Raysa, they were cute together. I'd never seen my best friend so flustered over a male, and it made my heart happy.

Devin folded into the seat beside her, then filched a roasted potato wedge from her plate and popped it into his mouth. "So, what are we chatting about?"

The three of us exchanged conspiratorial glances before Rue waved a dismissive hand. "Nothing important."

"It's definitely time for a subject change," Sy mumbled around another bite.

"I think I have something interesting for us to discuss." Liora materialized over my friend's shoulder, flashing an eager smile. "I heard the infamous Bacchanalia is happening tonight in Arcanum." She waggled her light brows, and my stomach heaved.

Had she heard about the Shadow Fae party from Ruhl? He wasn't still speaking to her, was he?

Rue clapped her hands, a sharp squeal squeezing through her teeth. "This is perfect! If you all recall, the fabled event is legendary across the academy and beyond."

"You can't be serious," I blurted. "Do none of you remember what happened last time we snuck over there?" I peered at each one of my friends, Liora included. Both she and Rue had consumed questionable potions and had been unconscious for some portion of the evening. Not to mention the fact that it had been the ill-fated night in which I'd been captured by Helroth.

"That wasn't a *real* Bacchanalia." Rue waved a dismissive hand. "Only a tiny taste. Besides, it'll be different this time, A," she continued, "Reign can come with us."

I nearly choked on a laugh. As if my broody mate would ever agree to a night of unsanctioned, wanton revelry across the Luminoc.

The moment I stepped inside the dark ballroom of Arcanum Citadel, the air changed. It crackled, wild and thick with *nox*, perfumed smoke, and something else... something darker. Lust. Power. Chaos. This was no ordinary celebration. This was a true Bacchanalia.

And I was walking straight into it, fingers laced with my *cuore's*, the Shadow and Light of us drawing stares like moths to flame. Anyone with eyes could see he was more than my mentor and I more than his student. But tonight, apparently, Reign didn't care. He wanted everyone to know I was his. I could feel the possessive surge through our bond, his barely restrained emotions coiled tight beneath his skin.

Gilded sconces burned low, casting molten shadows on the black marble walls. Scarlet and amethyst orbs drifted lazily above the crowd, pulsing with each beat of the haunting music. Velvet drapes hung like liquid blood, hiding alcoves where moans and bodies tangled in equal measure. The entire place was drenched in hedonism.

The cuorem pulsed to life at my core, ignited by the scent of sex in the air. I squeezed my thighs together to quell the sudden burst of heat.

Rue gasped beside me. "Oh, gods, I want to live here."

Devin was already pulling her toward a glittering bar made of onyx and bone. Symon grinned as he downed something that glowed green, eyes sparkling with mischief— where he'd gotten a drink so quickly, I had no idea. And Liora had vanished into the shadows soon after we'd arrived, of course.

I glanced up at Reign. He hated everything about this. I didn't even need the cuorem to know that.

The only reason he'd agreed to come at all was Malakar. He hoped to skulk away to the headmaster's office and steal into his mind to determine his true intentions regarding the joint training sessions.

Reign's jaw was tight, his shadows even tighter. They curled around his shoulders like wary sentries, reacting to the proximity of so much unbound power. His fingers never once loosened from mine.

"Relax," I murmured, brushing my thumb across his knuckles. "I'm not going to get seduced by a Shadow Fae drunk on too much absinthe."

His shadows flared, just slightly. "You assume I'm worried about you falling for someone else?"

"Aren't you?"

"No," he said, voice low and dark as obsidian. "I'm worried about the bodies I'll leave behind if anyone touches you. In any capacity."

I laughed. Gods, he was lethal and ridiculous. But truthfully, I didn't entirely disagree with his assessment.

Everywhere we walked, eyes followed. Whispers trailed. They all recognized me, even here, deep in the heart of Arcanum, the girl who should've been dead.

And Reign? They believed they knew exactly who he was. The banished, disgraced Shadow Fae professor who'd betrayed his own kind to serve the Light at the Conservatory.

The tension thickened as we passed through the main hall toward the onyx fountain spilling spiced wine into a shallow pool surrounded by velvet cushions and bodies that writhed like smoke.

A flicker of dark shadows caught my eye, and I spun around. Ruhl.

He lounged against a stone column, goblet in hand and hair loose around his face, with a smear of lipstick still fresh on his throat. The instant he saw me, he froze. The goblet slipped from his fingers and shattered at his feet.

Reign mumbled a curse beside me, but still we moved toward his brother.

"Aelia," Ruhl murmured once we'd reached him, voice caught somewhere between surprise and disbelief.

"Ruhl," I replied, even as Reign's hand tightened around my own.

The Shadow heir pushed off the column, staggering slightly—as he had the last time I'd seen him—his eyes flicking from my face to our joined hands, as if he could somehow sense the ethereal cuorem between us. And despised it.

The anger that flared in his expression wasn't subtle. "You're here," he said hollowly. "Why?"

"My friends forced me to come," I replied, tilting my chin toward them.

"And you, brother?" He ticked his head at Reign. "What could possibly bring you to this depraved gathering?"

"I had my own reasons."

"I bet you did." A smirk tipped up the corners of his mouth. His eyes burned, but his voice came out cool as he regarded me. "And what's the verdict? Is the infamous Bacchanalia all you could have imagined and more?"

I smirked right back. "I've seen better orgies."

A choked laugh escaped Symon nearby. I hadn't even realized he'd been listening as he guzzled down another potion—where was he getting them? This one was a vibrant purple in hue. Raysa, that would not turn out well.

Reign didn't move, but I could feel the shadows curling tighter around his spine, his *nox* and his raging jealousy held only by the thinnest thread of self-control.

"Enjoy your evening, then. I know I will relish mine." Ruhl looked like he wanted to say more, but he just shook his head and turned away, vanishing into a dark corner of the chamber without another word.

I let out a breath I hadn't realized I was holding as soon as he disappeared.

"Are you alright?" Reign asked.

I nodded. "I just hate the tension between us. Between *all* of us."

"You know I nearly threw my brother through that blasted column, right?"

"I do," I said, brushing my shoulder against his. "That's why I didn't let go of your hand."

Before Reign could reply, Devin and Rue reappeared, my best friend holding two glowing drinks and zero inhibitions remaining. "Did we just witness a passive-aggressive standoff between two handsome princes over a female in a den of pure debauchery? Because that's peak academia drama, and I am so here for it."

I groaned, but I couldn't stop the smile tugging at my lips. Even in a dark lair of orgies and shadows, she could lighten the mood.

"Go find Malakar," I whispered to Reign.

"As if I would ever leave you alone in this place." His lip curled in disgust.

"I won't be alone. I'll have Rue, Devin and Symon with me." I ticked my head at my friends, who were now taking turns pouring vials of colorful liquids down each other's throats.

He grunted, following my line of sight. "That's not in the least bit comforting, starlight."

"Just go, Reign. Otherwise, this entire night will have been a complete waste of our time."

His hand lingered on my waist, eyes locking with mine one last time. "I don't like this," he said quietly, shadows licking at his boots.

I threw him a devilish smile. "Which part? The music, the drinks, or the naked Fae dancing on the table behind you?"

His jaw clenched. "All of it."

I reached up on my tiptoes, brushing my lips across his cheek. Through the bond, I could feel his control fraying. "Hurry back, professor. Or I might end up dancing too."

A deep growl rumbled in his throat. "Not funny."

"Then go," I whispered in his ear. "Before I give you a real reason not to leave."

"Fine," he growled before a shadow peeled off his cloak and curled around the back of my neck. My umbral bodyguard. The tiny hairs at my nape stood at attention, minute nerve endings flaring at its icy touch. "Behave yourself."

"Always." I pressed a quick kiss to his mouth this time. "And hurry back. After all this sin and seduction unfolding around us, I find myself hungering for my mate."

Another growl vibrated low in his throat, nostrils flaring. "Oh, princess, you always know exactly what to say to drive me absolutely wild." He remained rooted to the spot, midnight orbs fixed to mine.

Before I lost all control myself and dragged my *cuoré* into our own dark corner to have my way with him, I nudged him toward the door. "Go, and for the love of Raysa, be quick."

Chapter Sixteen

R^{eign}

Every bone in my body screamed to remain with Aelia in the madness of that Bacchanalia. The entire chamber reeked of lust and debauchery. The way the Shadow Fae stared at her... Gods, it was a miracle I hadn't turned the entire erotic revelry into a bloodbath. There was nothing I desired more than to rip out their eyes for daring to look at my mate. And Ruhl's presence only exacerbated my nerves. What game was he playing at? Or was he telling the truth the other day, and he'd merely gone back to his old ways?

Shaking my head to rid myself of the pointless thoughts, I strode down the quiet hallway, cloaked in shadows. The halls of Arcanum Citadel were exactly as I remembered them: sharp, cold, and humming with restrained cruelty.

Noxus, I hated this place.

The sconces still burned with shadowflame, casting flickering azure light across the dark stone walls. I'd spent years walking beneath them as a student, dreaming of freedom. Now I was back, not as a boy desperate to escape, but as a male who had finally tasted it and would burn this place to ash if I had to. Anything for *her*.

Focusing on the task at hand was nearly impossible. Not when I could feel Aelia's desire pulsing through our bond, her scent still lingering in my nostrils.

Everything all right over there? I shot the question through the glittering strands that connected us.

Yes, Reign. You only left moments ago.

And yet, it feels like a lifetime to me. What are you doing?

Just watching Rue and Symon feed each other absinthe-infused grapes. I could almost hear her laugh in my mind.

Oh, realms, help us all.

Stop worrying about me and find Malakar. The sooner you do, the more quickly you can return, and I promise it will be worth it.

Another wave of lust crashed over me, this one so potent it nearly knocked me off my feet. My hand shot out, clinging to the wall to keep myself upright. *I'm coming, princess.*

Not yet, but hopefully soon.

Noxus, what has gotten into you?

Her teasing laugh flitted through our connection before the bond went silent. Muttering a curse, I adjusted my trousers, which had suddenly become too tight, and quickened my pace down the corridor.

The heavy door to Malakar's office loomed at the end of the hallway like a gaping maw. I didn't knock. I didn't have the patience.

I let myself in.

The room hadn't changed one bit in ten years. Sprawling tomes and shadowed artifacts littered the obsidian desk. Black banners hung limp on the walls, stitched with runes that slithered when I looked too long. A jagged window cut across the back of the chamber, revealing a view of the Nightbloom Gardens and the edge of the Luminoc River.

And there, seated behind the desk like he hadn't aged a day, was Headmaster Malakar.

He didn't look up. "I wondered when the ghost would return."

I didn't speak. Not yet.

He set his quill aside with surgical precision, then slowly raised his eyes to mine. They were just as I remembered; deep, dark pools of void, ancient and eerily still. The kind of stare that flayed you open and cataloged every secret inside.

"You shouldn't be here, Reign." His voice was low and velvety, like oil dripping from a blade.

"I've come for your cooperation."

His lips twitched. Almost a smile. "So bold. As if you've forgotten who made you."

"I've forgotten nothing," I said coldly, my shadows curling at my feet. I was a product of Malakar's brutal instruction as much as my own sire's.

"Mm. Haven't you?" He stood, robes whispering across the floor. "You wiped your own name from these halls. Took great care, didn't you? To erase the stain of your existence. And yet..." His gaze swept over me slowly, curiously. "Here you are. Again."

Not willingly.

He stepped closer. "Tell me, how did you manage to disappear? How many minds did you poison, how much memory did you alter to vanish like smoke?"

"Enough." I didn't have time for games or to reminisce on the past. "We're uniting the courts for battle. Training has already begun at Luce. You're to do the same here."

Malakar arched a brow. "And who appointed you steward of both academies?"

"No one," I said. "But I'm not asking."

The air shifted.

Malakar's shadows coiled behind him like a nest of snakes, mirroring mine. "You always had a defiant streak. Even as a student. Dangerous. Foolish."

I clenched my jaw. "You will begin joint training with the Conservatory of Luce. Immediately. Draven will be expecting your students first thing in the morning."

"I will not." He circled his desk. "King Tenebris has forbidden it. I spoke to him just yesterday."

Of course he had. My father's hand reached farther than I liked.

"I'm not concerned with my father's orders."

"You should be," Malakar replied, voice sinking low. "He's already suspicious of you. If he learns you dared to return to the Citadel—"

"I said I. Do not. Care." I stepped forward, letting the darkness bleed from my fingertips. "This alliance is happening. If you won't lead it, I'll have you replaced."

He chuckled, a sound completely devoid of humor. "You overestimate your reach, bastard. Or perhaps you're forgetting that I trained you once. I know the limits of your power."

I smiled slowly. "Then let me show you how far I've surpassed them."

Before he could react, I unleashed the *nox*.

It surged like a tide, wrapping the room in shadow, blotting out the torchlight, warping the air until the walls pulsed like a living heart. Malakar reeled back, summoning his own defense, but I was faster.

Then I drew from the well of *zar*. The true secret. The forbidden energy licked across my skin like hellfire and frost, threading through my thoughts as I dove straight into his.

His gasp echoed through the chamber. His mind was a fortress. Ancient and barbed, coated in centuries of mental wards. But I'd been trained to unravel minds. And I knew how to tear down his.

He snarled, his voice a blade inside my skull. *Get out!*

"No," I growled aloud, forcing the shadows deeper.

Memory shards flared. His promise to Tenebris. The orders. The fear. The doubt.

Finally, I found the crack. He actually wanted to fight Helroth. It was my father who deterred him, so I drove my will into the lingering doubt.

"You will initiate joint training with the Conservatory," I commanded. "You will tell Tenebris nothing. If he asks, you will inform him the students are preparing for a separate incursion, a rebellion in the Wilds, if you must. But he will not know the truth."

Malakar's hands trembled. Blood trickled from his nose, coating his upper lip. "You are not... strong enough," he rasped.

But he was wrong. For Aelia, I was strong enough for anything.

"War is coming," I snarled. "And I will drag every corner of this realm into the light, whether they want it or not."

The cuorem blinked to life, igniting with the fury of a thousand burning stars. I drove the command deeper, sealing it with a twisted thread of *zar*. A compulsion. One I had yet to attempt but felt fairly certain I could master.

A warning flared in the back of my mind. I'd never used *zar* this deeply before, not like this. If I pushed too far, I might unravel him... or worse, myself.

Too late.

Finally, Malakar gasped and crumpled to his knees, his shadows hissing and scattering like frightened things. The torches flared back to life.

I stood over him, breathing hard. "You will do as I said," I commanded. "And you will forget I was ever here."

Malakar didn't speak. His eyes were glazed, distant. The compulsion had taken root. I could feel the toxic *zar* flooding his awareness, stealing his will.

And just like that, I understood how Helroth had strode into Aelia's mind and forced her to do unspeakable acts. Now, if I could only find a way to undo it.

His expression remained unreadable, continuing to stare into nothingness as I turned and walked away. My thoughts were heavy, leaving the headmaster on the floor. But there would be no more delays.

My *cuoré* was waiting for me, and I would walk through hell, through my dark past, even through my own damned blood to return to her.

⚔

Aelia's eyes met mine from across the ballroom, as if she'd sensed my approach and had been waiting. And gods, the satisfaction that brought was inconceivable. Before I made it more than a few steps into the lavish chamber, she darted toward me and tangled her fingers through mine.

"Finally," she purred, her dark pupils flaring with need.

"Aelia, did you—"

"No. I didn't drink or eat anything. But I cannot be certain they're not pumping something potent through the air vents." Shrugging, she spun me around, toward a narrow hallway adjacent to the doorway through which I'd just entered. "Come with me."

Our eager footfalls echoed across the dark stone walls, her excitement and lust thrumming through our bond, fueling me. Finally, at the end of the corridor, I saw it.

The moment the door of the closet slammed shut behind us, I lost control. The scent of lust permeating the ballroom coupled with the intense desire surging through our bond for the past half hour had me in a chokehold.

With the lingering pulse of seductive music throbbing faintly through the obsidian walls, I pinned Aelia to the back of the door. In the next heartbeat, my hands were braced on either side of her head. My breath was ragged against her skin, shadows curling across the stone like smoke caught in a storm.

"I told you we shouldn't have come here," I growled, every word edged in frustration and something far darker.

"What happened with Malakar?" she shot back, her voice sharp, but breathless, laced with fire.

"Later," I growled.

But I didn't kiss her. Not yet.

I just stared, devoured her with my eyes, trying to read her. Searching for any flicker of doubt now that her inhibitions were lowered. Any regret. Any lingering thread of whatever the hell that look was Ruhl had given her when we'd first arrived. Like he'd bled out the moment she walked in.

"Stop thinking about him," she whispered, plucking the thought from my mind as she pressed her palms to my chest.

"I'm not," I growled, voice low and tight.

My thumb traced the hollow of her throat reverently, because even in my anger, I couldn't stop touching her. Couldn't stop needing to *feel* that she was mine. "You don't know what kind of darkness festers in Arcanum's bones, in the Bacchanalia, in Shadow Fae themselves. It's ancient. Hungry. It doesn't just tempt, it consumes. And you..." I swallowed hard. "You walked into that dark revelry glowing like sunlight, and every shadow in that den wanted to claim you."

She leaned in, fingers fisting my tunic, her voice a whisper that shattered the last thread of my restraint. "Then it's a good thing I've already been claimed."

Gods, that broke me.

I crushed my mouth to hers. It was hungry, reckless, and ruined by her. The kiss was rough and desperate, a storm I couldn't keep caged any longer. Her head hit the door with a soft thud as I tangled one hand in her hair and the other gripped her hip, grounding myself in her.

The cuorem pulsed between us, burning bright and deep.

She gasped against me as my shadows spilled over her skin, slick and possessive. They slid around her waist, slipping beneath her dress like they had minds of their own.

I pressed my thigh between hers and she arched against me, a needy sound escaping her throat that nearly undid me. "Tell me to stop," I growled into her mouth.

"Never," she breathed.

With a snarl, I lifted her, her legs wrapping around my waist like they belonged there. And they did. *She* did.

My kiss seared the truth to her lips. That I needed her. That I would burn for her.

Her scent. Her skin. Her light.

Gods, I was drowning in her.

Aelia arched against me as my hands traveled her perfect form, sparks of gold illuminating her body like sunlight incarnate. She was everything I wasn't, warmth, purity, light, and yet she looked at me like I was made for her.

She was *mine*.

"Are you sure?" I asked, my fingers hovering just inches from her panties, my control fraying by the second. "Someone could come..."

"I've never been more sure of anything, outside of cementing our bond, of course."

The words splintered through me, undoing me inch by inch. My lips found hers again, more softly now, before I untied laces and kissed my way down her body like a sinner before a goddess. I wanted her undone. I wanted her worshipped.

Kneeling before her, I slid her panties down, my hands shaking with barely restrained desire.

"Reign," she whispered, voice trembling, and that was it.

Sloughing off my trousers, I stood up, then slid into her with a groan, every part of me scorching as she wrapped around me, body and soul. The cuorem roared to life, blinding and endless, binding us tighter with every pulse of pleasure between us.

Our powers answered each other, light curling into shadow, shadow kissing light.

My mouth moved over hers as her hands tangled in my hair, nails digging into my back. She met every thrust with a gasp, her fingers gripping me like I was something worth holding onto.

"You're mine," I rasped, and she nodded, eyes glassy and dazed with need.

"I'm yours. Always."

I lost myself in her. In her body, her fierce, wild love, and the trio of powers coursing between us. The world narrowed to the space between our hearts, the steady thrum of the cuorem anchoring us. When we shattered together only moments later, her name was on my lips, and mine on hers.

And as we stood there, tangled and breathless in the darkness with her cheek resting against my chest, I was certain of it. Returning here, seeing Malakar and waking all the dark memories of the past, it only confirmed what I knew all along.

I could, and I *would* serve up my own father for slaughter to protect her.

Chapter Seventeen

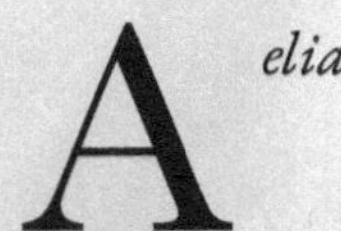

A *elia*

With Reign's forehead pressed against mine, our ragged breaths filling the small closet I'd dragged him into, my heart rapped out a contented beat. Echoes of pleasure still hummed through my veins, skimming over my sensitive flesh.

Gods, in all the times Reign had taken me, it had never been like *that*. So wild, so raw and primal. My knees wobbled as he lowered me to the ground, only the strength of the muscled arms still roped around my body keeping me upright. Raysa, what I wouldn't give for a bed right now. And then maybe another round.

"Let's go home, starlight." Reign's husky whisper at my ear had goosebumps spilling down my arms.

"That sounds wonderful. Just as soon as I can get my legs to cooperate." I crouched to retrieve my discarded panties.

A warm chuckle vibrated his chest, echoing against my own. As if I weighed nothing, he bent down and scooped me into his arms, a smile playing on his lips as he regarded me. "Have I told you how much I love you?"

"Not recently, no." I grinned right back at him.

Reign's smile deepened as he tucked a strand of hair behind my ear, his voice low and rough with emotion. "Then let me remedy that immediately. I love you, Aelia. More than the soothing embrace of shadows, more than the cool kiss of midnight. More than anything this realm could ever offer me. And I'll keep saying it until you never forget."

"I doubt I ever could."

Opening the door only a crack, he peered through the opening. Further down the hallway, the drunken revelry continued in full swing, writhing bodies rubbing against each other in the middle of the grand chamber and half-naked ones grinding in the shadows.

"Let's make a run for it before anyone sees us," I whispered into Reign's ear. I was certain my friends were in the midst of the Bacchanalia, enjoying every moment of unfettered debauchery.

And they deserved it.

"Just send one of your shadow messengers to let them know we left."

"As you wish, my love."

The scent of spiced wine and smoke still clung to my dress as Reign carried me toward the shadow-draped exit. The mesmerizing beats of the music echoed in the air behind us, the taste of him still on my lips, when a sudden tremor rocked the walls of the citadel.

Then a scream. High. Raw. Panicked. It was in the distance but still unmistakable.

We froze, my fingers tightening around Reign's arm.

Then the ground quaked again, more screams, more chaos. This time it was closer, louder, real.

Reign's shadows exploded from his back in a jagged burst, reacting before his voice even did. "Luce," he hissed, eyes darkening to pure midnight. "The students at the Conservatory."

No.

I wriggled out of his arms, my heart plummeting to the pit of my stomach as we ran through a great archway toward an overlook. The cool night air sent a chill up my spine, the moon shining bright and pale over the river, casting a silver sheen across the shimmering spires of Luce on the opposite bank.

Only, they weren't shimmering anymore. They were burning.

Pillars of smoke and hellfire rose into the night sky, while flares of violet and inky black energy lit up the dark like lightning strikes. Shadows surged across the lawn; shadows that weren't Reign's. Not natural. Not familiar.

Night Fae.

"Oh gods, they've come," I hissed, fear blocking my airway even as my *rais* surged to the surface.

Rue and Symon skidded to a halt behind us, breathless and wide-eyed. Devin followed close behind, and even Liora, her ever-smug expression finally stripped to horror, stood stunned at the railing.

"Raysa," Rue breathed, "are those...?"

"Night Fae," Reign confirmed, his voice pure steel.

I glanced over my shoulder to the ballroom of the Bacchanalia, still alive with music and laughter, and to the Shadow Fae oblivious to the hell unfolding across the river.

"We have to go, now!" I shouted, turning back toward the party. "We need to get everyone, anyone who'll fight—"

"You won't convince the Shadow Fae," Reign said quietly, jaw clenched.

"We'll see about that."

I stormed back into the shadowed chamber, raising my voice above the pounding music, my light flaring in the dark, raw and uncontrolled. "The Conservatory is under attack!" I yelled, the words sharp enough to silence the quadrant of dancers.

A few heads turned. A few smirks. But most ignored me entirely.

"We need reinforcements, students, anyone with training," I continued. "They're attacking our home!"

"And what does that have to do with us?" sneered a tall male near the dancefloor, a golden chain looping his ear to his collar. "This is the Light Court's war. Not ours."

"We're Shadow Fae," someone else muttered. "Not their shield."

"You're pathetic is what you are," Reign snarled beside me, his shadows unfurling across his shoulders.

"You're one to talk, traitor," a male hissed, nostrils flaring. "You stink of Light Fae. You're nothing but a sympathizer, drunk on the sweetness between that female's thighs." He curled his lip in disgust, eyeing me.

Reign lunged in a blur of hissing shadows before I could unravel my arms from against my chest.

"Reign, no!" I shouted, but he already had the foolish male by the throat, dangling a few feet off the ground.

Inky tendrils of *nox* and *zar* whipped around his tense form in a frenzy. The male's eyes widened, pure, unadulterated fear slashing across his pale skin. "Apologize," he growled.

I darted to Reign's side, curling my hand around his upper arm. The Fae dangled from my mate's shadows, his legs kicking wildly as they tightened like a noose. "Reign, please. We don't have time for this. All the students at the academy..."

With a growl of frustration, he called back his shadow wraiths, and the male crumpled to the floor.

"We'll never fight for you," he rasped, clutching his throat even as the mottled bruises began to form.

I opened my mouth to respond, rage and disbelief flaring through me, when a dark, amused voice beat me to it.

"Well, then," Ruhl drawled, stepping through the crowd like a prince among peasants. Like the prince he was. His hair was tousled, his tunic undone, but his gaze was sharp as shadowglass. "I guess the rumors are true then."

He stopped beside me and Reign, eyes flicking between the

crowd. "The mighty Arcanum Citadel, content to drink and fuck while the realm burns."

Silence fell.

Ruhl's smirk faded, replaced by something harder. "Let me make it simple. The Night Court, the legends of nightmares, have crossed the Wilds. They are attacking Luce now. *Tonight.* And if you think for a single second that they'll stop there, you're more foolish than you look."

"You expect us to die for Light?" another student spat.

"No," Ruhl said. "I expect you to fight for yourselves. For me, your prince. For *Aetheria.* Because once King Helroth and his Demons raze Luce, they will come here next. And you'll all be too drunk to lift a blade."

The crowd shifted. Whispers. Doubt. A flicker of fear.

Ruhl took another step forward. "I'm going. Anyone with a spine should follow."

The effect was immediate. A few older students exchanged glances. One stepped forward, sword appearing in his hand in a blink of smoke.

Then another. And another.

Soon, two dozen Fae stood ready. Still not enough. Not even half of the attendees, but it was something.

I looked at Ruhl, and for a moment, he was back. The Shadow Prince who had helped me through the trials, the one who actually gave a damn. Gratitude caught in my throat.

He nodded once, not quite looking at me. "Let's go."

"Well done, brother." Reign dipped his chin. "Nice to see the prince rising to the surface."

"Don't you dare get sentimental on me now, Reign. Besides, it's too soon to celebrate."

Reign's hand closed around mine. "Starlight, it begins now."

I didn't answer. I turned toward the flames in the distance, toward Luce, and let my wings unfurl in a shimmer of gold and midnight.

Chapter Eighteen

A*elia*

The moment my boots hit the scorched lawn of the Conservatory, the stench of burning stone and blood filled my lungs. Reign landed by my side a moment later, a curse slipping through his clenched teeth at the sight that greeted us.

Oh, Raysa, help us.

Luce was in *ruins*.

The western side of the academy, the Hall of Enlightenment, was gone, nothing but rubble and smoke. Arcs of unearthly hellfire scorched across the lawn like lightning strikes, blasting holes into the once-pristine marble paths. Students and instructors alike fought and fell amidst the chaos, their luminous weapons clashing against Night-forged blades that glowed like an infernal void.

A shriek pierced the air, inhuman, guttural.

I spun just in time to see one of them, my voluminous skirts twirling in the thick atmosphere. A Night Fae rider sat atop a monstrous, four-legged beast formed entirely of smoke and bone.

Its molten eyes locked on me, mouth gaping wide to release a plume of hellfire. I barely threw up a radiant shield over us in time, *rais* blazing from my palms as the flames seared across the barrier's edge.

The shield flickered against the onslaught but ultimately held. Pain lanced up my arms, and I gritted my teeth.

"Aelia!" Reign growled, his shadows coiling around my limbs like armor. "Behind me."

"No." I surged forward instead, summoning cool *nox* to fortify the fraying shield with a blast of swirling shadows, forcing the beast back.

Another enormous shadow exploded above us, and this one I recognized.

Solanthus.

He roared from the heavens, wings spread wide and shimmering beneath the sun's faltering rays. A second later, Phantom tore through the smoke, Reign's dragon trailing tendrils of shadows in her wake. The two beasts collided midair with another Night creature, claws raking against unnatural scales. Jaws snapped, wings battering the battlefield with hurricane winds.

The Night Fae rider shrieked as Solanthus barreled into him, flinging him from his beast and slamming him into the ground with a sound like splintering bone.

I searched the skies, the fields, the utter bedlam for any sign of the Night King, but there were too many bodies and too much chaos.

"Stay with me," Reign called out an instant before he shot forward. His shadows were like spears, impaling two Night Fae as they surged toward a cluster of frightened students. He fought like a male possessed, fury in every savage strike.

Gods, he was beautiful.

I could do nothing but watch him for a long moment, mesmerized by his brutal force and startlingly efficient violence. Jerking free the daggers beneath my trailing skirts, I tore through the flowing material, allowing myself a freer range of movement.

Scanning the field, I found my friends, each battling their own Night Fae. Symon appeared on the opposite ridge, raining light arrows down with terrifying precision. Rue and Devin moved like twin flames, slicing through dark riders as one, while Ruhl took on a Night Fae swinging a battleaxe. Gideon had appeared too, Reign's faithful friend arcing an umbral sword at a Demon soldier bathed in pure night.

Where was Liora?

Searching the blur of light and dark for her head of blonde hair, I finally gave up. Wherever she was, I hoped she was safe. Even if I didn't trust her, I didn't want her to die.

It was complicated.

Reassured that at least my friends were unharmed, I focused on my powers, on the steady thrum of the trio of energies lashing at my insides. I *was* the storm.

Movement suddenly twitched in the piles of Night Fae bodies we'd taken down. I blinked, breath caught in my throat, as tendrils of *zar* coiled through the debris, stitching together fragments of bone and skin. Fingers, skeletal and sharp, clawed from the charred earth, dragging ruined bodies upright again.

My stomach lurched. What in all the realms?

The Night Fae soldiers we had just destroyed... rose.

Only, they weren't the same. Their eyes were hollow now, pits of obsidian night instead of citrine or violet. They were moving closer. Their faces held no expression, no fear, no hatred. Only hunger. Their mouths hung open in silent screams, black ichor trailing from the corners of their lips.

Oh, gods.

"Reign!" I gasped, stumbling back as one lunged for me. I spun, slicing with my dagger, severing the thing's arm, but it kept coming. It seemed heedless of pain, oblivious of anything but the drive to kill.

Reign appeared at my side a moment later.

"What is that?" I cried, my power flaring, my light trying to push them back.

His voice came steady and deadly calm despite the chaos. "Necromancy." His shadow blade whipped through one of the revenants, slicing it in half only for the creature to crawl forward, dragging itself across the stones with skeletal claws. "It's one of the Night Fae's gifts. *Zar* can reanimate the dead."

This was *necromancy*? I vaguely recalled Helroth mentioning it during my captivity at Helspire, but Kaelith had never gotten around to teaching me that particular ghastly ability before Reign came for me.

My stomach hollowed, bile rising. "But they're not the same. They're not... *alive*."

"No," he confirmed, shadows bristling at his shoulders. "They're cursed. Hollowed out. Just husks of what they once were."

One of the things shrieked, lunging for a Light Fae student who screamed and froze in terror. Reign's shadows snapped it back, tearing it apart with *zar*-infused *nox*.

"They don't feel pain, as I'm sure you've noticed," he added grimly, his eyes locked on mine. "They don't stop. They don't die, not unless we destroy the *zar* that's animating them."

With *rais*. The unspoken words were clear. I forced my powers to stabilize, but my hands trembled. My throat went dry. These weren't Fae anymore... they were monsters. And weapons of pure destruction.

"Starlight, we don't have time for horror," Reign growled, dragging me back into the fight. "We kill them, now."

Together, we surged forward again, light and shadow entwining, pushing back the literal tide of death Helroth had unleashed. But in the back of my mind, one thought kept repeating, a whisper curling colder than even the *zar*.

What if this is what I become?

The cuorem pulsed at my core, Reign's presence a steady drumbeat in my mind, anchoring me even as the world fell apart. Light and shadow spiraled from my hands in waves, colliding with our enemies, alive and undead, unraveling them into raw energy that splintered the battlefield in radiant destruction.

The ground shook. The Hall of Ether collapsed in on itself in the distance, sending up a roar of fire and glass. Students were crushed beneath the debris, and my heart along with it.

"No more," I growled. "This ends *now!*"

I threw back my head and screamed, a burst of raw, divine power ripping from my chest and arcing through the air like a comet. It struck the lead Night beast dead center, searing it into ash, along with its rider.

From across the way, Reign raised his fist, and I felt it. The connection.

Power surged between us, light and shadow, *rais, nox* and *zar* braiding together in perfect harmony. My wings flared across my back, casting beams of pure gold into the smoke-cloaked sky. Our gazes collided in a perfect storm, and we ran straight into the heart of the battle.

Smoke churned in towering plumes all around us, blotting out the sunlight. The gentle glow of the Hall of Glory's spires was now scorched and fractured. The dormitories. Our home. The once-pristine towers were shattered, sections of the gilded façade collapsed, and craters marred the field where students had trained only hours ago. Pure power crackled in the air, *rais* and *nox* colliding with *zar* in bursts of wild energy. Screams echoed across the night like a haunting lullaby.

Both Light and Shadow Fae students fought the invaders, umbral blades moving alongside their glittering counterparts. I caught sight of Ruhl and Gideon, both moving like avenging shadows through the fray. It was brutal and horrible, and yet beautiful all in the same moment. For once, Luce and Arcanum were fighting as one. Unified against the enemy.

As I raced across the field with my daggers clenched in my fists, I once again registered the stench of scorched stone, sulfur, and blood, and my stomach turned. So much death, so much destruction.

And for what? More power?

Shadow beasts surged through the flames, massive things stitched together from smoke and skeletons. Molten fire spewed from their mouths, melting through both the umbral and luminescent weapons like they were paper.

My fingers tightened around the hilts of my daggers and brushed the shimmering crystals. They glowed beneath my touch, and a thought flickered to the surface. Infernium vein. It cut through *rais* and *nox* like magic. Would it be impervious to *zar* too?

I had to find out.

Another wave of Night Fae rode in, cloaked in armor etched with runes that shimmered like obsidian oil. Their eyes glowed violet, citrine and crimson in the dark, hollow and soulless. Their weapons gleamed with darkness not born of any realm I knew.

I flared my wings, blasting upward with a burst of light to scan the battlefield. My heart twisted at the carnage. Nearly a third of Luce's campus had collapsed, and the infirmary tower now burned in shades of sickly green. Students, both Light and Shadow Fae, fought wherever they could, disorganized, terrified. Too many of them were injured. Too many didn't stand a chance.

If I could find a way to imbue my radiant shield with the power of the infernium vein and cast it around the campus, I could protect everyone.

No. Reign's voice filtered through my thoughts.

I can do it.

It'll be too much for you, starlight. The fear in his voice lanced through me. *Wait for the Royal Guardians to arrive. They should be here any moment.*

"It'll be too late; I have no other choice. I can't let everyone die!" I yelled down to Reign as I hovered above the chaos, my hands blazing with light and shadow.

Rue and Symon were already flanking a faltering squad of Shadow Fae students, dragging them behind a crumbled archway where Devin knelt, drawing protective glyphs with trembling fingers. Liora had reappeared, her blonde mane of hair glowing like a halo as she weaved between the wave of darkness.

"Belmore! Ariadne! Over there!" I pointed to the eastern edge of the campus where the Night Fae were circling, picking off the students one by one. They hesitated, bloodied and pale, but nodded, surging forward with the other Shadow Fae Reign had managed to rally.

Still, it wasn't enough.

Lightning split the clouds, and a thunderous roar tore through the sky. A great winged form soared through the heavens, scales gleaming like golden fire.

Sol.

And no sign of the enormous winged beast of smoke.

A breath later, Phantom followed, her obsidian hide shimmering with veins of deep blue flame. Together, the dragons descended like wrath made flesh, crashing into the Night Fae's line with an ear-splitting impact.

Solanthus clamped his massive jaws around another beast's neck, wrenching the thing back into smoke. Phantom swept through the flames with her wings wide, unleashing a blast of shadowfire that disintegrated two more hellish creatures and sent their riders tumbling into the wreckage below.

Hope surged in my chest.

Sol, you have to take out the rest of those smoke creatures. They're destroying the campus.

We're trying, little Kin. It's not as simple as we make it look.

Can you distract them, at least, so I can try something?

I will do whatever I can.

I dove toward Reign, his dark blade clashing with a masked Night Fae whose power rippled through the air like a festering wound. I landed beside him, driving my blade into the Fae's chest. With eyes wide and mouth curving into a sickening scream, his body exploded to ash.

Reign's wary gaze met mine, dark and penetrating. "The infernium vein..." he murmured.

I nodded quickly before summoning a pulse of pure *rais* to knock back the other Night Fae encroaching on our flank.

"Together?" I asked, breath ragged.

"Always," he growled, shadows swirling around us like a tornado.

Our powers joined with a hum through the cuorem, fire and dark, starlight and smoke. We swept across the battlefield, carving a path toward the Hall of Luminescence. If I could only summon that shield, we could at least hold the line. For as long as we needed.

Before we reached the steps of the hall, I planted my feet at the heart of the burning courtyard, the chaos of war roaring around me. With a guttural cry, I summoned the storm inside me —Light, Shadow, and Night—each one crackling as they spiraled around me in perfect tandem. Reign stood beside me, clutching my hand. My powers merged into a radiant tempest, wild and unstoppable.

Heat pulsed through my twin daggers, the infernium vein blades glowing molten red as if they knew what was coming. I slammed them into the scorched earth with all the force I had left. Power surged through me and into the foundation of Luce itself.

The ground answered.

A shimmering shield erupted over the campus like a second sunrise cloaked in twilight, celestial glyphs etched in starlight and darkness rippling across its surface. I poured everything I had into it, every sliver of *rais, nox,* and *zar,* fusing it with the infernium's resistance to the Night.

Every single Demon Fae within the glittering orb burst into a pile of ash, leaving all the others unharmed. It was as if it had somehow sought out only the *zar* running through the Night Fae's veins. Stunned students glanced around the battlefield, eyes wide and relief rounding their shoulders.

And then, the hellfire came.

The flames from the Night Fae on the other side of the orb slammed into my shield, sending a tremor across the scorched earth, and fizzled. Repelled. It burned out against the wall of pure, fused power.

By the gods, it worked.

"You did it!" Reign's voice slid against my ear, his arms enveloping me in their firm hold, and it was only then I realized I was still crouching on the ground.

Then, something shifted under my boots. The soil beneath me trembled, not from the battle, but from something deeper. A pull. Familiar. Ageless.

I froze.

Reign tugged me off the ground, instantly sensing the change. "Aelia?"

"I feel him," I whispered. "He's here."

The world tilted. My surroundings flickered. And then, everything else was gone.

I stood alone in a sea of nothing. No flames. No battle. Just dark water lapping at my feet and mist rising from the void.

He stepped forward from it. King Helroth.

He was cloaked in night and forgotten souls, the stump that was left of his arm hidden in darkness. His hair, silver as ice, and his smile carved from cruelty. His eyes, burning pure crimson and hatred, pinned me in place like a butterfly under glass.

"So strong now," he purred, voice coiling through my thoughts. "So bright. But even the brightest stars burn out eventually without the proper flame."

"You won't win," I hissed, trying to push him out, to shove my power through the bond like Reign taught me.

Helroth only laughed. "You still think this is your story, child? You've only just begun to understand. I am not your end, Aelia. I am your beginning."

"You're wrong," I snarled. "You're not my anything." Summoning my powers along with the furious ones now surging through the cuorem, I shoved him from my mind.

The void shattered.

And I was back on the battlefield, the roar of dragons and

cries of desperate Night Fae attempting to break through the shield crashing into my ears.

Reign was there, gripping me tight, shadows tangled with mine as he shielded my body with his own.

"Aelia!" he breathed. "What happened?"

I stared across the field.

Helroth was gone. But his voice still echoed through my mind. *Don't forget your vow, princess. The final act draws near.*

Chapter Nineteen

R*eign*

Noxus, for a terrifying moment I thought I'd lost her again.

Sweeping a lock of platinum hair behind Aelia's ear, I tightened my hold around her waist, nestling us deeper beneath the warm blanket of my bed. A soft sigh parted her lips, her breath skating across the undone laces of my tunic and skimming over my chest, and I forced the suffocating fear aside, unwilling to wake my *cuoré*.

We survived.

More than that, she'd been incredible. Not only had she managed to summon a radiant shield around the entire campus, but she'd also tossed the Night Fae King right out of her mind.

When Aelia's eyes had glazed over in the middle of the battle, I knew Helroth had taken control. I could feel him through the cuorem, that invasive, sickening *zar* surging through the mystical strands that connected us.

The only good thing was that if I could feel him, it meant I could fight him.

The first time he'd stolen into her mind, I hadn't been aware of it. Now, everything had changed. The cuorem was growing stronger, our bond more resilient. At this rate, I was certain we'd soon be able to overpower him all together.

Aelia stirred beside me again.

Brilliant light seeped into my chamber, bathing the dim room in Raysa's glory. As if nothing had happened last night, as if nearly half of the campus and dozens of students hadn't been razed by Helroth's resurrected Court.

Glancing around the room, I took them all in, a blur of limbs, blankets and utter exhaustion. With half of the student dormitories destroyed, I'd taken them all in: Rue, Symon, Liora, Devin, and even Ariadne. The latter had begged me to allow Belmore in, but after all that Aelia had suffered at his hands upon her arrival at the academy, I refused. The arrogant Fae slept outside the door, and he'd been lucky I'd given him a blanket. At Aelia's insistence. Ruhl and Gideon had returned to their side of the Luminoc once the Night Fae had retreated. It was only when the invaders realized they had no hope of permeating Aelia's impenetrable shield that they'd scurried off into the Wilds.

They'd been left with only two options once my mate had let loose her power: retreat or die at the fangs of Solanthus and Phantom. A few of the other skyriders had joined the fight, as well, but most were powerless against the serpentine beasts of smoke.

Gods, it had been a massacre.

If Aelia hadn't managed that shield, the Conservatory would no longer be standing. By the time King Elian's Royal Guardians arrived, there would have been little more than bones and ash remaining.

Which reminded me, I had a bone to pick with that dawdling bastard.

I'd sent word of the attack before we left Arcanum and still, it had taken his forces nearly a half hour to arrive. Had he held them back on purpose?

A part of me hated to even consider that, but how could I not? The untimely death of the true king's heir would be very convenient for the Light royal.

"Morning..." Aelia's rough voice dismissed all further contemplation.

I peered down at my mate and pressed a kiss to her forehead. "It certainly is," I whispered, attempting not to wake the others. After the chaos of last night, I would give anything for a few private moments with my *cuoré*. I needed the reassuring feel of her all around me, but this would have to do for now. "How do you feel?"

"Not bad, considering."

"Considering the enormous amount of energy you must have expended last night." And continued to expend, maintaining the wards around the academy.

She nodded, nuzzling into my chest. "Do you suppose there's anything left of the banquet hall?"

"I'm afraid not." The Hall of Elysia had been one of the first reduced to rubble. "Hungry, starlight?"

"Starved."

"I'll send word to Ruhl to see if he and Gideon can pilfer some food from the Arcanum reserves."

Aelia glanced around the chamber at the sleeping Fae stretched out across the floor. "There will be hundreds of hungry mouths to feed, Reign, not just mine."

"But your mouth is the only one I care about." Gripping her chin, I pulled her face to mine and captured her lips. The kiss was much too short, but I couldn't risk the moment becoming too heated with a roomful of my students. Reluctantly pulling away, I whispered, "I'm sure Elian will send supplies along with the extra healers he promised today."

Last night, once the campus had been secured, I'd found Draven blockaded in his office. He trembled beneath his desk like a coward while the students he was charged with died at the hands of the ruthless Fae. He, too, claimed to have sent for reinforcements when the battle had begun, but who knew if he spoke the truth? At least, the king's healers had arrived shortly after his Royal Guardians.

They'd been just in time to help collect the wounded. The dead still littered the academy grounds.

Today would be a grisly day.

Ash coated the courtyard like snow. It clung to my boots, my leathers, and the bloodied wrapping on my palm where hellfire had met my flesh. Every breath tasted of smoke and loss. The sun was high in the sky, but its golden light couldn't quite cut through the deathly pall that hung over Luce. Not with so many voices silenced. Not with the scent of charred flesh still curling through the air.

I stepped over the cracked remains of the Hall of Elysia, careful not to jostle the scorched beam that hung precariously above. Somewhere beneath the rubble, Symon had heard groaning earlier. Now, Rue and a few of the Arcanum students Ruhl had gathered this morning were digging through it, their fingers raw and faces grim.

Aelia knelt nearby, her hands wrapped around the body of a fallen student. Light Fae, a first-year. The boy's face was frozen in shock, mouth parted like he hadn't expected to die so young. None of them had.

Her brow furrowed as she eased the boy's arm across his chest, lips moving in a silent prayer I couldn't quite make out. The cuorem hummed low between us, laced with sorrow and exhaustion, but also resolve. She was still fighting. Even in the face of all this destruction.

"Let me," I said softly, crouching beside her.

She didn't argue. Just leaned into my shoulder as I lifted the boy and carried him toward the long pyre being constructed at the edge of the training field. Dozens of students were already laid to rest in rows. Some wrapped in sheets, others barely more than scorched bones.

Aelia followed silently, fingers brushing mine as I set the boy down alongside the others.

"I hate this," she whispered. "The stillness of it. The way the training field has gone silent, and suddenly you realize how many voices will never fill it again."

"I know," I murmured, looping an arm around her waist and pulling her close. "But they died protecting something worth saving. And we'll make damn sure it wasn't in vain."

Aelia's head dropped against my chest. Her hair smelled like smoke and starlight. "I don't know if I'll ever be able to forget their faces."

"Don't," I said, tipping her chin up to meet her eyes. "Remember them. Every single one. We owe them that."

A soft snort left her lips. "Gods, Reign. Where did the cold, ruthless Shadow Fae I met all those months ago disappear to?"

A small smile tugged at my mouth despite everything. "I suppose that's your influence on me."

"Mm. Must be." Her fingers slipped easily into mine. "Come on, Professor Darkthorn. There's still much to do."

We made our way toward the shattered remains of the dormitory in the Hall of Luminescence. Most of the roof had caved in, and part of the eastern wall lay in ruins, a cascade of glittering stone and wood littered with ash-soaked bedding and half-burned scrolls. Ruhl and Gideon were already there, grim-faced as they shifted debris aside.

"I thought I'd never see the day," Ruhl muttered, hauling a scorched bedframe off a collapsed stairwell. "The infamous Shadow Fae professor, willingly participating in manual labor."

"I was about to say the same to you, my prince," I replied dryly. "You're right though. You've caught me. This is all an elaborate ploy to improve my image at the Conservatory."

Aelia rolled her eyes. "He's had worse plans."

"I'll take that as a compliment." I leaned closer and brushed soot from her soft cheek.

Symon and Rue reappeared with a trio of Arcanum students, dragging out a still-intact weapons rack and a collection of salvaged books. Rue looked relieved to have found something not burned beyond recognition.

"There's still some hope for the library in the Hall of Enlightenment," she said, hugging the stack like a lifeline. "Most of the Night Fae went after the dorms and the classrooms. Maybe they hate the professors' boring lectures too." She turned to me with a smirk. "Present company excepted."

A hollow laugh rippled through the group.

Even amidst the ruin, there were moments like those. There were flickers of warmth, of light. They didn't erase the horror, but they softened the edges.

We worked for hours. Hauling bodies. Clearing paths. Binding wounds. Elisa coordinated efforts from what remained of the infirmary wing along with the healers the king had sent. Phantom and Solanthus kept watch in the skies.

By the time the sun dipped low along the horizon again, the pyres were ready. Draven stood atop a dais, murmuring a prayer to Raysa, or perhaps he was cursing Noxus—either was plausible with that male. Aelia and I stood shoulder to shoulder, the rest of Flare Squad behind us, and Ruhl, Gideon and the other Shadow Fae students lingering nearby.

The headmaster ticked his head at Aelia. "Will you have Solanthus do the honors?"

Her head dipped slowly and, seconds later, a torrent of dragonfire lit up the sky. The scorching heat razed over our heads, warming the tip of my nose.

"They deserve more than fire and silence," Aelia whispered. "More than their remains sent home in a gilded urn."

I reached for her hand. "Then we give them more. We give their remaining families and friends a future."

She turned to me, eyes shadowed but steady. "Do you think this will be enough? Do you think Elian and Tenebris will finally see the truth now? That the Night Court won't stop until all of Aetheria burns?"

I looked past the flames to the broken ruins of Luce.

"I think this is the moment that forces them to choose," I said. "There's no more pretending. No more neutrality. Either they stand together or we fall apart."

She squeezed my hand, and I felt the bond between us settle, a steady thrum of belief.

"Then we make them see," she said. "Together."

"Always." I leaned down, brushing a kiss to her temple.

The fire roared in front of us. The dead would not be forgotten. And from their ashes, we would rise. Light and Shadow, side by side.

And gods help Helroth when we did.

Chapter Twenty

The training field still smelled like smoke. Even after days of repair potions procured from Draven's sources in Mysthallia, intense physical labor to rebuild crumbling buildings, and countless celestial wind glyphs, that charred scent clung to the edges of everything. It was like the memory of the battle refused to let go. Cracks still split the marble foundations of numerous halls, and scorched grass crunched beneath our boots, but somehow, that made it feel more real. It would ensure we'd never forget.

Hundreds of Light and Shadow Fae students moved in unison across the field, blades clashing, glyphs sparking, *rais* and *nox* humming in the air like an electric storm waiting to snap. I watched them from the edge of the battle-scarred training ring, arms folded. They were both beautiful and terrifying in the same instant. A Shadow male with dark ebony skin and navy hair sparred with a fierce-looking Ariadne whose glowing luminescent blade mirrored the dozens surrounding them. The pair circled each other warily before lunging at once, power flaring and blades ringing.

Reign stood beside me as always, silent, shadows licking at his leathers like a lazy mist. His arms were crossed as well, but I could tell he was pleased. He wouldn't say it, of course. That would imply too much emotion, and he'd already come dangerously too close to that in recent days.

"You're smiling," I said without turning.

"I am not."

"You are." I nudged him with my elbow. "The great Professor Darkthorn, secretly proud of his students."

"I will have you know I'm deeply disappointed in all of them," he deadpanned. "Their footwork is atrocious."

"You're a terrible liar."

"And you're distracting me."

I arched a brow. "You? Distracted? That doesn't sound very Shadow Fae of you."

That earned a small smirk. "Careful, starlight. Keep that up and I might be tempted to prove I'm still the superior warrior here."

"Oh?" I glanced up at him, feigning innocence. "Are you challenging me, Professor?"

"Absolutely. We should show these students how it's really done." He stepped onto the edge of the field, conjuring his umbral blade with a flick of his hand. "Unless you're too tired from all the supervising."

I drew my twin daggers in a single, fluid motion. "Bring it on."

The students paused, clearing a wide circle for us, murmurs rising as they gathered at the periphery. Rue and Symon were already placing bets, and I couldn't help the smile that followed.

I took my stance, drawing in a slow breath as I centered the gale within me, rubbing the worn medallion beneath my tunic. Light hummed along my skin, shadow curled beneath it, and *zar* pulsed in my blood like another heartbeat. Across from me, Reign stood motionless. He was calm, collected, a predator waiting for the perfect moment.

Then, he moved.

Shadows erupted across his shoulders, launching him forward with a burst of speed. I countered with a blast of pure light, the force driving him back just enough to let me duck and spin. My blade met his in a hiss of sparks. His second strike was faster, powered by *zar*, and I felt the heavy pressure of it slam into my defenses.

I gritted my teeth, drawing on my trio of energies. *Nox* surged with my shadows, twining through the light and strengthening the shield around me. I twisted beneath his blade, slid to his flank, and lashed out with a burst of light-laced shadow. He deflected it with a surge of raw *zar*, the air cracking like thunder.

"Sloppy," he murmured.

"You're bluffing."

He smirked and vanished in a wisp of black smoke.

I spun instinctively. Too late.

He appeared behind me, blade poised. I dropped low, sweeping my leg out to knock him off balance. Reign stumbled, but recovered quickly, pressing the attack with a storm of *zar*-infused slashes. Summoning my radiant shield, I blocked each blow. As the onslaught grew more powerful, my shield held, barely, flaring with starlight and shadow.

Then I released the full tempest.

All three powers poured from me in a radiant pulse—*rais* to blind, *nox* to cloak, and *zar* to strike. He blinked, just for a second, and I used it to dart around him. My luminescent wings flared, lifting me off the ground, and I crossed my daggers at his throat from behind.

The crowd went silent.

"I win," I whispered in his ear, breathless.

He laughed, low and dark. "You cheated."

"I simply used all my tools."

He turned his head slightly, the heat in his gaze melting straight through me. "Then I taught you well."

I let the daggers drop and stepped back, heart pounding. The applause from the students rang out around us, but I barely heard it. Not over the bond humming like a flame between us. Not over the quiet pride in Reign's eyes.

"Bravo!" A booming clap resounded over the silence an instant before Ruhl materialized from a mist of shadows. He eyed his brother, then me, a satisfied grin playing on his lips. Something had shifted in the aftermath of the Night Fae attack and seeing that smile on Ruhl's face settled some of the unease that had taken permanent residence in my core. "If only the two of you could save all of Aetheria with your fancy footwork."

Rolling his eyes at his half-brother, Reign turned back to his awaiting students. "Continue with the sparring exercises, everyone. You have another half hour before you get another break."

Muttered groans rolled through the crowd, but Reign ignored them, now focusing on his brother who stood beside me at the edge of the training ground. Ruhl had been sent to request an audience with King Tenebris in the aftermath of the attack. We'd hoped that after seeing the damage the Night Fae had wreaked at the Conservatory, the Shadow King would amend his position on the matter.

Reign leveled his dark gaze on the younger prince. "Any luck with Father?"

He snorted on a laugh. "It went about as well as last time." He cocked his head forward, offering it to Reign's snaking shadows. "Care to take a look?"

"No, there's no need. I can already imagine how it went." Reign's anger poured through our bond, the intense emotion drawing my thoughts to his.

It's time to deliver my father to King Elian. I'm done waiting. He's outgrown his usefulness to us. With Ruhl as king, at least we'll have the full power of the Court of Umbral Shadows behind us.

It hit me like a slap of ice water. The thought zipped through my mind as clearly as if it had been my own. I was certain Reign hadn't meant for me to hear it, but I did. Lifting my gaze to his, I searched those piercing midnight orbs.

Ruhl continued on about the chaotic state at Arcanum and the reluctance of half the student body to fight King Elian's war. Reign wasn't wrong. With Ruhl ascending the throne, unifying the Light and Shadow Courts would be much less challenging.

But what would it cost Reign?

Though Tenebris had been a horrible father, he was still his sire, his blood. Without knowing anything about his birth mother, he was the only parent he'd ever known. Surely, ushering him to his death at the hands of the Light King would have devastating effects.

"...Why don't you have a go at our stubborn sire, Reign?"

Ruhl's question drew me from the spiral of inner musings.

My mate remained silent for a long moment. A tendon in his jaw fluttered before he clenched his teeth and slowly nodded. "You're right, brother. It's time for me to pay the king a visit."

"Or perhaps, Malakar could do it," I blurted.

Both princes whirled in my direction. "Why Malakar?" Ruhl's dark eyes narrowed.

"Well, since Reign has already succeeded in forcing his will upon him, perhaps your father would be more willing to hear the truth from a neutral third party."

Ruhl laughed again. "The king doesn't take suggestions from anyone well. Just because Malakar oversees Arcanum, doesn't mean my father cares one lick about what he says."

Reign nodded, resignation settling across his grim gaze. "Ruhl's right. It must be me."

"But Reign—"

Slowly shaking his head, he reached out his hand. "Come, starlight, let's speak in private." Then he pivoted toward his brother. "Can you take over the training session?"

I fully expected a resounding *no* from the mercurial Shadow Prince, but surprisingly, a wicked grin curled the corners of his lips. "There is nothing I would enjoy more." With that, he turned on his heel and marched into the center of the sparring students. "All right, warriors, listen up..."

"Ruhl as a professor? I never thought I'd see the day." I grinned as I watched him rally the first- and second-years.

"Really? You couldn't imagine the future king taking pleasure in commanding others?"

"Well, when you put it that way..." I curled my arm around Reign's, and he immediately turned me toward the shadows of the Hall of Luce's crumbling remains. My feet dragged across the scorched lawn, knowing full well what he would say next.

When we reached a quiet niche with an overhang blocking the incessant sunlight, Reign drew in a pained breath. "You already know what I'm going to say, don't you?"

"I do."

A rueful grin crept along his lips. "You need to stop stealing into my thoughts, starlight." His hand cupped my cheek, drawing my gaze to his burning one.

"I can't help myself. Not when you continue to make foolish decisions without consulting me."

He loosed a frustrated breath. "King Tenebris's death is inevitable in this. It is the only way to ensure your safety and that of the entire realm."

"And what about you, Reign?" I pressed my palm to his chest, eyes fixed to his. "Who will guard your heart? Your soul? I know you love me; I feel it in every breath you take. I know you'd shatter the vow your father bound you to if you could. But he's still your blood, the last tie to the life you once had. Can you truly let that go?"

"Tenebris means nothing to me. To him, I was never a son. I was only a weapon, forged in cruelty and sharpened by pain. My sole purpose was to destroy the child of twilight. To destroy *you*, my mate. For that alone, he has earned his death. And when the moment comes, I will feel nothing but satisfaction as I watch him fall."

I swallowed hard, the violence in his tone and the fury surging between us driving the truth home.

"Please, do not worry for me, my love. You are all I need in this world to survive." He closed the distance between us, sealing the vow with a kiss that burned with promise and desperation. It was as if he was branding the memory of me into his bones before fate could steal it away.

Chapter Twenty-One

R*eign*

Stay out of sight, old girl.

Phantom snorted, dark plumes of smoke curling from her long snout. *It would be safer if I remained close. Only Noxus knows how this foolish mission will end.*

I appreciate the vote of confidence. With a rueful smile, I stepped out from the shadows of the looming darkwoods that surrounded Father's fortress home. The ebony turrets climbed high into the night sky, skeletal fingers reaching to the low hung full moon.

I paused at the edge of the forest, taking in the place that had been more penitentiary than home, the stone that had heard my screams and the traitorous shadows that had cloaked every bruise. It had been more than four years since I'd stepped foot inside. There wasn't a single thing about the grand castle that incited any sort of pleasant memories. It was nothing more to me than a prison crafted of stone and sorrow.

It was where Father made me into a monster, his weapon forged to destroy the child of twilight. Darkness crept into the corners of my vision as memories of the past uncoiled like smoke.

I was fifteen the first time he nearly killed me.

The training yard behind the Fortress of Umbral Shadows was nothing but black stone and cold mist, the sky a permanent slate of storm clouds. It was always cold there, even when the sun shone devastatingly bright across the Luminoc. That morning, frost still clung to the edges of the iron railings, and my breath misted with every exhale as I stood, blade in hand, facing the only shadow I could never conquer.

My father.

King Tenebris moved like a wraith across the yard, his own blade an extension of his arm and just as sharp as his piercing gaze. I was already bleeding from a slice above my brow, and the iron tang of it mixed with the chill, grounding me in a way that was almost comforting. Almost.

"Again," he said, eyes like pits of endless night.

I lifted my blade, somehow gripping it tighter even though my arms shook. I lunged, aiming for the opening I thought I saw, but he was faster. He always was. He knocked my blade aside with a flick of his wrist, stepping in close enough that I could smell the cold on him as he pressed his sword into my neck. I winced as the sharp blade pierced my skin. The scent of ash, steel and shadow closed in around me.

For an instant, I thought he would do it. End me for my incompetence.

"You are too slow," he growled, finally withdrawing his blade and striking my ribs with the hilt instead. Pain exploded through my side, but I didn't drop, didn't falter. I forced my eyes up to meet his.

He sneered. "Your hesitation will cost you everything."

I bit back a retort, swallowing blood from where I'd bitten my tongue, and repositioned. My shadows flickered around me, thin and weak, but there. I reached for the tendril of nox, *forcing it to form into a shield, just as he'd taught me.*

Tenebris's eyes glinted. "Better."

He struck again, and the shadow caught the blade, but the force of it sent me skidding across the slick stones. I hit the ground with a smack. My breath came ragged, pain flaring up my spine, but I didn't cry out. I didn't give him that.

"On your feet," he ordered.

I pushed up, every muscle screaming, and faced him again. My blade was heavy, my arms trembling, but I lifted it and positioned myself in the stance he'd drilled into me day after day.

"Your purpose is clear, Reign," he said, circling me like a predator. "You were born for one reason alone: to destroy the child of twilight. To end her before she can plunge all of Aetheria into eternal dusk."

His words seared into me, carving themselves into the marrow of my bones. He'd been saying them for as long as I could remember. Father had been whispering them in my ear since I was too young to understand, drilling them into me when I could barely hold a blade. And he reminded me with every bruise, every scar.

"She is your enemy," he continued, voice a cold promise. "There is no room for weakness. No room for hesitation. When the time comes, you will strike, and you will not falter. Because if you do, Reign..." He stopped in front of me, the tip of his blade pressing lightly against my sternum, right over my hammering heart. "If you do, I will finish what you could not."

The shadows around us shifted, drawn to him like iron to a magnet. I felt them pressing against my skin, cold and heavy, reminding me of what I was. What I was meant to be.

"Yes, Father," I forced out, the words like ice on my tongue.

He pulled back, lowering his blade, but his eyes never softened. They never did.

"Again."

And so I lifted my sword, blood dripping onto the cold stone, and I lunged. Because in that moment, I believed him. I believed that was all I was meant for.

The dark memories faded, shoved back by sheer will. I wasn't that helpless, young boy anymore.

No, you are not. Phantom's voice sailed through my mind, banishing the lingering images.

Twisting my head over my shoulder, I found a pair of silver orbs locked on my own. My skyrider's dread leeched through our bond, an unexpected twist of anger, pain and fear. *I hate what Tenebris did to you, Reign. Still, there must be another way to ensure Aelia's safety from the vow.*

There isn't. And don't tell me you wouldn't do the exact same thing for Solanthus if the situation were reversed.

Another huff.

I can defeat him, Phantom. I know I can. I'm stronger than he is now.

I believe you. There was reluctance in her tone, but her response was still satisfying.

And I appreciate the concern all the same. Offering her a reassuring smile, I forced my legs toward the fortress, wrapped in a dense cloak of concealing shadows.

✕

The air inside the fortress was cold, sharp and biting, much like I remembered it as a young boy. Flames flickered from the torches hung on the obsidian walls, faltering against the darkness that seemed to swallow everything whole. Unease churned in my gut, but I forced it down, steeling my nerves for the moment I'd waited for my entire life.

A heady swirl of *nox* and *zar* swam through my veins, my boots silent across the stone floor as I passed unsuspecting guards and traversed the quiet corridors leading to Father's private chambers.

Would he recognize the change in me? Would he sense the *zar* and question its origin?

If he sensed the cuorem, I'd have to move quickly before he put two and two together.

Shadows seeped from the cracks in the obsidian walls, and the long, narrow corridors whispered with every step I took. It was as if the fortress itself remembered every order he ever barked, every punishment he ever gave.

When I reached his private chambers, I paused and drew in a breath to slow the wild drumbeat beneath my ribcage. Slowly, I pulled open the door and peered into the dark room. The king was seated behind a massive onyx desk littered with scrolls. The hearth burned low in the corner, throwing jagged shadows across the chamber and catching on the edges of the blackened armor mounted along the walls.

Ordering my concealing shadows away, I revealed myself to the male who'd been more tyrant than father. Tenebris didn't look up right away, dipping his quill in ink as if I were nothing more than another shadow drifting in. His aura coiled around him like a living thing, thick with *nox*, oppressive even now.

"Reign." His voice was the same, cold and clipped, cutting through the quiet. "What in Noxus's name are you doing here?"

I stepped inside, boots silent on the polished stone, and looked him in the eye. "I came to speak to you."

He placed the quill down with precise care before leaning back, his eyes narrowing slightly as they met mine. "Speak to me? And what if someone had seen you? Did it slip your mind that you were banished from Shadow lands?"

I clenched my jaw, feeling the familiar burn of rage beneath my skin. Shadows flickered at my feet, restless and hungry. "This is more important than the damned farce you forced me into all those years ago."

His mouth twitched, a cold mockery of amusement. "Careful."

"No." My voice was steady, even as my hands curled into fists at my sides. "You don't get to tell me that anymore. I am not a boy, and I am done pretending you were ever a father to me."

His gaze darkened, shadows pulsing around him in warning. "You tread dangerous ground, Reign."

"You were never a father," I pressed on, stepping closer, ignoring the cold prickle of *nox* in the air. "You were a tormenter. A taskmaster. You forged me in pain and shadow and called it duty. You told me my only purpose was to kill the child of twilight. You made me believe that was all I was meant for."

For a moment, silence pressed down on the room, broken only by the crackle of the hearth. Then his gaze dropped, narrowing on the shadows twisting around my boots, weaving with something darker, sharper—the *zar*, rippling beneath the surface.

His eyes snapped back up to mine. "What is that?" he demanded, voice low and dangerous. "What have you done?"

I drew in a breath, the bond with Aelia thrumming steadily in the back of my mind. Before she woke and found me missing, I focused on the onyx wall I'd perfected over the years, blocking her out.

"Why are you really here, Reign?" he asked, his shadows pulsing. They thickened, filling the chamber like smoke. "Why now after all these years?"

I met his gaze, unflinching. "I'm here to deliver you to King Elian, Father." The words fell between us like a blade, sharp and final.

Shock flickered across his face, then it was gone an instant later, replaced by cold fury. "You would betray your blood for the Light Fae?"

"For Aetheria," I growled, not daring to mention Aelia yet. "For the realm you claim to care about while you sit in your fortress doing nothing."

His shadows roared fully to life, swirling around him in a violent storm, darkening the sky overhead. "How dare you?" he hissed, summoning an umbral blade in his palm as he rose, power crackling along its edge. "You come into my court, into my fortress, and speak to me of betrayal?"

I let the *nox* surge through me, felt the *zar* ignite, explosive beneath my skin.

"What have you done for your kingdom? You've spent years at the Conservatory and have nothing to show for it. What of your mission? You are a failure, Reign, and that is all you'll ever be."

Fury rose, burning and relentless, at his words. My shadows unfurled, meeting his, colliding in the space between us with a deafening crack.

His blade came down, faster than lightning, but I moved with the shadows letting them carry me to the side. I deflected his strike with a burst of *zar* that sent sparks of hellfire across the stone. His eyes widened for only an instant before he came at me again, faster this time, his blade a blur as he pressed the attack.

Shadow clanged against shadow, the hiss of it sharp, echoing across the chamber. Each strike rattled up my arms, jarring my bones, but I held my ground. Shadows swirled at my feet, rising to meet his with every blow.

His dark minions slammed into mine, not just pressing, but tearing. They clawed through my defenses with razor edges that bit into my skin, leaving trails of blood in their wake. I gritted my teeth and forced my shadows to hold, to stitch the tears before he could push through.

"You've grown strong," he spat. His blade moved like a phantom in the dim light as he struck again, forcing me back step by step. "But not strong enough."

He twisted, feinting low before driving the hilt of his blade into my ribs, knocking the air from my lungs just as he had when I was only a boy. Pain flared white-hot as I stumbled, shadows faltering.

You're injured. Phantom's concerned voice cut through the turmoil.

Later, I'm a little busy. I shot the thought through our bond, careful to keep the wall up across the cuorem so Aelia wouldn't feel the pain. Despite the note I left her, I knew she would not be pleased.

"You have no idea how strong I am now," I growled, refocusing to block his next strike. The force of it numbed my arms. Our blades locked, shadows groaning and sparks hissing between us. "How strong *she* makes me."

"She?" His eyes glowed with cold fire. His shadows thickened, choking the air and pressing down on me like the weight of the abyss.

He broke the lock, slashing low and tearing through the edge of my tunic. The umbral blade sliced into my flesh. I hissed, staggering, blood dripping onto the black stone. Before I could recover, he unleashed a wave of shadow so dense it felt as if I were drowning. It slammed me against the far wall with a crack that rattled my skull.

I tasted blood. The room spun, darkness closing in, but I forced my eyes open. I compelled my shadows forward, to fight back, even as he advanced.

"You will never be strong enough to defeat me, boy," he snarled. "I made you." He lifted his blade as he prepared to end it. To end *me.*

"No." My voice was hoarse but steady. I pushed off the wall, finally summoning the tempest raging inside me. The cuorem pulsed, steady and fierce, the bond with Aelia burning like a star within me. Power thrummed through my veins. Hers and mine. "Not a boy. Not anymore."

He swung, the blade arcing toward my throat, but I ducked. Twisting, my shadows laced in *zar* flared around me. I caught his wrist, shoving the blade aside, and drove my knee into his gut. He grunted, but even winded, he retaliated with a headbutt that sent stars bursting behind my eyes.

Pain lanced through me, but I didn't let go. I couldn't.

We grappled, shadows tearing at each other like wolves, his *nox* slamming into mine. He tried to overpower my shadows again and again, but I pushed back, letting the *zar* flood my veins. It burned cold and piercing, weaving through the *nox*, making me stronger, faster.

Tenebris tried to pull away, but I held on, shadows binding his arms as I pressed closer. Our faces were only inches apart now.

"You think you can kill me?" he snarled, power crackling between us and searing the air.

"I don't need to kill you," I panted, pressing harder. The *zar* slipped into the cracks of his defenses. They wrapped around the shadows he tried to summon, suffocating them, forcing them still. "I just need to stop you."

His eyes widened, just for a moment, before they darkened. With a primal roar, he threw everything at me. Shadows, *nox*, and his own raw power slammed into me like a tidal wave, driving me to my knees.

I roared, the shadows tearing at me, trying to rip me apart, but I held on. Calling the *zar* from my depths, I let it merge with my shadows and allowed it to *become* the shadows.

I pushed back.

Light flared in the darkness, not *rais*, but Aelia. Somehow, I could feel her through the bond. I drew on her power, the steady glow as the *zar* fused with the *nox* wrapping around him before he could counter. It bound his arms to his sides, slithering over his throat.

My father struggled, fury and disbelief in his eyes, shadows writhing around him like snakes caught in a snare. I forced the binding tighter, pressing the *zar* into his mind, the shadows holding him as his strength faltered.

His scream rent the thickening air as my dark tendrils infiltrated his mind. Pure night coiled through every crevice, stealing his consciousness. "No," he growled. "It's not possible..." His eyes met mine, hate and shock mingling there.

"Oh, but it is, Father. You see? I told you I wasn't the same boy you tortured for years."

"How is it possible?" he hissed, the cold fire in his eyes flickering. A whisper of something like regret, or maybe fear, flashed before his eyes rolled back, and he collapsed. His knees hit the stone with a crack that echoed across the chamber.

I stood over him, gasping. Blood dripped from my wounds, shadows slowly fading around us as silence reclaimed the chamber.

It was done.

I dropped to one knee, pressing two fingers to his throat. His pulse still beat, slow and steady. Good. He would live long enough to return to the Court of Ethereal Light. Then his life would be in King Elian's hands.

I lifted him, throwing him over my shoulder with a grunt. With his dark cloak trailing across the stone, I turned toward the entryway.

"Nice work, brother." The voice came from the shadows, smooth and amused.

I looked up to see Ruhl stepping out from behind the door, arms crossed, and a grin on his lips that didn't quite reach his eyes.

Chapter Twenty-Two

R*eign*

"What in Noxus's sake do you think you're doing?" Ruhl asked, glancing at Tenebris's unconscious form. "Though, I must say, whatever it is, I wished you would have waited for me. I would have loved to see the look on Father's face."

I adjusted my grip on the king, allowing my shadows to bear some of the weight, and met my brother's gaze. "Go, Ruhl," I snarled. "You shouldn't be here."

"Shouldn't be here to save our father?" His dark eyes narrowed. "As the Shadow heir, this is exactly where I should be."

"Let me leave with him, and you'll no longer just be the heir. You'll be the king."

His eyes widened, understanding flashing across his features. "That's how you secured Elian's loyalty... Not because he is Aelia's uncle, but because you promised him our father in return for his protection?" He paused, a vein pulsing across his forehead.

"Yes," I rasped.

"Noxus, I never knew the depth of your hatred for our father." He dragged his hand over his face.

"We weren't all his great Shadow heir."

Ruhl barked out a laugh. "You're the one who's gravely mistaken now if you believe my relationship with our father was any better than yours."

"You have no idea—"

"Neither do you," he snapped, cutting me off. His jaw ticked. "Does Aelia know? Surely, she wouldn't approve..."

"You don't know my *cuoré* as well as you think. Of course, she knows. I don't keep secrets from her anymore." I didn't exactly tell her I was coming for Tenebris beforehand, but there was no need to worry her, but he certainly didn't need to know that.

"Gods, Reign... When did you become so devious?" He cocked his head to the side.

"I have no choice."

"No, of course not. And isn't it convenient that by handing over Father, you'll also be ridding yourself of the ramifications of the pesky blood vow?"

"Yes," I gritted out. "And if you think you can talk me out of it, you couldn't be more mistaken." My shadows swirled around me despite the exhaustion, a frenzy of darkness coiled to strike.

"Would you cut me down, too, brother?" A flicker of resentment flashed across those piercing eyes.

Yes. The answer came without a second thought. For Aelia, I would see the entire kingdom in ruins if it meant saving her.

"I suppose I have my answer, then," Ruhl murmured when I failed to respond. We remained there for a long moment, eyes locked, neither one of us moving, barely breathing.

"Are you going to try to stop me?" I finally gritted out.

"Are you going to deliver our father to his death?"

"Yes." I shifted Tenebris's weight, feeling the bond with Aelia warm in the back of my mind. It was all I needed. "You should be thanking me, Ruhl. You'll finally get to sit the throne of the Court of Umbral Shadows."

"What makes you think that's what I want?"

I scoffed. "Because I know you, brother. With Father gone and you as king, you have no need to fear the words of your mirror image from that damned trial any longer. Either it was wrong, or we've altered its dreaded prediction somehow." Drawing in a deep breath, I softened the hard set of my jaw. "Either way, it ends now."

An interminable minute later, he dipped his head, something unreadable in that dark gaze. Then, he moved to the side.

Tightening my hold on our father's motionless form, I marched through the door without a second glance, leaving my half-brother and the ghosts of my past far behind.

The Royal Guardians stole my father from my arms the moment I stepped through the gates of the Castle of Ethereal Light. A mixture of surprise and suspicion was etched into each of their faces as I handed over the notorious Shadow King without so much as a word.

I felt no guilt, no regret.

Tenebris was still unconscious, thanks to my *zar*, his dark cloak trailing like a torn shadow across the pristine marble floors as the royal's guards dragged him inside. I remained there, frozen in the threshold for a long moment. The air here always felt too clean, too bright, the scent of *rais* thick enough to choke me. It was nothing like the warm energy that radiated from Aelia.

King Elian appeared at the top of the grand staircase, a serene smile curving his lips as he looked down at me. Light glinted off the golden circlet in his pale hair. "Reign," he said, his voice calm. "You've brought me quite a gift. I must admit, I didn't truly believe you would follow through on your promise."

I said nothing, breathing hard, the wounds from my father's shadows still burning beneath my tunic. I wasted no time before coming straight here, eager to be finished with this ugliness. The moment my father breathed his last breath was when I would finally be free. Freed of that damned vow. Free to love my mate without fear.

Elian's gaze flickered to the guards. "Take him to the dungeons. I will decide what to do with him later."

Something in me snapped at his words. "Later?" My voice echoed across the vast hall, the glow of the crystal lanterns trembling with the force of it. "You said you wanted him gone. You said—"

Elian's eyes slid back to mine, patient, almost pitying. "I said many things, Reign. Things change. After seeing the destruction Helroth ravaged upon the academy—"

I took a step forward, the shadows at my fingertips flickering despite the oppressive light around us. "That was not the deal, Elian," I growled.

"Watch your tone, Shadow Fae," he snarled right back. "I can always call back the legion of Royal Guardians I've deployed to keep my precious niece safe."

The growl died in my throat. "So you're going to let Tenebris live?"

His calm smile returned, thin as a blade. "I haven't decided yet."

My fists clenched, the bond with Aelia flaring in the back of my mind, grounding me before the shadows could slip free. I had done this for her. For the realm. For the war that was coming. And now the bastard Light King *didn't know*?

Elian's hand rested lightly on the banister as he turned to leave. "Your service to the realm is noted, Reign. Feel free to stay and rest for a bit. Perhaps, clean up before your return to the academy." His light eyes razed over me in disgust, the torn clothes, the blood splatter. "We will speak again."

And just like that, he spun around, the rustle of his robes the only sound left in the hall.

Again, I just stood there, unmoving. Ice surged through my veins, but it did nothing to dull the fury. The Royal Guardians turned for a corridor, and suddenly, I was moving again. Trailing behind them. And no one stopped me, surprisingly.

After never-ending minutes of circling the vast castle, I followed the guards down an endless spiral staircase. They took my father to the deepest cell, one lined with light-forged runes that would weaken even the strongest of Shadow Fae. I could feel their power rippling over my skin.

After they dragged my father into the cell and slammed the door shut behind him, they simply... left. I stood there, just beyond the bars, the scent of earth and damp stone curling in the air. Tenebris was slumped against the far wall, chains binding his wrists. His head was tilted back, dark hair falling across his face. For a moment, he looked younger, smaller, like the man he could have been if power hadn't twisted him into what he was.

And then his eyes opened. Cold, dark, and furious.

"Traitor," he hissed, his voice raw. The shadows around him flickered weakly, unable to take form within his cage of light. "You bring me here to this gilded prison to rot at the feet of that Lightborn whelp?"

I said nothing at first, stepping closer until I could see the lines of rage and bitterness etched deep into his face.

"I should have expected no less from the son of—from a bastard," he hissed.

I bristled. "You brought this on yourself."

His lips curled into a snarl. "You think you've won something, boy? You think you've freed yourself from me?"

I swallowed hard, the truth pressing against my tongue, heavy and sharp. "It was the only way," I snarled.

His eyes narrowed, something dangerous flickering there.

My breath caught as I eyed the celestial glyphs. Their power pulsed in the air, strong enough to bind my father's *nox*. This was it. The moment I admitted everything, the moment I freed myself.

"That prophecy you forced down my throat since I could hold a blade..." My voice shook, just a little. "The child of twilight. She's my *cuoré*." I never meant to tell him. Not truly. It was as if something had taken over me, ripping the dreaded truth from my mouth. Maybe a foolish part of me hoped if he knew the truth, that Aelia was my mate, he would change his mind. That a tiny shred of humanity was still alive in the cold, unfeeling male who raised me. And that maybe, just maybe, he would willingly release me from my vow.

For a moment, everything went still.

Then, he laughed. Low, dark, and hollow. "Oh, Reign," he whispered, leaning back against the wall, a cruel smile twisting his lips. "You think I didn't know? That I could be so blind?"

The world tilted. "...What?"

He chuckled again, the sound raising the hair at my nape. "You truly are my son, you know, to bind yourself to a power like hers." He leaned forward, the chains rattling softly as his eyes bored into mine. "You think you could hide her from me? From the moment I first laid eyes on her, I knew."

No.

"And now," he purred, voice dark with triumph, "you've given me exactly what I need."

I felt it, then. The blood vow. Ancient and vile, stirring in my veins, crawling across my skin like ice and coiling around my heart. The curse he had placed on me when I was too young to fight it, to question it.

"Reign of Umbra, by the blood that binds you to me, by the vow you swore in shadow and in flesh, I command you—"

"No." The word tore from me, raw and desperate, before he could finish. Cold sweat dribbled down my nape. Still, the vow tightened, burning beneath my skin and pulling me toward him, toward the command that would force me to kill her. The runes along the bars sparked to life, hissing, as his *nox* attempted to break free.

They should have been strong enough to smother his powers, but still, I could feel it... It was internal, blood-forged, and stronger than any external mystical bindings.

"No!" Shadows exploded from me, slamming into the bars and rattling the entire cell. I spun around, forcing my dark minions to carry me away. My vision narrowed as I raced through the corridors. And with every step, the vow clawed at me, screaming inside me.

I ran. The light of the castle burned, searing my vision as I tore through the halls. The command echoed, a dark drumbeat in my skull. Each step was a promise of the doom I carried inside me. I ran faster, putting as much distance between my father and me as possible.

The moment the gilded front gates swung open, I dropped to my knees, sucking in a breath of air. Gods, how could I have been so stupid? Another second with my father and he could have finished that command... And I would have been powerless to stop him.

"Fuck," I snarled, digging my nails into the earth. I never should have trusted King Elian. With Tenebris still alive and that blood vow hanging over my head, Aelia would never be safe from me.

Chapter Twenty-Three

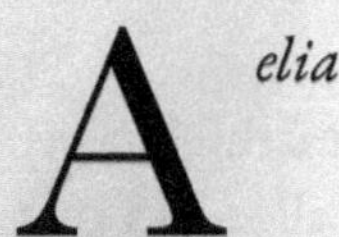

A*elia*

Dread coiled in my gut, a living thing clawing to get out. I forced myself to breathe, slow, controlled, as my blade cut through the air in measured arcs. The training field was silent, save for the harsh rasp of my breath and the whisper of *rais* slicing the breeze. When I'd awoken with a chill in my bones and an empty bed, I'd searched the chamber for Reign only to find a hastily written note scrawled on a parchment atop the nightstand.

He'd gone for the king...

I'd immediately sought him out through our bond, only to find a wall of pure obsidian blocking our connection. Still, I could feel a trickle of fury and an occasional whisper of pain. It had taken every ounce of restraint I possessed to keep from using my *zar* to rip through the mental barrier. Instead, I'd come out here to burn some nervous energy and attempt to center myself. I had to learn to trust my mate if I wished for him to do the same.

There was no denying that his abilities had grown more powerful—albeit, more out of control—since our bonding, but I had to believe he could handle his father. *Please, Raysa, keep him safe.*

The lethal tangle of powers that dwelled in my core were on edge, a battle of its own waging within my darkest depths. This had been the longest time and furthest distance we'd spent apart since my days at Helspire. The forced separation had me unsettled.

Which was odd since it had only been a few hours at most...

My *rais* seemed sluggish, the *nox* in an anxious frenzy, and the *zar*, ever more consuming. Perhaps, the cuorem truly did ground me and tether my unruly powers. Without Reign, would I lose control of my fragile restraint? Would Helroth's hold on me surge to the surface? My heart hammered at the mere thought.

No. I would never let him control me again. Gritting my teeth, I swung my sword, the trail of shimmering light arcing overhead.

Still, a dark voice echoed through the recesses of my mind.

Swear now, child of twilight, to bring down the Courts of Light and Shadow, until none but Night remains to rule the realm.

Shaking my head, I sought to loosen the lethal timbre stealing through my innermost thoughts. This time, it wasn't my grandsire in my head. It was my own fear clawing at my nerves. With every day that passed, I couldn't help but wonder if the twilight prophecy were coming true.

Hadn't I already brought darkness into the realm? Wind rattled through the ruined halls of the campus, raising the tiny hairs on my nape. I'd already harmed, already annihilated. Who knew how many Fae had been killed by my hand when Helroth had stolen into my mind and taken over my body? As selfish as it sounded, a part of me was relieved I couldn't remember.

Gods, it felt like no matter what we did, I was doomed to play the role of the dreaded child of twilight.

You are not doomed, little Kin. Sol's voice streaked through my mind, the gentle caress drowning out some of the blossoming dread. *Fate is merely a path others lay before you. It is not a prison, unless you choose to let it be.*

Isn't it though? Even in my head, I could hear the whiney twinge. *It feels as if every step I take isn't really my own, like all of this was decided long before I ever had a choice. My parents, the secrets, Helroth, the prophecy, even the cuorem bond...*

The spiraling words fell away even as I thought them. The fated mate bond may have been preordained, but it was I who'd made the choice to tie myself to Reign—to link myself forever— for whatever remained of our chaotic lives. And it had been the best decision I'd ever made.

You see... Sol's voice echoed through my mind, smug and self-righteous. *You've always had control, Aelia. You must only exert it.*

He was right, gods' damn it. *Thank you, Sol. I'm sorry if I don't say that often enough. I don't believe I ever would have survived any of this without you.*

You are doing just fine, little Kin. Thanks to my tireless efforts.

Before I could come up with a colorful retort of my own, a roar ripped through the air, sending my thoughts scrambling and head tipping back to face the sun-drenched sky. The powerful pounding of wings reached my sensitive ears a second before Phantom's sleek form appeared on the horizon.

Oh, thank the gods. I released a breath, allowing myself to let the relief settle.

Where in all the realms have you been? I shot the question through the cuorem, anger lacing my tone, the shimmering strands that connected us once again radiant.

You know where. Reign's voice filtered through my mind, so dismal and dejected, it stole the fire from my veins.

Gods, are you all right?

No. But I will be.

As Phantom drew closer, Reign's hunched form coalesced

across the brilliant azure sky. Lifting my finger, I summoned my *rais*, and radiant light glittered across the tip. Tracing the air in the shape of the familiar celestial glyph, Raysa's blessed powers skimmed over my flesh, then I focused my gaze, amplifying it until I could make out every detail of Reign's haggard face.

I hissed out a breath as I took in the blood and gore streaking his face. More than his physical state, it was the look of utter brokenness that had my stomach in knots. My wings flared unbidden, light bursting across the field as they lifted me. Every instinct screamed to fly to him, to reach him, to hold him, but I forced them down, my boots hitting the ground with a thud. Instead, I paced, restless, the bond between us a live wire humming with his pain.

Phantom said he's unharmed. Sol's voice staunched some of the worry.

Good, because once I get my hands on him...

The rumble of the earth beneath my feet put an abrupt pause to my anger. Branches rattled and snapped as Phantom landed within the cover of the Lightwood Forest, just beyond the academy. My feet were moving before I'd made the conscious effort.

With Phantom's frequent visits, the students had begun to question his dragon's repeated appearances. Stealing into their memories and erasing them every time had no longer been a viable option. Nor was it something I particularly relished Reign doing. Instead, Sol and Phantom had helped us come up with a lie based on a partial truth. That the female had been wild, living on the barren Eryndral Isle, and had been drawn to Sol because of the dragon mate bond. As a result, Reign had been able to tame the feral creature and claim her as his own.

The dragons insisted this would be the only believable scenario, so we'd heeded their advice. So far, the lie had been surprisingly well-received, and no one had batted a questioning eye. Then again, when the Night Fae were looming just beyond the gates, an additional dragon was more than welcome.

When I finally reached the edge of the forest, Phantom's obsidian scales glistened in the sunlight, the iridescent shimmer poking through the dense canopy of green.

"Reign." His name was a plea and a prayer.

His shadows curled around his back, lifting his sluggish form from Phantom's back and depositing him on the earth in front of me. Relief slammed into me so hard it nearly knocked me to my knees. He was here. He was alive.

But the moment my eyes truly took him in, the momentary respite turned to horror.

What I had seen from afar was nothing compared to witnessing it up close. Blood matted his hair, streaking down the side of his face and drying in dark rivulets along his jaw. His leathers were torn, scorched, soaked through with crimson and something darker. Shadows clung to him like smoke, curling sluggishly around his boots, flickering in and out as if even they struggled to hold form.

His eyes... Gods, his eyes. They were hollow, bruised with exhaustion, the light in them dimmed to a dying ember.

My heart lifted, only to drop again, the brief reprieve turning to ash as I saw him sway, as I noticed the way his hand shook when he reached to steady himself against Phantom's side.

Alive. But broken.

A dozen unanswered questions streaked through my mind, and it only took one word from Reign to answer them.

"Tenebris," he muttered, his voice hoarse.

"Is he..." I reached for him, but he took a step back and an unexpected pang lanced through my chest.

"Still alive." He looked away, jaw clenching.

I wrapped my arms around my middle, a whisper of ice dousing my veins. "What happened?"

He eyed me, then the charred remains of the Hall of Enlightenment beside us, then beyond to the blackened ruins of the academy. "I underestimated the enemy. As apparently, I am now known to do."

"Don't say that," I hissed.

His gaze dropped to the ground beneath our feet, to his blood-spattered boots. "I keep failing you, Aelia—"

"That's not true." My breath caught as I reached for him, fingers trembling, *needing* to touch him, to remind us both that we were still here, still together. Again, he winced, backing away another step. "Why are you acting like this?" I snapped.

"Because I failed!" he roared, shadows coming to life with his fury and billowing around his form like a storm unleashed. "My father knows about you, about us, about all of it. He's been playing me for a fool all this time."

Oh, gods.

He dragged his hands over his face, streaking sweat and blood across his skin. "He nearly invoked the vow, Aelia. He almost forced me to *kill* you. I could feel his power surging beneath my flesh, and I couldn't fight it. I tried so damned hard, but gods, it was impossible. I thought I could defeat him, overpower his influence, for *you*. But I failed..."

All the air caught in my throat, my vision tunneling. No. This couldn't be. "But Elian..." I rasped. "He has him imprisoned, right?"

He nodded slowly, shadows shifting across his shoulders in agitation.

"So, all you have to do is stay away."

"It's not that simple, Aelia. There is no doubt in my mind that my father will find a way to escape. There is no cell, no runes powerful enough to keep him prisoner. And when he does..."

"No. I'll speak to Elian, force him to ki—" Gods, what was I saying? Hadn't I been the one wishing Reign wouldn't be responsible for his father's death? And now, here I was, condemning him.

Reign's eyes finally lifted to mine, the depth of despair flashing across his midnight orbs gut-wrenching. "I can't be near you. It's not safe. All it would take is for one of my father's shadows to slip free, to whisper the dreaded words, and I would not be able to stop myself, princess."

"So what are you saying?" I hissed.

Reign dragged his hands across his face again, heaving out a breath. "I have to go." His voice cracked, shadows curling around his boots like chains. "I can't stay, Aelia."

Chapter Twenty-Four

R *eign*

I took one step back, then another. The bond between us pulled tight, a thread of light and shadow straining between our chests, quivering with every unspoken word, every fear.

"Reign," Aelia whispered, her hand still outstretched.

And gods, it nearly broke me. The look on her face, the pain in her voice.

I lifted my eyes to meet hers, wading through a cloud of nothing but darkness and perpetual torment, before tearing my gaze away. Shadows swirled around my fingertips as I took another step back.

And the bond snapped.

The pain was so sharp, it lanced across my chest, scorching my insides. The cuorem pulsed, vengeful and furious. As if even the mere mention of another forced separation had it eager for blood.

Aelia's hand was clasped across her chest as if she'd felt it too. "No," she growled, launching herself at me.

Her warmth seared through the cold that had been clawing at me since I'd left her side. Her fists curled into my tunic, bunching the blood-speckled fabric, pulling me down so our foreheads touched.

"You don't get to leave me," she hissed, breathless and trembling. "Not like this. Not ever."

"Aelia," I rasped, forcing down the ache in my throat. The cuorem screamed for me to stay, to *hold her*. "You don't understand. If he finishes the command, if he slips even a whisper of the vow through the shadows, I won't be able to stop myself. I will become the blade he made me, and I will—" My voice broke. "I will *kill you*."

She shook her head fiercely, tears glittering in her eyes like shattered stars. "I don't believe that. You would never hurt me."

"I'd have no choice!" I roared, frustration gnawing at my last shreds of restraint.

"There has to be another way. We will find it. We will *fight it*."

"I can't take that risk." My voice was raw, torn from somewhere deep and bleeding. "I would rather leave you and live with the agony of this bond tearing me apart than ever risk hurting you."

Her grip tightened, her power flaring beneath her skin. Light and shadow danced around us as the cuorem pulsed, thrumming in the space between our bodies. "You think I'll let you walk away? That I will stand here and watch you rip this bond apart, piece by piece, just to protect me?"

"Aelia—"

"No!" Her voice cracked, but her eyes were wildfire, the vivid blue I loved blazing. "I would rather die by your hand than live in a world without you."

The words punched the air from my lungs. The cuorem flared, her words echoing in my mind.

She pressed closer, the glittering strands that stretched between us pulling tight, already mending what had snapped. The warmth flooded back into the hollow places inside me. Her hand cupped my jaw, forcing me to meet her gaze and to see the unyielding promise there.

"We *will* find a way to break the vow," she whispered, softer now. "You and me. Together. There is always another way, Reign."

I squeezed my eyes shut, shadows shaking around me, trembling with the effort to pull away even as every part of me begged to stay.

She pressed her forehead to mine again, and I felt her tears mingle with my own. I could feel her light seep into the cracks the darkness had left behind.

"I can't lose you," I choked.

"Then don't," she whispered.

The cuorem pulsed once more, a single, defiant thrum between us. And for a moment, I let myself believe her. Because the alternative was simply too terrible to bear.

I hadn't told her yet, but I'd already sent word to Gideon. I needed him to double his efforts researching the scope of a blood vow and its effect on a cuorem. I prayed to Noxus he'd discover something before it was too late.

"Gideon?" Her eyes met mine, the flash of hope like a gut punch.

"He's cross-referencing any instances of a blood vow when a cuorem was at play." My shoulders lifted, then sagged at the weight of it all. "I'd had him researching the topic months ago before Helroth captured you, then once you were gone, we shifted focus."

"Did he find anything?"

I shook my head slowly. "Aelia, if—"

"No." She pressed her finger to my lips silencing me. "Don't you dare say it. You will not, under any circumstances, leave me for my own good."

My mouth curved into a reluctant smile beneath her touch. I knew she would never accept my leaving as an option, and it was exactly that stubbornness and endless optimism that made me love her so. But I'd had to try.

"Now, come with me." She weaved her arm through mine and tugged me forward. "You look and smell awful. It's time for a bath."

The scent of burnt bread and charred wood clung to the newly mended banquet hall, refusing to leave even as the morning breeze drifted through the cracked windows. Plates clattered softly, spoons scraping against bowls in the quiet, but the usual chatter was gone.

I sat beside Aelia, close enough to feel the warmth of her thigh against mine. The steady hum of the cuorem was a muted pulse under my skin. It should have soothed me, but at this point, nothing could. Not after what I'd done. Not after what I'd *nearly* done.

His face flickered in my mind: Tenebris's cold, merciless eyes glinting in the dark as he leaned forward, the chains rattling around his wrists and a cruel smile twisting his mouth. *"Reign of Umbra, by the blood that binds you—"* The words had crawled across my skin like ice. They'd sunken into my veins, wrapping around my lungs until I couldn't breathe.

I squeezed my eyes closed to banish the memories. When I reopened them, Aelia's face replaced his. Her eyes were wide and shimmering, pulling me back, grounding me. But the echo of my father's words clung to me, still, a phantom pain in my chest that wouldn't let me forget.

My plate was still mostly full. Steam from the porridge curled into the air before fading. I couldn't find the strength to lift my spoon. Across the table, Rue was picking at her eggs with a scowl, stabbing them with more force than necessary. Symon sat beside her, rolling a small piece of bread between his fingers. His gaze darted around the hall, to anywhere but me.

"This place smells like smoke and defeat," Rue muttered, twisting her fork.

"At least it's quiet," Symon replied.

I kept my eyes on the dark wood of the table, tracing the grain with my gaze as Aelia's hand inched closer to mine. Her pinky brushed against my knuckles. I should have taken her hand. I should have pulled her into my arms and told her that I would fix all of this somehow.

But all I could think about was how close I had come to killing her. How close I still was.

The whispers started quietly, a few seats down. Low voices carried over the hush of the hall.

"They say King Elian captured the Shadow King..."

My jaw tightened, shadows flickering across my shoulders before I forced them to still.

"...locked him away in the dungeons of the Castle of Ethereal Light..."

Rue froze, her fork halfway to her mouth as she turned to look at me, eyes sharp. "Reign?"

Symon's gaze followed hers, wide and uncertain. "Is it true?"

My temples throbbed, hot and furious, reminding me of everything I had done. Everything I had failed to do. I kept my eyes on the table, my hand curling into a fist so tight my knuckles burned.

"We might as well tell them." Aelia's voice was soft, but it cut deeper than any blade. Her hand slid over mine, her fingers warm and steady.

I looked up, meeting her eyes first. Gods, the way she looked at me, as if I wasn't the monster I felt like. As if she still saw me. My gaze shifted to Rue, then Symon, both of them waiting, bracing for whatever truth I was about to unleash.

"It's true." My voice was low and rough, scraping against the silence. "Elian has Tenebris. I delivered him to the Light King."

The air shifted, the murmurs in the hall turning from quiet to heavy, pressing down on us.

"You *what*?" Rue whisper-hissed, her fork clattering onto her plate.

"I brought him there," I continued, voice barely above a whisper, each word a confession I hadn't meant to give. "I fought him. I subdued him. I took him to the Light Court. I thought Elian would end him, end the vow and free me from him."

Symon swallowed hard, glancing at Aelia before looking back at me. "And... did he?"

I shook my head once, shadows flickering around my wrist before I smothered them. My throat tightened, but I still managed the word. "No."

Rue's chair scraped back as she stood, leaning over the table, eyes blazing. "Reign, gods, why didn't you tell us the plan?"

"What would you have done?" I snapped, before I could stop myself, shadows flaring. "It was my choice. My burden. He's my gods' damned father."

Rue's lips parted, her anger faltering as her gaze softened, then hurt flashed across her face. "Aelia is our family, Reign. And now you've bound yourself to her for all eternity, which means you are too. You don't have to carry it alone."

Silence streamed in again between us, thick and suffocating. Before I forced myself to look up and meet each of their eyes, I drew in a breath. "But I do," I finally replied, my voice quiet and hollow. "I am Aelia's *cuoré*, and it is my duty to protect her."

"And she's our best friend, so we're more than happy to share some of that burden."

"Right, what she said." Symon pointed his fork at me.

Aelia's hand squeezed mine, the cuorem thrumming between us, even as everything else felt like it was falling apart.

"You did what you thought you had to," she whispered, her eyes shining. "But they're right, you're not alone in this. You're never going to be alone again."

I looked at her, allowing her light to burn into me. I let it chase the shadows back, even if just for a breath.

"Now what?" Symon asked, his voice barely above a whisper.

I closed my eyes, exhaling, the weight of everything pressing down on my shoulders. When I opened them, I let them see the promise there, the raging resolve I had left. "Now, we find a way to break the blood vow, or I go back and finish this with my father myself."

"You can't..." Aelia murmured. "Elian would never allow it—"

"Then I'll kill him too."

Chapter Twenty-Five

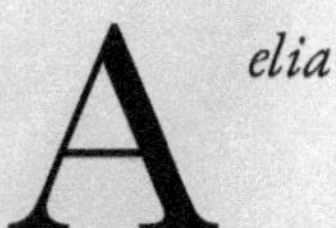

The Hall of Luce thrummed with excitement, a steady chorus of murmurs filling the grand chamber. Even the brilliant rays of blessed sun streaming through the skylight seemed more radiant today. After the past melancholy week of restoration efforts, burying bodies and mourning all those lost in the battle, we were in dire need of some light.

Still, as I sat between Sy and Rue, in the midst of Flare Squad, a hint of unease curled through my innards. This morning when I awoke, Reign was gone. Again. I'd barely had a moment to dwell on his absence before I spied the glittering parchment upon my nightstand. It was the first one that had appeared in weeks. The instructions were minimal: to convene at the Hall of Luce immediately.

Once I'd ensured my *cuoré* hadn't fled campus to murder his father, and potentially start a war with my uncle, I'd woken my roommate. Rue and I had quickly pulled on our training leathers then hurried into the hallway, where we'd found the rest of the students making their way out of the dormitories.

So here we were, the near three hundred students that remained. Across all four years. Most of the upperclassmen had already been called to the front, to patrol the borders of the Wilds. But from everything we'd learned, the Night Fae had gone back into hiding. *What in gods' name are you waiting for Helroth?*

Frustration lanced through my insides with each day that passed without a sign or move indicating their whereabouts. We were no more than sitting ducks, waiting for my grandsire and his Demon Fae to attack. The training sessions with our Arcanum counterparts had been going well, but we still hadn't learned to fight as a team. The centuries of mistrust were ingrained in our blood, and I hated to admit that unifying the courts might prove more difficult than defeating the Night Fae themselves.

The sharp whine of ancient hinges raised the hair on the back of my neck. I didn't have to twist around to know who was stalking in. I could feel him. Feel the surge of *nox* and now *zar* that accompanied my mate.

Which reminded me... Raysa, I had to find a way to discover more about Reign's past without him knowing. At least not until I had some answers to give. Only the gods knew if his current emotional state could handle Kaelith's speculations.

"*Where is the* zar *coming from, Kae?*"

"*The same place all power stems from, Light Fae. His blood.*"

His blood... Stars, who was his mother?

Reign's power bled through the room, billowing his dark cloak and pushing against me as he passed, drawing my thoughts back to the present. He took his place beside the other professors on the dais before his eyes met mine. Raging fury blazed through our bond, the rush of emotion so powerful it stole the air from my lungs.

What's happened? I sent the question through our mental connection.

Before he could respond, a flood of ethereal light bathed the chamber, and my skin prickled from the familiar intensity. The grand doors opened, and Elian strode in. He was dressed in pale robes that shimmered with light glyphs, his golden circlet catching the luminescent glow from the skylight. His calm smile swept across the room, so reassuring, so practiced, that it took everything in me not to flinch from it.

He glided down the aisle as if floating on a cloud as the students' hushed whispers filled the space.

"What is *he* doing here?" Rue whispered.

"I have no idea." That hint of unease grew more volatile.

Once my uncle stood upon the dais beside the headmaster, he began, his voice clear and warm echoing across the hall. "My dear students of Luce, you have endured much in the past weeks. You have shown courage and resilience, and now, your realm calls upon you to act once more."

A hush fell, thicker than the smell of smoke that still clung to the rafters. My fingers curled around the hilt of my dagger, the cuorem suddenly pulsing faster.

Elian spread his arms, the light around him seeming to brighten as if Raysa herself favored him in this moment. "Today, I bring news of victory. Our long-time enemy, the tyrant King Tenebris of the Court of Umbral Shadows, has been captured and is now locked away in the dungeons of Ethereal Light."

A murmur swept through the students, shock and confusion rippling outward like a stone dropped in still water. Heads turned, whispers rose, and questions formed in wide, frightened eyes.

I felt Reign go still atop the dais. Utterly, terrifyingly still.

Elian's gaze swept the room again, landing briefly on me this time. It softened for just a fraction of a second before turning hard again. "Now is the moment, children of Light. With Tenebris captured, the Court of Umbral Shadows is weakened, leaderless, and vulnerable. We will march on the border immediately to secure their lands and bring an end to the darkness that has plagued our realm for far too long."

My breath caught, the world narrowing as his words sank in. *March on the border... take the Shadow Court...*

No. No, he couldn't. Not like this. We were supposed to fight together. Fight the Night Fae! How could he betray us like this? He was supposed to be family, my gods' damned uncle.

Rue gripped my wrist, a gasp squeezing past her lips as I shot to my feet. More gasps echoed across the hall, some students cheering faintly, others frozen, eyes darting toward me. Toward Reign.

Reign's shadows flared, a whirlwind across his shoulders plummeting half the dais into darkness. His jaw was clenched so tight I could feel the crack of tension through the bond.

"You lied to us," I mouthed, but Elian kept speaking, kept smiling as if he were all righteous and hadn't just plunged a dagger into my back.

"You will gather your belongings and be ready within the hour. All capable students will join the Royal Guardians at the border to march with us in this momentous push against the dark," Elian continued, his voice a blade wrapped in silk. "Together, we will bring peace to Aetheria!"

"Peace?" Reign's voice was low, deadly, echoing like thunder in the hush that followed.

Elian's eyes flickered to him across the stage, the smile faltering for just a moment. "Professor Darkthorn, surely you understand this is necessary—"

"*Necessary?*" Shadows erupted around us, the sunlight flickering as the darkness thickened, spreading throughout the room. "You call a slaughter *necessary*? You call the invasion of my people's home *peace*? You are marching against the very Fae you need to destroy the true threat, the Night King!"

Students shrank back, the whispers turning to terrified silence as Reign's shadows roiled and billowed around us.

"Watch your tone, professor," the king growled. "You are forgetting your place."

"And you are risking *all of Aetheria*," he bellowed.

"King Elian," I hissed, stepping forward. My wings flared in a shimmer of light as I felt the cuorem's pulse grow more frenzied, the storm inside me rising to meet Reign's fury. "We need the Shadow Fae on our side. To fight against Helroth's forces. You promised us unity."

His eyes met mine, cool and calm. "This *is* unity, Aelia. Light will prevail, and the darkness, Shadow *and* Night, will fall, once and for all."

Gods, he thinks he can force the Shadow Fae into submission. My thoughts slipped through the bond.

He can't. Reign's voice was a low growl through my mind. *He'll only end up dividing our forces and killing us all.*

But what of his vow to protect me?

Technically, he hasn't broken it, starlight. In his twisted mind, perhaps marching across the Luminoc is protecting you.

"No," I snapped, my voice shaking with rage. "You're using us. Using *them*." I gestured to the students, to Rue's pale face, then to Symon's trembling hands. "The majority of students remaining are only first- and second-years. You're forcing us to fight your war. A war we cannot win divided."

A muscle ticked in Elian's jaw, but he kept his voice soft. "You, of all people, should understand the necessity of this moment." The veiled threat was clear.

Careful... Reign's voice surged through my thoughts again.

Still, I took another step forward, shadows and light dancing around me as the bond with Reign burned. "And you, your Ethereal Highness, of all people, should know I won't stand by and watch you destroy what's left of this realm for your pride."

Another round of gasps echoed across the chamber.

My uncle's eyes hardened, the light around him brightening in warning. "I am your king. How dare you speak to me like this?"

"I am not yours to command," I spat, wings lifting as the trio of gods' given powers roared. *I* was the true heir. But I kept the traitorous thoughts tucked behind my teeth, despite the urge to spill the secret that would change everything.

The hall erupted in whispers again, fear and uncertainty filling every crack as the tension between us grew sharp enough to cut.

Reign disappeared from the dais in a tornado of shadows, reappearing beside me a moment later. His hand brushed mine, shadows coiling protectively around my waist. "If you think we will let you use these students as your soldiers," he said, his voice a quiet threat, "you are gravely mistaken."

Elian's gaze flickered between us, then landed on Draven, who shrank beneath it like a wilting flower. A glint of cold calculation flashed in the king's eyes as sharp and bright as the light that pulsed around him. "As I understood it, it was Draven that led this academy, not either of you."

Reign's glare lanced in Draven's direction. The headmaster shrank behind the king. *Coward.*

"You would betray your own court, your own king, to defend the Shadow monsters?" Elian barked at me.

I lifted my chin, my hand closing around Reign's. "No. We will protect this realm. All of it. Even if we have to protect it from you."

The silence that followed was deafening.

Chapter Twenty-Six

R*eign*

Aelia, no. I growled the command through our bond, already certain it would go unheeded. I knew very well my mate's stubborn streak was rivaled only by her unflinching loyalty.

Her hand closed around mine, tightening with the breadth of her wrath as she glared at her uncle. *Elian betrayed us, Reign. You were right, he'll never overcome his hatred for the Shadow Fae, and because of that, we'll never be able to truly work together. There is only one way to force them all to listen.*

If you declare yourself as heir, you will never be able to take it back, starlight. You will have enemies coming at you from all sides.

And we'll deal with them together, as we always have. She took another step forward.

Gods, princess, you're going to be my ruin.

Was there ever a doubt? A hint of amusement crinkled the corners of her eyes. Just for a moment. Then, it was gone, replaced by pure determination.

Noxus, protect us.

Her wings flared, a whisper of shadow weaving between the blinding light. "I have a confession to make," she called, her voice brimming with determination. Every head in the room turned in her direction. "You know me as Aelia Ravenwood, powerless Kin, but there are some things you don't know. I was born of both Light *and* Shadow. Some of you may have heard of the prophecy, of the one destined to bring about our kingdom's ruin. I am that child, the child of twilight. You were all raised to fear me, fear what my presence represented but today, I ask you to forget everything we were all taught. Because I vow never to be that harbinger of oblivion, but rather, the one to bring forth a new dawn."

Again, a ripple of shocked murmurs tore through the grand hall.

"But I am not only the child of the prophecy—" she paused, glancing around the room at her fellow classmates, her people, meeting each of them in the eyes, "—I am also Princess Aelia of Ether, daughter of the fallen King Alaric and true heir to the Court of Ethereal Light."

The entire sprawling chamber fell silent, the air so thick my lungs ceased to function all together.

For a heartbeat, all I could hear was the rush of blood in my ears and the bond crackling between us, alive with her defiance, her fire. Gods, I wanted to drag her into my arms and kiss her senseless—and then shield her from the war she had just declared.

Elian blinked, once, twice, the confident smirk slipping from his face before he forced it back on like a mask. "Bold words for a powerless Kin," he said softly, the light around him pulsing in warning. "But where is your proof, child?"

Aelia's chin lifted, wings folding neatly behind her as the light flared around her, casting shadows that danced with the frenzied whispers now rising throughout the hall.

"You dare to claim the throne of Ether with nothing more than your word?" Elian pressed, voice rising as anger bled into each syllable. "You expect these students to believe a child of Light and Shadow, a—"

His words cut off as a roar split the sky, rattling the stained-glass windows until shards of colored light trembled across the marble floors. The ground itself seemed to quake beneath our boots as the cry rolled through the heavens.

Solanthus.

His power pressed against the hall like a storm, the primal promise of a dragon's allegiance in every breath of flame that seared the air.

Aelia's eyes flickered with fierce light, and she turned her gaze back to Elian, her voice calm despite the power that now thrummed around her. "You wanted proof. There it is. Solanthus is not only my bonded skyrider, but also the reincarnation of the dragon bonded to my father, King Alaric."

Elian's jaw clenched, his fingers curling around the edge of the wooden stand at the dais. "A dragon's roar proves nothing."

"Then let's get proof you can't deny." My voice was low, lethal. Shadows flickered at my feet as I stepped forward, brushing my shoulder against Aelia's. "Summon the healer. A simple blood test will reveal her true lineage."

Elian's nostrils flared, his composure fracturing for the first time as the students' murmurs rose into a wave, their wide eyes flicking between Aelia, me, and their so-called king.

"Enough." Elian's voice boomed across the chamber, drenched in powerful *rais* that made the shadows hiss where they met. "You all stand here, questioning your king, ready to believe the wild claims of a child of light and dark?" His eyes swept over the students, a sneer curling his lips. "You must choose. Today."

His gaze swung back to Aelia, cold and unyielding. "You will choose between your king and a usurper. Between your realm and the ruin she will bring. Between me and the self-proclaimed harbinger of destruction."

Aelia's fingers found mine, threading together, the cuorem vibrating so violently it hurt. The room split into hushed chaos with students turning to each other, questioning, doubting, fearing. I felt the truth slice between us like a blade.

War wasn't coming. It was already here.

"Who will stand with me?" Aelia's voice shot across the room, splintering the weighty silence. "With all of Aetheria?"

Rue and Symon were the first to their feet.

No one else moved.

Rue's hand threaded through Aelia's free one, and Sy lifted his chin in defiance. Aelia's hopeful gaze flickered across the remnants of Flare Squad, to Belmore, Ariadne, Zephyr and the others. Each of them squirmed uncomfortably beneath her roving stare.

Then, Devin stood, one aisle over, and marched to stand beside Rue. She threw him an appreciative smile before linking their hands. Then it was Liora who moved at the end of Flare team's row, sidling past all the others. I could *feel* my *cuoré's* surprise through our bond.

Belmore pushed to his feet next, something unreadable flashing across those ivy green eyes. I tensed, my shadows hissing and spitting, readying for the Light Fae to raise a hand against our mate. Instead, he dipped his head in a silent apology and moved toward Aelia.

One by one the rest of the squad stood, surrounding her. She greeted each of them with a relieved smile. Even Belmore. I supposed it was a good thing Ruhl hadn't killed him after all.

Tension crackled in the air, each second more pressing than the last. I glared across the room of students I'd spent the last four years of my life with. Would no one else stand against this Light tyrant?

Shadows slithered across my spine, flaring with indignation. Perhaps, it was time for my truth to be told.

No, don't. Aelia's voice rushed down the bond. *They'll only see it as another lie told by the deceitful Shadow Fae. They won't trust you.*

I heaved out a frustrated sigh. She was right, as much as I

hated to admit it. But that didn't mean I couldn't frighten some of these Light fools into submission, as I'd been doing for years now.

I stepped forward, shadows curling around my back until my wings coalesced, their breadth spanning across the entirety of Flare Squad. The silence parted like a wound as I let my gaze sweep across the room, meeting the eyes of the students I had trained, had bled for, and believed in.

"You all know me," I commanded, my voice low but laced with shadows rumbling beneath each word. "You know what I am capable of. But you have no idea how far I will go to protect those I love."

I let the silence stretch, let the shadows flicker across my arms, cold, dark and alive.

"If you wish to stand here and side with a false king who would lead you to your deaths and who would turn you into weapons to fight *his* war, then you are no students of mine."

A twist of *nox* and *zar* pulsed beneath my skin, a warning and a promise, as I let my eyes burn into theirs.

"But if you stand with the true heir, *your princess*—" I paused, my voice softening for only a breath before hardening again, "— then you will live. You will fight for Aetheria's future, not for its destruction."

My shadows coiled tighter, spreading out like a storm across the marble floor. "Choose wisely. Because if you side against her, you side against me. And I will not hesitate."

The hall fell silent, the weight of the promise hanging heavy in the air as the students looked back at me, wide-eyed, their fear filling the chamber.

The squeal of chair legs against marble echoed triumphantly across the space. Nearly half of the students rose to stand behind Aelia and me. Most were second- and third-years. Even a few of the professors joined our ranks. I couldn't blame the new first-years, not really. They had no idea what they'd been thrown into.

With half the hall standing on our side of the aisle, Elian

tipped his long nose in our direction and growled. His fury coiled in gilded threads, vibrating the air. "You will regret this, *princess*." He spat her title with disdain.

"You will address *my mate* with the respect her blood demands," I snarled, shadows snapping around me.

Another wave of gasps rippled across the chamber. A slow grin curved across my lips. It was time they all knew the truth. Aelia was mine. My *cuoré*. My mate. And now, more than ever, they needed to understand what that meant. A move against her was a move against me, and I would answer it with blood.

"Your Ethereal Highness will do," Aelia added with a smirk.

Elian's cheeks burned, crimson flushing his pallid features. Light flares cracked the marble, rattling the hall. "Get off my land, all of you, before I levy the mark of the banished on each one of you," he hissed. "You are traitors to the Court of Ethereal Light."

"No, Uncle," Aelia replied, a calmness in her voice I envied. "You're the one who betrayed this court, betrayed Raysa, and everything the goddess stands for. Remember that. Because the next time I see you, it will be with my dagger at your throat."

With a feral smile that had my heart thundering with pride, my mate spun on her heel. With her wings flaring in a blaze of Raysa's light, she led half the academy through the gilded doors without looking back.

Chapter Twenty-Seven

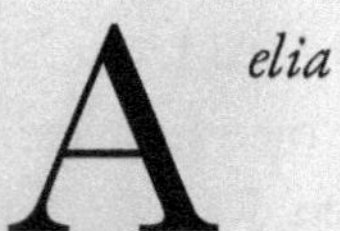

The cold wind off the Luminoc River stung my cheeks as I stood at its edge, the water churning dark and restless despite the burn of Raysa's ever-present light. Behind me, Reign, Flare Squad, and nearly a hundred other students who had chosen to follow us shifted in uneasy silence, the air crackling with tension and uncertainty.

Across the river, chaos had already begun.

I could see it all unfolding, dread scraping at my insides. Farther down the Luminoc, Elian's Royal Guardians, in their white and gold armor that flashed like shards of light, clashed with the black-clad Umbral Guard. The Shadow Fae fought back with wild, desperate precision, despite likely having been completely caught off guard by the attack. Smoke curled up from the banks, shadows rippling across the water as *nox* and *rais* collided, the clang of steel and the screams of the wounded carrying across the wind.

I clenched my hands into fists, the mate bond thumping beneath my ribs, a steady reassurance urging me forward. "This is madness," I whispered as I scanned the battle lines, searching for any sign of peace that might still exist. There had to be a way to stop the bloodshed before it drowned us all.

Beside me, Reign's shadows brushed against my wrist like a tether, grounding and protective. "We'll stop it, Aelia," he said, voice low and rough, the river wind snatching at his words.

Fury snapped at my veins. "This is exactly what Helroth wants, for us to tear each other apart so that he can step in and reap the spoils of war."

His hand replaced his shadows, capturing my wrist and spinning me to face him. "You're right, but you can't just race out there into the middle of a battle—or worse, drag these students along with you. You'd be no better than Elian."

The admonition stung, but the logical part of me knew he wasn't wrong.

"Fine, then where is Ruhl?" I demanded, my eyes still on the battlefield, searching the shifting lines of shadows and light. "With Tenebris captured, doesn't the role of king fall on his shoulders? He should be here, stopping this."

"I'm sure he's here somewhere," Reign said, jaw tightening. "But if you'll recall, it was Elian who was the aggressor. The Umbral Guard are only protecting their lands from an invader."

"I know that!" I hissed. Realms, this was a disaster.

"And even as interim king, Ruhl's power is fragile. He must undergo the Ritual of the Shadow Throne before he can hold any real sway as ruler."

"You really don't believe the Umbral Guard will obey him?"

"I don't know," he gritted it. "Besides, Elian came for blood, and some in the Shadow Court are more than eager to spill it in return."

"Then I'll stop it," I hissed, my wings flickering with light as they threatened to unfurl. "I'll tell the Royal Guardians the truth, just as I did at Luce. They'll have no choice but to back down."

Reign's hand moved up my arm, shadows flaring in warning. "You can't. If you go out there, they could cut you down before you have a chance to even speak a word. Let me go instead."

"No." My voice was steady, even as fear tried to claw at the edges of my resolve. "They need to hear it from me. They need to see that I am real."

"Aelia—" His grip tightened around my arm, his shadows twisting around my wrists like chains. "Please. Let me protect you."

I turned to face him, the wind whipping my hair around us, the cuorem burning as my power met his. "You can't protect me from this, Reign. This is what I was born for."

His shadows pressed closer, desperate, but I lifted my free hand, the tendrils of night loosening enough for me to reach up and press it against his cheek. Then, tilting his face, I forced him to meet my gaze. His eyes were wild with fear and love, and for a heartbeat, I let myself feel it all. The flurry of emotions swept through our bond, more powerful than the will of Raysa herself.

"You're going to be my ruin," he whispered again, shadows trembling.

A sad smile touched my lips. "Isn't that what the prophecy proclaimed?"

I tore myself from his grip, the shadows snapping away as I stepped toward the river. My wings burst forth in a flare of light and shadow that sent ripples across the dark water. Power gathered around me, raising the wind, lifting me off the ground as I prepared to cross the river.

"Aelia, no!" Behind me, Reign's roar echoed, torn between fury and fear.

But I didn't look back.

I launched myself into the air, the wind screaming past me as I flew toward the battlefield, racing to stop a war before it swallowed us all.

An answering cry filled the air an instant before powerful wingbeats thrummed across the sky. Not just one dragon, but two. Sol and Phantom streaked closer, cutting through the silky midnight across Shadow lands.

Do you know what you're doing, little Kin? Sol's admonishing tone reminded me a bit too much of my mate's.

No, but I have to try.

Forcing my ethereal wings to flap harder, I skirted the edge of the battleground from above. Steel clashed against steel, the air thick with the scent of blood and scorched earth. *Rais* flared, clashing with the deep, pulsing shadows of the Shadow Fae as they fought back with a desperation that tore at my heart. Screams and battle cries tangled in the wind, each one carving another notch into my resolve.

Already, I could feel Reign quickly approaching, his wrath surging through the glittering strands that connected us. I had to move now.

I dropped lower, taking in the chaos from close up. Luminescent blades clashed against umbral weapons in a maddening staccato, blood and gore already staining the dark earth. A blast of searing light exploded ahead, forcing me to throw up a shield as shards of burning air pelted my skin. When the dust cleared, in the center of it all, I saw him.

"Ruhl!" I shouted, angling my wings to land in the midst of the melee.

His shadows lashed out in sharp spears as he parried the relentless strikes of a Royal Guardian twice his size. The Guardian's blade, gleaming with light runes, slammed down, forcing Ruhl to one knee. His teeth were bared in a snarl.

"No!" The word tore from my throat as I surged forward.

The Guardian raised his sword for the killing blow, but before it could fall, I lunged. My daggers rippled with infernium vein as I crossed them above Ruhl's head, catching the blade with a shower of sparks.

"Get *off him*," I hissed, light flooding my being and rippling down my arms.

A burst of *rais* exploded from my blades, sending the

Guardian stumbling backward. Ruhl's stunned gaze snapped to mine, shadows flickering around him.

"Aelia?" he rasped.

"Get up, my king," I ordered with a smirk, pulling him to his feet as light and shadow curled together around us, shielding us from the anarchy.

Behind me, a thunderous crack split the air as shadows erupted, swallowing a dozen Light Guardians in darkness. Reign. Flare Squad fanned out behind him, Rue's arrows glowing with light and Symon's luminescent sword sparking as they pushed into the fray. One by one, they forced back the attackers to form a loose circle around us.

"Aelia!" Rue shouted, sweat and blood splatter already streaking her face as she fired another arrow into the dirt to block an advancing Guardian.

"Are you all right?" I cried, one eye on her and the other on my mate, who was now cleaving through the battlefield with his raging shadows.

She waved a nonchalant hand. "Oh, I'm fine. It's not my blood."

Sy grimaced beside her. "She got a little too close when an Umbral Guard's shadow blade sliced off a Light Fae's arm."

"That's gruesome." Shaking my head, I shouted, "Be careful," before stepping into the center of the chaos, and the storm within me raged to life.

I lifted my hands, the trio of powers—*rais*, *nox*, and *zar*—twisting together in a spiral of light and shadow, along with the deep, cold hum of the night. Power crackled across my skin and blinding light streaked with pure darkness as it built. The wind whipped around me in a furious gale.

"Get down!" I shouted at my teammates, just before I released it.

The blast erupted outward in a wave, rolling over the field in a pulse that sent Light and Shadow Fae alike stumbling, weapons dropping as light flashed before their eyes and shadows tangled around their feet. The ground trembled under the force, momentarily dazing everyone and freezing the chaos.

Silence rang out, sharp and merciless.

I stepped forward, wings flaring and catching the moonlight. *Rais* burned across the battlefield as shadows coiled around me. Sol and Phantom circled overhead, their mere presence bolstering my conviction.

"My name is Aelia," I called out, cutting through the smoke and fear. "Some of you may have known me as the powerless Kin, the weak student who didn't belong at the great Conservatory of Luce."

Faces turned to me, bloodied and dirt-streaked and eyes widening with disbelief.

"But today, I tell you the truth in hopes of ending a pointless war." I lifted my chin, letting the power settle around me like a mantle, letting them see me. All of me. "I am the daughter of King Alaric of Ether, the heir to the Court of Ethereal Light. And I am also the child of Light and Shadow. I was born bound by a prophecy, but I refuse to be the child it speaks of. I will not destroy this realm, but rather, I am here to save it."

The sounds of shock rippled across the field, some stepping back, others forward, uncertainty and hope tangling in their expressions.

"You have all been lied to, used, and turned against each other by those who would see Aetheria burn to protect their own power. But this ends now. We are not enemies." I swept my gaze across them—Royal Guardians, Shadow Fae, students, and my own Flare Squad as Reign's dark, steady figure watched me with pride burning in his eyes. "We are Aetheria's last hope."

I let the silence stretch. I allowed it to settle over them as the weight of the moment pressed into their souls.

"And I will not stand by and watch you tear each other apart while the true enemy, the Night Fae, gather in the dark."

My wings folded behind me, the cuorem thundering through my veins with a single, defiant beat. "Choose now. Not between Light and Shadow. Not between your courts or your kings. Choose Aetheria. Choose the future."

Chapter Twenty-Eight

R*eign*

The silence across the battlefield was crushing, so much so, it was as if time stood still. No one breathed. No one dared to move.

Aelia stood in the center of the clearing, more radiant than gods' damned Raysa herself with Light Fae to her back and Shadow Fae looming before her. But she didn't falter, didn't blink.

And in that moment, I loved her more than I ever thought possible. Because I realized she wasn't only my *cuoré*, she *was* the child of twilight, a princess of two courts, destined to rule them all.

I hoped she could feel the overwhelming pride surging through our bond. I was so distracted by my mate I almost didn't notice him. from the shadows at the edge of the circle, he stepped forward.

Ruhl.

His dark hair was matted with sweat and blood, a barely

perceptible circlet hanging over his brow. Shadows clung to his skin like a second layer, but his eyes were clear, burning with resolve as he moved to stand at Aelia's side.

"My fellow Shadow Fae," he called out, his voice low but still carrying across the hushed field with quiet authority, "I am Prince Ruhl of Umbra. Son of Tenebris, and now, by right and by blood, Shadow Regent and your future king."

Surprise rippled through the Shadow Fae ranks. Some dropped to their knees, while others tightened their grips on their weapons, clearly torn between loyalty to our father and fear of him, of the uncertainty.

Ruhl's jaw tightened. "I know what you have suffered. I know what it means to serve under a king who wielded fear like a blade and demanded loyalty without earning it. I am his son, after all." His eyes glinted, and for a moment, the shadows around him flared like wings. "But I am not my father."

Another murmur rippled through the lines, the wind carrying it like a prayer.

"I will not force you to lower your weapons for me." His voice softened, shadows curling around his hands, wrapping around the hilt of his sword before he dropped it into the dirt at his feet. "I will *ask* you to lower them for *her*."

He turned to Aelia, inclining his head in a show of respect that made the breath catch in my throat.

"For Aelia, heir of Ether, the child of Light and Shadow, who has risked everything to save us from tearing each other apart while Helroth waits to strike. Lay down your weapons, not for kings or courts, but for the realm we all share."

Ruhl looked back at his people, our people, shadows swirling gently around him. "Lay them down so that when the true enemy comes, we will be ready to fight him together."

The world seemed to hold its breath.

And then, slowly, one by one, blades hit the dirt.

The soft clatter of steel on stone and earth rang out like bells across the field as the Shadow Fae then the Light Fae lowered their weapons, their eyes lifting to Ruhl, then to Aelia, and to the future we were all trying to save.

The air grew less oppressive, the suffocating *nox* and *rais* dissipating as ethereal weapons vanished. Half of the Royal Guardians dropped to their knees, while the others slowly retreated.

I remained rooted to the spot, a few yards from my triumphant half-brother, the future king, and my radiant *cuoré*, a queen in her own right. And for the first time since I learned of the cuorem, I wondered if the gods *had* chosen wrong.

Ruhl was the heir to the Shadow throne, and Aelia was born to unite the Court of Ethereal Light with the damned Night Fae. They were destined to rule together.

Then why, by all the gods, had fate chosen to tie us as *cuoré*?

"We did it." Aelia's soft voice tore me from my dark musings. Realms, I hadn't even heard her move toward me.

"No, *you* did it, princess." Even I could hear the hollow echo in my tone.

She laced her fingers through mine and pressed her body close. Despite the hundreds of Fae, both Light and Shadow, surrounding us. "I never could have done any of this without you, Reign."

A grunt squeezed past my lips. "Oh, starlight, that's not true at all. You were destined to do this. To be a princess, a great ruler." My fingers itched to curl into fists, the unfairness of it all boring into me.

Her brows knitted, expression pinching. "And you are my *cuoré*. Two-halves of the same soul, remember?"

"Mmm." My jaw clenched.

Those brilliant sliver-blue eyes met mine, a surge of her concern coursing through our bond. "Reign, what's wrong?"

"Nothing," I muttered, my shadows spilling around us. Now was not the time or place to discuss the matter. But now that I'd considered it, I wasn't certain I could simply dismiss it. With Father out of the way, and the truth of Aelia's bloodline surfacing as a result of Elian's betrayal, joining the Light and Shadow

Courts under their new rulers would be the most logical course of action.

Gods, I'd been a selfish fool not to consider it more seriously when Aidan had brought it up months ago.

"Reign!" Aelia barked.

I blinked quickly, meeting her gaze. There was hurt there. And anger.

Curses, damned mental connection.

Silky shadows coiled around us, wrapping us both in an impenetrable cocoon of night. Before I could decipher which were mine or hers, a void of night dragged us in. Seconds later, we materialized in a quiet corner of the clearing, far away from curious gazes.

Realms, she'd shadowtraveled us both over a hundred yards.

"How could you even consider that?" Aelia growled, sparks of light flickering across her fingertips, blending effortlessly with the shadows spiraling around her form. "You are my mate, damn it. How could you think for even a second that the gods chose wrong? Or that I would tie myself to Ruhl simply to—"

"To save our kingdom, Aelia!" The words whooshed through my clenched teeth, harsher than intended. Drawing in a deep breath to temper the growing rage, I continued more calmly, "Royals do it all the time. They marry, not for love, but for duty, for strategic alliances."

"I refuse to even consider what you're saying right now." She threw her hands in the air, frustration deepening the faint lines between her brows.

Taking her hands, I forced her wild gaze to meet mine. "I love you, Aelia, more than anything. There is nothing I wouldn't do to protect you. Even if that means allowing you to marry my brother, for your safety, and for the sake of our realm."

"This is ludicrous." She wriggled free of my hold, crossing her arms over her chest like a flesh and blood shield. "I love *you*. I want to be with *you*."

"It would be in name only—"

"And you could live with that?" she snarled, anger pulsing through our mystical tie. "I would be Ruhl's *wife*. Even if I did not share his bed, we would be bound all the same. We would make appearances together, travel the realms together, do everything together as king and queen."

The cuorem pounded a violent beat, thrashing against my ribs. Sharp claws raked across my heart, squeezing my lungs until I could scarcely breathe.

Noxus, *could* I live with it?

Could I watch her stand beside Ruhl, see them rule together, lead the realms, and smile for the people while I stood in the shadows, nothing more than a ghost at her side?

Even if it was in name only, could I stand by and watch her become *his* queen?

Aelia's breath came fast, her eyes glinting like stormlight as the shadows and light flickering around her caught in the chaos of her rage, fear and love. "Look at me," she hissed, stepping closer, so close I could feel the heat of her power against my skin. "Don't you dare shut me out."

I forced my eyes up, meeting hers, letting her see the truth I could no longer hide.

"I don't know if I can," I rasped, voice cracking. Shadows shivered around me in a vengeful fury. "Gods, Aelia, I don't know if I'm selfless enough to let you go, even if it's what this realm needs. Even if it's what *you* need to be who you're meant to be."

Her mouth parted, a small, pained sound slipping free before she bit it back. "You are who I'm meant to be with," she whispered fiercely, pressing a hand against my chest over the frantic thrum of the cuorem. "Don't you feel this? Don't you understand? There is no kingdom, no throne, and no prophecy that will ever change that."

"I know," I breathed. I closed my eyes as her power sank into me, washing over the darkness that threatened to consume me. "But what if the gods ask it of us anyway? What if to save Aetheria, we have to—"

"No." Her hand slammed against my chest this time, light flaring, searing through the shadows. "No, Reign. I will not let the gods, or my uncle, or the prophecy take you from me. I would burn down every court before I let them."

My eyes snapped open, locking with hers, and for just a moment, the storm of fear and doubt broke, replaced by the blazing certainty in her gaze.

She would fight for me, for us, even if the world demanded otherwise.

"I love you," she whispered, tears glinting in her eyes. Her voice shook as she pressed her forehead against mine. "I will *always* choose you."

And as the cuorem pulsed between us, steady and fierce, I realized I would always choose her, too.

Even if it destroyed everything else.

Chapter Twenty-Nine

A *elia*

Reign and I stood there, foreheads pressed together, our ragged breaths mingling, bathed in a thick cloak of our shadows for an endless moment. Despite his declaration, I could still feel his uncertainty stretching across the taut tendrils of our bond.

He was wrong.

Aidan was wrong.

I didn't need to be Ruhl's wife to save Aetheria; we would find another way, together. I opened my mouth to say as much when a scream rent the air.

The cool tornado of whirling shadows dissipated instantly, revealing the chaos beyond.

Another roar split the night as a dark, writhing shape lunged from the treeline, smoke trailing like tattered banners. It slammed into the nearest line of Light Fae, sending bodies scattering, claws raking through radiant shields with horrifying ease.

Oh gods, not now.

All around us, the air thickened with the scent of scorched earth and acrid *zar* as creatures of smoke and bone, alive and undead, tore through the ranks of stunned Guardians. Half were caught as they attempted to flee across the Luminoc. Those were the loyalists, the ones who'd chosen to stand with King Elian. Serpent-like beasts, their eyes molten gold and mouths brimming with hellfire, slithered across the battlefield. Their roars shook the ground, my knees trembling from the force.

"Raysa, no..." I whispered, heart hammering.

Reign's shadows flared around us, summoned by the call of the encroaching darkness, his jaw set. "They didn't wait long."

No, they didn't. But neither would we.

Reign's *nox* skimmed over my skin, pulling us into the icy void. An instant later, we were transported across the clearing, standing in the middle of the turmoil once again.

Light and Shadow Fae scrambled, blades and shadows rising in tandem as they turned, for the first time, not on each other, but on the true enemy. Ruhl was already shouting orders to the Umbral Guard, his voice ringing with authority. Only a few yards away, Rue, Symon, and the rest of Flare Squad rallied the students and remaining Royal Guardians, forming defensive circles.

I grabbed Reign's hand, meeting his gaze as power thrummed between us. "Time to remind them who we are."

A slow, fierce grin curved across his lips, the heated discussion from only a moment ago forgotten in the face of our true enemy. "After you, princess."

I took a single step before spinning back and crushing my mouth to his. The kiss was hard and hungry, desperate and raw. I poured everything words couldn't say into that moment.

Above us, another roar, one sounding like thunder, split the sky as Sol descended, his golden wings scattering the smoke below him in swirling eddies of light. Phantom was a shadow streak beside him, her onyx-flamed eyes burning as she circled, releasing a shriek that rattled the Night Fae lines.

"Rue, take your archers to the ridge. Clip the wings off those monsters before they reach the lines!" I called out. "Symon, hold the left flank with the Guardians. Push them back, give Sol room to strike!"

My friends each responded with a fierce nod. Please, Raysa, protect them. Protect us all.

"Together on Sol," Reign called out beside me. "Phantom has her own agenda."

I nodded quickly as we ran side by side toward my skyrider, shadows and light weaving around our feet. As the dragons grew closer, we leapt, the wind catching in our wings as Sol dipped lower, extending a clawed foreleg. I grabbed hold, Reign's shadows coiling around us and lifting us onto the dragon's back as Phantom fell into formation beside us.

Little Kin, ready yourself. Sol's deep voice rumbled through my mind as his wings flared, launching us skyward.

Always. Resting one hand on my blade already alight with *rais* and *nox*, I twisted my head over my shoulder to meet Reign's determined gaze. I couldn't help but revel in the feel of him seated behind me, his unyielding form draped around me.

"I think I could get used to this." I tossed him a smirk.

"I'm not sure your skyrider would say the same."

Sol huffed out a grunt of agreement, flames shooting from his nostrils.

The ground was a mass of chaos, but for once, it was not chaos born of division. Light Guardians and Shadow Fae Guards fought side by side, their powers clashing not with each other, but against the Night Fae warriors and their monstrous abominations as they surged forward.

Cleary, they hadn't expected us to stand together. In fact, I couldn't help but wonder if this had been a planned attack. They had likely thought to find us fighting each other, a perfect chance to swoop in and finish us all.

"I tend to agree." Reign's voice zipped across the shell of my ear, over the whipping winds.

"How did they know they'd find us at our most vulnerable?" I shouted back.

"Obviously, someone told them." He paused, but I could feel the spiral of dark thoughts swirling through his mind. "It's a matter to deal with later. Now, we need to focus on that." He tipped his head at the beast of smoke and shadows hurtling toward us.

Reign's hand found mine where it gripped the spiked ridge along Solanthus's back, the cuorem blazing as we drew on each other's strength. "Aim for the serpent's eyes," he shouted over the wind, shadows dancing in his palms.

I nodded, wings flaring, and together we launched ourselves off Solanthus's back as my skyrider dove, fire streaming from his jaws to incinerate the smoke-beasts below. Phantom appeared below us, unleashing a torrent of silver dragonfire that carved a path through the Night Fae lines.

The wind tore at my hair, the world a blur of color and power as I angled downward, raising my hands as light and shadow converged, twisting together with the icy rush of *zar*. The blast struck the nearest serpent square in its citrine eye, sending it reeling with a shriek of agony before it crumbled into ash.

Another one lunged from the smoke, jaws gaping, but Reign was already there, shadows lashing out like spears. The umbral blades drove into its throat and pulled, tearing the darkness from within until it fell, lifeless.

Below us, the Light and Shadow Fae rallied, pushing forward with renewed vigor as they saw the creatures fall, their cries of fear turning into shouts of triumph. Ruhl was a dark streak among them, cutting down the Night Fae soldiers who scrambled to regroup.

"Together!" I shouted as I landed on Sol's back again, raising my blade as power built within me, a storm of light and darkness ready to break.

Reign slipped behind me. His shadows wrapped around my middle, grounding me as I unleashed the tempest. A blinding burst of white streaked with black tore across the battlefield in a wave that incinerated the creatures of smoke and sent the Night Fae soldiers fleeing.

The dawn light broke through the clouds across the border as the last serpent fell. The battlefield suddenly quieted, the only sound the ragged breaths of the united Fae below.

With my heart pounding, I searched the retreating mass of darkness for that streak of silver hair, that grisly cloak of forgotten souls. Nothing. Where are you, Helroth?

As I forced my gaze away from the escaping Demon Fae, a familiar head of pale blond hair, tied back in a neat tail, caught my eye. All the air siphoned from my lungs.

Heaton.

"Oh, gods, Heaton!" I cried as I slid off Sol's back.

Somewhere across the field, Rue must have heard me, because her shout echoed a moment later. Before Reign could stop me, my wings were pounding. I flew directly for the mass of retreating Demon Fae, my mate's howls echoing in the distance and vibrating through our bond.

"Heaton!" I shouted as I flew over the Night Fae warriors surrounding him.

His head tipped up, a flicker of recognition in those pale blue eyes before it vanished. Before I could fully adjust my grip on my blades, one of the Night Fae saw me coming. I twisted in the air, wings flaring with light as I raised my hands, but I was too slow, too exposed.

The Night Fae's blade swung out, catching my arm. I hissed out a cry as the metal split the skin.

Be careful, little Kin. Sol's voice crackled in my mind, a mixture of exasperation and protectiveness as he banked overhead.

"I'm trying," I hissed, breathless, forcing myself forward.

Heaton was within reach, his light hair matted to his face, eyes wide with confusion as the Night Fae tried to drag him back into their lines. Before I could reach him, another Demon Fae slammed a gauntleted fist into his gut, folding him over.

A scream ripped from my throat as I hurled a blade of light, severing the demon's arm before it could strike again. Shadows coiled from my other hand, threading between the enemy ranks and wrapping around Heaton's chest.

He fought, snarling, but my shadows held him fast.

Oh, gods, what had they done to him?

Reign appeared beside me in a blink, shadows snapping like whips around his arms, eyes black with fury. "I've got him," he snarled as he extended his hand past me. His shadows seized Heaton, ripping him from the grasp of the Night Fae.

The ground below erupted in chaos as another warrior lunged, claws snapping toward Heaton's legs. I dove, wings straining, catching Heaton's wrist and pulling him higher just as the demon grazed his boot.

My *rais* flared and Reign's shadows closed around us as we fell back, tumbling onto the torn earth behind the lines.

"Reign, we have to go!" I shouted, clutching Heaton as he gasped, struggling weakly in my hold.

Reign's shadows coiled around us, and I caught one last glimpse of the Night Fae before the world blinked into darkness. We slipped through the void, Heaton's ragged breath echoing in my ear.

Seconds later, when we emerged across the field, I let out a breath. Heaton collapsed in the dirt, coughing and gagging. But he was alive and safe.

Reign's eyes met mine, dark and wild, shadows still flickering around him as he stepped close, curling his arms around my waist. "Never," he growled, voice low enough so only I could hear, "do that without me again."

"Okay," I breathed, a faint smile tugging at the corner of my lips.

My shoulders rounded as I drew in a steadying breath, surveying the ravaged land around us. The Night Fae had vanished, likely having escaped through a portal of Helroth's making. And only a few yards away, Light Guardians helped

Shadow Fae to their feet, the lines between them fading for the first time.

The mighty flap of wings turned my gaze upward to the moonlit sky. To the two dragons sailing side by side, scales shimmering beneath the stars.

Are you all right, Sol?

Just fine, little Kin. And you?

Still surviving.

They didn't count on us standing together. His voice sailed through my mind, a hint of pride lacing his gruff tone.

No, they didn't. I allowed a smile to melt across my face. *But they will now.*

And as the moonlight claimed the battlefield, bathing both the Light and Shadow forces in an ethereal glow, I realized there was indeed still hope.

Chapter Thirty

R*eign*

Ghosts lingered in the halls of the Fortress of Umbral Shadows, Tenebris's former domain, each turn down a dark corridor toward the barracks resurrecting nightmares of my past. An icy chill frosted the air with even the flames flickering in the sconces wavering as if the obsidian stone threatened to swallow every ounce of its light.

Noxus, I hated this fortress.

Of all the places in the realm, I never thought we'd end up here.

Once the Night Fae had fled, Ruhl had suggested returning to our old home to rest and regroup. He'd sent his mother and our youngest brother, Dom, away to the seaside for safekeeping. The boy was too young to witness war and my stepmother too weak. It was best to safeguard them from all of this.

None of us were soldiers, not true warriors honed by battle; most of the Fae that fled with us were little more than children.

The brutal trials at Luce and Arcanum were nothing compared to the horrors of real war. A war that loomed at our doorstep now.

One that could no longer be ignored.

And with Light divided because of that damned traitor, Elian, we would have to fight twice as hard to combat the impending doom. How many Night Fae warriors did Helroth truly have? We had no real notion what we were up against. Neither Ruhl nor I had any real battle experience beyond our training at the Citadel. And now we were forced to lead a ragtag group of students, Royal Guardians, and the Umbral Guard into a war?

Gods, this was madness.

My steps quickened as I passed the door to Father's private chambers. It was ajar, just as I'd left it all those days ago. Did our blood still stain the stone floor? Or had one of the servants cleaned it after I'd captured my father and handed him over to his greatest enemy? The bastard who'd then turned around and plunged a knife into my back at his earliest opportunity. Realms, I'd been such a fool to trust Elian for even a moment.

I tore my gaze away from that door, forcing my boots to keep moving, the pull of the cuorem like a lifeline in the choking gloom. Aelia. She was here, somewhere within these walls that had once broken me, and now, she was the only reason I was still breathing.

I reached the barracks, the thick wooden doors hanging slightly ajar, just as my father's had been. But instead of silence and ghosts, voices spilled out. Some were frantic, others hushed, but all were scared. The whispers layered into a chaos that prickled against my senses like needles.

Pushing inside, I was hit by a wall of tension. The large, cold space was packed with bodies. Flare Team was huddled near the hearth, while Royal Guardians stripped off their gleaming armor, their faces drawn and haunted. Shadow Fae, a mixture of Arcanum students and the court's Umbral Guard, lined the edges of the sprawling chamber, weapons within arm's reach despite the truce that still held—barely.

And there in the center, a tether of light in the gloom, stood my Aelia.

She was surrounded by them, her hair mussed from battle and shadowtravel. Her steady gaze scanned each person with that impossible blend of command and compassion that made people follow her. That made them *choose* her.

The moment her eyes found mine, the disorder in the room seemed to pause. The cuorem thrummed between us like a drumbeat, steadying the storm inside me for just a breath. But only for a breath.

"Reign." Her voice was soft, but the weight in it made my shoulders tense.

Scanning the hall, I found Rue kneeling near one of the cots only a few feet away from Aelia, her eyes hollow. I followed her line of sight and felt my stomach clench.

Heaton lay there, pale and too still, his chest rising and falling shallowly. His hands twitched now and then, his eyes fluttering beneath closed lids. It seemed as if he were caught in some nightmare he couldn't wake from.

"How is he?" I asked, striding toward them.

"He hasn't woken since we pulled him from the Night Fae lines," Rue said, her voice cracking, though she tried to hide it. "It's like he's trapped."

"We've tried everything," Aelia added, moving to my side. Her hand found my wrist, grounding me. "*Rais* healing, shadow coaxing, even *zar*. Nothing reaches him."

The Guardians surrounding us exchanged uncertain glances, and one of them muttered, "We don't even know what we're fighting anymore."

The words echoed the fear already pressing against my ribs.

"And how can we be sure she truly is the heir?" Another voice.

A few more muttered whispers of agreement.

Then, yet another voice, this a quiet, rough one. "Shut up, you imbeciles, don't you see it? It's in her eyes. There is no doubt in my mind, she *is* Alaric's daughter."

Aelia's gaze zipped toward the older Light Fae male who leaned against the wall in the corner. He appeared to be around Aidan's age, but it was difficult to tell with elder Fae. Aelia's feet were moving toward him before I could stop her.

"You knew my father?"

The Fae dipped his head, strands of silver falling across his brow. "I did, your Ethereal Highness. It was my greatest honor to fight beside him at the end of the Two Hundred Years' War."

Aelia's breath hitched, a whirlwind of emotions streaking through our bond. Excitement. Pride. Grief.

"What is your name, sir?"

"I am Eryndor Dawnmere, and I am at your service." He spoke with his head bowed, body folded over, and eyes cast down to his boots.

"Please, rise, Eryndor."

"Losing King Alaric was the greatest tragedy to befall the Light Court during the war. Elian..." his words fell away. "Well, that doesn't matter anymore, princess. You are here now, and that's what is important." He dropped to one knee and raised a luminescent sword. My hands were nearly at his neck before his head dipped in reverence.

"By the light of Raysa, I swear my blade, my breath, and my blood to you, Princess Aelia of Ether. I vow to stand between you and the darkness, to fight at your side until the blessed sun falls from the sky, and to protect your life above my own."

Echoing footfalls reverberated across the room as the rest of the Royal Guardians dropped to their knees, each and every one repeating the soldier's vow.

Aelia stood impossibly still, her eyes gleaming with emotion, hands trembling. Through our mental connection, I could feel her uncertainty, her fear. She wasn't only afraid of failing them, but of losing everything she loved to save them. "Thank you," she finally murmured.

The moment stretched on, the weight of their declarations

thickening the air. Then, finally, one by one, they rose and scattered around the barracks once again.

Inching closer, I laced my fingers through hers and gave a gentle squeeze. "They're your men now, princess."

"That seems like quite a responsibility to take on."

"Nonsense. You were born for this, starlight."

I scanned the room, taking in the exhaustion and quiet dread on the students' faces. Despite the moving display from the troop of Royal Guardians, there was still so much unknown. They looked to Aelia, to me, and even to Ruhl for answers. My half-brother paced near the far wall, shadows flickering at his heels as they all waited for someone to tell them what to do next.

But the truth was, I didn't know.

Gods, we were children leading children into war.

Aelia's hand tightened around mine, pulling me back from the edge of that thought. Her eyes were hard, glinting like a blade in the dim light. "We need to make a plan," she said, loud enough for the room to hear. "Helroth wants to tear this realm apart, but we will not let him. Not while we still stand. Not while we stand together."

A few heads lifted, hope sparking in tired eyes.

"Ruhl," she called, her gaze flicking to where he stood, "we need scouts on the borders. We need healers working shifts, and we need the Guardians and the Umbral Guard training together, not across from each other. We must learn to move as one, light and shadow intertwined, if we're to stand against the Night Fae."

Ruhl's jaw ticked, but he nodded once, his eyes softening as they found hers. "Consider it done, Your Highness."

She released my hand, *rais* flickering on her fingertips as she turned back to the room. Her voice was stronger now. "We don't have the luxury of fear anymore. We have each other, and that's enough. Together, we will defeat Helroth." Releasing a breath, she glanced to each corner of the room. "For now, we rest and recuperate. Tomorrow is a new day."

As the room stirred, moving with renewed—if shaky—

purpose, she leaned into me. Despite dreading the onslaught of curious gazes, my arm curled around her shoulders, drawing her closer. Her forehead brushed against mine for a heartbeat.

"I meant what I said earlier," she whispered. "We will find another way, Reign. You and me."

I closed my eyes, letting the warmth of her promise bleed into the cold places the fortress always left in me. "I know," I whispered back, though the fear still pressed against my ribs like a blade.

When I opened my eyes again, I let the bastard Shadow Prince slip away and the leader they needed return. "Rue, you and Symon are in charge. I'll send the staff down to feed the troops and set up the barracks to accommodate everyone for the foreseeable future."

She offered a half smile in return as she gripped her brother's hand. "Yes, professor."

"And as for Heaton, if he so much as twitches, I want to know."

The faint smile slipped away, but she nodded all the same. I hated to even think it, but if Helroth had found a way to infiltrate Heaton's mind, we could have a spy within our midst.

"Aelia, Ruhl, with me," I said, my shadows sliding across the stone as I turned toward my father's war room. "It's time to plan our next move."

Chapter Thirty-One

An hour later and Tenebris's war room was teeming with activity. Not only had the general of the Umbral Guard joined us, but also a few of the other Shadow commanders who'd been stationed nearby. But perhaps, my most favorite addition of all was Aidan.

It had taken every ounce of willpower I possessed not to throw my arms around my adoptive father and give into the tears that had threatened the moment he walked in. Even now, I was barely holding it together. I couldn't wait to have a minute alone with the male who'd raised me. The male who'd given me everything he could, not because he had to, but because he'd chosen to. But right now, he wasn't my kind, caring adoptive father, he was the formidable general who'd led the king's armies into war.

Maps littered the massive obsidian table, weighed down by daggers and rusted pieces of armor, each mark and scribbled rune another reminder of the blood already spilled. The blood I was responsible for when Helroth had skulked into my mind and forced my hand.

A lantern flickered above us, the dim light casting harsh shadows across the faces of the assembled commanders. The general of the Umbral Guard, a grizzled male with hair like onyx stone and eyes like cold steel, stabbed a finger at the map. "We hold the Light Fae here." His voice was clipped, final. "Now, as for the bigger issue..." His finger ran across the schematic. "The Night Fae hadn't expected us to fight together, which was what gave us the edge today, but that surely won't be the case next time. Beyond that, we do not know the breadth of their forces. I suggest we wait, fortify, and strike only when we are certain of victory."

Murmurs of agreement rose from the other Umbral commanders, each wearing the exhaustion of the last battle like a second skin.

"We *wait*?" Shadows licked up Reign's forearms, restless. "And let Helroth gather strength while we sit in the dark? Let him choose when and where to strike again?"

Ruhl crossed his arms, shadows shifting across his shoulders as he leaned forward. "Reign's right. If we wait, we risk Helroth regaining control of the Wilds and moving into the vulnerable Kin lands of Feywood. We need to move now before they understand the full breadth of *our* power."

"And leave our lands undefended? For Elian to attack again?" another commander barked, slamming his fist against the table. "We're fighting a war on two fronts. We'll be slaughtered!"

"Better that than waiting like sheep for the blade to fall," Reign snapped, eyes flashing. The cuorem zipped to life between us, pounding with his frustration.

Aidan cleared his throat, drawing every eye as his calloused fingers smoothed a crease on the map. His presence alone quieted the room, the bickering stuttering into silence.

"There is merit in caution," Aidan said, his voice even, but the steel beneath it was clear. "You are not wrong, Reign. Helroth will not stop unless we make him. But if we march now, exhausted and scattered, with half-trained students at our flanks, we risk a massacre we cannot afford. We need time to regroup and to train together, Light and Shadow as one."

Reign's jaw clenched, his shadows twitching and poised to strike, but he said nothing.

Across the table, I stood with my arms crossed, the cold stone seeping into my boots. I watched as Aidan, Reign, Ruhl, and the commanders argued, counter-argued, and circled the same truth they were all too stubborn to admit.

They were terrified.

And so was I.

Every moment they argued, my thoughts wandered. To Heaton's pale face, the way his hands twitched in that nightmare sleep he couldn't wake from. To the haggard expressions of the students who'd fled with us. And most of all, to the argument with Reign. It haunted me. The idea of sacrificing the male I loved for a realm that might never be grateful, that might never be saved, churned like acid in my stomach.

I pressed a hand against my ribs, where the cuorem vibrated softly, anchoring me and reminding me of who I was. Who I had to be.

But not yet.

Not tonight.

"Enough." Aidan's voice cut through the tension like a blade. "We are all tired. We will gain nothing by tearing at each other in this state."

Ruhl exhaled, running a hand through his tangled hair. "Agreed."

Reign didn't move, his eyes locked on the map and jaw working.

I stepped closer to him, close enough for my shoulder to brush his. The cuorem thudded in quiet acknowledgment between us.

"We will decide in the morning," I announced softly, but firmly. "Rest, all of you. We need to be clear-headed if we are to stand a chance against Helroth."

For a moment, no one moved.

It was Aidan who first nodded, then Ruhl, the final signal needed to send the commanders shuffling out. As they moved, some muttered while others were silent, but at least we'd decided to leave the decision for tomorrow.

When they were gone, only Reign, Ruhl, Aidan and I remained, the war room quieter now, but no less heavy, for the conversations yet to come. Reign's hand found mine, our fingers tangling, and the bond snapped tight. My heart throbbed in response, a reminder that even here, even now, we still had each other.

But as we stood in the silence, listening to the fortress creak around us, I couldn't shake the cold certainty curling in my chest.

Tomorrow, we would have to choose.

※

"What is it like, being back here in your old home?" I voiced the question the turmoil of emotions surging through our bond already hinted at the answer to. But I asked it all the same, hoping to help Reign somehow.

Perhaps, if he shared what had him in such turmoil, it would help him begin to heal.

He scoffed, ripping his gaze from the window that overlooked the courtyard. After the meeting in the war room, we'd all gone our separate ways, and Reign had escorted me to this chamber for the first time since our arrival. It was dark and sumptuous, with a sprawling bed and shadows that hung in every corner. I wondered if this had been his childhood bedroom, although somehow, I doubted it.

His gaze flickered through the open window once again and

held for a long moment. Beyond the ramparts, the dark waves of the Shadowmere Sea churned. Was he thinking about our time at Duskridge Manor? Or had his thoughts traveled farther back in time?

He finally exhaled, shadows coiling and uncoiling through his fingertips, restless. "What is it like?" he repeated, voice low. His gaze roamed across the cold, obsidian walls, the flickering torchlight that couldn't quite banish the darkness clinging to the corners. "It's like walking through a mausoleum." His jaw tightened. "Every hallway, every stone in this place remembers the worst parts of me. The boy I was, the monster he made me into. The expectations, the punishments. The blood on the floors that never really washed away."

Sorrow tore at my insides for that young boy. He never spoke of what his father had done to him, what brutal methods he'd employed to hone him into his own personal weapon.

He glanced at me, swallowing hard. "It's like coming home to a nightmare I can't wake up from." Then softer, barely above a whisper as he let his shadows reach for me, he murmured, "But having you here... makes it bearable."

I didn't think, didn't speak. Only launched myself into his arms.

His breath caught as I collided with him, my arms wrapping around his neck, pulling him down to me. Shadows coiled around us instinctively, dark and protective, and gods, I reveled in their silky touch. I pressed closer, needing him to feel how deeply I believed him, how desperately I wanted to chase away the ghosts clinging to his skin. To show him that he didn't always have to be strong, that I could help shoulder that weight for him. That I would.

"Reign," I whispered against his throat, my lips brushing the pulse pounding there. "You're not that boy anymore."

His hands fisted in my hair, in the fabric at my back, pulling me against him so hard I could barely breathe. The cuorem thundered, a wild, reckless drum between us. Heat slowly built as our powers tangled, light flickering across the shadows curling around us.

I tipped my head back, meeting the storm roiling in his midnight eyes. "And you're not alone anymore. You never will be."

His jaw clenched, a muscle ticking as his gaze roved over my face like he was memorizing every line. "Aelia, I—"

I cut off his words with my mouth, pressing my lips to his with a hunger that tore the breath from us both. He froze for a heartbeat before he began to kiss me back in earnest. His shadows flared, wrapping around us in a cocoon as if even they couldn't bear to let the world see what was ours alone.

His hands slid down to my waist, lifting me effortlessly until I was pressed against the cold stone wall, warmth sparking wherever we touched. I gasped into his mouth, my legs instinctively wrapping around him, and he swallowed the sound, his tongue sweeping against mine, claiming, desperate, *home*.

I threaded my fingers through his hair, tugging him closer. I guided my light to bleed into him, hoping to soothe the darkness that trembled in his shadows. His hands gripped my thighs, pinning me against him. The friction of our bodies had the cuorem flaring with desire, our powers sparking and hissing where they met.

"Starlight," he rasped against my lips, his forehead pressing to mine as we both struggled to catch our breath, our bodies still moving, seeking more, seeking everything from each other. "Tell me to stop."

I shook my head, breathless, a small, wild laugh slipping free as I cupped his face. "Never."

His answering growl vibrated through me. Then his mouth was on mine again, slower now, deeper, as if he was trying to pour everything he felt into the kiss. And, maybe, he was, because I felt it all—his fear, his desire, his love—wrapping around me as surely as his shadows.

In that moment, there was no fortress, no tyrant of a father, and no looming war.

There was only *us*.

As his shadows worked to peel away every shred of clothing between us, I lost myself in the heat of his desperate kisses and in the overwhelming desire raging between us. This was supposed to be for him, but I hadn't realized how much I needed it, too.

And when not a scrap of clothing lay between us, he swept me into his arms, carrying me across the room where he laid me down and stretched me out across the bed. As he hovered over me, his eyes locked on mine, wild and yet reverent, he fitted himself between my thighs. Then, ever so slowly, he thrust inside me, and I saw stars.

A gasp tore from my lips, caught between pleasure and the burn of the cuorem flaring to life in a way it never had before. The bond thrummed so fiercely it almost hurt. His name slipped past my lips like a prayer as I clung to him. Legs wrapping around his hips once again, I grounded myself in the searing heat of him, in the way his shadows caressed my skin while he held me like I was something precious.

As his hands roamed my body, his fingers traced the mark of the cuorem on my chest. Sparks of light glittered beneath his fingertip, stealing the breath from my lungs. "Mine," he growled.

"Yours," I replied, finding the matching mark below his collarbone. "Always yours."

"Gods, Aelia," he groaned against my neck, his breath hot and ragged as I met each of his fevered thrusts. His shadows trembled as they rippled across my back, dancing with the light pulsing from my skin. "I need—"

"I know," I whispered, pressing my lips to his jaw, then his cheek, before finding his mouth again. I poured everything I couldn't say into the kiss. Every fear, every promise, every broken piece we'd been trying to hold together.

He moved inside me with a desperation that matched the thunder of my heart, each thrust pulling a cry from my throat as the pleasure built, sharp and sweet. The world narrowed until there was nothing but him, us, and the storm we created together.

Light and shadow twined around us, a dance of darkness and dawn that mirrored the rhythm of our bodies. I was shaking, the heat coiling tight, so close to breaking apart.

"Look at me," he growled, pulling back just enough to catch my gaze. Those midnight irises blazed, shadows coiling like smoke around the bright glow of the cuorem between us. "I need you to see how much I love you."

"I see you," I gasped. Tears slipped free as I arched into him, feeling the world shatter around us as the wave of pleasure crested.

And then, I fell, the stars exploding behind my eyes as pure ecstasy crashed through me, stealing my breath. *Rais* pulsed around me, bright enough to banish every shadow in the room. Until the dark wraiths returned, curling around me like a lover's embrace, Reign's embrace, as he followed me over the edge with a hoarse cry of my name.

For a moment, we didn't move, our bodies pressed together, trembling. Our hearts pounded in sync as the cuorem pulsed, warm, soft, and alive between us. For once satiated.

"I love you more than anything, Aelia," he murmured against my parted lips as I still struggled for air.

"I know," I whispered back.

"And I was wrong before... As much as it would gut me, I do love you enough to let you go."

My breath hitched, head already whipping back and forth. "No..."

"If only for the public eye, for the sake of unifying Aetheria," he amended. "But behind closed doors, you will always be *mine*."

I framed his face with my trembling hands. "You, my Prince Reign of Umbra, may be selfless enough to allow such a thing, but I am not. I cannot tie myself to another, even if it is in paper only. I belong to you, wholly and completely. We will find another way to unify the courts without a royal marriage."

A lopsided smile quirked up the corner of his lips. "Is that your royal decree, my princess?"

"It is. And you, as my humble servant, have no other choice but to comply."

A deep rumble of laughter vibrated through his chest, reverberating against my own. And it was the most glorious sound I'd ever heard.

Chapter Thirty-Two

R *eign*

Aelia slept curled against me. Her breath warmed my chest, the glow of the cuorem between us a quiet promise in the dark. Gods, she was everything. The light I never deserved, the future this realm needed.

And I hated it.

Hated that every moment I held onto my mate was a moment closer to losing her. Hated that the gods might demand I give her up, that the realm might need her to stand beside another, to rule beside my brother, to secure the unity we all fought for.

The thought of her hand in Ruhl's, of her smiling for the court while I stood in the shadows like some loyal ghost... Just imagining it made a growl rumble in my throat, shadows curling around my fists as I gripped the sheets, fighting the urge to pull her closer and to swear I'd never let her go.

Mine.

The word burned in my mind, possessive and raw.

But duty clawed back, reminding me that love wasn't always enough. That to protect her, to protect all of Aetheria, I might have to let her go one day. Even when every bone in my body told me to do the complete opposite. I closed my eyes, pressing my lips to her temple and breathed her in.

"Just a little longer," I whispered to the night, the promise tasting like a lie. "Let me have this, before the gods come to take her away."

No one is taking me away from you. Aelia's silky voice slipped through my dismal thoughts, something bright and shining amongst the darkness gathering. Even in my mind, her voice was rough from sleep. She stirred beside me, her hand trailing over my abdomen.

Not while I still draw breath, that's for certain. The words rushed between us.

Her lids slowly opened, blazing silver-blue irises meeting my own. I rolled her on top of me, needing the warmth of her skin against mine. When we were like this, alone, together, everything felt so right. We could take on legions of demon Night Fae, break prophecies, battle anyone and anything that came for us; I was certain of it. It was when I was left alone to my wandering thoughts that the future grew bleak. Devoid of her light, I was simply consumed by shadow... by the insidious *zar*.

Curses. I jolted straight up, nearly sending Aelia tumbling off me.

"What's wrong?" she squealed, her arms encircling my neck in an attempt to steady herself.

"I—I'm not certain... but all these doubts I've been having, the suffocating fear of losing you, of believing it better if you were with Ruhl..."

"Helroth?" she bit out.

"Maybe. Could he possibly be exerting his influence through the *zar* that's seeping through our bond?"

Her lips twisted as she sat up, straddling me. Typically, having her in this position would immediately have had heat streaking to my lower half, but right now, only ice skimmed my skin. There was something in her expression that had unease coiling low in my gut.

Searching our mental connection, I found nothing but a wall of radiant light blocking her thoughts.

"Aelia..."

She drew in her bottom lip, gnawing on the soft pillow much as I had only last night.

"What is it you're not telling me?"

Her gaze dropped to my bare chest, her finger drawing lazy circles across the glittering mate mark. "It's nothing."

"It's not *nothing*." I reached for her, clasping her chin in a firm grip and forcing her eyes to meet mine once again. "Tell me, love."

"I can't—I'm not sure..."

"Not sure about what?"

"The *zar* and where it's coming from."

Brows furrowed, I regarded her, that hint of unease growing ever more substantial. "Where else would it be coming from, if not you?"

"From you, Reign," she whispered, hands framing my face. "From your blood."

Ice doused my veins, a flurry of emotions battering my insides. "It can't be..." Sudden, violent images from my childhood rose unbidden. Tenebris sneering across the training yard, whispering about the *darkness in my veins*. I'd thought it metaphorical then. Hadn't it been?

"Kae said—"

"Kaelith?" I growled, squirming free of her hold before my hands closed around her hips, lifting then dropping her onto the mattress beside me. "You spoke to Kaelith about *me*?"

"No, it wasn't like that. He mentioned it in passing... after you'd nearly killed him in the dungeons at Duskridge Manor."

I leapt up, pacing the length of the bed. "That was weeks ago, Aelia! And you're just now mentioning it?"

"I don't know anything for sure... And you were so volatile then, your powers completely out of control. I was afraid to tell you—"

"What did he say?"

"That the *zar* he felt from you was familiar... and not familiar because he'd witnessed it in me. He said it came from *you*. From your blood."

"No, it's not possible."

"Isn't it though?" She slid to the edge of the bed and stood, halting my manic footsteps. "You've told me before you knew little of your mother."

"I would have known if I was part Night Fae, Aelia," I hissed, the violence in my tone, surprising even me. Gods, I couldn't be one of *them*.

"You've always said you were stronger than most, Reign. That you, as a half-royal, should not have been able to overpower your own brother, a prince, let alone your father, King Elian, and so many others." She extended her hand, caressing my cheek, eyes intent on my own. "Look at me, my love."

But I couldn't.

Fuck, it was bad enough I was a bastard in love with a princess, but a Night Fae bastard? The very monsters who were trying to destroy us.

"You are *not* a Night Fae bastard," she snarled. Once more she framed my face, this time with surprisingly firm hands so I was forced to her fierce gaze. "And need I remind you that I, too, am part Night Fae? Does that make me a monster as well?"

"No, of course not. Never you. You are light and love and everything that is good in this gods' forsaken realm."

"Then what in all the stars is the difference?"

"You are *good*, Aelia. Inherently so. And I am not. I'm selfish. I'm ruthless. And for the longest time, I told myself it was survival. But if you're right, maybe now I finally understand the truth—maybe I became this way because I have the blood of demons running through my veins."

She pressed her palm against my heart, right over the cuorem where it pounded in response to our chaotic emotions. "Then I guess we'll be demons together. And we'll use every jagged piece of ourselves to destroy the real monsters. Because, maybe, the only way to defeat darkness is to become something it fears."

The fire in those blazing orbs made me want to believe every single word that fell from those perfect lips. She always had that effect on me.

Pulling my mate close, I cradled her face in my hands, then dropped my forehead to hers. "Just when I think I couldn't possibly love you any more, you say something that carves me open and makes me yours all over again."

"Good," she whispered, before brushing her lips against mine. "Because you are mine, as I am yours. Whether you're Shadow Fae or Night Fae, or even a gods' damned blood-thirsty Immortalis, you will always be my *cuoré*."

A growl tore up my throat, the beastly sound erupting from my very core. It was a roar of love, utter devotion, and wild possessiveness. And gods, if war wasn't knocking on our door, I would have thrown her over my shoulder, carried her back to the bed and had my way with her all over again.

Instead, I cradled her neck, deepening the kiss for one last moment before forcing myself away.

Deciding to dismiss the possibilities of Night Fae blood running through my veins for now, I chose to focus on a problem I could solve. With everything that stood against us, eliminating at least one obstacle would lighten the load.

"I love you, starlight." I spoke the words with the hushed reverence they deserved as I compelled my feet toward the armoire. If I didn't leave now, we would end up back in that bed, in a tangle of limbs and sheets, despite the duty that now called us.

Her brows knitted as she regarded me. "Where are you going?"

"Don't worry, I'm not running off to Shadowmere to torture

Kaelith for more information about the possibilities of Night Fae blood running through my veins."

"Good. Because I honestly don't believe he has any."

A huff squeezed out through my clenched teeth. "I suppose time will tell."

"Well, if you're not going to pay him a 'visit', then where are you going?"

"I must see Gideon before we meet with Ruhl and his generals this afternoon." I reached for a pair of dark leathers and speared my legs through them, then drew a clean tunic over my head. "Before we make a decision to hunt down your grandfather, I must confirm the rituals required of my brother before he can legitimately claim the Shadow Throne."

"Why?"

As I buckled my tunic, shadows curled under my skin, whispering questions I couldn't yet answer. "Because, Aelia, if he is calling the Court of Umbral Shadows to war, he may need the full power of the throne behind him."

Chapter Thirty-Three

R*eign*

Noxus, I despised lying to Aelia.

But to my point, I'd warned her many times that I was not a good Fae, nor was I ever to be trusted. And what I was about to do now, it was for her safety, and more importantly, for our future.

She would never agree to it because of the inherent risks it presented. But none of that mattered. This was my mess, and now it was my duty to clean it up.

I slipped through the fortress gates under the cover of shadow, my *nox* cloaking me in a veil of cold silence. Everyone believed I was heading to Arcanum to see Gideon, to strategize about my brother's ascension to the throne and then join the others to plan our strike. Except, I had no intention of visiting that war room until this was done.

This wasn't a decision I could trust anyone else with.

Not Aelia. Not Ruhl. Not even myself, if I thought too hard about it.

It was incredibly risky, but I was prepared this time.

The cuorem pulsed in protest as I crept past the outer walls of father's dreaded fortress. I felt Aelia's stirrings in the bond, her worry like a ripple of light trying to pierce my darkness.

Just this once, starlight. Forgive me. I let that final thought seep through our connection before I tightened the walls of my mind, locking her out.

With a twist of *nox* and a sliver of *zar*, I vanished into shadow and reappeared moments later inside the Castle of Ethereal Light. The scent of gilded stone and *rais*-choked air wrapped around me like a noose. Even the corridors glowed faintly beneath my boots, every inch of this palace adorned in Raysa's splendor. I wasn't certain which castle I despised more—this one or the one I'd grown up in.

Two Royal Guardians rounded the bend, their gold-rimmed alabaster cloaks snapping behind them. Their eyes widened as I materialized from the dark, but they had no time to raise their weapons or shout an alert.

I struck first.

Nox lashed out from my palms, twisting into black tendrils that coiled around their throats and wrists. They struggled, blades dropping as my shadows struck, binding them still. Then, I pressed a sliver of *zar* into their minds, enough to knock them unconscious without killing them. Aelia's mercy had certainly rubbed off on me.

Their bodies crumpled to the polished marble with a dull thud.

"Sorry, boys," I muttered as I stepped over their motionless forms. "Wrong place. Wrong time."

Moving swiftly—that entire ordeal taking only moments—I cut through the next corridor, bypassing the guards in the central court with a flicker of concealing shadows. The castle walls tightened around me, footfalls echoing from all directions, but I tuned them out and focused only on the prize at the end of the interminable corridors.

Not only would I finally put an end to the threat of the blood vow hanging over my head, but I would also skulk into my father's mind and discover the truth of my heritage. Gods, if Kaelith was right... who had my mother been? She couldn't have been a mere servant in my father's household. Had she been of royal blood? My stomach soured for an instant as I considered a horrible truth. Could I have descended from Helroth's line? If Aelia and I shared blood...

My heart kicked at my ribs, sending a tremor through my innards.

No, it couldn't be. The gods would never have bound us as *cuoré* if we were related. That seemed too cruel, even for their sadistic games. Horrible thoughts assuaged for now, I continued the endless descent.

If I was, in fact, Night Fae, why had my powers suddenly emerged? Sure, it wasn't uncommon for half-bloods to develop later, but why now? The cuorem pulsed, low and steady, just under my skin as if in silent reply. My thoughts flickered back in time. Back to when I had first suspected the truth about Aelia and me, and I'd spent endless hours at the Arcanum library with Gideon at my side, researching the effects of the cuorem bond.

...enhances the abilities of each Fae, with each partner amplifying the other's power. This can manifest as increased strength, enhanced healing, greater mystical capacity, or even new abilities that neither possessed before.

That was it. It had to be.

The cuorem had woken my dormant Night Fae abilities, even before we'd sealed the bond. It had coaxed the *zar* to the surface, and I'd stupidly believed it had been coming from Aelia. I'd been so distraught I hadn't seen the truth when it had been plain all along.

My mind spun with the breadth of powers the demons were fabled to have:

Infernal Manipulation
Soul Draining
Cursed Illusions
Necromancy
Pact Making
Cursed Enchantments
Blood Magic
Astral Possession
Nightmare Realms

Night Fae *zar* was poison wrapped in silk. Gods, if that darkness lived inside me, what did that make *me*?

By the time I finally reached the dungeons, a pit had formed in my stomach. The air grew colder, scattering my thoughts. The *rais* heavier. Runes of light shimmered along the walls, warding off my *nox*. I felt the glistening barrier skim over my skin, like thousands of tiny pinpricks. But I was more than shadow now. *Zar* thrummed through my veins, potent and deadly. And this time, I was more than ready to use it.

The runes fizzled as I passed, unable to completely repel me. I followed the path down, boots silent on the stone steps. Pausing at the corner, I steeled myself. After the last encounter with my father, I knew I had to be the first strike. If I gave him so much as a second of time to call upon the vow, I would be a slave to his whims.

Drawing in a steadying breath, I summoned the icy *nox*, then the dark, twisted tendrils of *zar*. Raw power blossomed in my core, the heady sensations forcing a growl through my gritted teeth.

I would strike silently and without mercy.

King Tenebris deserved none. He'd never shown me any. He had never been a father to me, only the male who'd filled my mother with his seed and turned me into a weapon of destruction. My shadows swirled in a tornado of night, a frenzy of hissing, writing power laced in that thick, powerful *zar*.

Unleashing a tempest of undiluted power that bathed the corridor in endless night, I strode around the corner toward the cell that had held my father—

Empty.

The wave of shadows I'd summoned dissipated, a hiss of frustration vibrating the suddenly silent space. "What in Noxus..." My breath fogged the suddenly icy air, heart slamming against my ribs.

The door I'd once thought impenetrable now hung open on broken hinges, its chains hanging uselessly from the walls. The manacles were curled and blackened as if burned by something older, darker than even Shadow or Light.

On the floor, resting where Tenebris had once stood taunting me with that gods' forsaken vow, lay a single parchment. The edges shimmered with glyphs of ancient magic, of *lys*, the words glittering like starlight and bleeding into the cracks of the stone.

I crouched, shadows curling at my feet as I picked it up and scanned the text.

When the child of twilight ascends, unshackled by fate, the veil between worlds shall fray. Her power, unbound, will call forth the end—whether of ruin or rebirth, none can yet say.

As the balance shatters, the stars shall dim, and shadows shall stretch to devour the light. The tides of fate will bow to her hand, and the realms shall tremble beneath her choice.

Either salvation or oblivion awaits, for when twilight reigns, the final hour begins.

My throat closed around the words, the parchment trembling in my grasp.

Another gods' damned prophecy?

Not the one I'd been taught. Not the one that spoke of the destruction wrought by the child of twilight, the one ingrained into my mind before I could barely walk. I stared at the words, attempting to understand the seers' cryptic message. Especially the last line: *When twilight reigns, the final hour begins.*

Twilight? Gods, when would that be?

This prophecy was something worse. This was about choice. And choice was dangerous in the wrong hands. It wasn't merely fate either. This was Aelia, standing at the edge of oblivion, with the power to tip the scales either way.

But I trusted Aelia. I knew her. She was good, and I was certain that as queen, she would be the salvation the divination spoke of.

I crushed the parchment in my fist, shadows leaking through my fingers. This new foretelling was the least of my worries. "Father," I hissed into the emptiness, my voice low and cold. "Where the realms are you, you bastard?"

The walls said nothing. But the air shifted, as if something unseen smiled back at me from the void.

Damn it. I had to find him.

Had he escaped somehow or, with our temporary pact broken, had Elian moved him for fear of exactly this happening?

I growled a curse. Apparently, I hadn't given the Light King enough credit. He'd been one step ahead of us all along.

Chapter Thirty-Four

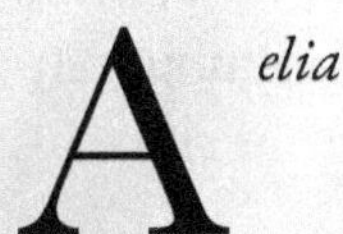

Heaton was alive.

Somehow, I still couldn't quite believe it as I stood in the archway, watching him. Pushing back the acrid taste of dread still coating my tongue from Reign's cryptic message, I focused on our team leader instead. Our lost friend, one of the few Light Fae who'd made my arrival at the Conservatory bearable over a year ago, was finally safe.

The barracks were unusually quiet, the typical hustle and bustle of constant movement and voices absent at this early hour. The Royal Guardians surrounding us slept the most soundly, unaccustomed to the absence of the ever-present sun. The interminable night had dulled their *rais* and their spirits. Today, we would have to commence training once again. Idle minds and bodies and all that...

Heaton shifted on his cot, legs curled into his chest, rocking ever so slightly. His cheeks were hollow, and dark smudges pooled beneath his lifeless eyes. Horror twisted his expression, gaze unblinking. He'd been like this since the moment we'd rescued him from the horde of Night Fae warriors nearly a week ago. Tiptoeing closer, I glanced at Rue, to where she slept in the cot beside his, exhaustion marring her typically perky features. She hadn't left his side for more than a quick trip to the bathroom. I'd watched, grief-stricken, last night as she alternated between soothing whispers and sweet lullabies, but nothing she did or said seemed to wake him from this nightmare-ridden, half-conscious state.

Guilt coiled through me, sharp and unwelcome, for not having rescued him sooner. Only the gods knew what sort of terror had been inflicted upon him all these months. Worse, I'd been so consumed with war strategizing, and my tumultuous relationship with Reign, that I'd also neglected my friend since his arrival at the fortress.

Slowly, afraid to startle him, I reached for his hand and offered a squeeze as I settled down beside him. "Heaton, it's me, Aelia. You're going to be okay. You're safe now, here with us."

Languid pale blue eyes lifted to meet mine, his pupils unfocused.

"Do you remember me, Heat?"

His eyes focused, for just an instant, and a faint smile slipped across his cracked lips. "Aelia..." he murmured. His lips formed my name again, a whisper so fragile it barely made a sound. Relief surged through me, loosening something tight in my chest.

He was still in there.

"Heaton." My throat tightened, and my vision went blurry, as I squeezed his hand again. "It's okay. You're back now."

"I'm back," he repeated, the deep lines between his brows softening.

For a heartbeat, I thought he was really back. His gaze locked on mine, sharp and lucid, like the Heaton I remembered—the leader, the protector, my friend.

"And you're okay..." he murmured.

"I am. We're all going to be okay. Helroth won't hurt us again—"

Then, something snapped. His eyes darkened, pupils constricting into narrow slits. A shadow passed across his features... not *nox*, but something else. Something fouler. *Zar*. Its presence slithered across my skin, summoning my own to the surface.

His palm slid from mine, and his fingers tightened around my wrist, steel strong.

"Heaton?" My pulse faltered. "It's... it's me."

His lips curled back, teeth bared like a cornered beast. "*Liar*," he hissed, his voice a rasp of something that wasn't entirely his own. "You're not Aelia. You're the darkness, the *infantum od twilit*. You're the one who—"

Before I could pull away, he sat up, his hands shooting to my throat. Cold fingers clamped around my neck, crushing, squeezing until black spots dotted my vision.

"Heaton—stop—" My hands clawed at his wrists, but I knew this wasn't truly him. I restrained the surge of *rais* threatening to erupt, barely fighting back. I couldn't hurt him. I wouldn't. Not after all he'd been through. Not after what Helroth had done to him.

This was my fault. I should have gone back for him sooner. As he would have done for me.

Tears stung my eyes as the room narrowed, spinning. His body trembled with rage, his lips moving in frantic whispers, over and over. "Destroyer. Child of twilight. Bringer of ruin, bringer of ruin..."

"No," I gasped, lips parting for air that wouldn't come. "It's... it's me... Heaton. *Please*."

A flash of light shifted in the corner of my blurred vision. Rue.

"Heat!" she screamed, lunging across the cot.

Her blade wasn't in her hand, but her arms—freakishly strong for such a little thing—were enough. The year of relentless training kicked in as she tore her brother off me, wrenching his hands from my throat. I slid to the floor, panting.

Heaton thrashed, snarling, eyes wild and tear-filled. He couldn't even recognize his own sister.

"Rue... be careful... he's... he's not himself!" I choked out, voice raw, clutching my neck as I sucked in ragged breaths.

"I can see that!" she snapped, wrestling him back against the mattress and pinning his arms, trying her best not to hurt him. "It's okay, Heat. Calm down. It's me, your sister." Her gaze flicked to me, panicked, but controlled as he continued to thrash.

A few of the Royal Guardians nearby finally stirred, awakened by the scuffle. The male that had served with my father, Eryndor, leapt to his feet. "Your Highness—"

"I'm fine," I rasped, even though my throat burned. "Please, go summon the healer. Hurry!"

He dipped his head without hesitation, silver strands of hair falling across his face. "Right away, princess."

As he ran off, Rue turned to me, eyes wide. "Aelia, are you—"

"Yes, I'm fine." I crawled to my knees, watching Heaton writhe, his body jerking beneath Rue's hold. His eyes were glassy again, but the whispers kept coming.

"Destroyer... destroyer..."

His hissed words carved through my mind like a blade. *Destroyer... child of twilight...* It shouldn't have mattered. I knew that. But it did. Because somewhere, in the deepest recesses of my soul, a small voice whispered back: *What if he's right?*

Helroth's blood vow over me still held. It was only a matter of time until he claimed it. The icy grip of fear the thought ignited threatened to consume me, but I shoved it back, refusing to succumb to its clutches. Now was most definitely not the time.

Rue's lip trembled. "He doesn't recognize you..."

"I know." My voice cracked, not only because of Heaton, but at the ache plain to see on my best friend's face. "It's the *zar*. It's infiltrated his mind too deeply."

This wasn't Heaton. Not really. This was whatever Helroth had left behind.

And gods help me; I had no idea how to fix it.

Elisa, the healer who'd fled the Conservatory shortly after us, rushed in a moment later with a glittering ampule clenched in her fist. Her healer's robes fluttered behind her, embroidered cuffs shimmering faintly with glyphs. Her normally serene expression was taut with worry.

"Heaton," she breathed, dropping to her knees beside the cot. Her eyes flicked to Rue, then to me, and finally to the bruises forming around my throat where Heaton's fingers had been.

"I'm fine," I rasped, yet again, even though my voice was barely a whisper now. Rue shot me a look, but she said nothing, her hands still trembling as we watched the healer with her brother.

Elisa pressed two glowing fingers to Heaton's temples, murmuring soft incantations. He thrashed once beneath her touch, but she was ready for it. With swift efficiency, she cracked the ampule, releasing a pulse of silvery mist. The scent of chamomile and dew drops filled the room, weaving calm through the air.

"Make sure he doesn't move," she instructed.

With a nod, Rue slid her hands from his arms to clamp them around Heaton's wrists instead. My best friend's jaw was tight, eyes glassy with unshed tears. I moved beside her to steady her shoulders, ignoring the sharp tremor in my own hands.

Elisa brushed the mist across Heaton's lips, whispering something too soft for me to catch. A moment later, his body slackened, the rigid tension in his muscles ebbing away. His breathing slowed and the jerky inhales smoothed into deep, even breaths.

Thank the gods.

"He'll sleep now," Elisa whispered, brushing a lock of damp hair from his brow. "The draught will keep him still for a few hours, at least. I infused it with both healing *rais* and a mild sedative from the vaults I ransacked at Luce before my hasty departure. Nothing that will harm him."

Rue exhaled shakily, her forehead dropping to Heaton's chest. A small, broken sound slipped from her lips. It sounded like a whisper of relief and grief intertwined.

I ran my palm over her shoulder. "He'll wake," I promised, though my throat tightened around the words. "And when he does, I'm sure he'll eventually remember who he is."

Elisa's gaze met mine over Rue's bowed head. Her eyes were grim, but gentle. "This is not just physical, princess. The Night Fae left their mark in his mind. We'll need time. Patience."

Time and patience. The very things we didn't have.

My stomach twisted as I looked down at Heaton's sleeping form. His face was peaceful now, but the bruises on my neck and the shadowed memories in his eyes told another story.

What if we couldn't bring him back? What if we'd already lost him, and this was just another ghost I'd have to carry?

I pushed the thought away, tightening my grip on Rue's shoulder, steadying myself against the storm that hadn't yet come.

Heaton would wake. He had to.

Dropping down beside him, I whispered into his ear, "I need you, Heaton. We all do. There's a war coming, and we won't survive it without you. Please come back to us."

A light hand landed on my shoulder, drawing me away from Heaton's soft breaths. "Let him rest, princess."

Straightening, I glanced back at Elisa and nodded.

"Do you have a moment?" she murmured. "I'd like to speak to you in private in my chambers, if I may."

Gaze darting between the now-sleeping Heaton and my friend, my shoulders slowly lifted. "Sure." Before I followed the healer out of the barracks, I turned to Rue with what I hoped was a reassuring smile. "We'll find a way to fix him. I promise."

Her head slowly dipped, but the uncertainty in her expression remained. It was more than just exhaustion, though, it was utter despair and anguish for her brother. "I know we will," she mumbled.

Compelling my leaden feet forward, I marched through the door after the healer, forcing myself not to look back.

Chapter Thirty-Five

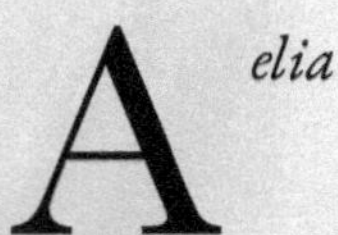

A elia

The scent of herbs and ancient magic permeated the air. Mossroot and moonflower tinctures woven through with something darker curled beneath my skin and perfumed every inch of the healer's chamber. My boots made no sound as I stepped through the threshold, shadows clinging to the corners of the room.

Elisa fiddled with something on her worktable before turning to face me, her usually calm eyes clouded with something sharper. Worry. Or maybe something more dangerous than that.

"It's hard to believe that only a year ago, Reign brought you, a powerless little Kin, to my door for healing." Her voice was soft, and there was no malice in her tone when she essentially called me weak. "And here you are now, a formidable princess of the Light Court."

I gave her a tight smile, unsure where this exchange was going.

"Come," she beckoned softly, her fingers fluttering in a quick, precise motion. "There's something you need to see."

I followed, my heart thudding in the back of my throat. She led me to the far corner of the chamber, to a thick curtain of midnight silk embroidered with *lys* runes I'd not noticed before. The fabric parted with a whisper, revealing a stone table. On it lay the still body of a Shadow Fae male.

He looked familiar. If I wasn't mistaken, he was one of the Umbral Guard who'd stood beside Ruhl during the last battle. His chest was bare now, the fatal wound across his ribs sealed cleanly with Elisa's stitches, but no breath stirred beneath them.

"I tried," Elisa whispered, smoothing a hand over his dark hair. Her voice held none of the healer's usual serenity. There was something harder beneath the surface. "I poured every celestial glyph, every elixir, every ounce of healing *rais* I could think of into saving him. But it didn't matter, the damage was too deep."

My throat tightened, still sore from Heaton's crushing grip. "Elisa..." My fingers curled into my palms, nails biting skin. "Why are you showing me this?"

Her gaze lifted to mine, steady and unblinking. "Because I think you can help me with something."

"I—I'm not a healer," I whispered, but my *rais* stirred uneasily, aware before I was at what was coming.

"No," she agreed softly. "You're something more." Her fingers traced the line of the corpse's shoulder, and when she looked at me again, her voice was quieter, but more unsettling somehow. "You've wielded *zar* before, haven't you?"

A chill sliced down my spine. "Yes..."

"And the child of twilight has many gifts." Her tone was gentle, coaxing. "Healing Light, icy Shadow... and death."

I shook my head, a sharp twist of horror in my gut. "What are you—" I cut myself off as understanding took hold. The Night Fae on the battlefield; the husks of their former selves reanimated by Helroth's *zar* surged to the forefront of my mind. Their glassy eyes, their unquenchable bloodlust had haunted my nightmares ever since. "I'm not a necromancer." I would never become the thing that made those monsters.

"Necromancy is just another tool, Aelia. Another branch of *zar*. You've felt it. I'm sure you have." Her eyes narrowed, though her voice remained soft. "And we are out of time and options. You saw the battlefield. We need every edge we can get."

I swallowed hard, my gaze flickering to the male's still face. His lips were pale, his skin cool. He had been loyal to his prince to the very end.

"I wouldn't want to make him into something he's not," I rasped, shame curdling in my stomach. "I won't turn him into one of Helroth's fiends."

I couldn't do this. I wouldn't.

Elisa stepped closer, her hand brushing mine. "Aelia, death magic is not inherently evil. It's how you use it that matters, like with any ability. And I wonder if entwined with your healing *rais*..." She sucked in her bottom lip. "We don't have to raise armies of dead. But think of what it would mean if you could bring back a single fallen ally. What that would do for morale. For survival."

I closed my eyes, bile rising in my throat. "I saw them, Elisa, witnessed those monsters up close. They're not... alive."

"But you wield all three powers, princess. What if you could do *more*?"

What if I could? What if I was meant to wield all three powers—*nox*, *rais*, and *zar*—for this? Even if it terrified me...

A beat of silence passed. Then another.

I had to try.

My hands trembled as I placed them over the Fae's chest. Shadows curled at my fingertips. The *zar* coiled beneath my skin like a cold serpent, waiting. Watching.

"Focus," Elisa whispered. "Not on his death. On his breath. Call it back."

I summoned the *zar*, letting it rise inside me, icing my veins. Next, I focused on the warm *rais*, the golden tendrils that lit up my soul. Power flooded my core, a tangle of ice and heat, a hollow ache radiating from my chest to my palms. The world narrowed, my vision rimmed in darkness as I pressed my hands to his still body.

For a moment, the air around us shifted. The shadows thickened. The cuorem throbbed, sensing my fear... but also something else. A pull from beyond the Veil. I felt it. I *felt* him.

Kairis.

His name came to me, unbidden, in a dark whisper.

"Kairis," I repeated, voice raw. "Come back to us."

At my words, his chest shuddered beneath my hands. My heart stopped. A shiver raced down my spine. And then... nothing.

The cold faded, leaving behind only the sweat on my brow and the sharp stab of disappointment in my gut. I staggered back, breathless.

I'd failed.

Elisa's eyes gleamed. "You felt something, didn't you?"

I nodded, unable to speak.

"You were close. Next time—"

"I'm not sure there should be a next time," I cut her off, my voice trembling. "This is dangerous." *And wrong.*

Elisa's lips pressed together, but she said nothing.

My thoughts spun, a jumble of light and dark, right and wrong. I barely knew where I stood anymore.

Maybe if Kaelith trained me... He knew *zar* better than anyone but bringing him here would ignite a war all its own. Reign would never allow it. And if I told him what I'd done here tonight, what I'd tried to do...

I wrapped my arms around myself, stepping back into the shadows. "I need to think," I whispered, the words still raw.

Elisa's gaze remained on me, calm and relentless. "Think quickly, Your Highness. War won't wait."

And neither would death.

It was nearly dinner time when I felt the familiar pulse of the cuorem squirming beneath my skin. My feet propelled me to the balcony, drawn by that all-consuming force that was my mate. A storm of shadows flickered across the moonlit sky an instant before Reign's imposing form appeared.

Powerful wings of night stretched wide, he emerged from the void with another familiar figure at his side.

Gideon.

What was he doing here? Reign had said he'd gone to Arcanum specifically to consult with his old friend. Why bring him back?

Always so curious. Reign's voice caressed my mind, at least somewhat easing my tumultuous thoughts.

When you have a mate who keeps secrets, it's difficult to behave otherwise. There was an edge to my tone, sharp and biting. But Raysa knew he deserved it.

I'm sorry, starlight. I promise to explain everything as soon as we're alone.

My feet inched closer to the parapet, wings flaring, aching to fly out to him. But I forced myself to remain still, reminding myself I was more than a little angry with my mate. *Aidan, Ruhl, and his generals are waiting for us to discuss our next steps. I've been delaying the meeting for hours.*

Well then, I guess we'll have to hold them off for a few more. With another powerful flap of his shadow wings, his boots hit the stone wall of the balcony.

Gideon landed beside him a moment later, a grin on his lips. "Please forgive the intrusion, Your Highness." He sketched an elaborate bow, and it was all I could do to keep a silly smile from breaking free.

"Aelia is just fine, Gideon. No need for the formalities."

"As you wish, princess." He dipped his head yet again.

"Gid, go tell my brother and the others that the meeting for tonight has been postponed until tomorrow," Reign barked.

Gideon's dark brows furrowed, unease pinching his expression. "...And what reason shall I give the uncrowned king and his generals?"

"None. Tell Ruhl to come see me immediately."

Poor Gideon looked like he was a second away from fainting. "Reign, he may only be a brother to you, but he's also the Shadow Regent, just a hairsbreadth from the throne."

He huffed out an exasperated breath. "I don't care what you tell Ruhl, just get him here."

With an exaggerated eyeroll in my direction, Gideon moved toward the door. But before he got far, he called out over his shoulder, "Careful, princess, he's in a mood."

I could see that. Now the question was: what had my mate in such a frenzied state?

"I told you I would explain everything once we were alone." Exhaustion and something darker laced Reign's tone, slicing into the marrow of my bones.

The turbulent state of my *cuoré's* emotions had the fury bleeding right out of me, replacing it, instead, with concern. Still, I attempted to hold onto a sliver of the anger for my own wounded pride. "Well, we're alone now, so speak."

Chapter Thirty-Six

R^{eign}

"What is the meaning of this?" Ruhl stormed into our chambers, shadows whipping across his agitated form as if he were king of the gods' damned castle.

Which, technically he was, but that was beside the point.

"Where have you been, brother?" he snarled in my direction, then glanced at Aelia, expression softening a tad.

As if it hadn't been bad enough to tell Aelia I'd lost our father, now, I had to admit it to Ruhl. Only a few days as Shadow Regent and the power had gone straight to his oversized head.

"We've been waiting for hours to convene in the war room." His heavy footfalls reverberated across the space. "Everyone's antsy, the soldiers are stumbling around with no purpose, the students are frightened—"

"I'm fully aware," I gritted out.

"Well, then, explain."

"Tenebris is gone." I hissed the words, anger and shame lacing my tone.

"What do you mean *gone*?"

"He's no longer being held prisoner in Elian's castle. That's where I went today... to attempt to clean up my damned mess."

"Oh, for fuck's sake, Reign." He dragged his hand through his short, dark locks, gaze flickering to Aelia once again.

"It doesn't mean he's escaped," Aelia interjected, seemingly reading my brother's dark glare. "Elian could have simply moved him somewhere for safekeeping now that our sham of an alliance has been severed."

Ruhl grunted. "Either way, it means that Reign is vulnerable to the blood vow, which in turn, puts you at risk."

"Which means it's simply another typical day for me." Aelia crossed her arms over her chest, scowling. "Elian wouldn't have just released him—"

"So, what if he's escaped?" my half-brother barked, the words carrying more venom than I'd expected.

"Don't you think he would have come by now?" Aelia replied.

"Who knows with Father..." I paced the length of the chamber, shadows trailing my frenzied steps. "He claimed to have known about you all along. If that was the case, then why wouldn't he have acted sooner? You've been at the Conservatory for a year!"

Ruhl hummed, a flash of something unreadable rushing across his face.

"What?" I snapped.

He took a step back, hitting the roughhewn wall. "Nothing..."

My brows furrowed as I took him in, then the sudden nervous flutter of his shadows. He was lying about something.

"Ruhl, so help me, now is not the time to hold anything back." My shadows surged toward him, my building frustration sending them scattering like wraiths. "If you know something, tell us."

"Please," Aelia added, inching closer as if to shield my brother from my billowing power.

Gods, one look from my *cuoré*, and my brother all but melted. The tight set of his jaw softened, something near to a smile quirking his lips. Could he still be harboring feelings for her?

Shadows pulsed beneath my skin, hot and volatile as I stared at my brother across the chamber. "You're hiding something," I growled, my voice a blade honed with suspicion.

Ruhl's gaze flicked to Aelia, then back to me, shoulders tightening once more, jaw locked. Shadows curled at his feet like restless snakes.

"Tell me," I snapped, stepping closer. "*Now.*"

His lips parted, then shut again. Gods, if he didn't speak soon, I wasn't sure I'd be able to hold back the building *zar*. I could simply force it out of him and be done with this.

Aelia's hand brushed my arm, a gentle tether to my roiling emotions. "Please, Ruhl," she whispered again, her voice softer, but somehow sharper. "No more lies."

Ruhl's shoulders sagged, as if the air had finally been crushed from his lungs. "I didn't think it mattered anymore," he whispered, his eyes fixed to the floor. "But maybe it always did."

"What are you talking about?" My voice sliced through the space between us, jagged and ice cold.

He looked up, and there was something there, something I hadn't seen in him before. Regret. Bone-deep, potent regret.

"Before I was born, before any of us were born—" Ruhl started, his voice hoarse, "Father made a pact."

My stomach dropped, shadows curling tighter.

"A pact?" Aelia's voice wavered, but she held firm beside me.

Ruhl nodded once, lips pressed into a thin line. "With the Night King."

The air thinned.

"Tenebris promised his heir," Ruhl whispered, "to a Night Fae princess."

The words hit like a punch to the ribs. I staggered back a step, but Aelia's hold only tightened, my jaw tight enough to crack. "You're lying." My voice was barely human.

"I'm not." His eyes met mine, full of guilt, and something worse. Truth. "I didn't know it was *her* back then. Father never realized he'd unknowingly tethered me to the child of twilight, or that he set you on a path to murder my future wife when he made the pact. I doubt Helroth did. Then, Aelia appeared at the Conservatory last year. Father never said it in so many words, but he hinted that she may have been 'the one'. He told me my marriage would unify the courts, strengthen his hold on power."

Aelia's breath caught beside me, her hand slipping from my arm as realization dawned. "At the ball..." she murmured. "That's why you asked me not to complete the cuorem bond with Reign. You knew then..."

"I suspected."

"Gods," she hissed.

And it was why he'd suggested the marriage back at Shadowmere all those weeks ago. He'd always wanted her and the power that came with binding himself to the child of twilight.

Ruhl's gaze darted to her, then back to me. "You have to understand that at the time, the Night Fae were extinct for all I knew. But now, I realize Father knew *exactly* who she was from the moment she set foot on campus. And if that's the case, maybe he's known for years that Helroth and his demons were still alive."

My fists clenched, shadows ripping from my skin like claws. "And you didn't think to mention this before?"

"I didn't know for sure until now," he shot back, but his tone was brittle. Weak. "Even after the truth came out about Aelia's bloodline, I told myself it was just a coincidence. She couldn't be the Night Fae princess I'd been bound to."

"But Father didn't forget," I snarled, the darkness twisting tighter, sharper. "That's why he never called in the vow. He wanted you to marry her. To tie her to *you*."

"I didn't *want* that," Ruhl snapped, shadows flaring behind him. "Don't you dare think for a second that I—"

"Didn't you?" The words cut from me, cold and merciless. "Don't lie to me, Ruhl. I see the way you look at her. Still."

His mouth clamped shut, his eyes darting toward Aelia for a breath, guilt bleeding through.

I stepped between them, shadows writhing at my back. "She's *mine*. She will *always* be mine." The words scraped raw from my throat, the *zar* lashing against my veins, all but begging to be released. "Father may have attempted to bind you to her, but the *gods* chose her for me." The cuorem burned in my chest, a wild, desperate ache.

"Reign..." Aelia's voice was soft, but it was enough to ground me before I snapped completely. "Let him speak."

I forced my breaths to steady, though every part of me screamed to drag Ruhl through my shadows and leave him broken and bleeding.

"I didn't want this," Ruhl repeated, but his words rang hollow now, and we all knew it. "I didn't ask for this."

"No, but you *knew*," I hissed. "And you kept it to yourself. All this time."

"Gods, it all makes so much sense now," Aelia murmured. "Why Helroth had wanted to remove Reign from my memories, why he wanted me to believe I loved Ruhl..."

Ruhl's shoulders slumped against the wall, shadows coiling at his feet like smoke. "I didn't know how to tell you. Either of you."

"You should have told us the moment you suspected," I spat, every word a blade. "We're not children playing court games anymore."

"You forget what our relationship was like before Helroth took her, Reign. You despised me. If I'd told you the truth about your precious mate, you would have destroyed me before I even had a chance to explain."

"Damn right," I growled.

Ruhl let out a rueful chuckle, that regret carved into his twisted lips once again. "You see? I had no choice but to keep it to myself until I knew for certain. Now that you've confirmed Father knew who Aelia was all along, it makes perfect sense."

"Fucking Tenebris." The words were a curse, a condemnation to the male who'd brought me nothing but pain my entire life.

Aelia's hand found mine as she moved to my side, her fingers threading through my own, but there was a tremor in her touch now. Her silence cut deeper than any dagger.

I turned to her, my heart twisting. "Starlight…"

She swallowed hard, her gaze locked on the floor, even as her grip tightened. "So all this time… all these months… we've been maneuvered like pieces on a gods' damned chessboard."

"Aelia, I swear—" Ruhl started.

"No." Her voice sharpened, *rais* flickering across her fingertips, eyes lifting to meet mine then settling on Ruhl's. "Whatever vow your father made to the Night King, it dies with him. I won't be anyone's pawn anymore." Her words echoed in the room, a final decree.

But my shadows still raged.

"We ensure the Light and Shadow Fae forces are prepared to fight, then we go after Helroth," she whispered, her voice steel wrapped in silk. "And after that, we *burn* the rest of his gods' forsaken court to ash. Then, and only then, we find Tenebris and put an end to this once and for all."

I held her hand tighter, but the pain didn't ease. Because deep down, I knew this wasn't over.

Not the war. Not the prophecy. And not the silent battle between the three of us.

Chapter Thirty-Seven

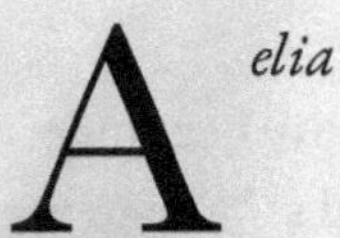

A*elia*

Another week of training and unnatural silence. Both from the Light King and my grandsire. Every day, our troops of Light and Shadow patrolled the border along the Luminoc, waiting for either one of our enemies to strike, and every damned day, there was nothing.

I almost wished they would come already.

Almost.

The full moon hung high in the sky, bathing the interminable darkness in its celestial glow. If it weren't for the unease skittering beneath my breastbone, I would have enjoyed the peaceful sight from where I perched, high on the balcony overlooking the Court of Umbral Shadows. An icy breeze lifted off the sea, threading through my dark locks and raising the hair on my arms. I couldn't stand it anymore, the waiting, the not knowing. I convinced myself we were doing the right thing, doing what Aidan and the

Shadow generals recommended: we were training our forces, preparing for war.

Still, I felt useless, trapped in this obsidian fortress.

I'd even ventured to Elisa's chamber once, considering a second attempt at honing my Night powers of necromancy. But I simply couldn't force my fist up to knock. The Night Fae possessed a whole slew of grisly abilities, but this was one I was certain I wanted no part of. Which was why I had yet to mention it to Reign.

My mate had grown ever more broody and sullen since Tenebris's disappearance and Ruhl's great reveal. Try as I might, nothing seemed to help his constant state of agitation. Worse, I could feel the overpowering *zar* stealing into his veins, only stoking his burgeoning wrath.

As if that wasn't bad enough, Sol and Phantom were still at odds over cementing their mate bond. Despite my constant coaxing, my stubborn dragon continued to waffle. I simply couldn't understand it. He loved Phantom, I could feel it through the mystical strands that connected us. There had to be something else holding him back, but what?

A sharp knock from my chambers snapped me from my spiraling thoughts.

I stiffened, hand drifting toward the dagger sheathed at my thigh out of habit, but as I marched into the room, I already knew who it was.

Ruhl.

His shadows crept beneath the doorway, their familiarity striking. A heavy pulse of dread coiled in my gut as I paused midway. The Shadow Regent had been remarkably absent all week, leaving his generals and Reign to lead the training exercises.

I'd assumed he'd been avoiding me. Apparently, the respite was over.

"Come in," I finally called out, wrapping my arms around myself as the weighty door heaved open.

Ruhl stood in the doorway, his face half-shadowed by moonlight, dark hair tousled from the wind, and eyes sharper than usual. He looked like a male who hadn't slept in days.

"I found something," he said without preamble, his voice rough, like it had been scraped raw from the inside. "A way to make this right."

My stomach dropped. "Ruhl..."

"Just hear me out."

I swallowed hard and nodded, motioning for him to enter. Shutting the door behind him, he stepped closer, shadows licking at his heels, but his expression was stripped bare. There was no royal mask tonight. Just my friend, my ally, and the male who apparently had once been promised to me in marriage.

"I've been working with Gideon," he started, his tone clipped but careful. "We've been searching through the oldest texts, and we discovered new information. That a blood vow isn't unbreakable."

My pulse quickened. "What did you find?"

"There's a way to sever it." His jaw tightened, muscles twitching beneath his skin. "A sacrificial substitution."

Cold crept down my spine. "What does that even mean?"

Ruhl's eyes met mine, steady and unflinching. "It means someone else takes on the burden of the vow. They absorb the magic binding Reign to Tenebris's control. They become the blade instead."

"Raysa, that's incredible. But who—" My words fell away as realization set in. "No." My voice sliced through the air before he could reply.

"Aelia—"

"No, Ruhl." I pressed a hand to my chest, where the cuorem suddenly throbbed. "You can't."

"I can." His voice softened, but the weight, the determination behind it pressed on my lungs. "It's the least I can do. I should've told you about the pact with Helroth as soon as I suspected. I could've—should've—stopped this before it began."

"That wasn't your fault."

"Wasn't it?" His eyes gleamed, shadows flickering in the corners of the room. "My father intended to use me to bind the courts together. And I stood by, pretending I had no part in it. But now, I can do something that matters."

"How?"

"I'll assume the vow and disappear, princess." A wicked smirk curled his lips.

My throat tightened. "You're the regent, Ruhl. You're the future king. You can't just vanish like that."

"I don't care about the crown." His words came fast, ragged. "I care about protecting *you*. About protecting Aetheria."

My lips parted, but no sound came out.

"I'm willing to leave it all behind," he whispered. "Disappear if I have to. You and Reign can lead together without this hanging over your heads."

"No," I rasped again, stepping toward him, anger and grief tightening in my chest. Ruhl had lied, kept the truth from us, but he didn't deserve this self-imposed banishment. "There has to be another way."

His gaze dropped, a shadow of something flickering there. But I saw it.

I waited for a long moment, allowing him time to muddle out what he wanted to say. "What?" I finally breathed when he made no sign of continuing. "You're still keeping something from me. Aren't you?"

He huffed out a breath.

"Just say it already," I hissed.

"There *may* be another possibility..."

My heart skipped. "What? What is it?"

He reached into his cloak and pulled out a parchment, unrolling it carefully on the table by the hearth. "The Moirai Shard."

The words glittered across the ancient text, the faded script humming with powerful energy.

"You couldn't have *started* with this option?" I threw him a playful grin, my relief at there being another possibility lightening the heaviness of just a moment ago.

"Maybe a part of me wanted to make sure you didn't want me gone."

I slowly shook my head. "We need you, Ruhl, all of us."

He barked out a rueful laugh. "Heavy is the crown, as they say."

"Now, tell me about this Moirai Shard."

"It's a relic said to be found in Lunaris," he explained, his voice low. "It's fabled to be one of the last remnants of the Threads of Fate, a shard of woven destiny itself. If the stories are true, it can sever any magical binding, curse, vow, or otherwise."

I drew in a hopeful breath.

"But no one knows if it truly exists, or if it even has the power claimed," he added.

Realms, this was the answer to our prayers. Not only could we use it to break the blood vow between Reign and his father, but also the one Helroth had imposed on me.

By blood and night, you are bound. Swear now, child of twilight, to bring down the Courts of Light and Shadow, until none but Night remains to rule the realm. By the will of the Night King, this vow shall hold.

Shaking my head to banish Helroth's gravelly voice as it scraped across my mind, I focused back on the parchment. Tracing my finger along the text, I scanned the ancient scroll, breath held. "Lunaris is Wolvryn territory," I finally rasped as I processed the words. A chill skirted up my spine at the mere mention of the savage Fae shifters that had been cursed by the primordial moon gods.

"No one has seen the Shard in centuries, but if it exists, I'll find it," Ruhl said, eyes locking on mine. "I'll go myself."

"It's too dangerous. I'll go with you," I shot back, despite the blossoming dread spreading through my body.

According to legend, the Wolvryn were bound by cycles of mystical transformation that completely stripped away their civility, awakening something primal within. Few dared tread on the island realm of Lunaris for fear of falling prey to the brutal, beastly Fae.

His jaw tightened. "Aelia, you know Reign will never allow that."

"Reign doesn't own me."

"I didn't say he did." His voice gentled, but the steel beneath it remained. "But you're the princess of two courts, and war is at our doorstep. We can't risk losing you."

"And we can't risk losing you either, Ruhl. You are the king, the future of the Court of Umbral Shadows." My throat burned. "We've already lost too many." My thoughts flickered to Heaton and the nightmarish torment in which he was trapped. I couldn't lose Ruhl to one of those bloodthirsty beasts in Lunaris.

Gods, there was no good option, was there? Allowing Ruhl to assume the vow would mean never seeing him again and relinquishing his chance at the Shadow throne. What would that mean for Reign? No, I could never ask that of his brother. He would be sacrificing too much. At least in seeking out the Moirai Shard, he stood a chance. But what cost would come with wielding such a powerful artifact? I doubted it would give us its magic without a price.

He reached out, brushing a stray lock of hair from my face. The touch was surprisingly gentle and entirely unlike the cocky Shadow Prince I'd met all those months ago. "Then we have to decide: Do I go alone, or do we risk sending more soldiers with me? Either way, I *will* do this for you, Aelia. I need to. I owe you, for everything."

A question clawed at my insides. One I'd been pushing down ever since the return of my memories after Helspire. If I didn't ask it now, I may never have the opportunity again. "Why are you really doing this, Ruhl? Are you so willing to sacrifice yourself because of duty, or is it because some part of you still wants me?"

A deep shade of crimson flushed his cheeks as a wry grin stretched across his face. "I see some of my brother's bluntness has rubbed off on you, duskling." His smile grew more brazen. "I like it."

I rolled my eyes, then whispered, "Well?"

He heaved out a sigh before answering. "Of course I want you, Aelia. There's not a single thing about you that I don't find incredibly desirable. Besides being absolutely stunning, you are one of the most formidable females I know." He shrugged as if he hadn't just stolen my breath with that declaration. "But I'm also not so delusional as to think you'd ever want me in return. I understand that you are mated to my brother, and that I have no place interfering in the games of love and fate that the gods play. But I can do this for you. For Reign. So, please, let me do the right thing for once."

The weight of it all settled between us. The Moirai Shard, Tenebris, Elian, the vow, and the war still looming like a blade at our necks.

And for the first time in days, I didn't know what to say. I wanted to believe there was still a right choice. But all I could see were different shades of sacrifice.

Chapter Thirty-Eight

R*eign*

"I'll go with Ruhl."

Aelia stared at me, mouth agape, from across the chamber. Shadows lingered in the corners of our room, a physical manifestation of the turmoil battering my insides. Noxus, when Aelia recounted the details of her encounter with my half-brother, I'd wanted to strangle the fool.

How could he even consider renouncing the throne simply to assume my blood vow? The Shadow Court needed a great ruler, a reliable one, one they were familiar with to lead during these dark times. Why would he do something so stupid and... noble? This was not the brother I knew, not at all.

Unless... My thoughts rushed back in time to the trial he'd undergone with Aelia their second term, the Mirror of Illusions. His mirror-self had claimed he would never take the throne of the Umbral Court. Was this all some elaborate attempt to evade that prediction?

"Reign..."

I blinked and Aelia stood before me, her fingers tangling with my own, anchoring the wild tempest of emotions throttling my lungs. "He cannot go alone," I muttered.

"He doesn't have to go at all. And neither do you."

"And we simply allow this vow to loom over us? Until Father emerges, from only the gods know where, and those dreaded words fall from his lips, forcing me to destroy you?" I shook my head, dark strands of hair falling across my brow. "No. I refuse to live like that, starlight."

"Then I will go with you, too."

Taking both her hands in mine, I pressed them against my chest, drawing her closer. "The three of us cannot go, my love. You are much too valuable to Aetheria."

"And you are too valuable to me." A swell of emotion rushed our bond—her love, her fear—a desperate tangle breathing life into my weary bones.

"This is exactly why I must go. Don't you see that? If we succeed, we'll finally be free, Aelia. It's all I've ever wanted, to be free to love you as you deserve, unshackled by blood vows, prophecies, or royal tyrants." I loosed a long breath, gaze trapped in hers. "It's not that I don't trust Ruhl to go alone, it's that the mission is much too important. We simply cannot fail."

"You won't," she breathed, her resignation bleeding through the words. "Just... promise that you'll come back to me."

Framing her face with unsteady hands, I whispered, "Always, starlight." Then I closed the distance between us, brushing my lips across hers. My shadows erupted from my fingertips, always so eager for her. The mate bond awoke as well, a relentless beast, illuminating the mystical strands that tied our hearts together. The kiss was meant to be gentle, reassuring, but as so often was the case, a chaste touch was never enough.

The cuorem demanded more.

My hand fell from her cheek, fingers tangling in the soft hair at her nape to angle her neck for a deeper kiss. The other hand slid down her torso to find the exposed skin between her tunic and leathers. Curling my fingers into her hip, I pressed her flush against me, eliciting a tempting moan. A growl vibrated in my throat at the rush of sensations flowing between us.

A sharp knock cracked through the haze of our bond, slowing the frantic beats of my heart. My jaw tightened as the door creaked open without waiting for permission.

Of course. My brother.

"Am I interrupting?" Ruhl's shadow slipped through the door first, followed by his looming frame. His eyes darted between us, guilt and something else flashing behind his usual smirk.

I pulled back from Aelia's lips with a growl still caught in my throat. My shadows recoiled from the intrusion but didn't vanish entirely. They slithered along the edges of the chamber, restless.

"You always did have impeccable timing, brother," I muttered, voice low and rough. Even the sight of him couldn't completely crush the fire Aelia had started.

Ruhl's smile faltered. "I came to say I'm leaving for Lunaris first thing tomorrow. Mordrin will accompany me to the island, then—"

"No," I snapped before he could say another word. "You're not going alone. That is to say, you're not going without me."

His brows lifted, surprise flickering across his face. "Reign—"

"I said *no*." My tone brooked no argument. "We go together, or not at all."

Ruhl's mouth parted, with what was surely an argument, but he closed it again, shadows weaving between his fingertips. "You're serious."

"As death."

Silence stretched between the three of us, a thick, heavy thing. I despised knowing that Ruhl still wanted my cuoré. And yet, I loved him for risking his life for her anyway. It was maddening, this tangle of blood and shadow surrounding us.

I sighed, running a hand through my hair and willing the edge from my voice before continuing. For Aelia's sake, if nothing else. "Look, I've despised you for most of my life. Thanks to Father, most likely. You know that as well as I. But today, you offered to take on a vow that would've surely destroyed you. For *her*." My throat tightened. "That's not something the Ruhl I knew would've done. Regardless of the circumstances."

His eyes narrowed, unsure whether to take the words as insult or praise.

"So, believe it or not, I'm proud of the male you've become, little brother." The words burned my tongue, but regardless, they were true. Even if part of me still wanted to rip his heart out for the way he looked at my mate.

Aelia's hand squeezed mine, her light rushing through the bond, softening the storm that had begun to brew in my chest.

"You don't have to do this," she whispered to me, then to Ruhl. "Either of you."

"Yes, we do," I said, voice steady now. "We're running out of time. The sooner we go, the better."

Her lips pressed into a thin line. "I wish I could go with you both, but as my stubborn mate reminded me, *someone* has to stay and rule the kingdom while you're gone." Her gaze shifted toward me, shining with love and a hint of fear. "Therefore, I'll hold the line here, my Shadow Princes," she said, looking to each of us, "but you must promise me, *both of you*, that you'll come back."

I brushed my thumb over her knuckles. "We'll come back. We are bonded for all eternity, remember?"

A soft smile parted her lips before she looked to my brother.

Ruhl nodded slowly, shadows quiet at his heels for once. "We'll find the Moirai Shard," he vowed. "And we'll break the chains that bind Reign to our father."

"Then the ones that Helroth has tethered to you," I added.

My heart pounded against my ribs at the words, at the weight of everything pressing down against us. We had no choice now. Tomorrow, we'd leave for Lunaris.

And gods help anyone who tried to stop us.

Moonlight spilled across our bed through the window, silver and cold against the dark sheets. But Aelia's body, where she lay pressed against my side, was nothing but heat.

Her breath ghosted over my skin, sending sparks down my spine with each exhale. Her fingers traced idle patterns across my chest, across the gleaming mate mark, soft and slow, as if she were trying to memorize me. As if she knew this could be the last night.

And Noxus, maybe it was.

The thought lodged in my throat, sharper than any weapon. My shadows curled beneath the sheets, restless and tense, but I forced them back. Tonight wasn't for fear. It wasn't for war or prophecies or blood vows.

Tonight was for her.

For *us*.

I buried my face in her hair, breathing deeply and taking it all in, everything she was, and imprinting it on every part of me. She was sunlight and shadow, light and dark, my mate, my *cuoré*. "Starlight," I rasped, my lips brushing her temple. "If you keep touching me like that, I'm not going to let you sleep."

Her fingers dipped intentionally lower, nails grazing over my ribs. "Maybe I don't want to sleep. Maybe you owe me from earlier when we were interrupted by your brother just as things were getting good."

I growled softly, the sound vibrating in my chest. It would be a difficult journey tomorrow, and I knew well that surrendering to my desire meant heading out on little to no sleep, because once we started this, there would be no stopping. Not with the torrent of emotions already simmering between us.

"Careful, princess," I whispered, taking a moment to memorize every detail of her face.

She tilted her head up, silver-blue eyes gleaming in the dim light, teasing and tender all at once. "What are you going to do about it, professor?"

And just like that, with her playfulness, her love, she shattered all my restraint. In a blink, I had her beneath me. My mouth swallowed her gasp as I claimed her lips, devouring the ache that had been building in my chest since the moment I'd found Tenebris's empty cell. Or perhaps, even longer than that, if I was being completely honest with myself.

She wasted no time. Her hands threaded into my hair, tugging, pulling me closer, as if she wanted to fuse me into her skin. But she already had. The cuorem throbbed between us, beating wildly, a tether of light and shadow tying us together even as fate threatened to tear us apart.

"I'm leaving in a few hours," I whispered against her lips, voice hoarse. "I should rest..." A flicker of disappointment crossed those blazing orbs, bringing a smile to my face. "But I need this, Aelia. I need *you*."

"I'm yours," she breathed, no hesitation. "Always."

The words snapped something loose in me. I kissed her like it was the last time. Like I'd never get another chance. My shadows whirled between us, desperate, as if they too sensed it.

My hands slid beneath her thin nightdress, pushing the silk up her thighs. I savored the way she arched into me, her body soft and molten under my touch. My lips trailed down her neck, across her collarbone and over her matching mate mark. I tasted every inch of her, marking her with shadows that only she could feel.

Her nails raked down my back, pulling me closer until not a sliver of space remained between us, and I growled again. This time, the sound was darker, more desperate.

"I want you to feel me even when I'm gone," I whispered, pressing my forehead to hers so that our breaths mingled. "I want you to remember this."

Her legs parted for me in unspoken invitation, and I easily nestled between her thighs. Exactly where I belonged.

"I couldn't forget if I tried." Her voice broke on a moan as I slid into her, slow and deep, her body welcoming me home.

The world fell away. There was only Aelia. Only this. Us.

We moved together, shadows and light twisting in the air around us. The cuorem pulsed in perfect sync with every breath, every stroke, and every desperate whisper of love against sweat-slicked skin.

"Aelia..." Her name left my lips like a prayer, a promise and a plea. "Gods, I love you."

"Never more than I love you."

The minutes slowed to hours as we each took turns worshipping each other, tongues and limbs entwined. And when we shattered together for the final time, our bodies trembling and our souls wrapped tight, I held her close and made the vow through our bond.

I will always come back to you. Even if I have to crawl through every realm of shadow to do it.

Chapter Thirty-Nine

R*eign*

The wind cut sharp and cold across the Shadowmere Sea, but Phantom's mighty wings sliced through the night like an umbral sword. Beside us—but not *too* close—Mordrin flew in a tight arc, his silver scales shimmering like moonlight over the water. Ruhl sat astride him, unusually quiet. Perhaps it was the early hour, or maybe it was something else entirely.

I still don't understand why he *had to come.* Phantom's voice sailed through my thoughts.

I'm assuming you're referring to Mordrin and not my brother.

She snorted, a plume of smoke rising from her nostrils. *Of course.*

I didn't think you would suffer two riders. Was I mistaken?

To avoid Mordrin's company, I just might have.

At times, I forgot just how complicated their past was. I doubted Phantom or Solanthus would ever forget Mordrin's treachery during the war all those decades ago. Running a soothing hand across the scales at her neck, I murmured, "We're almost there. You'll be rid of him soon enough."

Another snort from my skyrider was her only reply.

Turning my thoughts from my dragon's drama to my other companion, I cast a glance over my shoulder. "Try to keep up, brother," I called over the wind, my shadows curling along Phantom's spine. "We wouldn't want you getting lost before we even land."

Ruhl snorted, his voice carried along the shadows between us. "Funny, coming from the male who spent half his life hiding out at Luce. I thought you liked being lost."

"I like being alive," I shot back, a grin tugging at my lips despite the dread simmering in my gut. "Which is why we'll need to stay sharp when we hit Lunaris. These beasts aren't your average cursed Fae."

"Right," Ruhl muttered, pulling a worn piece of parchment from the satchel at his hip. The ancient map fluttered in the wind but held steady under the cloak of his shadows. "This drawing better be right. Gideon found it in one of Father's old tomes; his personal, private collection. He believes it's accurate, but..."

I arched a brow. "That's reassuring."

"It's the only frame of reference we have." His eyes narrowed as he studied the glowing glyphs shifting across the surface. "The Shard's supposed to be hidden at the heart of the Lupherium, the Temple of the Moon. The problem is, the Wolvryn guard it like rabid hounds."

"They *are* rabid hounds," I muttered, my jaw tightening.

The Wolvryn weren't simply shapeshifters. They were cursed Fae, once regal warriors of Lunaris who'd been bound by ancient moon gods. Some claimed they'd been protectors, guardians of balance. Others said they were a failed trial, a punishment for their pride. Either way, they'd become something primal. Savage.

They were forced to shift with the moon, but even in their Fae forms, the beast was never far beneath the surface. I had yet to see one in person, but according to the texts, the Wolvryn were hulking forms with wolfish features, claws that could rip through shadow wards and teeth sharp enough to tear through bone.

And according to every source we'd found, the Wolvryn had no allegiance. They didn't care about kings or crowns or realms.

Only blood.

Phantom let out a low growl beneath me, her onyx eyes flashing in the dark. *I don't like this.*

Easy, old girl. Once again, I brushed a hand over her scales, sending a calming pulse through the bond. *I know you hate leaving me on the ground, but we can't risk you getting caught by those things.* They would hear a dragon from miles away.

I'll stay close. Her voice slithered through my mind like silk. *If you call, I'll come. I don't care how many of those mongrels I have to burn alive to get to you.*

Thank you. I pushed the final thought to her before turning back to Ruhl. "We ground here."

We dipped low over the cliffs of Lunaris, the jagged shoreline jutting from the sea like the ribs of some long-dead beast. Phantom and Mordrin hovered just over the land a few yards apart, wings flared to keep us airborne.

The air here was different. Thicker. Wilder. The scent of rain-drenched pine mingled with something sharper beneath it. My nostrils flared at the unfamiliar odors: iron, fur, blood.

The Wolvryn had marked this land.

I slid from Phantom's back, my boots sinking into the mist-laced moss. Shadows coiled instinctively around my arms and through my fingers.

Ruhl dismounted beside me, rolling his shoulders. "You think this is the best place to start?"

"No idea," I muttered, watching as our dragons soared into the skies again, disappearing into the darkening clouds to circle high above.

His smirk was laced with something darker. "Spoken like a true royal."

"Careful," I said, shadows flickering at my fingertips. "I might take that insult personally. Besides, you're the only future king amongst us."

Ruhl's head tipped back, a nearly silent laugh vibrating his shoulders. "You know, my whole life, I've waited for this moment. For the chance to finally take the Shadow Throne..."

"And now?"

Ruhl's smirk faded, darkness settling across his features. His gaze dropped to the dew-coated moss between us, then lifted again, eyes sharper now. Something like exhaustion bled through the cracks in his usual bravado.

"And now?" His throat bobbed. "Now, I'm not sure the title is worth a damn thing. Why would I want to sit atop a throne of ash and bones?" His voice was raw, quiet, like a secret he hadn't meant to share.

I remained silent, allowing him the time to get his thoughts together.

"I used to think ruling was everything," he continued, his eyes narrowing on the horizon where the mist curled thicker. "Power. Control. Proving I was more than Tenebris's simpering loyal heir. But standing here, hunting for some cursed shard in the middle of Wolvryn territory to save you and Aelia, I realize the throne means nothing if the two of you don't survive this."

I remained perfectly still, taking aback by his words.

His lips quirked, but it wasn't really a smile. "Maybe that's what makes me fit to rule now. I don't want it anymore."

I nodded, letting his final words hang in the air between us. He was right. And I was so gods' damned proud of my younger brother that unexpected heat pricked at the corners of my eyes. He would be a great king, one that they would write about for centuries to come. I was certain of it. All we had to do was survive the day, and the coming war...

"Shall we?" Ruhl motioned toward the mountain range to our right.

"After you, Shadow Regent." I dipped into an elaborate bow, coaxing a smirk from his lips.

We moved silently through the underbrush, the map glowing faintly in Ruhl's hand as he tracked the glyphs. The Lupherium was supposedly hidden deep in the northern cliffs, past the Crags of Moira. If the shard truly existed, it was no doubt buried beneath ancient wards. It was yet another issue we'd have to solve once we found it.

The mist thickened as we walked, wrapping around our ankles, our waists, until the world narrowed to little more than shadow and breath.

Then, I felt it, the prickle at the base of my spine.

"Ruhl," I whispered, shadows curling around me, poised to strike. "We're not alone."

A low growl echoed from the trees, so deep it rumbled through my ribs. Shapes emerged from the fog, hulking figures, taller than any male should be, with eyes glowing amber in the gloom. Their fur bristled, dark and mottled, claws flexing as they closed in.

Wolvryn.

There were six of them, circling like wolves on the hunt. And by the looks of it, they weren't here to negotiate. Their claws gleamed like obsidian blades as they moved, forged from something older than any realm. When they breathed, the atmosphere thickened, iron and rot filling the air.

"Stay back," I snarled, *nox* surging from my hands. But the beasts only pressed closer, saliva dripping from fangs too long for their jaws.

From within, the *zar* thrummed louder, cold and seductive, whispering promises of annihilation. It wanted me to let go. To destroy them.

One leapt.

I ducked, shadows snapping around its neck midair, slamming it into the rocks. Another came at Ruhl, but he spun, his umbral blade arcing across its chest. Blood splattered the moss, thick and dark crimson.

Still, they kept coming.

Another Wolvryn lunged, claws scraping my side. I spun, shadows lashing out like vipers and wrapping around its limbs, but it writhed free. Fast. Too fast. And damned strong.

Ruhl shouted, slicing another across the thigh. "They won't stop coming!"

"Then neither do we," I growled, the *zar* rising in my blood, colder and sharper, harder to keep in. It fed the storm inside me. I threw out my hand, finally summoning the twisted tendrils of Night that now coursed through my veins. The shadows thickened, a snarl of ebony that wrapped around two of the beasts, crushing them to the ground.

They howled but didn't die.

Gods, they just kept moving.

The biggest one pinned Ruhl against a boulder, jaws snapping inches from his throat. "Reign!" he shouted, eyes wild.

I leapt, shadows streaming from my palms. The blast knocked the Wolvryn back, just long enough for Ruhl to ram his blade through its chest. It shuddered, let out a final, guttural growl, then went still.

As we stood there panting, I watched in horror as the fallen Wolvryn's bones cracked and mangy dark fur receded, revealing an enormous male. A very dead one.

Something rippled through the remaining beasts; a flux of raw power. Could the Wolvryn be linked somehow? Before I could think on it longer, something cracked, not just bone, but magic. I'd read tales of small packs led by an Alpha, the strongest of the lot. Perhaps their abilities stemmed from a bond similar to the one that flowed through Aelia and me.

As if in answer to my unspoken question, a flash of moonlight across the beasts' chests caught my eye. A faint glyph, etched in slivers of moonbeams, pulsed once then dimmed. They staggered, their amber eyes flickering, like the death of one had siphoned the strength from them all.

Releasing another wave of shadows laced with the potent *zar*, my wraiths easily tore through the remainders of the weakened pack. The others followed their leader soon after, one by one, until the clearing was soaked in Wolvryn blood and our shadows heaved a ragged breath.

My knees nearly buckled, the weight of exhaustion dragging at my limbs as if made of lead chains. Every breath burned, shadows flickering at the edges of my vision. The *zar* still pulsed beneath my skin, but it was weaker now. The dark power was finally spent from the battle—or maybe that was just me.

Ruhl wiped a smear of blood from his jaw, his hand trembling as his umbral blade sputtered out. "Remind me why we didn't bring the dragons all the way to the temple?" His grin was weak, but it was there. "Next time, let them do the heavy lifting."

Panting, I gave in and dropped to one knee, wiping the sweat from my brow. "Next time," I muttered, "you're going first."

Ruhl chuckled, a rough sound that didn't quite reach his eyes. "Next time, I'll summon more blades. Or better yet, perhaps you can let me borrow some of that *zar*."

"If only I knew how I got it in the first place."

"I'm sure you have theories..." A flicker of amusement, of curiosity, brightened his eyes.

"It's not from Aelia," I admitted.

"I didn't think it was." He regarded me for a long moment, and then it clicked. I saw it the moment he put the pieces together. How had he come to the realization so quickly, and how had I not realized it sooner? "Your mother..."

"Mmm," I murmured. "Whoever she may have been."

He nodded slowly, then heaved out a breath.

We stood there, side by side, for an endless moment, bloodied but alive.

For now.

Finally, I glanced at him, my chest tightening, not from the battle, but from something heavier. "Ruhl," I murmured, voice gruff. "I know I've never been easy on you, brother. But you've become a better male than I ever thought you would."

Ruhl's gaze snapped to mine, startled. "Did you just compliment me?"

"Don't get used to it," I muttered with a smirk. "I know you still want my mate."

His grin was rueful but real. "And I know I'd have to kill you before you'd let me take her."

"And if you succeeded, I'd only come back to haunt you in the afterlife," I whispered, shadows flickering at my fingertips.

"Well, then, it's a good thing I have no intention of ever trying."

"Good." A reluctant smile parted my lips.

The mist shifted again, curling between us, and the map in Ruhl's hand flared brighter, pulling us from the moment.

"We're close," he blurted.

"Then what are we waiting for?"

Chapter Forty

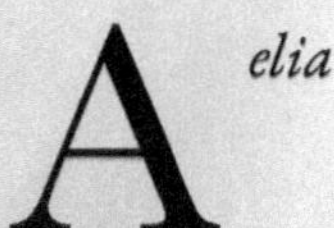

A ^{elia}

Stars, I hated sleeping without Reign. Moonlight slid through the crack in the velvet curtain, kissing the vacant side of the bed, another reminder that he wasn't there, and why. The cuorem throbbed, angry and relentless at the absence of its mate. I tossed and turned beneath the silky coverlet but sleep simply wouldn't come. Here I was, the first night with him away, and I was minutes away from giving up on rest all together. Or succumbing to the temptation of the sleeping draught Elisa had concocted for me. I eyed the small ampule on the nightstand, its glittering liquid enticing. A good night's rest was exactly what I needed.

Still, my thoughts spun, a jumble of fear and hope, laced in anxiety. If Reign and Ruhl succeeded in their risky mission, we would finally be free of Tenebris and Helroth. Then, we could fully concentrate on the war to come and on ending the threat of the Night Fae once and for all.

Gods, if only it were that easy.

With a sigh of defeat, I reached for the small glass vessel and, tipping my head back, swallowed down the foul-tasting contents. "Thank you, Elisa," I whispered when I lay my head back down on the pillow. As the warmth of the liquid slid down my throat, settling, my mind slowly grew hazy. The healer's words echoed, images of the lifeless Shadow Fae rising to the surface. *Think quickly, Your Highness. War won't wait.*

I'd avoided descending to her chambers for days, fearing she would ask me to attempt to use my *zar* again on another dead Fae. But I couldn't... I *shouldn't.*

The darkness came softly, at first. A whisper of night curling beneath my skin. I dreamt of shadows. Of cold wind threading through my hair, of silver mist coiling around my ankles, pulling me into a void where no light existed.

Then the voice came.

Smooth. Silk-wrapped poison. "Princess."

My throat tightened. I knew that voice. Helroth.

"No," I breathed, but the word was swallowed up by the void.

I tried to wake. To force my eyes open. Only, the sheets weren't beneath me anymore. My body just... floated, weightless, while tendrils of night wrapped around my ribs like chains. No matter how I struggled, how hard I fought, my lungs filled only with frost.

"You've grown stronger," he murmured, his tone almost... admiring. "But strength is irrelevant when your fate is already written."

His presence pressed against me, prickly and cold, like night wrapped in barbed wire. The last time he'd invaded my mind, I'd managed to force him out. But this... this was different. Reign wasn't here.

I spun in place, searching the nothingness, forcing my powers to rise. "Get. Out," I snarled, summoning light to my fingertips. Shadow too. The combination crackled through me, but it did nothing to dispel him. He didn't appear phased in the slightest.

His laughter echoed, low and hollow. "Oh, princess. You

think light and shadow will save you? It's too late. You've already set it all in motion."

I gritted my teeth. "I won't be your puppet, nor will I be controlled by you. I'll fight the blood vow until the very end. Just like I fought against the lies you tried to feed me about Ruhl. Yes, that's right, I know about your marriage pact with Tenebris. And still, I found my way back to Reign, to my real mate, my *cuoré*."

"Good for you, princess, but the Shadow Prince is inconsequential now anyway." His chuckle slithered through my thoughts. "And no, child. You're no puppet. You're the tempest. The harbinger. The child of twilight who will unravel Aetheria's last threads of balance."

The mist thickened, twisting into shapes, into images around me: me on a throne of bones, my wings bleeding both light and shadow; Reign's lifeless body sprawled at my feet; Ruhl beside him, shadows devouring him whole.

"No," I whispered, shaking my head. "That's not my future."

"Isn't it?" His crimson gaze flashed in the mist, twin coals burning in the void. "You carry the power of destruction in your veins, princess. Light, shadow... and death. You will break this realm, Aelia. Whether you wish to or not."

"I *will choose*," I hissed, pushing against the illusion, the nightmare... whatever this was. "I have choice."

"You do." His voice hardened, velvet turning to steel. "But the price of choice is consequence."

Then the mist recoiled, dragging him back, but not before his final words scraped across my mind: *When twilight reigns, the final hour begins.*

I bolted upright, a cry stuck in my throat, sweat slicking my skin. The second prophecy, the one Reign had told me he'd found in Tenebris's empty prison cell. My heart raced, the cuorem pulsing wildly under my ribs.

Reign.

The bond reached for him instinctively, but the tether stretched thin, distant, extending across the Shadowmere Sea to

Lunaris... That was it, wasn't it? With him gone, with his shadows no longer guarding my mind, Helroth had found a crack in the armor. A way in.

Aelia, are you all right? Reign's voice slid through the chaos, the warm timbre anchoring me, even from so far away.

Yes, I'm fine. I'm sorry to startle you. It was... it was just a nightmare. Or was it more? My hands trembled, gripping the sheets.

You're sure?

Yes, get some rest. It's late, and you *have a mystical artifact to retrieve.*

Goodnight, my love. I'll update you on the search in the morning.

I look forward to it.

Pressing my palms to my face, I lay back down and tried to steady my breathing.

Weeks of silence from my grandfather. And now this.

I knew it had been too good to be true. Hadn't I worried he would sneak in when we least expected it?

But what I didn't understand was why now? Was it Reign's distance or the sleeping draught which had dulled my mental walls?

A part of me feared it was because I was vulnerable without Reign. And Helroth knew it. I let my hands drop, staring at the ceiling of the obsidian chamber. Cold dread slithered down my spine, but beneath it, something else sparked.

Resolve.

I couldn't afford to be weak. Not anymore. If I was to survive this war, if I was to protect Reign, Aidan, my friends and our entire realm, I needed to be ready. For anything. Even the darkness Helroth claimed I'd bring.

I had to master it all. I would accept nothing less.

Rais. Nox. And yes... the dreaded *zar.*

Even the necromancy and soul draining I still feared so much.

My fingers trembled for a moment, then stilled. I would not

allow Helroth to decide who I became. *I* would decide that for myself.

Pushing back the covers, I rose from the bed, moving toward the window, toward the moon-silvered night beyond.

The time for fear was over. It was time to become what I was meant to be.

Even if that meant becoming something monstrous.

⚔

"You're certain about this, Aelia?" Aidan's weary eyes met mine.

I nodded slowly, though there wasn't much I was certain of these days. All I knew for sure was that I had to exhaust any and all options if I wanted to defeat my grandsire and the Night Fae. I glanced over his shoulder at the hulking male standing in the wake of Solanthus's enormous form. My dragon eyed the Demon Fae, nostrils flared, maw gaping.

I will eat him if he so much as twitches. Sol's voice echoed through my mind.

It had taken hours of pleading to force my dragon to collect my former jailor from Duskridge Manor. It was bad enough getting him to agree to allow Aidan to ride him, but Kaelith? It had been quite a battle.

But in the end, I'd won.

It wasn't as if you'd given me a choice. He huffed.

I told you why I needed Kae here.

It's all very risky, little Kin. And don't think I haven't noticed this was conveniently done in the absence of your mate.

Reign will understand. Or, at least, that was what I hoped.

Have you told him yet?

Of course not. What he doesn't know won't hurt him. And I needed him to focus on his mission. The last thing I wanted was for him to get distracted, fearing for my well-being.

Aidan lifted his hand and signaled to Kaelith. "You may approach," he called out.

Kaelith stalked forward, a dark, grimy cloak hanging over his shoulders. His eyes, those brilliant citrine orbs, glinted beneath the moonlight, curious and wary all at once.

"So..." His lips curved, sharp and knowing. "The little Light Fae princess calls on the Night Fae after all."

"This isn't about you," I snapped, though my voice lacked any real bite. My heart was pounding too fast for it. "This is about survival."

Kaelith's gaze drifted to Solanthus, then back to me. "Your skyrider looks ready to rip out my throat."

He's not wrong, Sol growled through the bond.

"I'll keep him on a leash," I murmured under my breath. Then, focusing on Kaelith, I raised my voice, steadying my tone. "I need you to teach me."

Kaelith's brow arched, head tilting just so. "Teach you what, exactly?"

I swallowed hard, knowing that once I set this in motion, there'd be no turning back. But still, I said, "Necromancy." The word left a bitter taste on my tongue. Aidan stiffened at my side, but I kept my shoulders squared.

Kaelith's lips parted into a grin, one that held no warmth. "Ah. So the princess of twilight has finally come to terms with what she is."

"I'm not asking for your commentary, Kaelith," I hissed. "I'm asking for your knowledge."

He studied me in silence, the wind lifting his long, maroon hair off his broad shoulders. "Why now?"

"Because Helroth isn't waiting anymore," I whispered. My throat closed for a beat, but I forced the next words out. "He was in my mind last night. I don't know how, but he slipped through. I can't let that happen again. I need to be ready and that means harnessing all my powers."

His smile faded, replaced by something sharper. "You're playing with blades you don't know how to wield, Aelia."

"That's why I need you to teach me."

"I could," he murmured, circling me like a predator sizing up prey. "But necromancy is not a spell, princess. It's not a trick of the hand or a clever glyph. It's hunger. Once you let it in, it changes you."

I held his gaze, forcing my voice to steady. "I've already changed."

Kaelith paused, eyes narrowing. "Do you even understand what you're asking for? Death magic takes. It doesn't just borrow power, it demands it. Your light, your shadow, even your soul. Are you willing to pay that price?"

My mouth went dry, but I nodded. "If it saves Aetheria, I'll pay whatever it takes."

A flicker of something unreadable passed through his gaze. Respect? "Very well." He flicked his hand, and ribbons of night coiled at his fingertips. "But understand this, Light Fae, once you cross this threshold, there's no going back."

I was well aware. "I crossed that threshold the moment Helroth unbound my powers."

Kaelith's grin returned, but it was sharper now. "Spoken like a true heir of twilight."

Aidan's jaw ticked beside me. "Aelia, think about this. Really think."

"I have." My voice was steel. "This is the only way."

My former jailor stepped closer, lowering his voice. "We'll start at midnight. I assume you have a body to practice on?"

My stomach twisted, but I nodded.

"Good, then I'll show you what it means to command the dead."

Aidan's head dipped grimly before he led Kaelith into the fortress. As the pair faded back into the shadows, I pressed a hand to my chest, the cuorem pulsing steadily, softly beneath my palm.

Forgive me, Reign, I whispered silently, eyes closing to the moon-drenched sky.

But maybe this was the way to finally win.

Chapter Forty-One

R*eign*

By the gods, I hated camping. I wouldn't consider myself a typical pampered royal, by any means, but this... this I absolutely despised.

I shifted against the damp cave wall, my leathers stiff with dried blood and Wolvryn fur. Ruhl lay sprawled beside me, one arm slung over his face, snoring just loud enough to make me consider shoving the moss beneath my palm into his mouth.

"Are you actually asleep," I muttered, "or just trying to piss me off?"

Ruhl's hand slid down, one dark eye cracking open. "Both."

I huffed a laugh despite myself. My shadows curled lazily around my fingers, restless but quiet. "Well, congratulations. Mission accomplished."

"You're just bitter because I got the better spot." He stretched, joints cracking, then winced as the wound in his side pulled. A fresh gash cut across his ribs from yesterday's encounter with the blood-thirsty beasts, but he'd refused to let me help him. Stubborn bastard.

"There's no *better spot*," I grumbled, flicking a small stone at him. "It's a cave."

"A *dry* cave." His smirk widened, teeth flashing in the low light. "At least, until you started crying in the middle of the night about missing your dear *cuoré*."

"Funny." I adjusted the knife hidden in my boot. Aelia had insisted I could never have too many weapons. "Maybe next time I'll let the Wolvryn rip you apart and save me the headache."

Ruhl's grin faded a notch, but his eyes softened. "You didn't last night."

"I didn't have much choice. You're the future king after all." I rubbed my jaw, eyes narrowing at the mouth of the cave where mist still clung to the rocks. The Wolvryn howls had echoed all night. Closer, then farther, then close again. It was like they were toying with us.

"You're not still brooding about my lack of interest in ruling, are you?" he asked.

"I'm always brooding, it's what I do," I muttered. "You know me."

His chuckle warmed the cold morning air. "True."

We sat in silence for a beat, the kind of silence that used to gnaw at me. But now, it was different. Less heavy. Something had changed between my brother and me. For a moment, when I found him in bed with Liora, I thought he'd returned to his old ways, but his selflessness regarding Aelia and this mission proved otherwise.

"We need to move soon," I grumbled, my broodiness out in full force as I pulled out the map. The glowing glyphs shifted as I traced my finger along the folds. "The Lupherium is still half a day north."

Ruhl shifted beside me, his own shadows curling lazily around his ankles. "We'll never make it if they keep tracking us."

"Then we shadowtravel."

He snorted. "Through unfamiliar terrain? Are you trying to get us spliced through a rock wall?"

"You scared?" I shot him a look. Though, he wasn't *entirely* wrong. Shadowtraveling without knowing the land was dangerous business.

"No," he snapped, then grimaced. "Okay, maybe a little."

"You never could shadowtravel properly," I teased, the old memory tugging a rare smile from me. "Remember the first time you tried when you visited me at Arcanum? You ended up in the girls' bathhouse."

His ears went crimson. "That was *on purpose*."

I rolled my eyes. "Sure, it was."

But his grin faded, seriousness slipping in. "I'm not like you, Reign. I'm not blessed by Zaroth with two gifts. My *nox* isn't strong enough for this."

"Yes, it is," I growled. "You just don't trust yourself."

"I trust you," he shot back. "That's why I didn't argue when you said you'd come."

My throat tightened, but I ignored it. "Good. Then shut up and let me focus."

I angled the map, orienting the glyphs with the ridges ahead. The Lupherium's coordinates shimmered faintly beneath my palm, and I locked onto the sensation like a predator scenting prey.

"We don't have a choice, Ruhl. If we run, they'll chase us. If we fight, they'll send more. If we call the dragons, we'll have every Wolvryn in Lunaris on our tails."

His jaw flexed. "So, what, we leap into shadows and hope for the best?"

"That's the plan."

"Wonderful," he muttered. "Typical move when it comes to your *cuoré*. All guts, no sanity. The unmated version of yourself would be horrified."

I almost laughed before a low growl rumbled from beyond the cave entrance. Then another, swiftly dampening the moment. Shadows slithered across the floor, claws tapping stone.

Damn it. It was too late. They were here.

I surged to my feet, grabbing Ruhl's arm. "Hold on."

"Wait—"

"Now."

The Wolvryn charged, snarls and teeth flashing through the mist, claws scraping the rock. One leapt for me, a blur of fur and fangs, but I didn't flinch. I seized Ruhl, fingers tight around his forearm before shadows exploded from my back in a storm of cold wind and pure *nox*. The cave split. And darkness swallowed us whole.

Then there was only silence, and the feel of my brother's arm clenched between my fingertips, grounding me. I guided my shadows, concentrating my scattered thoughts on the map.

It was like threading a needle blindfolded. Shadows rippled around me, the currents cold and unfamiliar. But I kept the glyphs in my mind, focused on the coordinates burned into my memory.

Ruhl gritted his teeth beside me, his arm locked in a steel grip. "Reign—"

"Quiet."

We spun through the void, flashes of mist and mountain crags flickering past. For a heartbeat, I thought I'd missed it. That we'd end up dead or worse, half-phased into the cliff face. But then my boots slammed into solid ground, and the shadows peeled away.

I released Ruhl with a gasp, both of us stumbling to our knees.

We were alive.

"Fuck," Ruhl panted, wide-eyed but grinning. "You did it."

"Of course I did." My chest heaved, sweat trickling down my back. "You think I'd let you die before you take that throne?"

"Didn't think you cared that much," he rasped.

I shot him a sidelong glance, shadows curling at my fingertips, but there was no bite to my voice. "Don't make me regret it."

We both laughed, breathless and shaken, but somehow still standing.

In the distance, the cliffs rose, sharp and gleaming. The Crags of Moira. My smile grew wider as I caught sight of an ancient moonstone embedded into the white bark of a nearby tree. It was carved into the form of an arrow, signaling toward the foreboding crags that marked the entrance to the Lupherium.

We'd made it.

By the time we finally reached the Lupherium, the last threads of night clung to the mist like reluctant shadows. Even after everything—two days without proper sleep, Wolvryn claws slicing too close to my ribs, and Ruhl's incessant banter—I froze at the sight of the temple.

It wasn't at all what I had expected.

The Lupherium wasn't some crumbling ruin buried by time. It was pristine. Untouched by war or decay. Its pale towers spiraled into the sky, like moonbeams made solid, carved from shimmering stone that pulsed faintly with soft, silver light. The architecture was unlike anything in Aetheria. No sharp edges, no brutal fortifications, just flowing curves and arches that hummed beneath our feet. It was as if the temple itself breathed with the tides.

At the heart of it all stood a massive circular dais, open to the sky. Moonlight poured through the clouds in cascading ribbons, illuminating a towering statue carved of iridescent stone.

Selraya. The Moon Goddess.

Her likeness loomed above us, arms outstretched. Her eyes were closed in a perfectly serene expression, veiled hair cascading down her back in rippling streams of light. A crown of crescent moons adorned her brow, and beneath her bare feet, a wolf lay curled in sleep, its silver pelt etched into the marble as if it were alive. A soft glow emanated from her chest, where a gemstone heart pulsed in rhythm with the temple's walls.

I swallowed hard, shadows curling tight around my spine as if they felt it too. This wasn't just a monument. This was something sacred. Alive.

Ruhl let out a breath beside me, his shadows subdued for once. "Gods," he whispered, voice reverent. "No wonder the Wolvryn are so damn protective."

And for the first time, I thought I understood why.

Maybe the Wolvryn weren't just cursed beasts but Selraya's chosen. Guardians of the moon's balance. Perhaps, their transformations weren't simply punishment, but also devotion, binding them to the goddess's cycle. Predators, yes, but protectors too. At least, they had been. Before the madness took them.

Clearing my throat, I reminded myself to focus on the reason we were here. "Come on." I forced my feet to move and my eyes away from the embodiment of the goddess in stone, and scanned the glyphs carved into the ruins before us. "We didn't come all this way to gawk."

The Lupherium itself pulsed with quiet energy. Pale moonlight filtered through the opening above, painting the ruins in ghostly silver and blue as we passed silent corridor after silent corridor. I didn't know how, but I could feel it in my bones. We were close.

"Not much farther," Ruhl confirmed, glancing down at the map again. His voice echoed slightly in the eerie quiet. "There's a chamber ahead. Marked with the symbol of the Moirai."

We ducked through a low archway, our boots gliding over smooth tile. A glimmer of light caught my eye, tucked away in an alcove carved directly into the ancient rock wall. A mirror.

Its frame was forged from midnight silver, swirling like smoke held in stasis, and strange glyphs glimmered faintly along its surface. The glass itself shimmered, shifting like moonlight on still water.

"What in all the realms?" I breathed as we inched closer.

An inscription was inked along the wall. My finger traced the swirling writing, lifting the tiny hairs at my nape. *The Mirror of Hidden Truths.*

Ruhl's brows shot up. "Have you ever heard of it?"

I nodded absently. "It's an old Lunarian myth. Gideon used to go on and on about it when we were at the Citadel. It's said to show a single truth. One *it* chooses. In exchange for blood."

The surface rippled at my words, glittering letters shimmering to life across its face. Slowly scanning the words, my gut twisted as the final letters appeared.

The mirror sees all. The mask shatters here. To walk the hidden path, you must confront the truth within yourselves.

Steeling myself, I stepped forward, my palm already tingling. "Well, it looks like we're about to get a truth whether we want it or not."

Ruhl's hand shot out, stopping me as I lifted my hand and the dagger I now held. "Are you sure? These kinds of mystical relics... there's no telling what it'll show."

"I need the Shard," I said, voice low. Then, without hesitation, I dragged the blade across my palm, letting the blood drip onto the mirror's surface. The silver glass rippled again. At first, with nothing. Then, movement.

A vision flickered to life. Not of me, not of the vow, but a memory. A truth.

One not of my choosing.

Of a dim chamber, lit only by crimson flame. A towering male knelt beside a woman cloaked in starlight and shadow. I squinted, narrowing my eyes at the familiar form. *Kaelith?* A much younger version, but it was him, I was certain of it. The female's features were obscured, save for the delicate curve of her jaw and the way her hand cradled a bundle wrapped in inky silk. The child inside didn't cry. Instead, it pulsed with shadow. I knew that presence, that *nox*. I knew it as well as I knew my own reflection.

It was... me. I was sure of it.

I staggered back, breath catching. "That's... that's impossible."

Ruhl moved beside me. "Is that—?"

"I think Kaelith is..." My voice faltered. "My real father."

It didn't make sense though. Why would Tenebris claim a bastard who wasn't his? And yet... the look on Kaelith's face. The grief. The protectiveness. The familiarity. My thoughts spiraled, but my heart *knew*.

Ruhl didn't say anything for a long moment. Then, softly, "You sure you want to keep looking for answers?"

I turned to him, jaw practically unhinged. If Tenebris wasn't my father, then Ruhl wasn't my half-brother either. Everything had been a lie. *Everything*. My thoughts spiraled, a tornado of torment shredding my insides. I knew what I was seeing was real. True. But right now, these were truths I simply couldn't contemplate. I'd never known my mother, and still, I'd survived. What difference did a father truly make? Besides, Aelia was my family now, and I had to find the Moirai Shard and return to her. My own complicated bloodline could wait.

"I don't think we have a choice anymore," I finally murmured.

Ruhl stepped closer to the mirror, then hesitated. "I'm not doing it," he muttered, stepping away. "I already know too much about my damned future. I don't need a cursed mirror rubbing it in."

I snorted. "Coward."

"Realist," he replied, rolling his eyes.

The mirror's light began to fade, swallowing the image. But not before a final flicker. A pair of glowing violet eyes and dark hair, set into a face that mirrored mine too closely to be coincidence. A Night Fae. One I'd never seen before.

"Did you see that?" I hissed.

But Ruhl had already begun to move down the hallway. His cocked his head over his shoulder, expression weary. "I've learned not to put too much stock in fate, brother. It's far too fickle."

Forcing my boots forward to catch up, I left the mirror and its images behind, burying the unsettling vision for now and focusing on Ruhl's words instead. One specifically. *Brother.* A dozen unspoken words sat perched on the tip of my tongue. After the years of hatred Father had sewn between us, to find out we weren't blood at all would be the ultimate irony.

But that was a truth to be left for another day. Now, we were here for the Shard. Quickening my pace, I shot past my brother as we turned a corner. Ruhl followed, shadows whispering at his heels. There, just a few yards ahead, was the central altar, where the Moirai Shard waited.

It wasn't just a sliver of crystal, as I'd imagined. The Shard was a prism of woven starlight and silver threads, suspended in air between twin crescent moons carved of obsidian and moonstone. It vibrated softly, like a hummingbird midflight.

There was something familiar about the prism, the way it refracted the light. It reminded me of something...

Ruhl reached for it, drawing me from my musings, but the moment his fingertips brushed the edge of the dais a shock of silver magic exploded outward. It hurled him back, and he hit the ground, hard. A hiss of pain squeezed through his lips.

"*Elra,*" he growled, pushing to his feet. "It's warded."

Elra. The power of Selraya. A blessed gift, much like *rais* or *nox*; moon-touched magic woven from lunar tides and shifting fate.

I stepped forward, testing the barrier. The *elra* rippled under my palm, cool, humming, and refusing to yield. Summoning one of my dark minions, shadows peeled from my skin attempting to infiltrate the orb. They poked and prodded, but the *elra* held, even with an extra shot of *zar* added to the effort.

A pang of frustration swelled through me, and a growl ripped from between my clenched teeth. "I'm not sure I can breach it..."

Ruhl dusted himself off, lips twitching in a smirk. "Are you asking for my help?"

I hadn't been, but maybe it wasn't the worst idea. I gave him a sidelong glance. "Do you have it in you, brother?"

"I've made it this far, haven't I?" His smile faded, eyes darkening and determination settling across his features. "Let's do it."

I closed my eyes, summoning *nox* first, and shadows coiled around my fingers, feeding off the temple's darkness. Then came the *zar*, that cold pulse of Night in my veins, drawn from somewhere deep in my bones. My mother, maybe.

Beside me, Ruhl did the same, shadows lashing from his fingertips in perfect sync with mine. His *nox* crackled more furiously than I'd ever seen it.

We stepped forward together, our power merging in a single burst, darkness and void, shadows and death. Not fighting the *elra* but weaving through it. Coaxing it.

The barrier trembled. The silver light cracked, splintering into a thousand shards of moonlight. With a sound like shattering ice, the ward dissolved.

We reached for the Shard together, our hands closing around it at the same time. Suddenly, the ground trembled, sending a tremor through my entire body. My free arm shot out to steady myself as I tightened my grip on the artifact, refusing to lose it after all we'd been through to get here.

A figure stepped from the shadows of the temple's inner sanctum just as the shaking stopped, silver robes whispering against the floor and feet bare. The female's face was veiled, but moonlight radiated from her skin, a soft, pulsing glow that made my chest tighten.

A priestess of Selraya.

I'd read about them in the few ancient tomes I'd scanned in the Arcanum library.

"Shadow Princes," she whispered, her voice like wind over water. "You have breached the Lupherium's defenses, not by force, but by unity."

Ruhl and I stood still, dread pooling low in my gut. This almost seemed too easy. There had to be a catch, there always was.

"I am not here to stop you," she continued, clearly having read my thoughts, her tone as gentle as a lullaby. "The Moirai Shard belongs to no one. It exists to balance fate. But know this —" She lifted her veil, revealing eyes like twin moons, one silver and one obsidian. "When the Shard is used to break a bond woven by gods, there is always a sacrifice. Be warned."

The Shard in our hands pulsed, brighter now, heavier.

"What kind of sacrifice?" I rasped, throat tight.

She tilted her head, almost sad. "That is not for me to say. The Moirai choose. But a thread must be cut, so another may be spun."

Ruhl and I exchanged a wary glance before his jaw ticked. "How do we use it?"

"You must only whisper the words to unlock it: '*Moirai incendiae*'. The Shard will do the rest."

I opened my mouth to ask more, but her form dissolved into silver mist before I could, leaving us alone beneath Selraya's watchful gaze. As the priestess vanished, the Shard in my palm pulsed again, once, twice. Like a heartbeat. Or perhaps a countdown.

Ruhl's fingers flexed around the shard, his jaw tightening. "Well," he muttered, voice dry but hollow. "That sounded promising."

I didn't answer. Because in my gut, I had a terrible feeling I knew exactly what sacrifice the Shard would demand.

Chapter Forty-Two

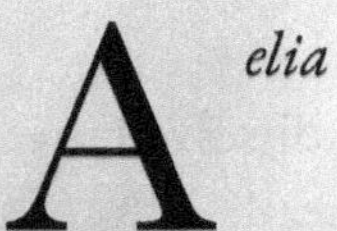

A elia

The old dungeons beneath the Shadow Fortress still stank of blood and rot, centuries of Fae cast into the darkness to be tortured and left to die. I squeezed my eyes closed, forcing back the grisly images threatening to surface. Was this where Tenebris had trained Reign? Where he'd forced his son to do unspeakable things? I drew in a breath, compelling my legs forward in spite of the urge to run in the opposite direction.

Despite the flickering lanterns lining the corridor, the relentless darkness clung to the stones. My boots echoed with every step as Kaelith led me deeper, past rusted chains and broken cages until we reached a circular chamber carved into black rock. At its center lay a stone slab etched with ancient runes that pulsed faintly in a language I couldn't understand.

My stomach twisted at what lay atop the stone.

"You brought me to a *tomb*?" I asked, voice tight.

Kaelith turned slowly. "You're here to master death, princess. Where else should we begin?"

I swallowed the bile clawing up my throat. Lying on the slab was a corpse. A young male; another Shadow Fae from the look of him. His skin was pale with the chill of death, his body marked with shallow gashes. My pulse quickened.

"Who was he?"

"A deserter," Kaelith replied coldly. "Or so the Shadow general said. Does it matter?"

"It does to me."

Kae stalked toward me, his eyes glowing faintly in the dimness. "This is the difference between us, Light Fae. You cling to morality, to mercy. But death has no such luxury. If you want to control it, you must become what you fear."

"I don't want to become a monster," I whispered.

He circled me slowly. "You already are. You carry light and shadow in equal measure, and now the *zar* curls in your veins like a starving beast. You cannot silence it forever."

"I'm not trying to silence it," I snapped. "I just... I want to *control* it. I don't want to be controlled."

Kaelith stopped in front of me, gaze sharp. "Then stop resisting."

He raised a hand, and the room dimmed. No, not dimmed. The darkness itself deepened, thickened, until it felt like I was breathing smoke. The *zar* within me stirred, drawn to the power pulsing from him.

"Reach into it," Kaelith instructed. "Summon it through your blood, through your veins. Let it rise."

I closed my eyes and obeyed.

It came fast. The *zar*. Pushing past my *rais* and *nox*, it was a rush of cold power, slicing through my chest like a blade of ice. It burned and numbed all at once, dragging my soul into a current I couldn't quite escape. My hands trembled as the darkness poured into my limbs.

"Now, command it," he whispered. "Will the dead to rise."

I gritted my teeth and lifted my hand toward the corpse.

A tendril of black mist slid from my palm, wrapping around the male's wrist. The mark on my chest, Reign's mark, throbbed. The cuorem pushed back, instinctively rejecting the *zar's* pull.

"No," I gasped. "It's too much."

"Let it consume you!" Kaelith barked. "Only then will you master it. You cannot control the darkness while fearing what it will make of you."

The corpse twitched.

A violent shudder ran down my spine.

"I can feel him," I whispered. "His soul is fading, but it's still tethered by a thread."

"Then bring it back. Bring him back to life."

Like last time in Elisa's chamber, I felt him. For an instant, I felt the pull from the Veil as my hands hovered over his chest. *Come back. Exsurge anima.* I repeated the foreign words forming unbidden in my mind, over and over. A grisly mantra on my trembling lips. My ribs tightened, a whirlwind of energies surging to life in my core. Warmth, then icy cold. I could feel his soul slipping right through my fingertips.

"I can't do it," I hissed. "It's too late."

"Drain it then," Kaelith urged. "Take his soul. Death answers only to those who command it without hesitation."

My hand trembled. The mist thickened. The power *wanted* me to take it.

But... I couldn't do it. Gods, necromancy was bad enough, but soul-draining? I dropped my hand, breath ragged. The mist dissipated, and the corpse stilled.

Kaelith hissed in frustration and turned away. "You're holding back. Still chained by your Light."

"I'm still *me*," I snapped, voice hoarse. "Regardless of my power. And I won't lose that, not even to win this gods' damned war. Then, it's only Helroth who wins."

Kae said nothing for a long moment. Then, softer, he whispered, "There will come a time when you must choose, Aelia. Between your soul and survival. Between who you are, and who Aetheria needs you to become."

My jaw clenched.

I didn't want to become a reaper. A goddess of death. But I was already halfway there, wasn't I?

Kaelith's expression was stone, unmoved by my trembling hands or thundering heart.

"You failed," he added coolly, "but you came close. Try again."

"I can't—"

"Yes, you can," he growled, closing the space between us. "You're afraid of what you'll see in yourself if you cross that line. But war doesn't care about your fear, princess. It only demands results."

My teeth ground together. I wanted to scream at him, to tell him he didn't understand, but gods help me, I knew he did. He knew my grandfather better than anyone else.

I stepped toward the slab.

The Shadow Fae's body lay still, a cruel echo of life. I reached out, slower this time, letting the *zar* slither down my arm like black fire. My light recoiled. My shadow pulsed. But this time, I didn't resist the addictive energy, I embraced it.

The room went cold. My fingertips hovered just inches from his heart.

"Speak the words I taught you," Kaelith whispered. "You know them."

My lips parted. "*Exsurge anima. Redde mihi veritatem.*" Rise soul. Return to the land of the living.

The air thickened. Light and shadow collided beneath my breastbone, mixing with the night, *rais*, *nox* and *zar* entwined in a tornado of unrelenting power. My fingers clamped around the icy slab in an effort to ground myself in the oncoming tempest.

I could feel him again. His soul flitted just beyond my grasp.

Balen. His name formed on my lips.

The corpse arched off the slab with a choked gasp, eyes snapping open, milky and wide. A hoarse rattle escaped his mouth, a fragment of breath stolen from the veil between life and death.

His eyes locked on mine. Panic punched through my chest. His mouth moved, soundless. Then I felt it again.

His soul.

Only, now, it flooded through me. Too fast. Too much.

My knees buckled, but I couldn't pull away. My hands were locked onto the slab, light and shadow screaming inside me, and beneath it all, the inexorable pull of the *zar.*

A void opened. Hungry.

"Aelia!" Kaelith's voice was distant. "Let go!"

But I couldn't. I *didn't want to.*

I felt *powerful.* Infinite.

A scream tore from my throat, not of pain, but absolute ecstasy.

Then, a sharp crack echoed across the chamber, and the stone slab shattered beneath the force of the onslaught.

I felt shadows wrap around me like silken chains. Familiar shadows.

"*Enough,*" came the voice, cracking like a whip through the storm. *Reign.*

The cuorem pulsed, tearing through the haze of bleeding power and jerking me back from the grisly line I danced along.

My head whipped toward the doorway. My mate stood there, eyes ablaze, shadows flaring like wings of vengeance behind him. His jaw clenched, his stance brimming with fury as he took in the sight of me, eyes wild, breath ragged, and hands still burning with *zar.*

"Reign..." I croaked, but my voice wasn't my own. It was something *other*, laced with that all-consuming *zar.*

He crossed the room in seconds, grabbing my wrists and yanking me back from the crumbling slab. Light exploded in my chest, the mate bond fully roaring to life at his touch. His shadows poured into me, cutting through the darkness clinging to my soul. I gasped and collapsed into him.

The corpse fell limp behind us.

I trembled against his chest, clutching him as if he were the only thing tethering me to myself. And maybe he was…

"You're back," I whispered, tears streaking down my cheeks.

His arms tightened around me. "Just in time." He held me until the tremors stopped, until the last ounce of energy bled from my veins.

Then, with a quick kiss to my forehead, he released me. And launched himself at Kaelith.

"You bastard," he roared, slamming the Night Fae against the stone wall with enough force to crack it.

Kaelith didn't fight back. He just smirked, only adding to my mate's fury, until he rasped out, "She asked for it."

Disbelief surged across Reign's expression for just a moment, and a hint of guilt pierced my chest. I should have told him. His gaze darted to mine before refocusing on my Demon trainer.

"It doesn't matter," he growled. "You pushed her past her limit."

"She *needed* to be pushed."

Reign's fist slammed into his jaw.

"Reign, stop!" I shouted. "He's telling the truth."

Kaelith coughed, bloodied but grinning. "She was magnificent. You should've seen it."

"Don't talk about her like she's some experiment." Reign's voice vibrated with lethal rage; shadows rising like a tempest.

"I wasn't experimenting," Kaelith sneered. "I was preparing your mate to survive."

Reign's hand tightened around his throat. "If you push her again without my permission, I'll cut out your heart and feed it to Solanthus."

Kaelith's grin only widened. "You won't need to. Because next time, she'll do it herself."

Reign finally let go, letting Kae drop to the floor.

I watched them from where I knelt, still too weak to move, the last of the *zar* retreating from my fingertips. I didn't recognize the look on Kaelith's face as he pushed to stand. It was equal parts pride and warning as he watched me.

And I didn't know what scared me more. That I'd succeeded. Or that, for a moment... I'd *liked* it.

Chapter Forty-Three

R*eign*

Anger still roared through my veins, red-hot and all-consuming as I slid to the floor beside Aelia, framing her still too pale face with trembling hands. How dare that Night bastard push her like this?

"I already told you I asked him to," Aelia muttered, invading my thoughts.

"But why? Why would you want to delve into that sort of darkness, princess?"

"Because I have to, Reign. We all must do everything we can to win this war, to protect Aetheria. You gave up your own father, for goddess' sake. This is the least I can do."

Father. The word rang hollow.

I couldn't help my gaze from twisting over my shoulder to Kaelith who leaned against the wall, blood dribbling down his split lip. Gods, could it really be true? I thought I could push it back to deal with at a better time—if such a thing existed—but I needed to know the truth now that fate had brought him right to me. I couldn't live with this new doubt. I'd gone long enough without answers.

"Did you find it?" Aelia's hopeful gaze seared into me as she drew my eyes back to hers. "The Moirai Shard?"

I nodded slowly.

"Oh, thank Raysa!" Her smile grew more brilliant. "You did it, Reign, you really did it."

"I helped a little." Ruhl appeared in the archway, his typical smirk twisting his lips before he scanned the dark chamber. "What in all the realms happened in here?"

"Just a little training," Aelia replied weakly, and if I wasn't mistaken with a bit of embarrassment as well.

Wrapping her in my arms, I heaved her off the floor and deposited her onto a stone bench in the corner. "Stay here," I whispered. "There's something I need to discuss with Kaelith."

She reached for me, hand curling around my arm. "Reign, don't."

"I won't hurt him." I gently cupped her chin. "For once, this isn't about you, princess." I offered a reassuring smile before I turned toward the male leaning against the far wall.

My shadows surged, sharp and biting, coiling around Kaelith's throat in an instant.

He didn't flinch as he stepped forward. "Reign, so nice to see you again."

"Where were you?" I snarled, dragging him back against the stone wall. "Thirty fucking years ago, where were you?"

His eyes narrowed, not with challenge but with confusion. "What are you talking about?"

"You tell me." My jaw clenched as I shoved him back again. He hit the wall hard and slid down onto his knees, scraping the obsidian floor. He didn't rise this time. "You were holding me," I hissed. "In the vision. From the mirror. That was *you*."

Kaelith blinked once. Then again. His lips parted, but no words came.

"You were younger," I went on, breath coming fast. "Your

hair was shorter. Your face softer. You were standing beside a woman with long, dark hair, violet eyes. She was holding a baby swaddled in shadows. That baby was *me*."

The words felt foreign in my mouth, but my soul had known the truth the moment the image seared into my mind.

"What in Zaroth's name are you talking about?" he growled, tipping his head back to look up at me.

"I saw it! In the Mirror of Hidden Truths at the Lupherium in Lunaris."

He stared at me for a long beat, something like haunted recognition blooming behind his eyes. A long-forgotten memory coming to life. "Gods..." he whispered. "You saw that?"

"You're not going to deny it?"

"No." He rose slowly, brushing dust from his cloak. "Because it's true. That was me."

I said nothing, my heart pounding so hard I could feel it in my temples.

"The woman," he said carefully, "was Elaris."

I froze at the sound of my mother's name. At the words that confirmed everything... I couldn't remember the last time I'd heard it spoken aloud. The Shadow Court acted as if she'd never existed.

Noxus, it was all true then. This man was my father—

"She was my niece," Kaelith said softly, interrupting my wild thoughts.

The floor might as well have vanished beneath my boots.

"She brought her son—you—to me once. Just once." His voice thickened. "You were only days old, and so small. Your shadows were already active, wrapping around you both like they were afraid of the world. She never said who your father was. I begged her to stay, but she wouldn't. She said she had to protect you. That staying would only bring danger."

"And then what?" I demanded. "She just... vanished?"

Kaelith nodded slowly. "I never saw her again."

My fists clenched. "So all this time... gods, you're my uncle?"

His expression turned pained. "Your great-uncle, technically. My brother, Karnax, must have been your grandfather. He ruled the Night Court long before Helroth. A brutal male, but not a tyrant. He tried to keep the balance. When Helroth rose to power, he betrayed Karnax. Killed him. Stole his crown. And his mate."

"Vaelora," Aelia breathed, having somehow appeared beside me.

Kaelith's jaw tightened. "Your grandmother, Reign. Helroth took her as a prize. A warning. He sent Elaris away when she was only a child. She was nothing more than a reminder of Karnax, his greatest enemy."

The room spun.

My blood. My family. My whole life had been built on lies. Tenebris. The court. My supposed destiny. I could feel Ruhl's heavy gaze boring into me from across the room.

I wasn't just Night Fae and Shadow Fae. I was heir to a stolen throne. Aelia's throne...

"You didn't know?" I asked quietly.

Kaelith shook his head. "If I had... Reign, if I had known you were hers, I would've come for you. I raised Elaris after Karnax's death. She was like a daughter to me. I loved her. Then, during the chaos of the war, she disappeared. I feared she was dead, until she returned that day, with you in her arms."

My shadows writhed violently, seething with the cold pulse of *zar* and *nox* combined. Not out of hatred for Kaelith, but for what had been taken. From my mother. From me. From him.

"You swear that's the truth?" I asked through gritted teeth.

"I swear it on Zaroth," he replied, solemn and raw. "I would've stormed the Shadow Fortress myself, scoured it from top to bottom had I known you were there. Had I known you were in Tenebris's clutches. I would have done anything to keep you and your mother safe, Reign. *Anything.*"

I staggered back a step, trying to breathe. Aelia's hand found mine, fingers tangling between my own.

All this time, I'd thought my fight with Helroth was simply about Aelia and the damned prophecy.

But it was so much more than that. This was about blood. Family. Revenge.

"I'm going to kill him," I said quietly. "Not just for the realm. Not just for my mate. But for Karnax. For Elaris. For Vaelora. I'll burn his kingdom to ash if I must."

Kaelith didn't argue. Didn't warn me against such foolishness. He simply bowed his head and murmured, "Then let me help you."

The balcony where I often came as a child to avoid my father jutted out from one of the highest spires of the Fortress of Umbral Shadows. It stood hidden behind sweeping obsidian arches that caught the moonlight and scattered it across the marble floor. I leaned against the balustrade, trying and failing to still my spiraling thoughts. Above, the stars burned bright, seemingly close enough to touch, their light weaving with the soft glow of the warding runes etched into the balcony's railings. A cool breeze carried the scent of rain and the faint sweetness of night-blooming flowers from the royal gardens below. It felt like the world was hushed and waiting.

But my mind was utter chaos.

Helroth had killed my grandfather, banished my mother, imprisoned my grandmother... Gods, it was too much. A heady surge of *zar* surged through my veins, coiling like deadly serpents. The flood of power was overwhelming, intoxicating.

Had Tenebris known who my mother was? And how had she ended up in the Shadow Court to begin with? And, the question weighing on me most: what became of her?

Noxus, if only I knew where the realms my father was so that I could finally get the answers I deserved.

"There you are..." Aelia's soft voice splintered through the agony waging havoc in my mind, breaking through when no one else could. She slipped her arms around my waist, resting her chin on my shoulder blade as we stared out over the slumbering realm. "Are you hiding from me?" she whispered into the folds of my cloak, her worry leeching through our bond.

"No." I heaved out a breath, the fury and overpowering *zar* receding at her touch. "Never you." And I meant it. I simply wasn't ready—or even knew how—to talk about the turmoil in my mind.

She began to hum, the familiar tune soaking into my very bones.

"Sleep, my starlight, soft and bright,
Drift on dreams through silver night.
Moonlight hums a tender tune,
I'll find you 'neath the fading moon."

The cuorem pulsed between us and the words suddenly filled my mind. Like a man possessed, my lips moved, singing the lullaby I didn't know I remembered. It was the one memory I had of my mother, her sweet voice cradling me in the darkness.

I whirled around, pulling Aelia into my arms. "Did you do that?"

She shrugged. "Possibly... I'm not quite certain. I was trying to remember the words to Vaelora's song and, somehow, together, we must have brought them to the surface."

I tugged her ever closer, holding her more firmly against my weary form. "Thank you," I whispered across the top of her head, pressing my lips to her forehead.

"There's something else I remembered from my chats with Vaelora, something she told me about her daughter."

My entire body tensed at the pinch of her brows, at the

anxiety racing through our bond. I pulled back to look at her. "Tell me."

"Vaelora once told me her daughter was taken prisoner by the Shadow Fae during the war. She heard rumors... ones that claimed she'd been made a slave by the king."

Not a servant as I'd surmised, but a slave. A low snarl built in my throat. My fists clenched at my sides, every muscle in my body tightening with fury.

Tenebris.

Of course it had been him. My father had kidnapped my mother. Enslaved and impregnated her. Then what? Had he banished her or had she simply abandoned me?

The air thickened with *nox*, shadows bleeding from my skin like wrath made tangible. Aelia's hand on my chest served to anchor me, her soft presence a balm to the storm raging in my blood.

Gods, I wasn't sure how I'd survive any of this without her.

"I swear it, Aelia," I ground out, my voice rough with fury. "I will discover the truth. Whatever Tenebris did to her... wherever he kept her..."

"I know you will," she whispered, and I felt her faith in me, her love. It surged through me as powerful as the anger and determination. It bolstered me. Gave me strength.

"And Helroth..." My eyes blazed as I turned back toward the sea of stars. "I'll rip him apart for what he did to my grandfather, to Vaelora, to Kaelith. To you. For what he stole from all of them. From all of us. I'm going to find Helroth and free my grandmother from that monster's grasp if it's the last gods' damned thing I do. He will never harm you or anyone else that is *mine* again."

The oath settled over me like iron. Heavy. Final. Binding.

This wasn't just about surviving the war or keeping Aelia safe anymore, though she would always be my priority. This... this was about legacy. My grandfather's. My mother's. And maybe, someday, my own.

Aelia's hands framed my face, her thumbs brushing the tension from my jaw. "Then we'll do it together," she whispered. "All of it. We'll make them pay."

I leaned into her touch, my heart hammering so loud I could feel it in my throat. "Just... not tonight."

Her brows drew together in quiet concern. "Reign?"

"I've missed you terribly, and I need to forget," I rasped. "Just for a little while. The blood. The pain. The gods' damned truths I never asked for." My hands skimmed down her arms, fingers tightening at her waist. "Make me forget, starlight. For a few hours, let it be just us. No courts. No thrones. No war."

Emotion flashed in her eyes, fierce and full of love. She rose onto her tiptoes and pressed her lips to mine.

The cuorem ignited between us, not in an eager frenzy, but in salvation as I deepened the kiss, tangling my fingers in her hair.

Because I knew in her arms, I would find peace. In her kiss, I would find purpose. And in her love, I'd find the strength to face whatever hell would come next.

Chapter Forty-Four

A *elia*

The moonlight caressed my bare shoulders as I ambled through the nightbloom gardens, the air heavily perfumed by the exotic flora. It was early and most of the inhabitants of the fortress still slept, pleasantly unaware of the new ancestral discoveries we'd made, or the ramifications they would bring.

After Reign and I had spent hours tangled in each other with our bodies moving as one, and the cuorem had finally been temporarily satiated, he'd confessed that today he would approach the Shadow generals to take a more active role in the upcoming war.

We still had the Ebonshard Compass, after all, and with it, we had the power to find Helroth. Now that Reign knew his grandmother lived, and under Helroth's control, no less, he wished to move immediately.

But with the tumultuous state of Reign's arrival, and the subsequent lifechanging discoveries, he'd yet to show me the legendary Moirai Shard, or give me many—or any—details of its recovery. He'd mentioned the encounters with the Wolvryn, and bits and pieces of their journey, but I still had no idea how exactly they'd acquired the mystical artifact, how it worked, or how the blood vow would be broken.

I had assumed he would wish to break the blood vow before moving against Helroth, and now with the Shard we could. Vaelora was his family, after all, and I understood his desire to rescue her as soon as possible.

A flicker of movement caught my attention near the edge of the reflecting pool, and I turned just in time to see a shadow detach itself from the hedges. Ruhl stepped into the moonlight, his black tunic rumpled and his hair wind tousled as if he'd just flown in, or as if he hadn't slept at all. Judging by the weariness etched into the lines around his eyes, it might have been both.

"You're up early," he said, voice low.

I offered a small smile. "So are you. Aren't you tired after that excursion to Lunaris?"

He shrugged. "I figured I'd steal a moment of quiet before Reign hauls me into yet another war council."

I shifted toward him, brushing my fingers along the petals of a deep violet blossom. "So, how was Lunaris? I still haven't heard about everything that happened." My gaze flicked to his, the question lingering in the silence between us. "Or how the Moirai Shard works."

His brows lifted slightly, clearly surprised. "Reign hasn't told you?"

I shook my head. "Not in full. Only that it exists. That you found it. And that it can break the vow."

Ruhl exhaled slowly, scrubbing a hand through his hair. "It's not that simple."

My stomach dipped. "It never is, is it?"

He looked away, jaw tightening, as if he wished my *cuoré* had imparted this knowledge to me instead. "There was a priestess. A servant of Selraya, the Moon Goddess. She didn't stop us from taking the Shard, but she did leave us with a warning." His voice grew quieter. "The Moirai Shard doesn't just sever bonds. It rewrites fate. But to do that, a thread must be cut."

My throat constricted. "What does that even mean?"

Ruhl's gaze met mine, solemn and shadowed. "She said a sacrifice is required. One we can't predict. That the Shard will choose what needs to be given up when it's used. It doesn't ask permission. It just takes."

A hush fell over the garden, the only sound the soft rustle of nightbloom leaves in the breeze and the sudden frantic thrumming in my chest. The Moirai Shard wasn't the key to our salvation. No. It was simply another blade. And someone, Reign, me, or maybe this realm, would bleed when it was drawn.

No wonder Reign hadn't told me yet. He likely had it in his stubborn head to do something stupidly selfless to save me.

"And if the price is too high?" I asked, the question tearing from me in a hoarse whisper. "What then?"

"I don't know," he admitted. I could feel the hurt behind his words. "But it's the only way we've found to truly break the blood vow. There's no other option, besides the one I offered before."

Having Ruhl assume the vow wasn't an option. Not a real one. The future king of the Court of Umbral Shadows couldn't just abandon his kingdom for me. I wouldn't let him.

I stared out at the glowing pool, my reflection rippling in the water, half in shadow, half in moonlight. The child of twilight.

Of course the Shard would demand a price. Power like that never came freely. Not even for someone like me, cursed with abilities she never asked for. Powerful beyond anything the realms had ever seen.

"Do you think the Moirai Shard will take him?" My voice shook. "Reign?"

Ruhl didn't answer right away. Instead, he stepped closer and placed a hand on my shoulder. "I think it will take whatever costs us the most. That's how fate works, isn't it?"

I closed my eyes, fighting the sting of tears. I wouldn't give him up. I simply wasn't capable. "Then we better be ready," I finally murmured, choking back the building sob. "Because if the Shard demands more than we can give, we'll have to decide—"

"How far we're willing to go to win this war," Ruhl finished for me.

I nodded, the weight of his words pressing deep into my chest. And for the first time in weeks, I wondered if we were truly ready for what was to come.

Because fate was cruel. And sacrifices were always steep.

"And not to make this just about me, but..." A flicker of mirth danced in Ruhl's dark eyes. "I can only serve as temporary king for so long before I must undertake the Ritual of the Shadow Throne. Otherwise, some other arrogant Shadow Fae lord, a far worse candidate than me with some distant claim to the throne, may come to fight me for it. Clearly, that would not be ideal during a war."

"Raysa, no, it wouldn't." I heaved out a breath, fighting the small smile at his feeble attempt at lightening the mood. "And what exactly does the ritual encompass?"

He grunted, rolling his eyes. "It's an overly complicated sacred rite passed down through generations of the Shadow Court to prove a prince's worth and bind him to the realm." He waved a dismissive hand. "It begins with a rare celestial event, then there's a trial, a binding of the crown, and, finally, culminates with the coronation at the Obsidian Lake. There I must stand before the mystical waters to determine what kind of king I will become. If the reflection accepts me, the waters will rise and cloak me in a royal mantle of living shadow, thereby crowning me as king. But if it does not deem me worthy, I'll be pulled into its murky depths, never to be seen again."

"Good gods, that sounds awful."

"And you wondered why I offered myself as the substitute..." He grinned, but a hint of worry flashed across those bottomless pitch irises. He was clearly more concerned about this ritual than he wanted to let on.

"Surely, this mystical lake will find you worthy, Ruhl." I stepped forward, placing my hands on his shoulders, needing him to hear the truth in my words. "You will be the greatest king this court has ever seen. At least ten times the ruler your father ever was."

"At least he set the bar low."

"Don't do that." I shook my head with a rueful smile. He truly didn't believe himself worthy and that gutted me.

"Do what, duskling?" He cocked his head to the side so that the stars twinkled in his eyes.

"Belittle yourself like that. We never would have come this far without you. You are the reason the Shadow and Light Court soldiers are here today, together and united. That's a tremendous accomplishment, Ruhl, not something to make light of. Those men already look up to you as their leader." I gave his shoulders a squeeze. "Undertaking the ritual now may not be ideal, but it could help to solidify the realm. Don't be afraid. You are *more* than worthy."

A slow smile crept across his lips. "Your faith in me, though very likely misplaced, means the world to me, princess."

For once, he used my title not in a mocking tone, not as a way to poke fun at his brother's pet name for me, but rather in what seemed like real reverence.

"In case you've forgotten," he added, growing serious once more, "there's also that pesky premonition from our trial last year. The one that said I'd never claim the Shadow Throne."

Now, it was my turn to wave a dismissive hand. "Prophecies can be fickle things, and we all know it's in the specific wording. Perhaps you won't claim it, maybe it'll simply fall into your lap. Or maybe it'll claim you."

He shook his head, the ghost of a smile twitching at his lips. "I certainly hope you're right, duskling." With that, he turned toward the pathway leading back to the fortress, holding out his arm in invitation. "Come on, we better get back inside before Reign comes out to hunt you down."

A laugh bubbled up as the truth of his words hit me. I'd just felt him stir through the bond, and Ruhl was right, even half-conscious, my mate was already searching for me. I only hoped when the time came, Helroth would be as easy to find.

An hour later and we were all seated in the war room. The table had been cleared of scrolls and war maps, save for one object that now held every eye in the chamber, the Ebonshard Compass. The face was a liquid mirror, reflective and shifting, emitting faint, eerie whispers. At its center, a shard of pure ebony crystal floated, pulsing with a crimson glow. The ancient artifact hovered inches above the polished obsidian table, spinning slowly, as if it could already sense its quarry.

Reign stood at the head of the room, hands braced on the edge of the table with Aidan by his side, the ever-faithful general. The full weight of Reign's presence pressed into every corner. Shadows clung to him like night, but his voice was clear and steady.

"It's time," he said simply. "We stop waiting. We stop hiding. We take the fight to Helroth."

The silence that followed was thick. Oppressive.

Aidan leaned forward, his eyes narrowed. "And if he sees us coming? Like when we rescued Aelia?"

"I don't care," Reign bit out. "He has Vaelora. My grandmother. And we've delayed long enough. We have the Compass and the Shard. Why not use them to our advantage? We can track him no matter where he runs. We can use the Shard to break the blood vows. No more waiting for him to strike first, to come after our courts or *my mate*."

A ripple of unease passed through the generals at the far end of the table. One of them, Commander Varek, tapped his fingers against the table's edge. "We've strengthened our forces, yes. But we still don't know the full extent of his army. Or their *zar*. Attacking blindly could cost us everything."

Reign's jaw flexed. "It's not blind. The Compass will lead us directly to him. And the longer we wait, the stronger he becomes. He's already sent his troops after us. He's wormed his way into Aelia's mind, and I won't let him get away with it again. He's watching. Listening. Every breath we take is another invitation for him to strike first."

I met Reign's eyes across the room. The cuorem pulsed softly, the storm of his resolve bleeding into me. And Gods, I knew he was right. I, too, was tired of waiting.

Ruhl let out a breath from beside him, arms crossed. "And what about the Shard? Do we use it before the assault? After?"

Reign hesitated, just barely, but I caught it. "We wait. We hold it until we know it's needed. If Helroth tries to activate the blood vow he has over Aelia, then we use it."

"And what if the price is too high?" Aidan asked grimly.

Reign's shadows stirred. "Then I'll pay it."

I swallowed hard, fighting the urge to shout across the room. To tell him he couldn't just offer himself up like a lamb to slaughter. But I knew this wasn't the time. Not here. Not in front of the others.

But we would definitely discuss it in private.

Silence fell again, and for a moment, I feared they would still deny him. That the council would once again vote for caution over action. That they'd let fear blind them to the danger at our doorstep.

Then Aidan's hand struck the table, the vibration resonating across the room. "We strike," he said, his voice like steel. "In two days' time. Let the bastard see us coming."

Commander Varek exchanged a glance with the other generals before nodding once. "It's risky, but the troops have come a long way. And I agree, we can't wait forever."

Ruhl smirked faintly, though there was little amusement behind it. "Guess we better start packing."

Relief surged through the bond as Reign's shoulders finally dropped a fraction. He met my gaze once more, the fire in his eyes no longer just fury, but hope.

And a hint of fear.

Because now that we'd set the plan in motion, there was no turning back.

Chapter Forty-Five

A *elia*

"After all this time, who knew you were a real prince?" I smirked up at Reign from the silky sheets of our bed, allowing the gentle rise and fall of his chest beneath my cheek soothe the turmoil of the past few weeks.

Pale moonlight cast through his dark hair, streaking it in strands of shimmering silver as he glanced down at me. He snorted on a laugh, leisurely running his fingers through my locks as if we had all the time in the world. "I'm no prince, starlight. As it turns out, I'm the forgotten heir of a usurped throne."

Clucking my tongue, I moved on top of him, meeting him square in the eyes and trying my damnedest to ignore the way his naked body reacted to my own. "A throne that rightly belonged to your grandfather and that Helroth stole." I shrugged. "Besides, I've got two already, I'm more than happy to give you one."

A deep chuckle, warm and true—something I'd gone far too long without hearing—rumbled through his chest, vibrating against my own. "How kind of you to offer me the key to one of our kingdoms."

"It's the least I can do after all you've done for me." I grinned before pressing my lips to his parted ones. "My love, my *cuoré*."

"You know," he mumbled against my mouth, "that my desire to kill Helroth has nothing to do with claiming the Court of Infernal Night's throne, right?"

I pulled back with a frustrated sigh, my entire body humming from the faint brush of our lips. "Of course I do."

"Good." His arms encircled my waist, pressing me flush against the length of his unyielding frame.

Once more trying to focus on something other than the firm, muscled body beneath me, I asked, "How do you feel about all of it? In all the commotion, the preparations for battle, we haven't had a moment to discuss the revelations."

Reign hissed out a slow breath between his teeth. "I'm afraid it's more than I care to handle at the moment. Right now, my main concern is you, then ridding the realm of Helroth. Everything else can wait."

A heavy silence descended between us for a long moment. The weight of the realms, of our choices, sometimes seemed too much to bear.

"I love you," I finally breathed before claiming his lips once more. There was so much more to discuss—the Moirai Shard, the elephant in the room that both of us refused to speak of. Breaking the blood vow would come at too steep of a price, I was certain of it.

And where would that leave us?

Still at the merciless hands of Tenebris.

But I decided now wasn't the time to fixate on that. Tonight, I was the one in need of forgetting, because in two short days, we'd go to war, and I feared nothing would ever be the same.

"Make love to me," I whispered.

His breath hitched. It was a quiet sound, but I felt it everywhere. In the tightening of his arms, in the stillness of his body beneath mine, in the soft tremor of the cuorem echoing against my own heart.

"Aelia..." My name left his lips like a prayer and a curse all at once, reverent and raw.

"I need to feel something that isn't war," I murmured, fingers trailing down his chest. "Something that isn't death or prophecy or gods' damned sacrifice."

His hands slid up my back, slow and reverent, like he was trying to memorize every curve, every piece of me he'd fought so hard to keep. "You are everything I feel," he said, voice rough and thick with emotion. "You are the only thing that's ever felt real."

The tears that stung my eyes weren't from sadness, but from the unbearable weight of love. Of hope. Of the fragile, precious thing we held between us.

He rolled us gently, reversing our positions until he hovered over me, dark hair falling in a silken veil around our faces. The stars watched in silence through the tall windows, and for a moment, it felt as if the whole realm had paused just for us.

"I will never let anything take you from me," he whispered, brushing his lips against my brow, then down to the hollow of my throat. "Not Helroth. Not Tenebris. Not fate."

My fingers gripped his shoulders, anchoring myself to the only certainty I had left. "Then show me," I breathed. "Show me we're still us. That no one can steal this away despite all we must still overcome."

And he did.

His hips fit perfectly between my thighs as he lined himself up against my entrance. A gasp parted my lips at the heady sensations. I burned for him, every inch of my body begging to be closer, to be one. He thrust into me with a desperate grace, like he'd been searching his whole life for the place he belonged, and he'd found it... in me. As we moved against each other, we were two halves finally made whole once again, destined to fit in the spaces only we could fill.

With every touch, every whispered word, he unraveled me. It

was both tender and fierce at the same time. Shadows danced across our skin, not as weapons, but as worship, wrapping us in a cocoon of moonlit midnight.

There was no prophecy in that moment. No vow. No war.

Only love. Only *us*.

And when we finally shattered, together, trembling and breathless in each other's arms, I clung to the hope that it would be enough.

Enough to survive the storm still coming. Enough to bring us back whole when it was all over.

Even if the Moirai demanded everything.

I woke before Reign began to stir, the ache of goodbye still echoing in my bones. Last night with my *cuoré* had been *everything*, simultaneously healing and grounding, but even love couldn't stop the war from creeping in.

A restless energy surged through the barracks before training exercises began, Light and Shadow students and soldiers milling about, awaiting orders from the generals. It had been decided that only a small force would accompany us to track down the Night King with the Ebonshard Compass. We hoped, somehow, we could end this war before it began.

Perhaps, we were foolish.

Perhaps, we were already too late.

The tension in the air was a living, breathing thing, pressing into every conversation, sharpening every glance. I weaved between groups of warriors gathering their weapons and armor, giving encouraging smiles and words to both Light and Shadow, all while my thoughts drifted toward the Ebonshard Compass pulsing quietly in the war room.

If it worked and led us to Helroth without him seeing us coming, we might end this before it truly began. But that was a mighty *if*.

I turned a corner, almost walking into Liora who spun on her heel with a start at my approach, her vibrant green eyes just a bit too wide before she smoothed her expression. She stood with Rue and Symon, the unlikely threesome whispering together, off to the side. Something unreadable flashed across my best friend's expression as she gave me a quick smile, but I couldn't decipher it before Liora spoke, drawing my attention.

"Aelia," she purred. "There you are. I was just asking if it's true, are you really going after Helroth tomorrow?"

I blinked at the question, thrown by her sudden boldness. "Yes…" I replied slowly, watching the way her fingers twisted in the folds of her tunic. "Ruhl and the generals have agreed. We leave at dawn."

Symon whistled low under his breath, arms crossed as he leaned back against a carved obsidian column. "About damn time."

"I thought the goal was to train the Light and Shadow forces to fight together," Liora said.

My brows drew together. "It still is. But we can't delay any longer. Why?"

Her lips curved into a smile that didn't quite reach her eyes. "Just worried for you, that's all. Facing Helroth sounds like a death sentence with such a small force, even with Reign by your side." Her voice held a strange undercurrent, and for a moment, I couldn't tell if it was concern or veiled mockery.

Before I could respond, Rue stepped forward and looped her arm through mine, a too-bright smile on her face. "Actually, I'm glad we ran into you. I was about to visit Heaton. He's still not himself, but I thought maybe a friendly face might help."

At the mention of Heaton, my stomach tightened. Guilt still clawed at me. I'd been so wrapped in war councils and Reign's unraveling heritage that I hadn't checked on him often since his return.

"Yes," I blurted. "I would love to see him."

Rue led us down the spiraling hall to the lower wing of the

infirmary, where the air was thick with warding runes and the tang of herbs. The scent of blood and burn salves lingered beneath it all.

She gently pushed open the door, with Sy and, unfortunately, Liora, following behind as I stepped into the dim chamber. Heaton lay on a narrow cot, his wrists bound loosely with light-woven thread to prevent him from harming himself. And others. His skin was pale, clammy, and a sheen of sweat coated his brow. His lips moved faintly, whispering words I couldn't hear.

"Still like this?" I whispered, my heart aching for my best friend and her brother.

Rue nodded. "He has good days and bad. Mostly bad. He doesn't sleep. He talks about darkness, about voices in his head. The Night Court broke something in him."

Symon moved to the other side of Heaton's bed and crouched down, murmuring something low and comforting.

Liora, however, lingered by the door with her arms folded, and her gaze oddly blank.

Heaton stirred, his head shifting toward the sound of our voices. For a moment, I thought he'd drift back into unconsciousness. Instead, his eyes snapped open. The moment his gaze landed on Liora, the wild flicker in his eyes went cold. Deadly cold and, for the first time in a long time, lucid.

Everyone froze.

"Heaton?" I murmured, inching closer, scared to frighten him after our last encounter.

His whispers halted, cut off by a silence so thick I could hear my own pulse.

Then, in a voice clearer than I'd heard in weeks, Heaton muttered, "She doesn't belong here."

All eyes turned in his direction. But his gaze was locked on Liora. "She walks in light, but she was born in darkness. A child of moonless blood. A liar. A traitor."

The words hit like a thunderclap.

Rue gasped, and the blood iced over in my veins.

Liora's face didn't change. Not even a twitch. "That's enough," she said lightly, stepping closer. "Poor Heaton. He gets worse by the day, doesn't he?"

"*He* sees truth," Heaton hissed, straining against his bonds. "She carries shade in her veins. Night Fae. *She's* one of *them*."

My thoughts flickered back to Heaton's last outburst weeks ago, when he'd lunged at me. He'd called me *infantum od twilit*. He may have been confused and frantic, but he hadn't been wrong. I *was* the child of twilight. I was everything he'd claimed.

"Stop it," Liora said, with a laugh that sounded far too forced. "He's clearly not in his right mind."

Symon turned slowly to face her, his usual easy-going smile absent. "You're not denying it."

She blinked. "Of course, I am. Gods, Symon. Are we really going to take the word of a broken soldier?"

But there was a faint tremble in her hands.

I stepped forward, heart pounding. "Liora," I said carefully, "is there something you want to tell us?"

She gave me a tight smile. "Only that your enemies are getting cleverer. They know how to twist even the most loyal minds into saying exactly what will tear you apart." And with that, she turned on her heel and swept from the room.

Could Helroth or some other Night Fae have skulked into Heaton's mind to sow the seeds of doubt and break us from within?

I stared after her, unease coiling in my chest like a snake.

Was Heaton delusional? Or had he just seen something the rest of us had missed?

Rue touched my arm, drawing my attention. "I told you. There's always been something off about her..."

"I don't know," I whispered, unable to take my eyes from the spot the female had just vacated. "But I intend to find out."

Because if Liora truly was one of them, and she'd been in our midst all this time, then Helroth wasn't just watching from afar.

He'd been here all along.

Chapter Forty-Six

R*eign*

In the quiet hours before dawn, I stole across the silent chamber where my *cuoré* still slept, to the armoire in the back of the room. A faint glow seeped through the doors, pulsing with energy. Steeling myself, I wrenched the dark timber open for the first time since Ruhl and I'd returned with the cursed artifact.

The Moirai Shard hung shimmering in the air, suspended between the crescent moons, one crafted of the darkest obsidian and the other of the purest alabaster moonstone. Power thrummed in the air, pushing against the *nox* and *zar* slithering over my skin. How could something so beautiful, so ethereal be the cause of such turmoil?

I'd barely slept last night, too consumed by what the dawn would bring. Would today be the day I'd be forced to use the Shard to sever the blood vow? If I failed, I wouldn't just lose Aelia. I'd be the blade Tenebris drove through her heart. I winced as the priestess's words echoed through my mind.

"When the Shard is used to break a bond woven by gods, there is always a sacrifice."

"What kind of sacrifice?" I rasped, throat tight.

"That is not for me to say. The Moirai choose. But a thread must be cut, so another may be spun."

Banishing the dismal thoughts, I slipped the shard into my cloak, then carefully closed the doors of the armoire and turned toward the balcony. The one in which Aelia and I had spent hours upon last night, staring up into the moonlit sky as I claimed her again and again, the cuorem surging with power between us.

But now that time was over. As soon as the sun crested the peaks of the Alucian range in the Court of Ethereal Light, we would move. And I had no idea what we would find on the other end of that Compass.

Aelia had recounted the details of the odd encounter with Heaton and Liora, but still, I refused to believe it. If Liora had been lying to us from the beginning, then the traitor hadn't just breached our defenses. They'd slept beneath our roof. Trained with us. Fought beside us. That kind of betrayal didn't just sting, it could cost us the war. And I couldn't help but wonder, if it were true, how could I have been so blind to it?

I vowed not to repeat that mistake again today. I'd already assigned Ruhl with the task of keeping an eye on her. Surely, that would keep my half-brother out of trouble, too. Gods knew, alone, they both had the uncanny ability to find trouble, but together? They *were* trouble.

As I stared out into the sleeping court below us, my thoughts circled back to the last time I'd used the Compass, to bring my Aelia home. Would we be forced to cross through the Nyxian Gate once again as we had last time? Or would the mystical compass require some other sacrifice?

So many ancient artifacts, and every one of them thirsting for blood. The gods certainly did enjoy playing their games.

A rustle of sheets behind me drew my attention. Aelia stirred in the massive bed, the brilliant moonlight bleeding softly across her bare shoulders, painting her in pale blue and shadow. My heart clenched at the sight. I would carve entire realms in half to preserve this version of her—safe, whole, and unburdened by the war that waited just beyond our walls.

Her eyes fluttered open, heavy with sleep, and landed on me. "Mmm... you're brooding again," she murmured, her voice warm and still husky with dreams.

I managed a small smile and padded back toward the bed, sinking down beside her. "Is it that obvious?"

"To me?" She propped herself up on one elbow, the sheet slipping low along her back. "Always."

My fingers found hers where they rested on the mattress, curling gently. "We leave soon."

She nodded, eyes searching mine—for what, I wasn't sure. "I know."

The silence that followed wasn't just heavy, it was reverent. Like we both understood we were standing on the edge of something that could either shatter or save us. And neither of us dared break it just yet.

"I'm ready," she whispered after a beat, squeezing my hand. "For whatever comes."

Before I could answer, a pulse of cold wind shivered through the room, followed by the familiar pounding of wings.

It's time. Phantom's voice slid through my mind like silk. Her presence rippled along the edge of my thoughts like an icy tide pulling back from the shore.

"I know," I replied loud enough she could hear through the open window before I rose to my feet, meeting my mate's eyes. "We'll be down shortly."

Aelia sat up fully now, drawing the sheet around her bare form like armor. She stared at me for a long moment before rising too, uncaring of the chill, of the war, of the world.

Just us.

She stepped into my arms, pressing her forehead to mine as I bent down to her. "We end this today. Do you hear me? We win. For the courts. For us. I will accept nothing else."

I swallowed hard and nodded, breathing her in like I could bottle her scent to carry with me through the battle. "I love you," I whispered, my voice low and firm. "No matter what the Moirai demand. That doesn't change."

"Then let's make sure they don't take anything we aren't willing to give," she said fiercely, pulling back.

I nodded, letting my shadows curl gently around her waist in silent agreement.

With my *cuoré* by my side, I was ready. Ready for whatever waited on the other side of the Compass.

✕

The Shadow courtyard was a hive of motion and energy, the sky streaked with the first rays of sunlight across the Luminoc River as our crew assembled at the base of the obsidian spire. Armor glinted in the pale light. Wings flapped. Hooves clattered against stone. Even the wind felt different today, sharper, hungrier.

Phantom landed first from her perch high atop the fortress, her shadow-wreathed wings unfurling with a thunderous beat that shook the entire keep. She lowered her massive head, onyx eyes locking on me with knowing focus.

Ready, my prince? The grin in her voice sailed across our bond. I wasn't certain I loved my new title.

"Not even close," I muttered, my shadows flaring into wings, lifting me easily onto her back.

Solanthus landed beside her a moment later with a blast of golden flame and heat, his tremendous sun-kissed form inciting gasps from the surrounding Light and Shadow warriors alike. Aelia flew onto his back a heartbeat later, flashing me a reassuring smile as she settled between the glittering golden scales of his wing bones. With only that smile, I felt the steady thrum of the cuorem press into my spine, her strength, her love, her confidence and trust pouring into me like sunlight through storm clouds.

Rue, clad in full golden armor with her braid whipping behind her like a banner, climbed up on Windy next. "You look like you've barely slept," she called up to me, never one for decorum.

"Sleep is for the living," I replied.

She laughed. "Let's hope we still qualify come tomorrow."

Behind her, Symon soared in on Griff, his hippogriff screeching as it banked hard and circled once before landing. The hybrid beast of talons and hooves kicked up dust as it settled, always a little more dramatic than necessary, much like its rider.

"Just went out for a quick hunt this morning," he explained.

"Someone was a little on edge," Rue added with a teasing smile.

Then came Liora, crimson wings aglow as her phoenix blazed overhead like a comet, its cry splitting the dawn. Her expression was unreadable, and for a moment, I felt that familiar flicker of unease. Ruhl had promised to keep an eye on her. I prayed he still was.

Speaking of the devil, Mordrin swooped in next, his scales gleaming like steel dipped in moonlight. Ruhl gave a lazy salute from his dragon's back before landing beside us.

Aidan and Kaelith moved between the troops, confirming each member of our unit had both a skyrider and weapons at the ready. The small unit of Light and Shadow soldiers assembled quickly, following their inspection, each with a mount of their own; pegasi, hippogriffs, and gryphons from the Conservatory of Luce. A force small enough to move quickly, but powerful enough to strike with precision.

I reached into my cloak and drew out the Compass. It pulsed in my hand like a living, breathing thing. The floating shard at its center spun slowly, drinking in the early morning moonlight. Whispers curled at the edges of my thoughts, teasing, taunting. I tuned them out and pressed my palm flat against the crystal.

The Compass flared.

Light and shadow exploded outward in twin rings. The artifact lifted into the air just as it had last time, spinning faster and faster until it suddenly jerked forward. The shard at its core pointed due northeast, into the skies above the Bloodhollow Mountains.

Everyone fell silent as the Compass stilled, the pull undeniable.

"That's where we go," I said, voice steady despite every fear, every hope, and every doubt rolling through me. "Helroth's waiting."

Phantom rumbled beneath me, her wings shifting in anticipation. *Then let's not make him wait any longer.*

Without another word, I dug my heels into her flank, and she launched into the sky with Aelia aboard Solanthus right behind me. Wind screamed past us as the others followed, an entire storm of wings and fury soaring toward the end of this war.

Toward Helroth. Toward fate.

Chapter Forty-Seven

Dread coiled low and tight in my belly as we soared over the Bloodhollow Mountains. I brushed the hilts of my daggers, needing the comfort of their presence, the familiar feel of them at my side bringing a sense of calm. The crystals pulsed with energy with each brush of my fingertips. Light crackled and shadows followed, twisting through their cores, refracting into a million brilliant stars. For the first time in a long while, I once again considered the gemstones' cryptic origins. Where had they come from, and what could they really do? It seemed to serve as a conduit for my hybrid powers, but had it served its *true* purpose yet?

A mystery for another day.

Are you ready, little Kin? Sol's voice growled through my subconscious.

This time, my hand closed around the hilt of my blade, and

searching the trove of powers that dwelled deep in my core, I allowed the trio of energies to flow through me. *I am.*

Good, because I am afraid that Helroth will not go quietly to rest in Noxus's eternal embrace.

Of course he wouldn't. Huffing out a breath, I pressed my other palm to Sol's scales, allowing the heat to warm the ice coating my veins. *A part of me foolishly hopes I can reason with him.*

Does your mate know that?

No...

Plumes of smoke lifted from Sol's nostrils as he snorted. *That will go over well.*

I was just hoping that, somehow, I could get through to him. He is my mother's father, after all. There has to be some good in him, right?

I didn't know your mother well, little Kin, but judging by the female you've become, she must have been an incredible Fae. And those are rarely forged in darkness alone.

Unexpected emotion tightened my throat. It wasn't often Sol doled out compliments. *Thank you, Sol.*

Now is not the time to get all weepy-eyed, princess.

Blinking quickly to banish the tears, I steeled myself and focused on the task at hand. *Of course not, I wouldn't think of it.*

The cuorem thrummed beneath my skin, a twist of fury and anxiety surging through the bond diverting my attention to Reign. He rode beside us, the tips of Phantom's wings nearly brushing Sol's with each powerful thrust. Mordrin, instead, wisely kept his distance, with Ruhl bringing up the rear of our troop.

Are you all right? I sent the thought through the mystical ties that bound us, despite the rush of dread zipping in both directions.

Mmm. Just anxious to have this over with. He glanced down at the Compass in his hand, the tendon across his jaw fluttering.

I want to try to talk to him, Reign.

To whom?

To my grandfather, of course.

His head whipped in my direction, fear and anger pulsing the dark depths of his gaze. *You can't be serious?*

What if I can stop this without any more bloodshed?

You can't! *This is the Night King. He's intent upon ravaging all of Aetheria, destroying Light and Shadow until only Night remains.* A wave of shadows consumed my mate, his powers surging to the surface, but I refused to allow it to deter me.

With your father missing and King Elian's forces divided, maybe we can find another way.

On the contrary, Helroth has created the perfect scenario for his complete and utter conquest of the realm.

I have to try.

Reign's shadows extended, curling across his shoulders until they morphed into wings. Thrusting off Phantom's back, he appeared beside me a moment later, settling in behind me. "Aelia, this is madness," he hissed into my ear.

Why is your cuoré on my back? Sol's jagged growl rushed through my mind.

Sorry, just give us a moment. I shot the thought back with anything but apology in my tone.

Canting my head over my shoulder, I glared at my infuriating mate. "Do you trust me or not?"

"Of course I do. But I also love you and want to protect you above anything else. Going to Helroth waving a white flag with efforts at diplomacy will ruin our chances at catching him off guard." He reached for me, hand cradling my cheek. "Please, starlight, allow me the chance to exact the revenge I deserve. For taking you away from me, for killing my grandfather... Helroth deserves no mercy." The haunted look in his eyes, the tremor racing through his form where it pressed against mine, stole my resolve. He was right. Reign did deserve this, after everything that had been torn away from him.

"Fine," I muttered. "But if the surprise attack doesn't work, I will do whatever possible to avoid bloodshed."

"Deal, princess." He chuckled at my pout and pressed a kiss to my lips before he was lost to the shadows, only to emerge upon Phantom's back seconds later. "I love you," he shouted over the blustering winds.

"Not more than I love you," I called back.

The Compass, where it still sat in Reign's hand, suddenly went wild, the crimson-lit shard spinning erratically in its center as if it had lost all sense of direction. Then, just as suddenly, it stilled, pointing directly toward a ridge below wreathed in black mist.

"That's it," Reign called over the wind, releasing his shadow messengers to the entire squadron, then lifting the artifact higher. "We land there."

Sol let out a guttural roar, his wings angling downward as we began our descent. Around us, the others followed suit. Phantom and Mordrin swooped low, flanked by pegasi and gryphons, the sky blooming with shadow and light-touched wings. The air shimmered with *rais* and *nox*, crackling like static against my skin.

As Sol landed atop the jagged, frost-dusted cliff, I immediately sensed it. An unnatural stillness clung to the air, as if the land itself held its breath. Once the entire team landed and dismounted, we all gathered around the mountaintop.

"Everyone ready?" Reign scanned our motley crew, the Compass once again writhing in his palm. He winced as if in pain.

Grim nods encircled us, and it occurred to me that they had all seen this before—Symon, Rue, Ruhl, even Liora. They had been with Reign when he'd come for me the first time. I was the only one who had no idea what came next.

The Compass dropped to the earth, and a sharp crack hissed through the air. Slivers of smoke rose from the ground, a wave of pitch-black curling around the artifact. Then, the ground shifted beneath my feet, and a vast chasm split the earth, wrapped in a vortex of swirling mist and violet-black shadow. Within the vortex, glimmering bands of light and starfire spun like threads of fate.

The air was suddenly impossibly thick. Cold. Ancient.

I moved around Reign, boots crunching over brittle rock as I approached the chasm. His arm extended protectively, pushing me back a step. "What is this?" I breathed, eyes locked on the swirling gate. It wasn't just a portal, not like what I'd seen Helroth use before, it was alive. It seemed to pulse with something more ancient than even the Courts themselves. Older than the gods even.

Kaelith stepped beside me, darkness blooming around him, his brows drawn. "I've heard of this," he murmured. "The Vesper Gate. A tear in the veil between worlds. They say it only opens when fate demands it."

"Another gods' damned test," Ruhl muttered behind us. "*Of course.*"

"Where does it lead?" I asked.

"To Helroth," Reign said quietly. "The Compass brought us here for a reason, just like last time."

"But how do we get through?" Aidan asked, stepping forward, his hand on the hilt of his sword. "It doesn't look stable."

I stepped closer to the edge, the vortex's pull brushing against my skin like icy fingers. The cuorem pulsed, a warning and invitation all at once.

"Maybe it needs blood," I said, voice tight. It seemed as if it was always about blood with these things. "Maybe from me? Since I'm the child of twilight, it makes sense—"

"No." Reign's voice cut across the cliff like a blade. "Let me try first."

I turned to him, startled. "Reign—"

"I have Night Fae blood, too," he said, striding past me. "Maybe that's what it's waiting for. Maybe it's not about Light and Shadow anymore. Maybe it's about the third option, which I have more than enough of."

Zar. The power of Night. Of Zaroth. Of destruction.

He reached the edge and drew one of his daggers from his boot then sliced it across his palm with barely a wince. His blood, dark crimson and shimmering like spilled twilight, hit the ground and the atmosphere instantly changed.

Nothing happened at first. The vortex hissed, a breeze curling with stardust, and then, with a tremor that shook the cliff beneath us, the entire gate shuddered.

With a roar like a thunderclap, the swirling vortex expanded, parting down the middle like a curtain being drawn. At its heart, a narrow bridge of obsidian shadow formed, leading into a void filled with stars.

It worked.

Reign turned to me, eyes glowing with power. "Looks like I was the key this time."

I stared at him, wonder and fear warring inside me. "You shouldn't have risked yourself for me—"

"I had to." His voice was low, but fierce. "This is my legacy too, Aelia. These are *our* people, *our* war."

With that, I watched as my *cuoré* turned for the vortex, holding out his hand. I wrapped my fingers around it without hesitation. One by one, the others began to follow, but I lingered at the edge for a moment longer, staring into the gate. The air thrummed with ancient power, the crystals in my daggers vibrating in response.

This was only the beginning. Because on the other side of that gate, the Night King waited.

Chapter Forty-Eight

R*eign*

Crossing the Vesper Gate was like falling through the bones of a dying star. Time folded in on itself, light collapsed into shadow, and every breath was a war against the weight of power pressing in on all sides. My fingers tightened around Aelia's hand. The bridge beneath our feet, obsidian, jagged, and laced with threads of starlight, stretched across a void where the sky bled violet and silver. Phantom flew just above us with Solanthus at her side, wings tucked close, their massive forms navigating the narrow path with eerie precision. Around us, our forces moved in hushed silence, too awed—or too terrified—to speak.

And maybe both were warranted.

Because with every step deeper into this rift, the shadows in my blood stirred. Responded. The closer we drew to the end of the bridge, the more the truth clawed its way to the surface.

I wasn't just Shadow Fae anymore. Not just some bastard

prince raised in secret. I wasn't even the brutal weapon I was made to be, the cursed son of Tenebris.

I was Night. Not by title, but by blood. By legacy. A royal, nonetheless.

The moment my blood had opened the gate, and the Vesper threads had wrapped around me like anointing chains, I'd felt it. The call of Zaroth. The echo of a kingdom buried deep in my bones. Karnax's throne might've been lost to time, but his blood still flowed in my veins.

And for the first time, I didn't fight it.

I *owned* it.

And if I had to burn every last remnant of the Night Court to keep Aelia and Aetheria safe, I'd still do it gladly. I would not run from the darkness inside me. Nor would I allow it to be a hindrance.

I would wield it.

The end of the bridge drew closer, the void fading into mist-slick stone. A massive, curved wall jutted from the mountainside like a scar carved deep into the land. Crimson torches of hellfire lit ancient battlements and smoke curled from vents chiseled into black iron towers.

Helspire Keep. The seat of the Night King.

My grandfather's throne turned tomb. My mother's first home. Aelia's prison.

A flicker of movement caught my eye, then another.

Dozens. Hundreds. Thousands.

As the mist cleared, a dark sea of Demon warriors came into view, their armor forged of molten obsidian and shadowed bone, each helm crowned with jagged nightsteel. Their eyes burned like coals in the gloom, fixed on us with unflinching menace.

Banners flapped above them, red and black, adorned with a twisted sigil of a bleeding crescent moon. The Court of Infernal Night.

A trap.

"Fuck," Ruhl gritted out from just behind me.

My stomach twisted as realization struck: The Night Fae had known we were coming. They hadn't just been prepared. They'd planned for this.

I reached for the Compass at my side. It still pulsed, but the tug was faint now, blurred. Muddled. Like something had warped its signal. Had Helroth corrupted it somehow? Had he twisted fate itself to lure us here?

Reign? Aelia's voice came through the bond, tight and wary. *This is not good.*

I didn't answer right away. My gaze swept the ridgeline, the towering walls of the Keep, the sharpened spears of *zar* ready to skewer us all.

Someone had tipped them off. And only one person had known about everything, the day, the time, the Compass...

Liora.

The understanding hit like a blade to the gut. I'd not only defended her, I'd trusted her. Not just with information, but with our lives. Our mission. *Aelia's safety.* Gods, how could I have been so stupid?

What Heaton said, it was all true. She was Night Fae. And worse, she was loyal to Helroth.

My shadows surged, wild and violent, wreathing my arms in darkness as I scanned our small troop for her pale blonde hair, already knowing what I'd find. She was gone. So much for Ruhl keeping an eye on her. Phantom hissed low, sensing my rising rage.

"She betrayed us," I whispered to Aelia who stood at my side, the words bitter in my mouth. "Liora."

Aelia didn't speak, she didn't need to. Instead, she only dipped her head, eyes following mine. Then a gasp from Rue, followed by another sharp curse from Ruhl as realization set in across our forces.

Kaelith moved forward, his expression twisted with fury.

"We should've known," Ruhl muttered.

"No," I growled. "*I* should've known. She was my acquisition. I should've listened."

Across the battlefield, a figure stepped out from the gate of the Keep, his armor like living night, his cloak of lost souls trailing tendrils of smoke. His face was sculpted in cruel perfection, silver hair bound back from eyes of gleaming red.

Helroth. King of Infernal Night.

He shifted, his cloak snapping in the icy wind, baring the jagged stump of his arm. Hope surged hot and fierce through my veins. The great king wasn't untouchable. He wasn't immortal. He bled just like the rest of us.

"Have you come home, princess?" His hard gaze landed on my *cuoré*, then darted toward me for only an instant before settling on her once again.

She was his ultimate prize, the child of twilight. Aelia was all he ever wanted, and I would ensure she would never be his.

The wind howled between us as he raised his remaining hand, and the sea of warriors behind him stepped forward in perfect unison. Shadow beasts writhed in the air, maws open and brimming with crimson hellfire. It was an army forged in night, bred for destruction.

Beside me, Aelia drew her daggers, the light-shadow crystal at the hilt glowing like a star on the edge of collapse, drawing my eye. And it was only then it hit me. The Moirai Shard. The crystal... That was why it had seemed so familiar. A piece of it resided inside Aelia's daggers.

That was why no one had recognized the mysterious gem.

"Aelia, your daggers!" Cloaking us in impenetrable shadows, I grabbed one and turned it upside down, pointing at the crystal. Within the hard casing was the same prism of woven starlight and silver threads I'd retrieved from the Lupherium. "Part of the Shard, it's inside the hilt."

She stared at it wide-eyed. "How... how did it end up in there? And what does it mean?"

"I don't know." I stared at the shimmering crystal, brows

furrowing. "But I hope to find out." Later. Now was not the time to ponder these new revelations.

Helroth was waiting, and he wanted blood.

He wasn't the only one.

Before I moved, Aelia's shoulder brushed my own as she took a step forward, reclaiming her dagger. "I have to stop this. I have to try to reason with him."

"No," I hissed.

"Reign, it's the only way." Her silver-blue eyes scanned the mass of darkness. We were a mere handful against an entire army. It would be a massacre.

"It's too dangerous." I spun at her, eyes wild, shadows writhing down my arms. "I will *not* lose you."

Her hand found my chest, pressing against the cuorem. "You won't. But if there's even the smallest chance I can stop this without bloodshed, without sacrificing you, or Aidan, or anyone else I care for, I must take it."

A low growl built in my throat. Phantom stirred above me, her wings battering the air, and I felt the tension bleed through the bond. This was madness. Helroth didn't negotiate. He destroyed. Manipulated. Consumed.

"You're not going alone," I growled.

"I love you, but I am not yours to keep, Prince Reign of Umbra." With those final words, her ethereal wings unfolded, illuminating the darkness and she shot into the night sky, my shadows dispersing in her wake.

No.

"King Helroth," her voice crackled through the tense air. "I ask for a word in private, as your granddaughter and heir to the Night Throne."

A wave of gasps rippled across the battlefield, echoing from both sides of the divide.

A wicked grin twisted Helroth's lips. Then a hush fell as the Night King's voice cut through the mist like a blade. "She may approach," he called out. "But only her."

Every muscle in my body locked.

No. Fucking. Way.

"No," I snapped again, louder this time. "That wasn't the deal, A—"

"There was no deal with my granddaughter," Helroth said, his tone cold and amused. "She has a mind of her own. She wishes to speak? Then she will come to me. Alone."

Aelia's eyes met mine, a reassuring smile on her lips. *Reign. Please. I need you to trust me.* Her voice seared across my mind.

"I *do* trust you." My voice cracked. I hadn't meant to speak the words out loud, but I continued anyway. "It's *him* I don't trust." My shadows surged into the sky, curling around her wrist, unwilling to let go.

Her gaze softened. "Then trust that I'm strong enough to face him. That I won't break."

"You're my heart," I whispered through my shadows, barely audible, so that only she could hear. "Don't make me watch it walk to its death."

She slowly shook her head, expression grim but resolute. The cuorem flared bright and steady between us. "I'll come back to you. Always."

And before I could stop her, before I could do something desperate, she turned, wings flaring with brilliant light twisted in shadow, and crossed the line between Light and Night.

Chapter Forty-Nine

A *elia*

The moment I passed the threshold, the chill hit me like a slap to the face. Night thickened around me, curling like mist at my ankles. The air itself felt heavier, more potent.

Helroth stood at the heart of it all, a dark monument of power. His crimson eyes tracked my approach like a predator watching prey. Still, he said nothing as I stopped a few feet away.

Aelia, are you all right? Reign's voice ricocheted through our bond, the cuorem like another heartbeat pounding beneath my ribs.

I'm fine. Please, just trust me. And be ready. With that, I slammed down the barrier between the ethereal strands that connected us. I had to focus.

"How brave of you, Aelia," Helroth murmured at last. "Or foolish."

"Maybe both," I answered, keeping my chin high. "But I'm not here as your powerless captive this time. I'm here to end this."

Despite the stiff upper lip, a whisper of doubt surged to the surface. *What if I'm wrong? What if I can't resist him again?* But shoving aside the fears, I strengthened my resolve, fisting my hands at my sides. Doubting myself wouldn't help anyone, much less stop this war.

His lips curved. "End it? The war that's been building for the past twenty years? You think one lost Light Princess can stop the tide?"

"I'm not just a princess or your helpless puppet," I said, voice steady. "I'm the daughter of King Alaric of Ether and Princess Sable of Inferna. I am heir to the thrones of Ethereal Light *and* Infernal Night. I know the truth now. About you. About my family. About your deal with Tenebris and Elian's betrayal."

He stilled. I felt the tension ripple beneath his skin like coiled steel.

"Go on," he said, curiosity flickering.

"My uncle Elian vowed to protect me against you, and the moment he had the chance, he betrayed us. He marched on the Shadow Court, forcing his people into yet another war. All of which I'm sure isn't news to you." I paused, watching the gleam in his eyes. "The moment Tenebris was captured, Elian sought only to take advantage of the weakened Shadow Court. It must have been his plan all along. However, Tenebris is no better. He refused to unite the courts, to spare Aetheria from the oncoming war. He doesn't deserve the Shadow Throne, any more than Elian does the Light."

Helroth's brows rose faintly.

"Maybe you're not the only monster with a crown," I continued. "But at least for you there's still a chance to make things right."

He let out a low, bitter laugh. "*Right*? You think there's any 'right' left in this realm?"

"I do." I took a step closer. "Ruhl will take the Shadow Throne. Elian can be removed from the Light Court. And you, you can end this, Helroth. Not as a tyrant or the Demon Fae who started another bloody war. But as the king who brought the realms back into balance. And more importantly, as my grandfather."

His gaze sharpened, jaw tightening. And for a breath, a single heartbeat, I saw something shift. A flicker of consideration. Maybe even longing.

"Aelia, you have no idea what you are asking..." There was something about his tone, a hint of warmth I'd never heard before as he said my name.

I held my breath. The moment dragging on for a lifetime.

But then it vanished.

"You weren't there before the war," he said, voice colder now. "You didn't see how the Night Fae were treated. Cast aside. Feared. Hunted. I was a royal without a throne, too, once. Do you know what it's like to beg for peace and be given chains? To kneel and be spat upon?"

I swallowed, throat tight.

"Balance is a myth," he spat. "Justice doesn't exist. The only language this realm understands is *power*."

"So, you want revenge," I whispered. "Revenge against Elian and Tenebris?"

"I want *reclamation*." His eyes glowed brighter. "For every Night Fae slaughtered. For every child who grew up believing they were cursed. I will remake this world, Aelia. Not for vengeance. For retribution."

My chest tightened. That word. *Reclamation*. He wanted to sit atop a throne made of smoke and ruin. "You'll burn all of Aetheria down for your own damned pride."

"I'll build a new one from the ashes."

My heart hammered. "And what about your granddaughter? What about your daughter, Sable's child? *Me*. What will you do when I stand in your way?"

His gaze locked on mine. "That depends on whether you still mean to."

And just like that, I felt it, the moment was gone. The brief window for peace closed, sealed behind centuries of pain and hatred.

I turned, the weight of his decision settling like lead on my shoulders.

He would not yield.

And now, we had no choice but to fight.

A bitter laugh erupted from my lips. "Of course I will fight you, Grandfather." *Grandfather.* It was the first time I'd used the term out loud, and it tasted sour on my tongue. "I will not let the Courts be plunged into decades of darkness again. I will be the harbinger of balance, the beacon of hope to bring forth a new dawn." I paused fingering the hilt of my dagger. "And if you stand in my way, I will cut you down like every tyrant before you, regardless of the shared blood running through our veins."

"Those are big words from a little girl," he spat. "And what do you think will happen after you cut me down? Will you rule both Courts, Aelia, or perhaps you have your gaze set on all three?"

"The Night Court isn't mine to rule, nor is it yours. Kaelith told us the truth, of how you stole the throne from his brother, the true king, Karnax."

He scoffed. "I thought I saw that traitor in your midst. Does he truly wish to claim his brother's cursed throne now? After all these years?"

"No. But maybe Reign will." I regretted it the moment the threat fled my loose lips.

His snide grin twisted, the arrogant mask retreating for an instant. "What do you mean?"

Raysa, he really didn't know. And he wouldn't discover the truth from me.

"We've come for Vaelora." I spoke the words calmly. "If you refuse to consider peace, then we will fight. But I'm not leaving today without the one soul who was kind to me during my captivity."

"Vaelora?" he repeated. "You would risk your tiny squadron against my entire army for a *servant*?"

"She's not just a servant, she's—" My words trailed off as I considered the implications. "She is Kaelith's sister-in-law, his family."

Silver brows furrowing, those crimson irises bored into me. Then, I felt it. The *zar* pushing at the edges of my subconscious. He was trying to infiltrate my thoughts, to rip the truth from my mind.

But I wouldn't let him. I'd never again allow him to control me.

The *zar* lashed through my skull like shadowed lightning, searching, clawing, desperate for cracks to slither through. But I had no cracks left. Not anymore.

"You owe me a blood vow," he growled. "You are to destroy Light and Shadow—"

"I don't owe you anything," I hissed, raw power lacing my tone.

I closed my eyes and reached inward, not just to the trio of gods' given gifts, but to the bond that pulsed like a living star beneath my skin. The cuorem. It was more than a connection. It was armor. An anchor. A promise between Reign and me forged by the gods themselves.

I pictured his hand in mine, the way he whispered my name in the dark. The way he looked at me like I was salvation instead of sacrifice. And I let that feeling rise, strong and sure, wrapping it around my mind like a wall of living flame.

Helroth's power slammed into it and recoiled. His eyes widened, just slightly. But it was enough. "You've grown stronger," he murmured, voice low and wary now. "Stronger than I thought possible."

"I'm not the girl you held in chains," I said softly, my power rising behind every word. "I'm not yours, to control or otherwise, and I never will be."

He watched me closely, crimson eyes narrowing, as if reevaluating everything he'd assumed.

I could have said more. Could have pleaded one last time. But

I saw the truth now, as clearly as I saw the hatred in his eyes. And gods, it was devastating.

There would be no peace. Not with him. So I took a single step back. Not enough to appear as if I were retreating, just enough to steel myself.

Then I reached through the bond again.

Reign. My voice echoed like a bell of fate. *Now.*

There was no need for further explanation.

The shadows around me pulsed, and in the distance, I felt the storm rise. A whisper of wind brushed my cheek, followed by familiar roars splitting the sky. Sol and Phantom. Then Mordrin.

Helroth spun toward the sound, frowning.

"You should have chosen peace," I said, my voice a blade of certainty. "Because I'm not the only one who's stronger now."

Above us, the skies cracked open, and the fury of war came roaring down.

Chapter Fifty

R *eign*

Now.

The second Aelia's voice echoed through the bond my shadows erupted like a tidal wave. "Attack!" I bellowed, my voice carrying over the ridge. My wings flared, propelling me into the sky and onto Phantom's back. The moment I was seated, she shrieked overhead and dove like a spear of living night.

Solanthus and Mordrin answered with a unified roar, flames streaming from their gaping maws in searing arcs that scorched the front line of Night warriors. Pegasi screamed, gryphons dove, and Light and Shadow warriors armed with spears of light and blades laced in *nox* met the enemy midair with brutal force.

All around me, the clash began.

Night Fae surrounded the king, and Aelia was swept into the cloud of darkness. Terror cut through me, sharper than any blade as I watched her disappear.

"Aelia!" I shouted futilely, my voice lost in the uproar.

I'm fine, Reign. Her answer breezed through my mind, as casually as if we were conversing over a cup of tea. Then I saw her in the midst of the fray, ethereal wings blazing as her luminescent daggers carved a path through the Night Fae hellions on the ground. A lavender-haired female tried to corner her, and my shadows whirled in a frenzy, desperate to reach their mate. But within seconds, Aelia had the Night Fae on her back and had moved onto the next.

With my *cuoré* safe, I turned my attention to the rest of our forces. Aidan cut a swath through the front lines with terrifying precision, his light-forged blade gleaming like a star in the smoke. He fought like a general possessed, his every strike a vow for a better realm.

Ruhl kept to the skies aboard Mordrin, my half-brother and his dragon battling the Demons mounted atop creatures of smoke and night. *Zar* and *nox* clashed midair, beastly screams ricocheting through the anarchy. I was relieved to have Ruhl on our side. My brother would make a formidable king.

Kaelith moved through the chaos like death incarnate, his *zar* pulsing with ancient power, tendrils of night coiling around enemies before they even had time to scream. His goal was simple: infiltrate Helspire Fortress and find Vaelora. I watched the male, my great-uncle, for an endless moment, imagining what my grandfather must have been like.

Symon launched himself from Griff's back, drawing my attention back to the sky, slicing through three Demon warriors before his boots even hit the ground. "For the record," he shouted over the din, "I so did not sign up for this!"

Rue streaked by overhead, her golden armor ablaze with *rais* as she slashed with twin sabers, Windy bucking through the storm like a thunderbolt. "Stay alive and I'll buy you a drink!" she called back.

"Fair enough."

I barely restrained the urge to growl at my students. Now was not the time for banter. They needed to focus. Everywhere, chaos ensued, blood raining down from the heavens.

I scanned the battlefield for Liora, but she was nowhere to be seen. She was simply... gone. Just like I feared. The traitor Rue had suspected for months.

My fury simmered beneath the surface as I moved my search of the battlefield onto Helroth, the monster responsible for all of this. He stood still amidst the blood and fire, untouched, calm, like a god watching ants destroy themselves.

Then his eyes locked on Aelia overhead, cutting a path through his Night Fae.

No. No.

I felt it the moment he reached for her again.

Zar lanced through our cuorem, thick and potent. Gods damn it, I was certain she'd managed to block him out before, but the bastard wouldn't give up. The blood vow ignited, a crimson tether sparking between Helroth and Aelia like a brand forged in hellfire. I could feel its pull, the *zar* infiltrating deep into my marrow. She faltered midair, clutching her chest, and the bond between us screamed.

Aelia.

She dropped low, barely catching herself on Solanthus's back, her form writhing like something inside her had broken loose. Her wings sputtered, her mouth open in a silent cry, and the shadows that surrounded her began to twist.

"No!" I roared.

Phantom wheeled toward her before I even spoke the command, but I could already feel it, the war raging inside her once again. The blood vow pushing. Forcing. Compelling.

Strike down the Light, it demanded. *Turn against the Shadow. Become his.*

My heart shattered. My shadows surged without control. I knew that feeling too well. The helplessness. The rage. The bitter shame of being nothing but a weapon to someone else's will.

Aelia! I sought her out through our bond, but the shimmering strands were dulled, a thick haze impeding our connection. Then I reached for the Moirai Shard hidden within the folds of my cloak. I could use it to sever the vow, once and for all. But what of the cost? Phantom's mighty wings flapped, propelling us closer.

Launching herself off Solanthus's back, she lashed out at a passing Light Fae, arcing her luminous blade and just barely missing his head.

"Aelia, no!" I shouted, my voice raw and desperate.

Gods, if she hurt someone, she would never forgive herself.

Again, I focused on our bond, on the tendrils of love and light that connected our souls. *Aelia, please, don't do this. You can fight him, I know you're strong enough. You are the strongest female I've ever laid eyes upon.*

Her eyes snapped up to mine and the murky fog blocking our connection began to lift. *Reign?*

I'm right here, starlight.

Her luminescent blade sputtered, eyes fully locked on mine. I could still feel the battle raging within her, Helroth's hold clawing at her insides. Her body convulsed, and a burst of energy exploded outward, not just *rais* or *zar* or *nox*, but *all of it*. Light. Shadow. Night.

A triune storm. The tether between her and Helroth snapped with a sound like a bell tolling for the damned.

She screamed, the defiant shriek echoing through the pandemonium. A shockwave of pure *rais* burst from her core, flattening warriors on both sides, and scattering Helroth's elite like leaves before a storm.

And in that moment, I truly saw her. The future queen of not just one Court, but all three. Light in her soul, Shadow in her blood, and Night in her bones. The beacon of balance. The child of twilight. My mate.

And gods help me, she was stronger than I was.

Because I'd failed. I hadn't been able to fight Tenebris' blood vow. But she'd just broken free from her grandsire's binding oath, all on her own. I hadn't needed the Shard at all...

A single tear slipped down my cheek, carved of awe and fury and love.

Helroth staggered backward, his crimson eyes wide with disbelief. "Impossible," he hissed. "You are bound to me!"

"I was," Aelia shouted, her voice ringing across the battlefield like a declaration. "But not anymore."

At that, I dove. Phantom roared as we hurtled toward the Night King, my umbral sword burning with a knot of *nox* and *zar*, the cuorem a battle drum in my chest.

"For everything you've taken," I whispered. "For Aelia and for my grandfather, Karnax."

Helroth's eyes of coal darkened, understanding flashing through the crimson abyss. He hesitated, only for a moment. But it was all I needed.

"This ends now," I roared, then struck with all the fury carved from bloodshed and ruin. Shadows exploded around me as Phantom launched me from her back. My sword, ablaze with *nox* and laced with *zar*, met Helroth's just before it could strike. The force of our blades colliding cracked the air like thunder.

He grinned, holding a blade of pure void in his one remaining hand. "You dare challenge me, Bastard Prince?"

"I'm not just a bastard anymore," I growled, forcing him back, step by step. "I'm the legitimate heir to the Night Throne, and today, I am your reckoning."

He twisted, a flare of *zar* crackling in his palm, and the very air around us screamed. My shoulder seared as his blood magic scraped past my armor, tearing skin from bone, but I didn't falter. I wouldn't. Not now, not ever.

"You're weaker than your grandfather," Helroth sneered. "Although, he begged too."

The words hit harder than his blade ever could. My vision went red, shadows flaring around me like a tempest. I lunged, roaring, our swords clashing in a whirl of steel and shadow.

Helroth was fast, faster than I'd expected, given his disadvantage of fighting one-handed. His movements were calculated, brutal, ancient. He fought like a god who had conquered death and decided to dance with it again.

But I didn't care.

This wasn't just war anymore.

It was vengeance.

My shadows struck out, bleeding from my fingertips like deadly wraiths. They curled around Helroth's neck, lifting him off the ground. Inky tendrils of night cut through the shadows, blades of pure black strangling the *nox*. My *zar* rose to the surface, but it wasn't strong enough. Not compared to his.

He knocked me back, blade slicing across my ribs. He stood over me as I gasped and staggered. No. I would not let him win. I strained, summoning my dwindling *nox* but before he could deliver the killing blow, a flare of light slammed between us.

Aelia.

She dropped from the sky like a comet, her wings spread wide, twin daggers spinning with pure fury as she struck between us.

"Enough!" she screamed, eyes burning silver-blue, cuorem thrumming so hard it rattled the air. "You'll have to kill me to get to him."

Helroth froze.

His blade hovered midair, inches from Aelia now. I leapt to my feet, trying to push her behind me, but she was an unmovable force.

"Aelia," he said, voice oddly hollow. "Move."

"I won't," she said, chest heaving. "If you wish to strike him, you'll have to kill me too. Regardless, the cuorem will likely break us both."

For a moment, everything stilled. Even the battlefield around us dimmed in my mind. All I could see was Aelia between us, the female I loved shielding me with her life.

An endless moment dragged on.

Then, Helroth began to lower his blade.

But before he sheathed his weapon, a golden sword arced between us.

I moved at the same time, shadows surging in a desperate wave. But it was too late.

Aidan. He'd been closing the gap behind us, his luminescent sword raised, light pulsing with purpose.

Helroth struck first.

A dagger of pure *zar* pierced Aidan's chest, right through his armor, right through the sun-forged plate I thought nothing could penetrate.

"Aidan!" Aelia screamed.

The male who had raised her, who was a father to her in every way but blood, fell to his knees.

"No!" Her cry echoed through my insides, her pain palpable.

Aidan crumpled to the ground, the golden glow in his eyes flickering, once, then twice. Aelia screamed again as she fell to her knees beside him, and I felt it, in the marrow of my bones, a grief too ancient for sound.

Light and shadow burst from Aelia in a violent wave, spiraling together into a blinding orb that detonated across the battlefield. The ground quaked beneath us. Fae from all sides were thrown back, weapons clattering from stunned hands. Even Helroth staggered, his crimson eyes narrowing as the surge of raw, unbridled power forced him to step away.

The cacophony of battle fell silent. Time itself seemed to hold its breath. Within the golden-black sphere of energy, only the three of us remained untouched—Aelia, Aidan, and me— suspended in a fragile sanctuary carved from her grief.

The protective orb thickened, shimmering threads of light stitched with shadow, pulsing in rhythm with her sobs.

"No! No, Aidan, please, stay with me." Aelia's voice was hoarse, broken, as she cradled his body in her arms. I dropped down beside them, winding my arm around her shoulders.

Blood soaked the ground beneath us, hot, bitter and final.

He looked up at me, blinking slowly. "Promise me... you'll take care of her."

"You're going to be fine," I murmured.

Aidan coughed, then managed a crooked grin. "Don't lie to me, professor. Now... swear it. Vow you will protect Aelia... with your life."

"Always and forever."

"Aidan, please, don't leave me." Her broken voice nearly undid me.

And then, his body went still. The light in his eyes vanished, faded like the final spark of a dying star.

Aelia knelt beside me, her hands trembling as she squeezed his hand, lips parted in a silent scream. Around us, the battlefield seemed to pause, as if even the air held its breath. Aelia pressed a kiss to his forehead, whispering softly, then dropped her head to his chest.

Rue sobbed from somewhere beyond the glittering orb, and Symon let out a strangled curse.

Helroth said nothing as he marched closer once again, on the other side of the impenetrable shield, blade dripping with blood and crimson eyes cold as winter.

And in that moment, something inside me snapped.

I rose, slow and shaking, Aidan's blood on my hands. "No more mercy," I whispered. The cuorem flared—rage, grief, power flooding through me—and this time, even the gods wouldn't be able to stop me.

Then, just as suddenly, Aelia's power dimmed, leaving a hushed, trembling silence in its wake. "No." Her voice was nothing more than a strangled whisper. Then her hand wrapped around mine, tear-filled eyes lifting to my own from where she still knelt on the ground, holding onto the male who'd loved her as his own. Shadows coiled around us. "This is over. We take Aidan home. Now."

"But—" I pointed toward the troops, where the dazed soldiers were beginning to rise.

"I need to take him *home*," she repeated, stronger now.

My head dipped, the swell of emotions coursing through our bond enough to silence my rebuttals, almost bringing me to my knees. Her shadows darkened, drawing us into the familiar, icy void.

Helroth's burning crimson glare was the last thing I saw before we were hauled into the murky abyss.

Chapter Fifty-One

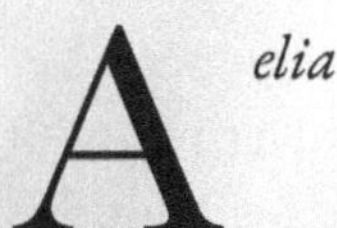

A*elia*

The world collapsed beneath my feet.

One moment, I held Aidan's broken body in my arms, bloodied, lifeless, and still warm. The next, a torrent of *rais* and *nox* blossomed, wrapping us in shadow and light, and I was dragged into the void.

It wasn't planned. It wasn't controlled. I didn't even know if I had the strength to pull us through, but the cuorem answered the call, and so did the shadows that loved Reign as fiercely as I did. They bent to my will, obeying the scream in my soul.

When we landed, it was with a jolt and a gasp of cold air, the scent of pine and earth rushing into my lungs. I blinked, the sudden sunlight shocking after the interminable black.

The cottage.

Our tiny haven in Feywood, half-wild and blooming in flowers, surrounded by the chorus of crickets and the babble of the creek just beyond the tree line. Where Aidan had raised me, where he'd first trained me to use my daggers. Where Reign had appeared at my doorstep and saved me from the hands of that dark Fae lord.

Where it had all begun.

I fell to my knees, again pulling Aidan's body into my lap, cradling him the way I had once imagined I would comfort a baby brother. If I'd had one.

His blood soaked my hands. My leathers. My soul.

His face... gods, his face was peaceful. Just like he looked when he'd sleep under the trees after sparring. One hand curled faintly near his chest, as if even in death, he was still trying to fight, to protect me.

"No," I whispered, rocking him, brushing a strand of silver hair from his brow. "No, you promised. You were supposed to take care of me. You said you'd never leave."

Reign was silent beside me, his shadows shivering with restrained grief. I felt it through the bond, though, his guilt, his fury, his helplessness.

But mine eclipsed it all.

Because Aidan had died trying to protect me.

Just like he had my entire life.

The warmth left his body gradually. As slowly as the sun setting into the horizon. I didn't even realize how long I sat there, holding him, until his skin turned cold beneath my touch and the weight of him settled into permanence.

"I can't..." I struggled to breathe, to get the words out. "I can't believe he's gone."

Reign knelt beside me. His voice was hoarse as he whispered, "Neither can I."

I held Aidan tighter still, refusing to let go of the only parent I'd ever known. The only one I would *ever* know. Mine were both long dead. Another round of grief enveloped me, and my entire body trembled with the force of the sob.

Reign's arm curled around my shoulders, drawing me into his

warmth. "Let's take him inside, starlight. It's time for us all to rest."

I hadn't even realized full night had descended. The crescent moon loomed overhead, the stars cast in shadows tonight, as if even they mourned. For my Aidan was gone.

Reign attempted to scoop me into his arms, but I held onto Aidan's hand, refusing to let go. So my mate, the male whose presence urged my heart to keep beating and my lungs to continue inflating, hauled us both off the dark earth and into our tiny cottage.

Once he'd gently laid Aidan on the threadbare couch, he carried me into the washroom where he took on the painstaking task of removing my blood-stained clothes. Here, in our modest home, there was no hot shower, no fine gilded basin. Instead, my *cuoré* filled buckets with water from the well, warmed them on the stove, then patiently spilled them over my trembling form.

Time and again, just when I thought it wasn't possible to love him any more, he would prove me wrong.

Once we were both clean, he swept me into his arms once again and carried me to Aidan's old bed. It was barely big enough for two, but tonight, I needed to be as close to Reign as physically possible. I needed the healing power of his touch, his gentle caresses, the brush of his lips on mine.

Because without Aidan, I was drowning, and only Reign could anchor me back to the surface before I disappeared beneath the grief.

✕

We buried Aidan at dawn.

There was no fanfare, no funeral procession of nobles, no courtly rites or royal headstones. Nothing befitting the burial of the king's most trusted general. Nothing for the male who'd given up everything to raise me in hiding. It was only us, the sky tinged in pale gold, and the field where we'd trained until our arms ached and our stomachs hurt from laughing.

The earth was soft beside the chicken coop. The baby chicks clucked at our approach, lifting my spirits for a moment as I recalled how Aidan had once threatened to turn one of the roosters into soup if it kept biting his ankles. I remembered how he used to grumble about chores, and how his eyes would crinkle when he smiled.

The happiest moments of my childhood were filled with images of Aidan. And now, with his death, my last connection to that *normal* upbringing was gone. My fingers lifted to the medallion that hung at my chest. The one he'd gifted me right before all of this began. My parents had fought so hard to deny fate her due, but all the terrible things had come to pass all the same.

Reign found a shovel and dug the grave himself.

I tried to help, but my hands trembled too much to hold the massive trowel. So I gathered stones for the marker instead, my fingers bleeding as I stacked each one with utmost care.

When it was done, I knelt at the foot of the grave and placed Aidan's sword on top, the golden hilt catching the light. I ran my fingers over it one last time. The leather grip was worn smooth, callused by a lifetime of war. Like him. Strong, stubborn... and now gone.

"I'll keep fighting," I whispered. "For the realm you believed in. For the peace you wanted us to have. I promise, Aidan, I won't let your sacrifice be in vain. I love you, *Father*."

Reign stood behind me, his hand resting on my shoulder, still grounding me—always grounding me.

"We'll finish what he started," he murmured. "Together."

Tears slid down my cheeks, unchecked. The wind stirred the tall grass, whispering through the trees like a lullaby. And in that sacred silence, in the heart of the woods that had once been our sanctuary, we let him go.

Not from memory.

Not from love.

But into the earth, where he would be part of Aetheria forever.

We spent the remainder of the day with a weighty silence hovering between us. I alternated between sitting at Aidan's grave, reminiscing while polishing my daggers, and cooing at the chicks as they ate.

All the while, I could feel Reign's steadying presence, both through the bond and in person. He always hovered nearby but still gave me my distance. Neither of us spoke much, but my spiraling thoughts were more than enough company.

Hours passed, then days.

Reign and I fell into an easy routine at the cottage, and for a few peaceful days, I allowed myself to believe there was no war beyond the quiet fields of Feywood, that our friends weren't waiting for us at the Fortress of Umbral Shadows, and that King Helroth would have to die.

I'd been foolish to hope for peace.

Perhaps, it was my fault that Aidan was dead.

If I'd only listened to Reign—

"No," my mate's voice broke through my dark musings.

I glanced up, releasing the blades of grass I'd woven into a braid, and met Reign's turbulent midnight orbs. He stood only a few yards away from the grave, watching me intently.

He walked toward me, a wreath of wildflowers in his hands, then knelt on the earth by my side. Placing the beautiful arrangement atop the loose dirt, he took my hand, squeezing. "Aidan's death is not your fault, starlight."

"We never should have gone... I'd been so foolish to believe my grandsire would ever consider peace."

"No, Aelia, I was the one who insisted we go. If it's anyone's fault, it's mine."

My bloodshot, swollen eyes snapped open. "Oh, goddess, Vaelora. How could I have forgotten?"

Reign slowly shook his head, a faint smile tugging on his lips. "You were in shock, love. You lost the male who was more a father to you than many royals ever are." There was something about his words that resonated in my darkest depths.

"Did Kaelith find her?" I finally managed. "Did they make it out?"

He nodded slowly. "Vaelora is safe and back at my father's castle. They all are, Rue and Symon too. That flux of power left most of the soldiers stunned for long enough that our forces were able to escape."

"Oh, thank Raysa." Gods, I hadn't even thought about my closest friends, my other family. What kind of a friend was I? I'd left them all there to deal with Helroth.

Before I could allow the guilt to consume me, Reign tugged me up to my feet and brushed his lips against the top of my head. "I don't want to rush you. You deserve all the time you need to grieve the male who raised you, who loved you like his own. But—"

"But Helroth is still out there, and we can't just hide out here forever while everyone is waiting on us."

His head dipped grimly.

A heavy silence settled between us, thick with mourning and the weight of everything still undone. The breeze stirred the wildflowers near Aidan's grave, rustling the tall grass like whispered farewells. I dropped to my knees once more and pressed a trembling hand to the fresh mound of earth, unwilling to leave him. Not yet.

"I know we have to go," I whispered, my voice raw. "But I don't know how to lead without him. He was always there, Reign. He was the one who made me believe I could do this. Be this."

"You don't have to be him," Reign said gently, crouching beside me. His shadows wrapped around my shoulders like a blanket, a quiet comfort in the cool morning air. "You only have to be you. That's more than enough. He knew it. And so do I. When you feel doubt, remember that."

Tears pricked my eyes again, but this time I didn't let them fall. I let his words settle deep in my soul, where Aidan's had once lived. Where they always would.

"I just don't want to fail him," I said, staring at the stone we'd etched with a simple carving of a sun and a sword. His two guiding principles.

"You won't." Reign rose and offered his hand. "But you will fail the realm if we don't finish this."

My fingers curled into his, steadying myself in his strength, on the unbreakable bond of the cuorem pulsing steadily between us. I turned for one last glance at the grave, then nodded.

"Let's end this," I said, my voice stronger now. "For Aidan."

Reign's shadows surged around us, and a moment later, we were gone. Back to the Fortress of Umbral Shadows. Back to the war.

Back to the fight for Aetheria's soul.

Chapter Fifty-Two

A *elia*

The Shadow Fortress hadn't changed, but I had. I wandered through the obsidian stone corridors, the scent of smoldering torches and iron still clinging to the walls like smoke after a wildfire. A week had passed since the battle with Helroth. A week since I'd shadowtraveled Reign and Aidan out of the blood-soaked ruin of that battlefield. A week since I'd felt Aidan's final heartbeat fade beneath my hands.

We were still breathing. Still standing. But nothing felt the same.

Only a dozen soldiers had been lost. That's what the Shadow generals kept saying. A miracle, really. But it didn't feel like a miracle. Not to me.

Aidan wasn't just a soldier. He was *mine*.

Rue had been trying to get me to eat all morning, taking over Reign's duty since our return. She'd even gone so far as to steal honeyed buns from the kitchen before the head cook could stop her. Symon helped her, naturally, flashing his ridiculous smile and bowing like a courtier while Rue stuffed her pockets.

Now we sat in the barracks common room, the three of us curled on one of the oversized couches as the rest of the soldiers trained or rested in the adjacent halls. Outside, the moon filtered in through one of the high arched windows, painting the black stone floor in pale blue light.

A shuffle of footfalls turned my attention to an approaching Royal Guardian. Eryndor Dawnmere. The male who'd served under my father during the Two Hundred Years' War. He bowed his head, eyes cast down to the floor. "If I may, Your Ethereal Highness, I wish to extend my condolences for the loss of General Solmere."

I stood there, blinking stupidly.

Sy elbowed me, whispering, "He's talking about Aidan, little Kin."

"Oh, yes, of course. Thank you," I rasped out.

"He was a fine male, King Alaric's greatest general. He will be missed." He dipped his head and scurried away before I could find the wherewithal to speak. To tell him that he was so much more than just a great general... That he was also a great father, a funny, kind, generous male even when he was stern. That he always kept me safe, while ensuring that I was more than capable of handling myself. And then I realized...

All this time, and I'd never asked Aidan his true surname. Throughout our years in Feywood, he'd been a Ravenwood, just like me. Now, he was nothing. Just... gone.

General Aidan Solmere. I wished I'd learned it before.

"Heaton's up," Rue said softly, nudging me with her shoulder and drawing me free of my solemn musings before I could sink down the well of despair I'd been living in the past week. "I've seen a huge difference these last few days. You want to see him?"

My breath hitched.

"I don't want to push," she added quickly. "But he's lucid

today. Really lucid. I thought... I thought maybe it would be good. For both of you."

I nodded, my throat too tight for words.

Symon popped up first, stretching like a lazy cat. "Come on, princess. Let's go see if the madman's still mad, or if he's finally sane enough to recognize me as his favorite from Flare Squad." He winked, then held out his hand with an exaggerated flair. "Shall we?"

Despite everything, a small laugh slipped through my lips. "Lead the way, my loyal court jester."

Together, we made our way through the halls, Rue's arm looped through mine. My steps faltered as we approached the infirmary door, but she gave my hand a gentle squeeze. I took a breath, then stepped inside.

Heaton sat propped up in bed, a mug of broth in his hands and a blanket tucked around his waist. His once-shaggy, wild hair had been trimmed, and though his skin was still pale, the madness in his eyes was gone.

For a heartbeat, I just stared at him. The last time I'd seen him, he'd been writhing in pain, mumbling half-nonsenses and lashing out. Though, as it turned out, he'd been right about Liora. A flare of anger rippled beneath my skin. That traitorous female had sold us out to Helroth. She was the reason Aidan was dead, and she would pay the price the next time I saw her.

Heaton cleared his throat, drawing my attention once more. His gaze lifted to mine, and he smiled. All the fury from a second ago vanished with that one look. I'd thought we'd lost him, truly lost him, to the craze of *zar* and the lingering trauma. But maybe...

"Highness," he said, his voice hoarse but warm. "You're a sight for sore eyes."

My knees buckled as the tears spilled over. I rushed to his side and wrapped my arms around him, careful not to jostle his healing wounds. He stiffened at first, then relaxed with a soft chuckle, his arms curling around me.

"I take it I missed a few things?"

"You have no idea," I whispered, pressing my forehead to his shoulder. "You came back to us."

"I told you I would," he murmured, squeezing me gently. "I just had to fight through a whole lot of darkness to get here."

"Gods, I missed you, Heat."

Behind me, Symon cleared his throat dramatically. "Not to interrupt this beautiful reunion, but I'd like it noted that I also missed him, probably more than you did, and—ow!" Rue elbowed him in the ribs.

Heaton laughed, and it was such a blessed sound I nearly wept all over again.

Releasing him, but still remaining by his side, I sat up before giving my dramatic friend a sarcastic eyeroll.

"I've missed you too, Symon," he said with a grin. "And Rue. Even after your awful attempts at soup."

"Excuse me?" Rue placed a hand on her chest, mock-offended. "That was the best onion broth this fortress has ever seen."

"Please don't force me to eat it again," Heaton said dryly. "I'd like to keep what's left of my stomach lining."

We all laughed. Real, *true* laughter. It echoed through the infirmary like sunlight breaking through clouds.

"How's Belmore's ear?" Heaton asked. "All healed up after its close encounter with Aelia's blade?"

"Raysa, Heat, that was over a year ago! You've only been gone for a few months."

His expression sobered for an instant, all of ours did. How badly had the Night Fae damaged my friend?

"It sure seems like a lot longer." The hint of a smile curved one side of his mouth. "I guess I was wrong, Rue. Putting up with you wasn't what made the time drag on endlessly."

"Very funny, big brother." Slipping onto the bed beside him, she jabbed her elbow into his side, and he rewarded her with a satisfying *oomf*.

For a few minutes, as the siblings' playful banter filled the infirmary, the grief faded. The weight of war, of loss, of everything we'd endured softened. Because Heaton was alive. Because we were still together.

And even in the heart of shadow, that was enough to give me hope.

Maybe the worst had yet to pass, but at least I could enjoy this little reprieve and some healing could begin.

Later that evening, I marched past the war room, unable to face the Shadow generals who were still alive, while mine was gone. Whispers drifted into the corridor, the familiar voices of Reign and Ruhl echoing the loudest. My last few conversations with Aidan had been across that table, arguing over battle plans. I wish it had been more meaningful. That I'd gotten the chance to thank him for everything he'd sacrificed for me. For loving me when he didn't have to, for being the father I'd so desperately needed.

The cuorem pulsed as I continued down the hall, as if Reign had sensed my presence. It was likely he had. He'd barely left my side since the battle with Helroth. I'd forced him to join the others today, to plan our next move. I simply didn't have the strength.

But soon, I would have to find it.

Ready or not.

"Where are you running off to, duskling?" Ruhl's familiar tambor echoed off the obsidian walls.

Spinning around, I met those dark, mischievous eyes. "Trying to avoid the war room, actually."

"Ah, I see." He stepped closer, running a hand through his hair. "Smart girl. Once you get sucked in, it's difficult to escape."

"So how is it that you managed?"

Ruhl leaned against the wall, a rueful grin on his lips. "Your *cuoré* sent me."

"He did?" My brows knitted as I regarded him. "That doesn't sound like my overly possessive mate at all."

"I know. I couldn't believe it myself. Perhaps, he finally trusts me around his precious *cuoré*."

"I hope you're right. There is nothing that would make me happier." And I meant it. Standing there, I drew my lip between my teeth as a moment of silence descended. "With all the chaos, I never got the chance to thank you for going with Reign to retrieve the Moirai Shard. I really appreciate your selflessness, Ruhl."

He waved a dismissive hand. "Didn't my brother teach you never to thank a Fae?"

I couldn't help the grin from parting my lips. Of course he had, but it never did stick.

"Besides, it was good for us," he continued. "We've spent our entire lives competing against one another, both jealous of the other. We despised each other. Our father made sure of that. And as it turns out, it was all for nothing. We are both princes, both powerful and capable, of two different courts. You, for all the heartache you've caused us"—he threw me a smirk—"are actually the one thing that finally brought us together."

"Well, I'm glad I could help... I think."

Ruhl chuckled, the sound echoing softly in the empty corridor. "You've always been good at that, bringing impossible things into being. Reign was a bitter shadow the last I saw him. Now, look at him. A king in all but name."

My throat tightened. "He's everything I never dared to hope for."

"And yet," Ruhl said gently, "even he can't fix all that was lost."

"No," I whispered. "He can't bring Aidan back."

We stood in silence for a beat, the air between us heavy with unspoken sorrow.

"But he can stand beside you while you build what comes next." Ruhl pushed off the wall. "We all can. You're not alone, duskling. Even when you feel like you are."

Tears pricked at my eyes, but I blinked them back. "You're not so bad, Shadow Regent."

"Don't let that get around," he said with a wink. "I've got a reputation to uphold."

A smile tugged at my lips as he turned and strode back toward the war room. I lingered for a moment longer, listening to the muted thrum of voices behind the doors. The pulse of the cuorem was steady in my chest as if Reign had heard every bit of our conversation.

Soon, I would have to step through that threshold. I would stand where Aidan once stood and finish what we started together.

But not tonight.

Tonight, I let the grief live beside the hope. And I let myself breathe.

Chapter Fifty-Three

R*eign*

The fortress slept,or at least it pretended to. Shadows pooled in the corners of the obsidian halls as I paced them in silence, my boots whispering over etched runes that pulsed faintly with old, flickering *nox*. I couldn't sleep, and I hated to wake Aelia, as she needed her rest to continue to heal from the grief, so instead, I paced. War had changed the rhythm of this place. We were in the eye of the storm, and the walls knew it. Every stone held its breath.

And so did I.

I should have killed the Night King.

The thought had looped in my mind so many times, it had worn a trench. I could see it, over and over. Helroth's blade arcing toward me, my own parried strike a second too slow. And Aelia jumping between us. Noxus, if he'd struck her instead... Agony ripped at my insides at just the thought. I would never survive losing her. I wouldn't want to.

Then Aidan... gods, why had Aidan stepped between us?

He'd taken the blow meant not for Aelia, but for me.

I clenched my fists until shadow coiled tightly around my fingers, the darkness biting into my skin. My shadows should have moved faster. My blade should have been sharper. I should have been stronger.

But I wasn't.

Instead, I'd stood, stunned, as Aidan crumpled, and all I could do was try to catch him before he hit the ground with my *cuoré's* shock and devastation rushing our bond.

You are spiraling again. Phantom's voice slipped into my mind, a cool wind brushing against scorched skin. I paused, leaning against one of the carved columns overlooking the dark training yard below.

Do you blame me? I asked her, my words raw in the bond. If I'd done what I was meant to, he'd still be alive. Aelia would still have her adoptive father, and at least it would have been one thing I could have given her.

A long silence followed.

You are not a god, Reign. You are a male who carries too many burdens and still walks upright. That is strength.

I scoffed under my breath. "Tell that to Aelia," I whispered, even though I knew well that she didn't blame me. It was Helroth and Liora who held that distinction. But still, I couldn't let it go, the feeling that I'd failed them. *Tell it to the grave we buried him in. To the blade I couldn't drive deep enough into Helroth's chest to rid this world of him forever. We're no closer to ending the war than we were a week, or even a month ago. We're only down a dozen soldiers and Aelia's adoptive father.*

Again, Phantom didn't answer right away, and for a moment, I thought she'd left me to wallow in peace.

There is something I've kept from you. Her voice was lower now, tinged with something I couldn't quite place. *A way, perhaps, to make you stronger. To awaken something greater. But not yet.*

My brows knit. *Why not now?*

Because, like all power, it does not come without a price. And I'm not certain we are ready to pay it.

Cryptic, as ever.

Phantom, if there's even a fragment of truth to what you said, if there's any way to make me stronger, to be the male she truly deserves, then you must tell me. Please. I would tear apart the stars and surrender every ounce of light left in me, if it meant keeping Aelia safe. There's nothing I wouldn't give. Not even myself.

I know that, Reign. And that is exactly what I fear.

I didn't get the chance to press her further. Footsteps sounded from the corridor ahead, deliberate and unhurried. I turned as Kaelith emerged from the shadows, dark robes trailing behind him like midnight smoke. And then, I saw her. Vaelora.

For some reason I couldn't quite explain, I'd avoided her all week. Upon our return from Feywood, I'd offered little more than a hello to my *grandmother*.

She kept to herself, remaining in her chambers and clinging to Kaelith's side when she did emerge. The ancient Night Fae great-uncle I hadn't known existed a few weeks ago, the male who had sat by and watched my *cuoré* as she was held captive for months and done nothing. As Vaelora had. Was that why I was wary to go to her? Was I still subconsciously harboring ill will toward them? It didn't matter that they had no idea who Aelia or I were at the time. I couldn't simply let that go.

I stiffened, instinct coiling under my skin. Avoiding Vaelora's guarded gaze, I turned to my great-uncle instead. "Come to offer more faulty intel on the Night King?" A part of me knew very well how unfair I was being, but I couldn't help it. Anger brewed just below my skin, and he was an easy target.

Kaelith didn't even flinch. "No. Just clarity."

I stared at him, jaw tight.

A shadow of something passed over his face. "I wish things had been different, Reign. We both do." He ticked his chin at Vaelora. "We wish we'd known of your existence years ago. I thought my brother's bloodline had ended in death. Clearly, I'd been wrong."

We stood there in silence, two Night Fae and a bastard bound by blood and decades of silence.

"I'm so sorry, Reign," Vaelora whispered, her voice wavering. "And thank you for the rescue. I never thought I would escape the walls of Helspire Keep alive."

I nodded, unexpected emotion tightening my throat. She had been a prisoner as much as Aelia had. They *both* had been.

"And I should have come to visit with you since my return." I awkwardly dragged a palm over my nape and huffed out a sigh. "I hope there will be more time for that soon."

"I pray to all the gods." She dipped her head. "It would be my greatest joy to get to know my grandson. I missed out on the chance to know your mother as an adult, and I'll be damned if I allow that to happen with you." A smile curled her lips as her eyes met mine, and another wave of longing crashed over me. Of the mother I never knew, the grandmother, the grandfather, an entire bloodline kept secret.

Then Kaelith stepped closer, raising my hackles and putting an end to the quiet moment. "Not that this family reunion isn't lovely, but there are more pressing matters to attend to." His eyes narrowed as they seared over me. "I saw what you did on the battlefield. You're powerful, Reign. But Helroth, he's had centuries to master the *zar*. You've had, what? A few months? Less?"

"I don't need a lecture from you right now," I growled.

"No. You need a teacher."

I blinked, not having expected that at all.

"I trained with your grandfather, Karnax," he said quietly. "And for a time, I trained Helroth, too. I know the way he fights. The way he thinks. If we want to beat him, truly beat him, you need to know it too. And not just in theory."

I crossed my arms, weighing the offer. "So you're offering to be *my* instructor?"

"I am," he said, blunt as a blade, as he'd been since the moment I'd met him. "Because we're running out of time. And because, like it or not, you and your *cuoré* are the last heirs of the Night line, one true and one stolen. That power in your blood? You haven't even scratched the surface."

I looked away, jaw ticking. "Let me guess, you think I'm not worthy of that great power," I muttered.

"Of course not," Vaelora hissed, jabbing her elbow into my great-uncle's side.

Kaelith shook his head, throwing my grandmother an eyeroll —not something I was sure I'd ever seen him do. "I think you're angry and scared. And that dulls the edge of power instead of sharpening it."

Another beat of silence passed.

"Do it, Kaelith," she murmured.

With a grunt, he extended his hand. "Come to the lower training court at six before the soldiers begin their exercises. If you want to learn."

I didn't take his hand, but I met his gaze. For the first time, I saw no manipulation there. Only honesty. And a strange flicker of something I'd never seen in the face of any Night Fae besides Aelia.

Hope.

"At six," I echoed.

And as Kaelith and Vaelora walked away, I realized I was already planning how I'd kill the Night King. I lingered a while longer, listening to their whispers and footsteps fade into the quiet, his words clanging around inside my skull like a bell that wouldn't stop ringing.

You haven't even scratched the surface.

Was that true? And if so, what would happen when I did?

Then Phantom's cryptic warning curled like smoke through the back of my mind.

A price. One you might not be ready to pay.

But Aidan had already paid the price, hadn't he? And so had

too many others. If there was a way to stop this war before Aelia lost anyone else, before I lost her, I'd take it, no matter the cost.

The corridor stretched ahead of me, lit by flickering torches that cast long shadows against the obsidian walls. I didn't know where I was going until I saw the faint sliver of light beneath our bedroom door.

Before I could reach it, it swung open.

Aelia stood there, barefoot, her robe hanging loosely over her shoulders, silver-blue eyes blinking against the light. Her hair was a mess, tangled from sleep, but to me, she looked like salvation incarnate.

"There you are," she murmured, stepping into the hall. "I was worried..."

"I didn't want to wake you," I said.

She studied me a moment, as if reading the wear etched into my bones, then she slipped her hand into mine. "Come to bed, Reign. Please."

I let her tug me into the room, unable to deny her, and closed the door behind us. The fire was still warm in the hearth. The bed rumpled. The chamber, ours. Not the one I'd grown up in all those years ago, but one we'd made our own, together.

I sat down on the edge of the mattress, and she curled in beside me, tucking her head against my shoulder, her presence securing me in the here and now.

"I ran into Vaelora and Kaelith," I whispered, watching the flames dance.

"Oh, Raysa, I have yet to see her. I feel awful. She'd been so kind to me at the Keep, and now that we know the truth..."

"There will be plenty of time to catch up with my new relatives once we've crushed the Night Fae." I shook my head, drawing in a steadying breath before continuing. "Kaelith offered to help me train my *zar*. Said he once trained with Helroth too."

Her hand squeezed mine, but the flash of surprise in her expression was there all the same. "Good," she finally replied. "You should take him up on it."

I turned to her, brushing a lock of hair from her cheek. "You're not worried he has some other motive?"

"I think Kaelith and Vaelora want the same thing we do. Peace." She sighed, nuzzling closer. "Besides, I trust you. And I know you'll do whatever it takes to protect Aetheria."

And you, I wanted to say. *Most of all, you.*

I didn't tell her about Phantom's cryptic words. Not yet. Not until I understood the cost.

Instead, I lay her down on the plush mattress and settled in beside her, letting the scent of her lull the storm in my mind, as only she could. She curled into my chest, her breath steadying against my skin.

And for the first time in what felt like days, I closed my eyes and let the stillness envelope me. I still didn't have all the answers. Still didn't know how we'd win this war, or what I'd have to sacrifice to make that happen.

But with her in my arms, her hand warm against my chest, and with a plan taking shape, I finally felt something I hadn't let myself feel since Tenebris's disappearance.

Purpose. Resolve. Like maybe we could actually win this.

Chapter Fifty-Four

"Come with me on patrol this morning?" Reign tugged a dark tunic over his head as I stepped into my leathers. Soft moonlight spilled into our chamber, the fortress still quiet at this early hour.

I'd planned to spend the day training with Kaelith, as my mate was supposed to be doing. After some reluctance, he'd agreed that learning to master his *zar* would prove to be the greatest aid when it came to the war effort. The whispers of troop movement along the border with the Wilds were growing in intensity. If Helroth's army materialized from the ether near Feywood, we had to be the first to know of it. The powerless Kin would be utterly defenseless against the Demons.

"How did you get roped into patrol duty?" Lacing up my boots, I glanced up at my mercurial mate.

"I volunteered."

"Trying to avoid Kaelith?"

He grunted before spearing his arms into his cloak, shadows already buzzing over his skin, a telltale sign of his emotional state.

"You are, aren't you?" I marched toward him, slapping my hands on my hips. "Why?"

Another grunt.

"Reign..." Curling my hands around his collar, I rose to my tiptoes to meet his conflicted gaze. "Don't make me delve into your mind uninvited."

A rueful grin curled the corner of his mouth. "Oh, princess, you are always invited anywhere I am."

"Then tell me, why are you avoiding this?"

Reign's expression tightened, shadows flickering across his cheekbones like restless spirits. He exhaled sharply, the sound edged with frustration.

"I'm not afraid of Kaelith," he said at last, voice low. "I'm afraid of what he'll find lacking."

I blinked. "*Lacking*?"

"My *zar*," he admitted. "What if it's not strong enough? What if I've reached my limit, and there's no more to unlock? Helroth has had centuries to master his. Mine still feels unruly. Incomplete."

My heart squeezed. "Reign..."

"I've tried everything, Aelia. I've betrayed my own damned father for this war, for this realm, for *you*. And still, I'm failing. I couldn't stop Aidan from dying. I couldn't kill Helroth when I had the chance. I don't want to face the truth that maybe—" He broke off, jaw clenched. "Maybe I won't be strong enough. That I will fail you when it matters most."

The words hung heavy between us. And gods, did I understand them.

I reached up, pressing my hand to his chest where the cuorem pulsed beneath skin and bone, connecting us on the deepest level two souls could be connected. "You are more than enough. You have strength no one else has, and not just power, but restraint.

Compassion. Purpose. You are not the same male I met at the foot of my cottage door in Feywood. You are so much more. The gods wouldn't have chosen to bestow the cuorem on someone weak, Reign. It chose *you* for me. *I* chose you."

His eyes flicked to mine, and for a moment, I saw it, the boy who had grown up unwanted, his origins kept secret, always doubting where he belonged.

"Kaelith might know the *zar*," I continued, "but you know what it means to wield power for something greater than yourself. You are the Night Court's true heir. My mate. The realm's last chance at balance. But more than that, you're the male I trust with my life. That has to count for something."

He stared at me for a long beat. Then, slowly, his shoulders eased, and he cupped my face in his hands. "You're infuriating when you're right, you know that?"

I grinned. "So I've been told."

Reign's expression softened, and something in him settled. The shadows no longer clung to him like regret. Instead, they stirred with purpose. He bent to kiss me, soft and reverent, then rested his forehead against mine. "All right. I'll go see Kaelith after patrol."

"Good," I said. "But first, let's go see our dragons. I could use a few hours in the sky, even if it is for patrolling. And besides, something tells me they've been waiting for us."

As we stepped out into the pale moonlight, hand in hand, the fortress behind us faded into shadow and the horizon ahead brimmed with sunlight and promise. Solanthus and Phantom clawed at the earth, luminescent eyes fixed to ours.

"See, I told you." I pointed at the anxious pair.

Reign cocked his head, shadows coalescing across his shoulders. "Yes, Phantom has been moodier than normal lately. Cryptic, too."

"Then let's find out what's going on." I squeezed his hand once more before releasing him and marching toward my skyrider.

Are you ready to fly, Sol?

With you, always, little Kin.

My wings flared, sparks of ethereal light igniting across my back, waking the *rais* deep in my core. Sometimes, I still couldn't believe I had luminescent wings, forged of light *and* shadow.

Once I was firmly settled between Sol's wing bones, I glanced across the way to my mate aboard Phantom. She clawed at the earth, nostrils flaring and a stream of tension vibrating the air around the onyx beast.

What's going on with Phantom? I threw the question at my dragon.

You mean besides the looming war, her brooding bonded rider, and the general chaos that has erupted since you dropped into our lives? He snorted, columns of smoke curling around his nostrils.

Very funny, Sol.

His gleaming golden wings unfolded, and with one powerful beat, we thrust skyward. My stomach dipped, legs tightening around his massive form.

You're really not going to tell me? I tried again once we were airborne with Phantom soaring beside us.

Not until we've decided.

Decided what?

Patience, little Kin. All in due time.

Gods, I hated when Sol kept things from me. Damned dragon secrecy.

I heard that. His gruff voice rumbled through my skull.

Good, I wanted you to. Then, after stewing for another moment, I added, *Just tell me what's going on.* I couldn't help the frustration that tinged my tone, even mentally.

Phantom is discussing the situation with your mate as we speak. Besides, we are supposed to be on patrol. Focus.

Right.

Wait... *How come Phantom can tell Reign, but you won't tell me?*

But instead of responding, my stubborn skyrider only pounded his wings harder, drowning out everything else.

While I silently stewed, I watched as the Court of Ethereal Light stretched ahead just beyond the Luminoc, the blessed sun already high in the sky, bathing the lands in Raysa's glory. In the past few months of residing in Shadow lands, I'd missed the sun more than I'd thought possible.

We soared higher, Sol coasting effortlessly while Phantom veered off slightly to the left, her wings like twin blades cutting through the morning light.

Below us, green hills unfurled into golden meadows, then dense thickets of woodland. As we crested a ridgeline, my chest tightened.

There it was. The Conservatory of Luce.

Where it had all started.

Its crystalline spires shimmered in the distance, catching the sunlight like mirrors reflecting heaven itself. The gardens still bloomed, even after the Night Court's siege weeks ago. The wards I'd put in place were holding strong, a golden glimmer pulsing faintly above the dome.

But all I could think about was what we'd lost. The bodies we'd buried. All the remaining students still haunted by the attack. Would I ever set foot in those halls again?

A lump rose in my throat, and I blinked away the sting of tears.

I miss it, too. Sol's murmur echoed through my mind, and I couldn't stay annoyed with him any longer.

I nodded, pressing a hand to his warm scales. We didn't linger for long, though. There was no time to wallow in memory. Onward we flew, past the outer villages of the Light Court, where the rooftops gleamed with sunstone tiles.

"Reign," I said aloud this time. "Do you see that?"

Umhmm. His grim reply rushed through the cuorem.

At the border, where the golden fields of Light bled into the smoky grays of Shadow, a host of tents had been pitched. Pale golden banners bearing the sigil of the Court of Ethereal Light fluttered in the wind.

"Elian's Royal Guardians," I murmured.

"They've been camped there since the king declared my father's capture," Reign said darkly. "Waiting. Watching. Either they're planning another strike, or they're simply too ashamed to return to the Light Court."

We circled overhead in silence, scanning the encampment. No immediate signs of aggression, just drills and watch rotations. It looked quiet. Too quiet.

Sol and Phantom kept their distance, their massive shadows rippling over the hills.

"All clear," I finally said, releasing a breath. "For now."

Reign let out a slow exhale, and I felt something tingle down the bond before he said, "Then maybe we can steal a moment to ourselves."

I glanced over my shoulder, raising a brow. "What are you suggesting, Night Prince?"

He grinned. "There's a waterfall a few miles south of here, hidden in the cliffs near the Whispering Groves. Phantom found it ages ago."

"A waterfall?" I laughed. "Reign, there's a war brewing."

"And we've just confirmed that, for today at least, it isn't erupting." His shadows danced along Phantom's spine. "Come on, starlight. One hour. Just us. Then we can continue south to Feywood."

A thrill curled through my chest, unexpected and welcome. "You want to go swimming?"

"Desperately," he said with mock solemnity. "Preferably naked."

I barked a laugh. "Gods, you're incorrigible."

"And you love it." He wasn't wrong.

Sol veered toward the southeast, and I let my heart follow him.

Maybe we were foolish to take even a sliver of peace for

ourselves in the midst of war. But after everything we'd lost, maybe we needed it. Maybe we deserved it.

Just one moment to breathe before the world demanded our blood again.

Chapter Fifty-Five

R *eign*

The majestic falls came into view like a secret whispered by the forest. Tucked deep into the folds of the Whispering Groves, the cascade shimmered like liquid sunlight. Pooling into a crystalline basin below, steam curled from the surface in lazy spirals.

Oh, Noxus, yes, we needed this. Especially after what Phantom had just alluded to.

I touched down in the glade first, my skyrider's massive form landing gracefully in the clearing. Sol followed moments later, wings folding in with a snap of wind and tension.

Aelia dismounted with fluid ease, her eyes already drinking in the serene beauty of the place. She turned to me, smiling with something soft and rare. Not the ferocity of battle or the weight of duty, but lightness. That alone was worth the temporary shirking of our duties.

We'll be nearby. Phantom's voice whispered through my mind. *Solanthus and I have much to discuss.*

Let us know when the decision has been made.

Her head dipped before she and Solanthus turned toward the grove, moving deeper into its shadows.

"We shouldn't be here," Aelia said, tugging off her jacket, "but I'm so glad we are."

I shrugged off my cloak and stepped toward her, letting the shadows slide off my skin like silk. "We've earned an hour, I'd say."

Her boots hit the mossy bank, and without waiting for another word, she slipped out of her leathers. Heady desire pooled low in my gut at the sight of my radiant *cuoré*. Before I lost all sense, I followed suit, tossing my tunic aside until I stood bare beneath the open sky.

The cuorem pulsed, strong and frenzied between us.

After a heated glance in my direction, she turned and stepped into the pool, a soft gasp escaping her lips as the warm water lapped at her thighs. Her wings shimmered behind her, ethereal and radiant even in the shade of the forest, a vision crafted of flame and starlight.

I followed her in, my feet urging me forward of their own accord.

The moment I touched the water, something shifted. My skin tingled. Not just from the heat but from her. From the bond. The cuorem stirred deeper, vibrating through every cell, tugging me toward her with an urgency that was almost primal.

She felt it too. I could scent it in the air, her arousal, her desire.

The cuorem flared brighter as if answering an ancient call. It vibrated beneath my skin, the line between dragon and rider, lover and mate, blurring with every breath. It wasn't just desire, it was something older. Something sacred.

Her breath hitched as I reached her, my hands sliding around her waist. "Do you feel that?" she whispered.

I nodded. "It's the cuorem... but something more." My thumb brushed over her bare hip, and she shivered.

Aelia arched against me, her lips brushing my jaw. "It's like something else is weaving through it. Amplifying it."

Scorching desire raced through my veins, heating my blood into a frenzy. Gods, I needed to touch her. To be inside her. *Now.* I couldn't understand what was happening. Wanting to be with my mate wasn't new, by any means—it was pretty much our normal, really—but this, this was *more.*

"Solanthus," I murmured.

"Phantom," she said at the same time.

The dragons weren't within view, but they were close, close enough for their lusty resonance to ripple between all four of us. The skyrider bond I'd always known as singular and sacred was now colliding with the cuorem, and gods, it was electric. Their presence surged through the bond we shared, magnifying every sensation, every breath.

I lowered my head, brushing my lips over hers, barely restraining myself. I wanted to devour her. Aelia sighed into my mouth, her fingers threading through my hair, her wings flaring slightly behind her. Droplets of warm water flicked into the air, spraying across my heated skin.

"You're sure they aren't watching?" she asked, laughing breathlessly against my lips.

"Right now, I couldn't care less if they were," I rasped, completely distracted by the feel of her body against mine. The way she fit so perfectly. "They're arguing now," I muttered against her lips. "Phantom's practically vibrating with rage."

"Sol's too calm," she whispered. "He only gets that way when he's trying not to start a fight."

Our uneasy laughter mingled, but the tension underneath, gods, it burned.

Unable to resist, I trailed kisses down her neck, my shadows curling in a frenzy across the water. She pulled me closer, our bond humming like a drawn bowstring, and I knew she felt it too. Everything was heat and light and the unspoken need to lose ourselves in each other, to drown in something holy before reality took it away again.

"Aelia..." I breathed against her lips. "I need you. Now."

"Then take me." Her legs parted for me, and a growl rumbled deep in my chest. I slipped my hand beneath her thigh, wrapping it around my waist before positioning my arousal at her center.

She groaned as I effortlessly slipped inside her.

"Oh, Noxus, starlight. This feels... incredible."

"Even more than usual," she groaned as I thrust deeper, "and that's pretty impressive."

The earth trembled beneath our feet, not a violent tremor, but rather quiet reverence. The trees fell silent, and even the waterfall's roar seemed to hush.

Then a sharp voice slammed into my thoughts. *Reign.*

I groaned aloud, resting my forehead against Aelia's. "We're in the middle of something, Phantom," I growled aloud, and my mate chuckled, still breathless.

This is important. Phantom's tone was clipped. *Solanthus and I have made our decision. We are completing the dragon bond.*

I blinked, stunned, still in Aelia's embrace. *You're certain?*

Yes. It's time, despite the risks. The war demands more from us than we can give as we are now. Together, we can be more. And so can you.

My heart thudded.

Aelia pulled back slightly, looking concerned. "What did she say?" Apparently, Sol had yet to impart the news.

I met her gaze, awe sparking beneath the shadows of my thoughts. "They're doing it," I whispered. "Phantom and Solanthus... They're completing the dragon mate bond."

Her eyes widened. "Now?"

"No, not exactly." I shook my head, still dazed, and still buried to the hilt inside my mate. "They need to speak to us."

She reached for me, breath catching as she rocked her hips against me once more. "I suppose it's too much to ask for them to wait a few more minutes?"

A rueful chuckle slid past my lips. "It's been decades, what's another half hour?"

The water shifted as a low rumble echoed through the trees. Phantom and Solanthus appeared through the thicket, their heads raised, eyes glowing and wings slowly unfurling as if stirred by some ancient instinct.

I muttered a curse before pressing a quick kiss to Aelia's mouth. "To be continued..." Then, reluctantly, I slid out of my mate, freeing myself of that intoxicating hold and turning toward our dragons, still semi-covered by the deep water. "Well, then, don't keep us in suspense. Now what happens?"

The ground trembled again, stronger now.

My arms shot out on instinct, reaching for Aelia and tucking her into my side. Only, it wasn't from an attack. The rumble below the earth was deeper. Older. As if something buried in the marrow of the world was beginning to stir.

Phantom turned toward me, her obsidian eyes glowing brighter than I'd ever seen them. It was a tethered storm straining at the edge of release.

We must leave. Her voice rolled through me, thunder against bone.

Aelia pressed closer, instinctively seeking my hand. Solanthus watched her, but his body was rigid with restraint, muscles quivering like he was barely keeping himself rooted to the earth.

"What do you mean, 'leave?'" I asked aloud, my fingers tightening around Aelia's as I tugged her out of the lagoon. After fetching her clothes, I slid into my leathers and glanced up at our dragons. "Now?"

Phantom nodded, dipping her massive head. *There is a place hidden from time. An isle born of fire and the blood of the gods. The Ancients of our kind called it Aekorith. It is where all true dragon pairs must go to seal the mate bond, to undertake the Rite of Syneris. We've made our decision and now have been summoned.*

"Aekorith," Aelia breathed, awe coloring her voice. Solanthus must have been echoing Phantom's words in her mind.

It is sacred. And secret. The island only appears to bonded dragons ready to complete the ritual. It calls to us, and we must answer.

My gut twisted. "But what about the war? We're on the brink, Helroth could strike any day. We need you. Both of you."

Phantom lowered her gaze, shadows flickering off her wings. *We know, which was what we were discussing. But without this bond, we will never reach our full potential. The strength we hold alone is a fraction of what we could become together. All of us.*

Aelia blinked. "What do you mean?"

The bond between us and you, it is deeper than rider and mount. It is soul to soul. When Solanthus and I seal our bond, yours will change too. Strengthen. The cuorem and the skyrider threads will fuse. You will gain more than just power.

I swallowed hard. "And the risks?"

Phantom looked me dead in the eye. *The ritual is dangerous. We must face the Trials of Aekorith. There are three in total: one of flesh, one of flame, and one of soul. If we fail...* She hesitated.

Aelia's hand clenched mine. "What happens if they fail?"

If we fail, we perish. Together. And the magic that binds us to you dies with us.

Silence fell like a blade between us.

I couldn't breathe.

We could *all* die.

After everything? After what we'd survived together? The thought hollowed me out.

Aelia stepped forward. "Why didn't you tell us this before?"

"They never planned on completing the bond..." I replied, echoing Phantom's answer. Gods, no wonder the call of the dragon mate bond is so relentless, lasting through lifetimes.

"We can't allow you to do this just for us," Aelia continued. "It's too much of a sacrifice."

It isn't only for you. Phantom's voice faltered. *Solanthus and I love each other. The mystical tethers drawing us together were never severed, and the pull is as strong today as it was all those years ago. We want this for us, too.*

A beaming smile split Aelia's lips, and I could feel her happiness surging through our connection. "Then we'll come with you."

You cannot. Phantom's voice rumbled low, regretful. *The island won't allow it. The ritual must be done in secrecy. In trust. In sacrifice. We go alone. And we return stronger or not at all.*

My dragon turned her massive head toward me again. *You must let me do this, Reign. For you. For her. For Aetheria.*

Tension clawed at my chest, sharp and unwieldy.

"I can't protect you there," I whispered.

You never could. Her voice softened. *That was never your job. But you gave me purpose, Reign. You gave me something to fight for. And now, I must become what I was always meant to be.*

Aelia swallowed, her voice shaking. "How long?"

Time moves strangely in Aekorith. It could be days. Weeks. Perhaps, longer. But we'll come back. If the gods are just, we'll come back stronger than you've ever dreamed.

I stepped forward, pressing my forehead to Phantom's sleek obsidian hide, the warmth of her scales anchoring me in this terrifying truth.

"I'll wait as long as it takes," I murmured. "But you better come back to me, old girl. You hear me?"

I will. She nuzzled my shoulder. *You'll know when it's done. The whole realm will.*

Aelia moved to Solanthus, a tear sliding down her cheek. She pressed her hand to his chest, and the golden dragon leaned into her touch with a rumble like distant thunder.

The sooner we go, the more quickly we can return. Phantom's final words thrummed across my mind.

At that, they turned as one, wings spreading wide like twin banners of war and legacy.

I wanted to stop them. Gods, I wanted to shout. But I didn't. Because this was the only path forward, and we all knew it.

So, we stood at the edge of the water, the falls still whispering behind us, and watched them rise into the sky—Phantom and

Solanthus, obsidian and gold, night and flame—soaring toward the unknown.

And though I'd never felt more hollow, I'd never been more proud.

Chapter Fifty-Six

A*elia*

It had been two entire days of silence across the mythical bond that connected me to Sol. It was as if a piece of me had been stolen. It was like losing a limb, one I could still feel even though it was no longer there. Every instinct screamed for him, but all I found was silence, a static void where his warmth had once been. Even my *rais* felt subdued, the gilded, ethereal energy burning less brightly without my skyrider at the other end.

First Aidan, and now Sol. I wasn't sure I could survive this.

Sitting on a grassy knoll overlooking the training arena below, I plucked a blade of grass and wove it between my fingers. The moonlight glistened overhead, setting the dewdrops aglow with starlight as the verdant stalk moved.

The moment Sol and Phantom had left us at the hidden cascades, the radiant, flickering tether between us went quiet. Somehow, I could still sense him for a while, and then a few hours later, he was just... gone. Nothing but a black, empty void remaining where his immense presence had once been.

The same was true for Reign and Phantom. My *cuoré* was handling it about as well as I was. Only the distraction of mastering his *zar* with Kae kept his mind occupied. My gaze dipped to the arena below where my mate and his great-uncle traded *zar*-fueled blows. On the bright side, he'd spent nearly the entire day with my former captor, and from the range of emotions whizzing through our bond, progress was being made.

"No rest for the wicked." Rue's voice tore me away from my thoughts, forcing my gaze up to meet a mischievous one.

Symon grinned beside her, throwing his arm across her shoulders. "She's right, you know." His fingers reached out for my ear, but I batted it away, earning a dramatic pout from my ridiculous friend. "What are you doing moping around up here all by yourself?"

Rue plopped down beside me. "Yes, why?" She ticked her head at the arena below, where dozens of former Royal Guardians and Umbral Guard trained together. "Shouldn't you be down there with your soldiers?"

"My soldiers?" I huffed out a laugh.

"Of course they're yours, little Kin. They worship you almost as much as I did those perfectly rounded, sexy ears." He heaved out a despondent sigh. "I only wish I'd had the chance to touch them more—"

"Sy!" I cried out with a laugh.

"I digress..." He waved a dismissive hand as he plopped down beside me. "The point was, those Guardians need you. They've abandoned the king they blindly served for years for *you*. You are their princess, their hope for a new and better future."

"I think you're overestimating my power." I fiddled with the blade of grass before dropping it to the ground.

Rue snorted. "Oh, please. You blasted a Night Fae battalion out of Luce with a triune shield no one thought possible."

"And convinced Reign not to kill Kaelith the first time they met," Symon added. "Frankly, I'd have let him take a swing after he helped Helroth keep you captive for all those months."

"You are uniting the Courts," Rue said softly, nudging me with her shoulder. "Shadow, Light, *and* Night. *And* you have a dragon!"

"Don't forget the adorable Kin children who are surely already asking for 'Princess Aelia' stories before bed," Symon chimed in with a grin. "You're practically a living legend."

I rolled my eyes. "You two are absolutely ludicrous."

Rue wrapped her arm around my shoulders. "Maybe. But we're also not wrong."

I glanced back down at the arena, where Reign spun, shadows lashing from his hands in controlled arcs. Kaelith deflected with a shield of pure *zar*, and the sound cracked through the night air like lightning.

"I just... I miss him," I whispered. "Sol. And I'm scared. About what's coming. About what it'll cost."

Symon's teasing faded, his hand resting lightly on mine. "Then lean on us until he comes back. That's what family does."

Family. That familiar ache of loss thrummed behind my ribs.

"Besides," Rue said, standing and dusting off her leathers, "you don't have to do it all alone. But you *do* need to stop sulking in the grass like some moody Faeling poet. Reign's going to think they've finally broken you."

Symon grinned, extending a hand to me as he stood too. "Come on, princess. Let's show your *cuoré* what he's fighting for."

With a half-laugh, half-sigh, I let them pull me to my feet.

The three of us descended the hill together, Rue linking her arm through mine while Symon sang some made-up battle song off-key beside us. As we reached the edge of the arena, Reign turned toward me, his bare chest glistening with sweat and shadows curling protectively around him. Kaelith stood to his side, stone-faced as ever, but I swore I saw a flicker of approval in his gaze when he saw me.

Reign's eyes locked with mine, and despite everything we had yet to face, I felt steadier. Because I wasn't alone.

"How's he doing, Kae?"

"Not bad," he gritted out before taking a swig from his leather skein.

"*Not bad*?" Reign echoed. "My *zar* swept the floor with yours."

Kaelith's lip twitched into a begrudging smile. "I'll admit you've progressed more quickly than I'd imagined in only two short days."

I curled my arm around Reign's waist, glancing up with an adoring smile. "That's because he's my mate."

Kaelith scoffed, rolling his eyes so hard the citrine of his irises all but disappeared. "Why don't you show him how it's done, Aelia?"

A sliver of unease rushed through me. Of the trio I'd been blessed with, *zar* was still the one I avoided using most. I'd even happily given up on the necromancy lessons with Kae now that he had Reign to instruct.

"Yes, show us what you've got!" Rue squealed as she and Sy clapped their hands excitedly.

"Use only *zar*," Kae commanded.

I exhaled, stretching my fingers at my sides as the *zar*-infused shadows responded instantly, eager and coiling, as if they'd been waiting for me to stop ignoring them.

"I don't know..." I hesitated, eyeing the target dummies still lined up at the far end of the arena.

"Oh, come on, princess," Reign goaded, stepping back and crossing his arms, that infuriatingly smug smirk that he knew would rile me on his lips. "You can't let your mate outshine you in front of your own army."

Rue and Symon whooped.

With a dramatic sigh, I stepped forward, drawing in a slow breath as I sank into the darker well of powers deep within me.

Unlike *rais*, which shimmered and danced, *zar* was heavier. It thrummed like the weight of midnight in my blood.

The arena quieted. Even some of the soldiers had stopped to watch.

The moment I tapped into the *zar*, my heart stuttered. It was denser than before, darker, like something coiled and waiting beneath my skin. I welcomed it anyway. I raised one hand, fingers splayed wide and summoned the night.

With the cuorem flickering to life, awakened by the ancient power, I used it to anchor myself. I knew only Reign could keep me grounded, keep me from losing myself in the abyss.

I moved on instinct, guided by something innate. The coils of *zar* obeyed, not like Reign's quick strikes, but slower, more controlled. When I launched the blast, it wasn't with precision. It was reflex. Rage. Grief. Power. It hit the first target like a storm split open from the inside.

It poured from me like a living veil, shadows stretching long and sharp across the stone floor. Again, tendrils of inky *zar* twisted up my arms, thick and sinuous, unlike the ethereal shadows Ruhl commanded. Then, with a flick of my wrist, I launched them.

The second dummy erupted in a blast of black hellfire, the *zar* consuming it whole.

Gasps rang out from the barracks above.

I stepped into a smooth spin, calling more *zar* to my other palm. This time, I shaped it, something I'd only ever seen Kae do. A sleek dagger formed, serrated and humming with volatile power. With a grunt, I hurled it at the third dummy. It impaled the center of the chest with deadly precision.

"Sweet Raysa's ass," Symon whispered. "Remind me not to get on her bad side."

"That was impressive," Kaelith said, blinking. "You've been holding back."

I turned toward Reign, breath stilling in my chest, waiting for his reaction.

But there was only awe in his midnight eyes. Pride. "You never cease to surprise me," he murmured.

A smile split my lips. Maybe I had been avoiding the *zar* because it reminded me of captivity. But now, it felt like something else entirely, something that actually belonged to me. And to Reign. It was power, not punishment.

Then my *cuoré* stepped forward, grinning. "Now, it's my turn." He moved into the center of the arena, raising one hand without flourish. His *zar* answered like a dog to its master, swift, silent, and lethal. A ring of smoky blades hovered around him, then flared with raw energy as he spun, launching them one by one.

Every blade found its mark.

The soldiers broke into stunned applause, but Reign was already walking toward me, shadows still pulsing around him.

"We're stronger than we've ever been," he said, his voice low and urgent, meant only for me. "When our dragons return, mated and even more powerful, we'll be ready."

I nodded, the lingering sting of *zar* still humming beneath my skin. For the first time in days, I didn't feel numb. I felt powerful.

Together, we turned to the training field as the soldiers resumed their drills. Light and darkness, united. And for one fleeting heartbeat, I believed we could win this war.

Then, an ear-splitting roar pierced through the moment of triumph.

Mordrin sailed overhead, wings pounding and silver scales glistening beneath the moonlight. All eyes turned upward as the Shadow Regent descended aboard his monstrous dragon. The moment his talons hit the earth shaking the ground beneath my boots, unease settled low in my belly.

Ruhl leapt off Mordrin's back and raced toward us, shadows buzzing across his lithe form and the expression on his face doing nothing to quell the brewing storm in my gut.

Reign must have sensed his brother's unease as much as I had.

His feet were already moving toward the uncrowned king the moment he hit the earth. "What's happened?" he growled.

"The Night Fae... they're here."

Ruhl's voice was a ragged whisper, but it cracked like thunder through the arena. Around us, drills stopped. Blades fell still. Even Kaelith's *zar* stilled mid-pulse. And just like that, the air shifted, as if the realm itself was holding its breath.

The war hadn't just begun. It had arrived.

Chapter Fifty-Seven

R^{eign}

The war room crackled with tension, full of unspoken fears and sharp opinions colliding like unsheathed blades. Shadowlight flickered across the obsidian walls, illuminating the gathered council of generals, strategists, and those who'd fought in the Two Hundred Years War and knew how fast it could all unravel.

Aelia stood beside me, arms folded tightly, her mouth a hard line of restraint. But I could feel her rage vibrating through the cuorem. Her fear. Her grief. Her power.

"Reports confirm it," said General Arven, his voice as brittle as dry bones. He'd served my father for decades. What would he do if he knew I'd been the one to betray him to Elian? I pushed the pointless thought aside for now as the male continued. "The Night Fae battalions are no longer lurking in the shadows of the Wilds. They're on the move, marching through Feywood."

Aelia drew in a sharp breath before her fist slammed against the stone table. "Then we ride to meet them. Today."

I touched her arm before I could think better of it. "We can't."

She rounded on me. "We *have* to. The Kin are powerless. You know that better than anyone. If Helroth's forces reach them—"

"They won't," I interrupted. "Not all of them. You heard what Ruhl said earlier, Helroth isn't riding with them. This is only a small force." I paused, lowering my voice another octave. Only our tightest circle of confidants knew our dragons were unreachable. "We're not ready. Not without Solanthus or Phantom."

The silence that followed was brutal.

Her eyes searched mine, desperation etched into every line of her face, and it was a punch to the gut. "So we wait? While they slaughter innocents?"

"No." I pulled away from the table, pacing to the edge of the chamber. My shadows stirred around me, restless. "This is only the first wave. Helroth is testing us, baiting us into moving too soon. If we rush out with half our strength, we'll lose everything."

"I wish Aidan were still here," she whispered. The raw ache in her voice nearly undid me. "He'd know what to do, and he wouldn't hesitate to protect them."

I stepped toward her, placing a hand over hers on the table. "Aidan trusted us to lead. You. Me. He knew this moment was coming."

She turned her face away, jaw trembling.

Ruhl stepped forward, his shadows still clinging to his back like smoke. "Then let me go."

Aelia blinked. "...What?"

"I'll take Mordrin and a squadron of Umbral Guards," Ruhl said. "We'll intercept the Night Fae before they reach Feywood. Harass their flank, slow their momentum. Long enough for our forces to prepare." And our dragons to return. The unspoken words were as clear as day.

"Absolutely not," Arven barked. "You are the Shadow Regent,

the future of the Court of Umbral Shadows. You are much too valuable."

"And you'll be outnumbered," Aelia said, voice tight.

His crooked grin surfaced. "Wouldn't be the first time. And if anyone knows how to fight dirty, it's me."

"You're serious?" Aelia's brows drew together.

Ruhl's expression sobered. "You think I'm going to stand here while Helroth's monsters carve up Kin villages?" Looking between me and my mate, he lowered his voice, directing his words only to us as the other generals argued. "We all know you two are tethered to those dragons. When they return, you'll be the realm's best chance. But not if you charge off now and die without them."

Aelia opened her mouth to argue, but I caught her hand in mine. "He's right." Two words I never thought I'd say where it concerned my half-brother.

Her stare pierced me, fury and heartbreak in equal measure. "I hate that he's right."

"So do I," I admitted. "But you and me? We're not just warriors anymore. We're the rallying point. The Courts need us, especially you. Strong and alive."

"And what about Ruhl? The general is right, too. He's the future king."

Ruhl shrugged nonchalantly. "Assuming I pass the Ritual of the Shadow Throne, which I am in no hurry to do."

Aelia squeezed my brother by the shoulders, forcing his gaze to her serious one. "You *are* the Shadow Court's future, Ruhl. You can't be so flippant with your life."

He snorted on a laugh. "And you're one to talk, princess." Then his dark eyes darted to mine. "Both of you. We are all heirs of some court or another. We are all equally valuable." Then he wriggled free of her hold. "Let me do this for you, for all of us. You two have carried the burden long enough."

Neither Aelia nor I spoke. I was too stunned by this selfless stranger posing as my once spoiled, arrogant younger brother. And gods help me, for the first time, I was afraid to lose him.

With the silence lingering, he turned toward the door. "I leave within the hour. Let's see how the Night Fae like a little fire of our own."

I watched him go, a dark streak of purpose and recklessness wrapped in shadows. Then I turned to Aelia and pulled her against me, anchoring her to the one thing I could still offer.

"We'll fight," I promised into her hair. "When the time is right, we'll burn the darkness from this realm. Together."

She didn't speak. But the weight of her heart pressed against mine.

A long minute later, with the generals still bickering in the background, she whispered against my tunic, "What do you think is happening with Sol and Phantom?"

"I wish I knew, starlight," I murmured against her hair.

"I hope they're back soon."

"As do I."

A heady tangle of *nox* and *rais* surged across the training arena, the entire space teeming with movement. We'd managed to bolster our forces in the past few days after sending out half a dozen scouts across both Light and Shadow Courts, summoning both fighting males and females to our cause.

Aelia had rallied Fae from both Courts like she was born to do it. A warrior princess with fire in her blood and stars in her veins, destined to unify all Aetheria. I felt it with increasing certainty with every day that passed. I only had to keep her alive so she could actually fulfill that destiny.

Another day had come and gone, and as if worrying about Phantom and Solanthus wasn't taxing enough, now I had my brother and our troops in the Wilds to fret about. From the shadow message I'd received yesterday, Ruhl had managed to keep the Night Fae forces at bay. They'd stopped them right at the border of Feywood. So far, no Kin lives had been lost.

Meanwhile, on the other boundary, along the Luminoc, that fool, King Elian, kept his Royal Guardians threatening Shadow Lands. Which forced us to split our soldiers across two fronts. This was exactly what we'd all feared. Fighting two enemies in a war was far from ideal.

A part of me wanted nothing more than to confront Elian head on and end this lunacy. But for all his faults, the male was still Aelia's uncle and her only living blood relative. I understood the dilemma well, seeing as I'd experienced it with my own bastard of a father.

Not for the first time, my thoughts turned to the male who'd sired me. *Where are you, Tenebris?* The Moirai Shard still waited in the armoire, poised to claim whatever sacrifice it deemed fit. At least we wouldn't be forced to use it to sever the blood vow Helroth held over Aelia. She wouldn't have to bear that steep price because she'd been able to overcome it on her own somehow.

I, on the other hand, was still fettered by its relentless hold.

Why? I simply couldn't understand it. Was it because she was the child of twilight? Did that give her some sort of godly power I could never attain?

Blowing out a breath, I tossed out the futile thoughts. None of that mattered right now. I just needed to focus. To train. To be strong enough to do what needed to be done when the time came.

As I marched along the periphery of the arena, the shadows around me shifted, then warped, and I knew before he stepped into view who was approaching.

"Still brooding, are we?" Kaelith drawled, his voice low and dry as old parchment.

I turned, jaw already tight. "I wasn't brooding. I was thinking."

"Same thing, in your case," he said, stepping into the flickering torchlight, arms folded across his chest. "I gave you half the morning, nephew. You've had your moment of reflection. Now it's time to bleed."

I arched a brow. More at the word *nephew* than his desire to make me bleed. "That's your motivational speech? I thought the ancient Night Court warriors—a royal, nonetheless—were supposed to be poetic."

He smirked, unamused. "Poetry doesn't keep you alive when your enemy's blade is at your throat. Power does. Discipline. Control. You want to stand against Helroth? Then move."

The speech was so familiar, something I'd said to my own students countless times before. It was as if it had been dragged from my own lips. Perhaps, I had more in common with my Night Fae great-uncle than I believed.

My hands curled into fists, shadows already flickering across my knuckles. "You always this charming before noon?"

"No. Usually, I'm worse," he said with a tilt of his head. "Now, get moving before I drag you into the sparring circle myself."

A muscle ticked in my jaw, but I forced a breath through my nose and stalked past him.

As we walked, his voice lowered. "You're strong, Reign. But you're still holding back. Still letting the past weigh your blade."

I didn't answer. Because he wasn't wrong.

But I would face it. All of it. The past. My father. Helroth. The war. And I would win.

Even if it meant bleeding for every damned inch. For *her*.

Chapter Fifty-Eight

A*elia*

The wind tugged at the ends of my cloak as I walked the upper ramparts of the Shadow Fortress, the ancient stones slick beneath my boots from the morning mist. Beneath the waning moon, I could see the wild, jagged terrain sprawling beyond the perimeter, dark, beautiful, and haunted by war.

A shadow message had arrived only hours ago from Ruhl.

The Night Fae had infiltrated Feywood.

My fingers curled into fists at my sides, breath catching painfully in my chest. My home. My quiet, beloved little village tucked into the folds of the forest like a secret. The place I'd spent so many years hiding, tilling the fields for the Fae, and training with Aidan in secret.

Gods, Aidan.

His name alone was enough to lance a hole through my composure.

And Sol. I missed him with a ferocity that made my bones

ache. It had been too many days of silence, the bond between us little more than a flicker in the void. I told myself he was alive. That both he and Phantom were. But telling and believing were two very different things.

A whisper of movement had me pausing at the northern tower, the cold wind sweeping down from the peaks. I turned and stilled.

Vaelora.

She stood with her back to the stone wall, white hair billowing like silk in the breeze, her navy eyes sharp, even in the dim light. There was something different about her now, the quiet, unassuming servant replaced by a forgotten queen.

It was the first time I'd seen her since Helspire Keep.

My steps faltered. We hadn't spoken since her arrival. Since I'd escaped. Since I'd survived.

"I didn't expect to see you out here," I said quietly, not wanting to startle her.

She inclined her head. "I walk out here to enjoy the night sky. I missed it for so many years."

For a moment, we simply stood in silence, the shadows casting long patterns between us.

"Thank you," I said, my voice rougher than I intended. "For what you did. For what you tried to do for me back in Helspire. You didn't have to."

"I did," she replied softly, brushing windblown hair behind her ear. "Not because of duty. But because you were alone. And scared. And strong." She paused, her gaze drifting toward the horizon. "You reminded me of someone my daughter could have been."

I didn't know what to say to that. So, instead, I asked, "Have you spoken to Reign?"

A sad smile curved her mouth. "Not truly. Not as I wish to. He keeps me at a distance. He's polite and respectful, but his heart is locked."

A pang tightened in my chest. I knew that lock well. I'd had to pry it open more than once.

"He's afraid to let me in," Vaelora continued, eyes clouding. "Maybe he simply doesn't trust me yet, or perhaps it's something else entirely. But I already see who he really is. He reminds me so much of his grandfather."

"Karnax," I said softly.

Her smile faltered. "The only male I ever loved."

My heart clenched. She didn't say it, but I could feel the grief behind those words. And the regret. Before I could respond, footsteps echoed behind me, heavy and sure, and familiar. I turned.

Reign.

He slowed as he approached, shadows rising faintly around his shoulders like a protective cloak. His gaze shifted from me to Vaelora, unreadable.

"Reign," she said, her voice calm, but there was hope there too. "You've been training hard with your great-uncle. I've barely seen either one of you in days."

He grunted. "Kaelith doesn't believe in moderation."

A hint of amusement touched her face, but it faded as quickly as it came. "You're both blessed with the same relentless strength. But strength isn't always what wins wars."

His jaw tightened.

"Sometimes, love does," she added.

A beat passed. Then another.

"I'll keep that in mind," he said at last, voice quiet but edged in something that wasn't quite resistance.

Vaelora nodded slowly, then turned to me. "Walk with me again sometime."

I nodded, and she slipped away into the shadows like a wraith, leaving me alone with my mate.

Reign stepped beside me and let out a slow breath. "I heard about Feywood. How bad is it?"

I shook my head. "Ruhl says they're battling near the edge.

But if they push deeper, there are Kin who won't survive that kind of assault."

He didn't speak for a long while. Then, his hand slid into mine, firm and warm. "We'll stop them," he whispered. "One way or another."

I leaned my head against his shoulder, grounding myself in the only thing that still felt steady in a world unraveling around me. "I know."

We stood there for an interminable moment, leaning on one another, basking in the pale moonlight and the twinkling stars casting their ethereal light on the endless darkness below.

"We can't just keep waiting," I murmured, tilting my head back to meet his troubled gaze.

"I know."

Steeling myself for what came next, I forced the sentence out. "I sent word back to Ruhl that I'll join him tomorrow."

"*What?*" Reign spun on me, shadows peeling from his broad shoulders to encircle me as if they could somehow keep me pinned to the spot.

"Those are *my* people, Reign, and unlike the Light and Shadow Fae, they are completely powerless. I will not stand by and allow those poor Kin to die."

"But Ruhl—"

"Ruhl is one male with one dragon. He cannot bear the responsibility for all of us."

"And I cannot bear the possibility of losing you," he growled.

His roar echoed across the ramparts, swallowed a moment later by the wind whistling off the cliffs. Shadows lashed out from his body, flickering like broken wings before dissipating into the night. I didn't flinch. He didn't scare me, he never truly had, even when he appeared at my door in Feywood a year ago.

"I've made up my mind," I said, my voice low but firm. "I owe it to them, Reign. To the Kin who work their fingers to the bones for the Fae. They were my neighbors and my friends, who whispered stories of a better world to their children even as monsters lurked at their doorstep. I am their princess, too. Their hope. If I don't go, what will happen to them?"

He dragged a hand through his ink-black hair, jaw clenching. "You are also my *cuoré*," he said hoarsely. "The bond between us —" His voice cracked. "If you fall... I fall. I could never live without you. There isn't a world in which I would want to."

My heart squeezed, the weight of his words anchoring themselves in the deepest parts of me. But I couldn't turn away from this path. "I know the risks," I whispered. "But I can't live with myself if I stay behind while innocent lives are ripped apart. I won't be a queen who hides behind stone walls."

He stepped closer, his hand cupping my cheek, his thumb brushing away a tear I hadn't realized had fallen.

"Then I'm coming with you," he said, shadows already curling up his spine, determination burning in his midnight eyes.

I shook my head. "You can't. You know that. If Phantom and Sol return while we're gone or if the final battle begins, your power is our last line of defense. If anything should happen to Ruhl, you are the Shadow Court's heir too. Their strength."

"And *you* are my strength." His voice broke like a vow, soft but irrevocable. His jaw ticked, shadows trembling at the edges of his form, like he was about to speak.

Then it hit me.

A violent jolt of energy ignited behind my ribs, flooding every vacant space within me with blinding, brilliant light. Pure *rais* surged through my veins like wildfire, searing away the cold void that had consumed me for days.

Solanthus.

His name thundered through my soul as the skyrider bond snapped back into place like a lifeline drawn taut. The hollowness I'd carried for a week was gone in an instant, replaced by a pulsing current of power, of presence, of him.

My breath hitched, knees buckling as the onslaught of energy crashed through me, staggering me backward. Tears blurred my vision, but I blinked them away in time to see Reign drop to his knees, eyes wide, lips parted in stunned disbelief.

"They're alive," I choked out, pressing a trembling hand to my chest. "Thank Raysa, they're alive."

Chapter Fifty-Nine

A *elia*

Sol! Even in my mind, his name erupted like a prayer, tears filling my eyes. *You're all right?*

Yes, little Kin. We're both fine. A bit exhausted, but we survived the sacred ritual.

Thank the gods. I could feel Reign hovering, his shadows sliding over my flesh, but I was too focused on the internal conversation to reassure him. Realms, I'd missed Sol so much. *Have you completed the mate bond?*

Not quite. We need you and your cuoré for that. A hint of irritation flared in the reawakened connection between us.

"What's going on?" Reign shouted, drawing me from the conversation.

"Wait," I hissed, smushing my finger against his lips. "That's what I'm trying to find out."

I pressed a palm to my chest, grounding myself as Sol's voice rippled through me once more, ancient and resonant.

We need you here. Now. You and your mate. The bond must be sealed in full with all four of us.

Where are you?

In Aekorith, the hidden isle of the dragons. Follow the mystical strands that connect us. Shadowtravel to me, Aelia. I'll guide you. Then his voice deepened, tinged with reverence. *But be warned… this is no place mortals were meant to tread.*

Yes, of course. I barely had time to grab Reign's hand. "We're going. Now."

"What?" he blinked. "Where?"

"No time to explain. Just trust me. Sol and Phantom need us."

He didn't hesitate. His fingers simply tightened around mine. "Always."

I closed my eyes, then focused on the flickering tether of energy sparking to life through both the cuorem and skyrider bonds. Shadows curled around us, buzzing and whirling in a desperate fury. It was as if they too could sense the importance of this moment.

Darkness swallowed us whole for endless minutes, then burst into brilliant, blinding color. We emerged into a realm that stole the breath straight from my lungs.

The air shimmered with auroral light, like the sky itself was woven from stardust and flame. Towering obsidian peaks jutted toward the heavens, crowned in violet mist, while crystalline waterfalls spilled from their cliffs, glowing faintly with ethereal fire.

Below, the land pulsed with life. Lush emerald fields were carpeted in soft, glowing moss and enormous blossoms that opened and closed like they were breathing. Rivers of molten gold wound like veins across the earth.

My jaw dropped, my head swiveling to take in every incredible detail. "It's beautiful," I murmured.

Reign's hand squeezed, fingers tightening as he took it all in.

Dragons. Dozens of them. Maybe more.

This must have been where they'd all fled to after the Two Hundred Years' War. They sat coiled atop the cliffs, gliding on wings of moonlight and fire. Their scales refracted light like living jewels of onyx and gold, sapphire and silver, and iridescent hues I didn't even have names for. None of them looked our way, but I could feel their awareness, their silent judgment.

They were all asking the same thing: *Why are* you *here?*

Reign staggered beside me. "Where in the gods' damned realms are we?"

"Dragonkind's secret isle," I whispered, voice trembling. "The place Sol called Aekorith, remember? This is where the ancient dragons completed their bonds."

Solanthus stood ahead of us, poised and waiting, gleaming like a god carved of celestial fire. Phantom loomed beside him, shadows rippling like smoke across her massive form.

"Welcome to the hidden cradle of our kind, little Kin." Sol's voice echoed through the valley like thunder.

I blinked once, then twice, my jaw nearly unhinging for the second time in as many minutes. "Sol... he spoke."

Reign nodded, lips parted. "I... I heard. Gods, I *felt* it." His voice was as strained as my own.

"And now, it's time," Sol announced.

I took a cautious step forward, heart pounding as I stared up at Sol and Phantom, side by side, glowing with power that made my bones ache. A warm wind swept over the isle, carrying the scent of smoke and starlight. It kissed my cheeks like a blessing. Or a warning.

Reign moved beside me, silent for once. I could feel his awe rippling through the cuorem, his shadows held tight and reverent against his skin like they, too, were bowing before this sacred place.

Come. Sol's voice rumbled inside me. *We must begin. The final ritual cannot wait.*

"What do we do?" I whispered aloud.

Solanthus dipped his massive head toward a stone ring etched into the glowing moss. The symbols were ancient. I squinted to make them all out—sprawling dragons, woven knots of magic, two mirrored suns along with two mirrored moons. One pair for rider. One pair for dragon.

"Step into the ring," Phantom instructed. "Together."

Reign and I exchanged a glance, his eyes as wide as mine likely were. After only communicating mentally for so long, hearing their voices aloud was incredibly jarring, even if they sounded exactly the same. We only paused for a moment before obeying. The moment our feet touched the stone, it pulsed with golden light.

My skin prickled, every nerve a live wire. Power coiled through my spine, golden and searing. My legs nearly buckled as the ancient sigils began to pulse beneath my feet.

"The Rite of Syneris is older than time," Phantom continued, her obsidian eyes locking to mine, then Reign's. "It requires not just power, but trust. Surrender. Unity."

Sol's wings stretched wide, golden light bleeding from every scale. "When mated riders and mated dragons are bonded as one, they form what the Ancients called *the Tetrum Cordis*, the Heart of Four. It is an incredibly rare phenomenon."

I couldn't help but wonder if Sol and Phantom had undertaken this very ritual with my parents all those years ago.

No, we didn't. Sol's voice sailed through my mind once again. *Phantom and I were already mated when she bonded with your mother. This is the first time for us all.*

"Each of us will offer a part of ourselves," Phantom explained, drawing me back to the present. "Our powers. Our pain. Our truth. It will weave us into a single current."

"And when it's done," Sol added, "no force in this realm, or the next, will be able to sever it."

Reign's hand found mine, fingers threading tightly. "What happens if we fail?"

Phantom's tail flicked like a blade. "Then the bond breaks, and all four of us will be destroyed."

A shiver danced down my spine, but I held firm. "Well, then, I guess failing isn't an option."

Sol nodded, then breathed a plume of gold fire into the sky. "Then let it begin."

With all of dragonkind watching us, the four of us were positioned at cardinal points around the circle. Sol to the north, Phantom to the south, Reign and I across from one another, east and west. The sigils beneath our feet blazed brighter, spinning slowly, like a great wheel being turned by unseen hands.

I felt it first, the call of the bond, deep and primal.

"Speak your truth," Solanthus said.

My voice quivered but didn't falter as words dribbled from my lips, seemingly of their own accord. "I am Aelia of Ether and Inferna, princess of light and darkness, child of twilight. I give my heart, my power, and my soul to this bond."

Reign followed, voice rough with emotion. "I am Reign of Umbra, lost heir of the Court of Infernal Night and bastard prince of Shadows. I offer my power, my blood, and my oath."

Phantom's growl resonated across the isle. "I am Phantom, the Death of Dawn, forged of shadow and storm. I surrender my fire, my fury, and my name."

Sol's voice was a song of triumph. "I am Solanthus, the Sun Chaser, of sunlight and flame, last of the Drakari line. I give my wisdom, my strength, and my truth."

The air thickened, then hummed, as if the isle itself was listening.

"Now," Phantom said, "you must give pain."

I didn't hesitate. I let it rise: Aidan's face; my parents' deaths; the loneliness of growing up without ever knowing them; Elian's betrayal; Helroth's refusal to stand down.

It poured from me like light cracking from glass. And when I looked across the circle, I saw Reign's shadows bleeding too, his pain made visible as dark as spilled ink.

Our dragons roared in tandem, wings unfurled, *rais*, *nox* and *zar* spinning around the ring in a cyclone of gold and black.

A memory rose to the surface, one of the first conversations I'd ever had with my skyrider when he was nothing more than a tiny dragonette. *Our souls reincarnate by the powers of the gods, the perfect balance of light and dark, and now Raysa has delivered me to you.*

All four of us, we were the perfect balance of light and dark.

"Now," Sol said, interrupting my mental musings, "you must leap and face the will of the gods."

The stone circle cracked open beneath us, revealing a pit of pure light and void, a swirling nexus of all our energies fused.

I eyed the yawning chasm, a whisper of fear kindling beneath my breastbone. What if we didn't survive this? I hesitated at the edge, heart hammering, glancing between the void and Reign. What if this was the gods' final test? A leap not into unity but oblivion. What if I lost him?

Not physical death, little Kin. But surrender. Sol's voice echoed through my mind, a soothing balm amidst the uncertainty. *I have no doubt in my mind that the gods will find us worthy.*

Reign's gaze lifted to meet mine. "We go together."

Drawing in a steadying breath, I nodded.

And we jumped.

The world disappeared.

Light consumed me. Shadow kissed my bones. Fire and smoke wrapped around my soul, branding me with something ancient and eternal.

I felt Reign, inside and around me, his power fusing with mine anew until I couldn't tell where I ended and he began. I felt Sol's warmth, fierce and vast as a sun reborn. Phantom's storm surged through me like a tidal wave of midnight and fury.

Our hearts. Our pain. Our power.

Their voices swirled through my mind in a flurry, words I couldn't quite understand but felt deep in my marrow.

A scream tore from my lips as the bond pierced deeper. Not just through flesh and mind. But soul. My essence fractured, shattering like a star imploding. Light and dark warred within me, pulling me apart, unraveling every thread that made me who I was.

Memories broke. Names blurred. Pain bloomed.

For one agonizing heartbeat, I was nothing. There was no Aelia. No light. No body. Just pieces.

And then, the threads reknit.

Stronger. Brighter. Whole.

But not as the girl I was before. I was something else now. Something almost divine, terrifying, and... complete.

We were *one*.

After what felt like an endless moment, we exploded from the nexus and were lifted into the sky by a mighty force older than the gods themselves. I landed atop Sol with Reign appearing beside us aboard Phantom.

Another scream erupted, but this time, it was a cry of joy. Power. Completion.

Our dragons soared, glowing like twin stars reborn. And between us and them, the bond flared like a golden bridge, braided with light, shadow, fire and storm.

We had done it.

We were bound. All four of us.

Aelia and Reign. Solanthus and Phantom. The Tetrum Cordis.

Chapter Sixty

Reign

The grass beneath my back pulsed faintly, as if the land itself hadn't quite settled from what we'd just done.

A tempest of *rais*, *nox* and *zar* still crackled in the air. It was almost too much, too bright, too alive. But for the first time in what felt like an eternity, I wasn't weighed down by fear or fury. It was just breathless awe.

Aelia lay beside me, her chest rising and falling in soft, rhythmic waves, her hand loosely laced with mine. Strands of dark hair, streaked with platinum and moonlight, clung to her dewy brow. She was glowing. Not just from the starlight scattered across the dragon isle's endless sky, but from something deep within.

The bond between us shimmered like molten starlight. Changed. Amplified. *Whole.*

Above us, Solanthus and Phantom still streaked through the clouds, twin meteors dancing in a sky that blazed in impossible hues of violet, obsidian, and duskfire gold. I didn't know where the isle ended, and the heavens began. Maybe that was the point. Maybe here, there was no end. Only eternity.

Solanthus and Phantom flew with the others now, more dragons than I'd ever seen together, even those written about in the ancient tomes of Aetheria. The enormous beasts seemed as old as the mountains, wings whispering forgotten songs. And I could feel all of them. Their power rushed my veins, the heady sensation like nothing I'd ever imagined.

That was more... than I expected. Phantom's dry voice licked across my mind like smoke and satisfaction.

You nearly exploded, Reign. Sol's thoughts were more amused than concerned as they drifted through my thoughts next.

Even though I'd expected it, hearing his deep voice rumble through my mind still came as a shock.

Sol! Don't say that. Aelia's enraged cry tore through our mental conversation.

Very funny. I shot the thought back to Aelia's dragon, finding the shimmering golden strands that now connected me to him. *I suppose there will be no secrets between us any longer.*

Now I can really keep my eyes on you, Shadow-Night Prince. Solanthus's growl was laced in menace.

Enough, Phantom cut in.

Aelia groaned beside me. "Tell them to keep it down. I can barely feel my fingers."

I laughed under my breath. "They *both* can hear you now, you know."

Her eyes cracked open, lashes fluttering. "Of course they can. We're all in each other's heads now. Forever."

My hand flexed in hers. "That part will take some getting used to."

But even as I said it, I felt it.

Not just her thoughts. Her *rais*.

For so long, I'd known her *rais* only as light. Beautiful, radiant, pure. But now, it sang through me. Like a symphony etched in stars. It curled around my shadows, not consuming them, not even battling them, but folding into them. Completing them.

I drew in a shaky breath, chest tightening. "Gods, Aelia... I can feel it. Not just *you*. But your *rais*."

Her head turned, eyes wide, searching my face. "You can?"

"It's like every piece of you is humming inside me now. Not just the cuorem. But your light. I didn't know—" I broke off, swallowing hard. "I didn't know it would feel like this."

Her fingers tightened around mine, and her voice went softer than I'd ever heard it. "I've always felt your *nox*. Like velvet and iron, coiling through me. But you've never felt my *rais*?"

I shook my head slowly. "Not like this. Not completely. Before it was just warmth. Now, it's a burning star inside me. It's like a sun, scorching through the dark. I don't know how to explain it."

Tears shimmered in her eyes, and it was something beautiful. It was wonder and gratitude all rolled into one.

Solanthus's voice swept gently across our thoughts. *This is the gift of the Tetrum Cordis. There is no longer separation. Not between dragon and rider. Not between mates. You are of one breath. One power. One soul.*

And gods help anyone who stands against that. Phantom's voice was a growl of approval.

Aelia laughed softly, then turned toward me, half-draping her body over mine. I wrapped my arm around her instinctively, needing to anchor her. Or maybe needing her to anchor me.

"I missed you," she whispered, burying her face in my neck.

"I was right here."

"You know what I mean."

I did. We lay in silence, wrapped in each other and the hum of a bond newly reborn. Somewhere high above, Solanthus roared, and Phantom answered with fire and shadow, light and thunder.

I smiled faintly, eyes drifting closed. I wasn't ready to leave this idyllic place just yet. But soon...

Let Helroth come. Now, we were ready.

The moment my boots touched stone, I felt the shift. My wings of shadow flared across my shoulders. The Fortress, so often cloaked in silence and shadows, was alive with tension. The air pulsed with it. A ripple in the atmosphere like a warning carried on smoke.

Looks like we've returned just in time. Sol's voice rumbled in my head as I crossed the courtyard.

Or perhaps too late. Phantom's grim reply came nearly instantaneously as she circled overhead.

Wait a minute. I sent the thought to Phantom, despite the guilt. I knew very well that the newly mated pair desired some time alone. I not only knew it, I could feel it. Their animalistic craving for each other rushed our mutual connection, spurring my own base instincts to life.

Fine, we wait. She all but growled back her response.

Aelia landed beside me a moment later, her eyes narrowing, wings tucked tight to her back. "Do you feel that?"

I nodded grimly. "It's time we found out what we missed while we were in Aekorith."

Solanthus and Phantom circled once more before landing with thunderous force in the outer courtyard, their presence drawing every eye. Whispers erupted along the ramparts. Soldiers dropped to one knee. And for the first time, it wasn't just awe that filled their gazes.

It was fear. And urgency.

Ruhl emerged from the arched gates, dust coating his leathers, a long gash trailing down his arm, half-sealed but still angry and red. Mordrin followed close behind, his silver scales dulled and scorched in places. His wings beat the air in agitation, his eyes a swirling storm.

"Reign," Ruhl called out, his voice hoarse, but still strong.

I met him halfway across the courtyard. "What happened?"

Aelia was at my side in a blink. "Feywood. Did they breach the border?"

Ruhl's head dipped. "Some of them, yes. We held them back as best we could, but it wasn't easy." He gave a short laugh devoid of humor. "Mordrin's wing caught fire. Twice. He's not thrilled about it."

Mordrin snorted behind him, shadows rippling off his flanks like waves of heat.

"But that's not the worst of it," Ruhl continued, although I wasn't sure his skyrider would agree with his assessment. "Your dragons completed the bond, didn't they?"

I exchanged a glance with Aelia. "They did. How did you know?"

"Mordrin nearly dropped me mid-flight," he muttered. "Said the entire mountain screamed with it, of the Twin Tempests. Any dragon across Aetheria must have felt the power resonate. Who knows who else could have too... That kind of ancient magic doesn't go unnoticed."

Aelia's voice dropped. "The Twin Tempests?"

"Your bonded dragons, duskling." He smirked.

Her brows puckered as she regarded my brother. "So what are you saying, exactly?"

"I'm saying"—Ruhl's tone sharpened—"that the world shifted and others sensed it. Those others possibly being Elian."

My stomach turned to stone. The prophecy.

"The Light King is moving?" I asked, already knowing the answer.

Ruhl nodded. "I saw the banners myself. Elian's Royal Guardians are on the march. Not toward the Wilds, toward here. Our Court, our castle. The fool likely thinks the two of you have grown too strong."

Aelia's jaw clenched. "He doesn't realize what's truly coming. That we need to fight Helroth, not each other."

"No, he doesn't," Ruhl said. "But Helroth does. And if I'm right, he'll let Elian thin us out before striking."

A perfect storm.

Two fronts. Two enemies. One fortress.

I turned toward the nearest guards, the ones that lined the gates. "Sound the horns. Ready every battalion. Call the scouts back. I want the outer perimeter doubled."

"Yes, my prince," the pair of Umbral Guards replied in unison, saluting before racing off.

I looked back to Ruhl. "How bad was it in Feywood?"

His shoulders sagged slightly. "Worse than I hoped. Not as bad as I feared. But we need reinforcements. A lot more if we want to keep the Kin safe."

"You'll have them," Aelia bit out. "I'll go myself if I have to."

"No," I growled, my voice firmer than steel. "We don't split up again. Not ever."

Her eyes searched mine, full of stubborn fire, but she didn't argue. Not yet.

Ruhl watched us both, something like approval flickering across his soot-streaked face. "Well, I'm glad to see the bond didn't break you."

"No," I said quietly. "It made us whole."

He gave a nod, then turned back toward Mordrin. "Then let's make sure we don't lose what we just gained."

Chapter Sixty-One

A *elia*

Across the Luminoc, the sky bled orange as the sun sank behind the blackened mountains. Long shadows trailed across the courtyard, as restless as my pounding heart. Soldiers moved like clockwork around us, cinching armor, checking weapons, and murmuring oaths into the starlit night.

Reign stood beside me, dark armor glinting with a violet sheen. A storm of shadows rippled just beneath his skin, the perfect counterpart to my own sun-kissed gilded trappings. He looked like a king forged in war, my mate, my love.

And tonight, we'd ride together.

"Feywood is just a few hours' flight," he murmured, his hand finding mine as I checked the binding on my vambrace. "Since Ruhl has held them back thus far, if we strike hard now, we can push them out before they can regroup."

I nodded, but my gaze drifted toward the trees. Then my thoughts traveled to the Feywood Forest and the Kin. The powerless. My childhood friends. The kind, hard-working neighbors I'd grown up with. I could already feel the copper tang of war clinging to the air, like the realm itself braced for blood.

A sharp wind rustled my hair, carrying with it the scent of pine and ash.

"We won't let them fall," Reign said softly, as if he'd plucked the fear straight from my chest. And given the new all-arching bond, he likely had.

Before I could answer, the piercing call of a horn shattered the evening hush.

Reign and I both snapped toward the sound. Luminescent wings lit up the sky, and half a dozen soldiers appeared, the golden sunburst crest of the Light Court glowing across their alabaster uniforms.

"What in the gods?" Reign growled, shadows flickering around his fingertips.

"Wait," I whispered, a strange chill creeping up my spine.

The first male landed, luminescent wings tucking behind his back, then the others filed in beside him. He held no weapon, only a scroll sealed with my family's crest. Elian's crest.

"My Lady Aelia," the envoy said, bowing low. His voice was strained. "By order of His Ethereal Highness, King Elian of the Court of Ethereal Light, I bring you word."

Reign stepped forward before I could speak, his voice like thunder. "You serve a usurper. Elian is not the true king. There is only one Fae with the right to sit atop that throne, and you will address the princess as her lineage demands. As *Your Ethereal Highness.*"

The male scoffed, a chuckle rippling through his fellow Royal Guardians.

Reign's shadows unfurled, a tempest of pure wrath descending across the field. The air thickened, a torrent of *nox* and *zar* pulsing in the air. Fear flashed across the males' faces, a visible tremor coursing through their feeble forms.

The male in the lead clenched his teeth then dipped his head lower. "Your Ethereal Highness," he gritted out.

"Now, why have you come?"

The envoy flinched beneath Reign's glare. "The king sends an invitation."

My brows pinched. "To what?"

"A meeting. He requests parley with the Princess of Twilight and the Shadow Prince."

Reign snorted. "Convenient timing."

But my blood ran colder than the northern winds. Elian never made a move without strategy. And for him to ask for a meeting now, on the eve of two wars, one political and the other prophesied, meant something had changed.

Was Ruhl right? Had he sensed the sealing of the Twin Tempests? Did he know of the Tetrum Cordis?

The envoy extended the scroll to me, and I hesitated for only a breath before breaking the wax. Elian's handwriting was as familiar as it was infuriating.

Aelia,

The time has come for us to speak, not as king and rebel, but as family. The realm cannot survive what is coming if we remain divided. I await you in an hour's time at the Elaren Summit. Come alone, or with your mate. But come.

—E.

I closed the scroll, fingers trembling.

"What does it say?" Reign asked, his voice low.

"He wants to talk." My gaze lifted to his. "At the Elaren Summit. In an hour."

Reign's jaw ticked. "It could be a trap."

"Maybe," I said. "But if there's a chance he's willing to listen... if there's a chance to avoid bloodshed, we have to take it."

"Aelia…"

"I know you think I'm naïve." I could feel it pulsing through the bond. "And I really don't believe his intentions are pure, but we owe the realm any chance at peace."

"This is just another ploy, starlight. He's already betrayed us twice. How many times must we allow him to do it again?"

"We'll be prepared this time. We go ready for war, and if we come back with peace, we'll be all the more blessed for it."

A beat passed. Then Reign nodded, just once. "Fine," he grumbled. "But gods' help us, Aelia, this will not end well."

I looked past him to where Sol and Phantom stood waiting at the edge of the courtyard, wings spread wide. Perhaps fate had offered us one final breath before the storm.

✕

The wind howled through the narrow pass as our dragons touched down on the sun-kissed plateau just north of Feywood at the foot of the Alucian Mountains. The sun hung over the peaks, casting radiant light over the summit's jagged stones and ivory spires. Once a sacred meeting place between all three Courts, Elaren was now nothing more than a deserted stretch of land.

I slid off Sol's back, my boots crunching against the crisp grass. Reign landed beside me with practiced ease, his shadows already curling along his arms like restless serpents sensing a trap.

"I don't like this," he muttered, scanning the cliffside where a trio of Light Guardians waited in their gleaming armor.

"Neither do I," I whispered, pressing my palm briefly to the spot over my heart. The cuorem beat steady, but beneath it something felt off.

Ruhl and Mordrin are at the ready with a troop of Umbral Guards should the need arise. Reign's deep, steady voice was like a caress to my chaotic thoughts.

Good.

A golden canopy had been erected between the cliffs, flanked by columns etched with the Light Court's ancient symbols. And beneath it stood the King.

Elian.

Draped in ivory robes chased with gold thread, he looked every bit the noble monarch. His crown sat low over his brow, his golden-blond hair shining like burnished metal in the fading light. His expression, however, was unreadable.

"My dear niece," he said, spreading his hands in welcome. "And the Shadow Prince."

The way he addressed us made my stomach knot. As if we were both pawns on some familial chessboard.

"Elian," I said coolly. "You've changed your mind? You finally want to discuss peace for Aetheria?"

"I do," he replied, voice warm and smooth. "Come. Sit with me. There's much to discuss." He motioned to the chairs placed in a neat circle around his throne.

Neither of us sat.

Elian smiled thinly. "Or stand, whatever you prefer."

I kept my posture poised, but every muscle in me was taut. "Why now?" I asked. "Why parley after marching your Royal Guardians toward the Shadow Court? After sending countless troops to the Luminoc border?"

His eyes met mine, calculating. "Because everything has changed."

My blood cooled a fraction. "What do you mean?"

He took a step closer, just enough for the sunlight to catch in his irises. "I've felt it, Aelia. The realm has felt it. Something ancient has stirred." His gaze drifted between Reign and me. "You carry something more. Both of you. The bond between you is no longer just that of bonded Fae. It is... other. Stronger."

I said nothing. Neither did Reign.

"With every day that passes, we come closer to fulfilling the prophecy. You can't be so blind as to not see that?"

"I will not be this realm's ruin," I gritted out. "You and Helroth are to blame for everything that's happened."

Elian's smile didn't reach his eyes. Ignoring me, he continued, "You're stronger now. And strength like that cannot be ignored, nor should it be fought."

"Forgive me if I don't believe you're suddenly ready to kneel before us," Reign said, speaking for the first time, his voice low and lethal. "Last I checked, you were still calling her a traitor."

"I was a fool." Elian's tone shifted into something almost vulnerable. "But even fools can see when the end is coming. You were right, Helroth won't stop at Shadow or Light. He wants all of Aetheria. Perhaps, even all of Crescentia. We must unify before it's too late."

"And what? You'll bend the knee?" I asked.

"No." His voice hardened. "But I will offer an alliance."

I arched a brow. "On what terms?"

He hesitated just a beat. And that pause was enough to crack the illusion of peace he was attempting to weave.

"You're not telling us everything." Reign stepped forward. "What else?"

Elian's jaw clenched. "I had hoped to speak plainly before revealing this. But I see now, truth earns trust." He turned toward his guards and gestured sharply. "Bring him."

I didn't move. Couldn't breathe.

Then I heard them, the chains. The scrape of iron against stone. Heavy footfalls. A presence that chilled the very marrow of my bones.

And then *he* emerged.

Gaunt but still regal. Bound at the wrists with enchanted cuffs imbued with *rais* that hissed against his skin. His once midnight hair was now streaked with silver. His face carved from shadow and fury.

Tenebris.

Reign stiffened beside me, his breath sharp and shallow. His hand drifted to the inside of his cloak where he'd tucked away the Moirai Shard. I never thought we'd need it today, but...

"Elian," I whispered, dread coiling beneath my skin. "What is this?"

The king didn't flinch. "A show of good faith, of course. Surely, your mate would be happy to see his sire alive and well. Wouldn't he?"

Reign didn't speak. He couldn't. I could feel the war raging inside him, the pull of blood and betrayal. But mostly of undiluted fear. For me.

Aelia, I can't leave you with them, but if I stay... His voice was frantic across the bond. His fear racing through the delicate strands of our connection, bloating my insides.

Tenebris lifted his chin, those eyes of pure void landing on us, and, for the first time, I saw something entirely unexpected as they darted toward Reign.

Pride.

"Hello, son."

Chapter Sixty-Two

R *eign*

No.

The word detonated in my skull like a curse, an explosion of shadow and dread that nearly buckled my knees.

No, no, no. It couldn't be.

My father stood before me. King Tenebris.

He was bound in iron cuffs etched with runes, eyes glowing like frozen stars. A creature of nightmares I'd clawed from my memories and buried in the darkest corners of my soul.

And he was here. Shackled but not broken. Never broken.

His eyes found mine. And for one eternal heartbeat, everything fell away. The slick stone beneath my boots, Aelia's presence at my side, even the war looming in the distance. All I could feel was the searing, ancient pull of blood.

The blood vow.

Still alive. Still binding and lethal. Still capable of forcing me to kill my mate.

My heart roared like Phantom mid-dive. If he spoke the words, if he commanded it, I wouldn't be able to stop. *I'll hurt her. I'll kill her.*

I couldn't. I took a step back and slid my hand beneath my cloak. The Moirai Shard. It was time to find out what the cost would be. The priestess's words echoed through my mind. *Moirai incendiae.* Two words and I could end this.

No, wait. Aelia's voice surged through my mind. *The cost…*

"Elian," I growled, my voice so raw I hardly recognized it. "What the hell are you doing?"

"Offering peace," he replied smoothly. "And answers."

"Answers?" My laugh was broken glass. "You just put the most dangerous male in Aetheria on a feeble leash and expect us to believe you're doing it for the good of the realm?"

Tenebris didn't flinch. His gaze never left mine. "I told you we would meet again, son."

The sound of that word—*son*—was a blade to the gut.

Despite the imminent danger, I couldn't stop my mouth from forming the words. I had to know. "What happened to my mother?"

Something dark flashed across my father's expression.

"I know Elaris was your prisoner, a slave in your grand castle. I need to know what became of her."

"How bold of you to ask something of *me* given the current circumstance." His tone was ice.

"Just tell me," I roared, shadows flaring with rage, hissing and writhing across my fingertips.

A flicker of amusement swam across those soulless eyes. "She tried to escape and I had her killed." A harsh laugh scraped from his throat. "She ran. She begged, but it changed nothing."

The world tunneled. My vision rimmed in black as the *nox* surged, hungry for blood. "You're lying."

"Am I?" Tenebris tilted his head, the ghost of a smile cutting his face. "Open your eyes, Reign. Mercy is a story mothers tell their sons so they grow soft."

Our bond thrummed. Aelia's voice was like a hand on my sternum, steadying. *Reign. Breathe.*

I swallowed glass. "Her name was Elaris," I hissed, each syllable a blade. "And you will speak it with respect when I carve your last breath from your throat."

Shadows roared up around me, a crown of midnight and ruin. Tenebris didn't step back. He simply extended a palm as if inviting a dance.

Elian released a sharp laugh, cold and menacing. He was enjoying this...

"Enough!" Aelia stepped forward, every inch the fiery princess, chin high, shadows and light dancing at her heels. She stood before me, hands gripping mine and eyes beseeching. *Reign, please. You can't. Not right now.*

Despite every bone in my body demanding his blood, I knew she was right. If I failed, if I remained a second longer than I should, I could be forced to do the unthinkable. I would *not* risk Aelia.

I nodded, rage still pounding through my veins, but I willed the calm to settle. The swell of furious shadows dissipated, retreating beneath my skin.

Aelia turned her attention back to the Light King. "Why did you bring Tenebris, Elian?"

"He wants to help," Elian answered.

Liar.

I turned to Aelia, panic rising in my throat once again. *We need to go. I knew this was a trap. And perhaps you were right, we cannot risk using the Shard right now without understanding the consequences.* Desperation laced my tone, a chaotic tangle of the raging desire to kill my father and keep Aelia safe.

A swarm of Aelia's shadows coiled around us, forming an impenetrable cloak. Darkness misted around us and the kings before us faded to nothing. *Reign, wait. You said it yourself, we've changed. Maybe you can fight his hold over you now. Maybe we don't need the Moirai Shard at all.*

I can't risk that! "We have to leave," I hissed aloud, sharper this time, not caring if they heard through the dark shield. "Now."

I grabbed her arm, already pulling her back toward Solanthus and away from the ruthless kings, but she resisted. "Please, Reign, I believe in you. In us. You can do this. You can't run from your father forever."

"I'm not the one in danger," I snapped. "He could activate the vow at any moment. You don't understand, if he speaks it, I won't be able to stop myself."

She cupped my cheek with one hand, grounding me with that single, stubborn touch. "You are my *cuoré*, and together we are strong enough to defeat anything and anyone."

"Aelia, please, I cannot live without you."

Shaking her head, she released a resigned sigh. "Then go. Please. I'll be fine."

"I'm not leaving you," I hissed.

Leave. Phantom's voice sliced into my thoughts like a whip of shadow. *Now, Reign. Get away from him.*

Aelia is not alone. Solanthus's voice boomed next, calm and firm as the sky. *I will protect her. I swear it. But you must break the proximity. It's the only way to keep Tenebris from enacting the vow.*

"I can't," I whispered aloud.

Despite knowing the consequences, I simply couldn't force my stubborn feet to move. To leave my mate with *them*. Did I dare attempt to activate the Moirai Shard? Every second I waited, I put her at risk. If Tenebris so much as whispered the binding command, I would become the blade that pierced the heart of the only female I'd ever truly loved. The female who was made just for me.

I turned to Aelia, my shadows writhing, my lungs barely working. "I won't leave you."

"Then stay with me and let's fight together." But her voice cracked. And that almost destroyed me.

I stepped back. One pace. Then two. The wall of shadows

dissipated, revealing the awaiting royals. Solanthus shifted behind her, wings flaring in silent promise. Phantom circled above, a shadow burning with fury.

I met Tenebris's gaze one last time. "You won't have me," I hissed, my voice like ice. "Never again."

He tilted his head, the barest flicker of amusement playing across his mouth.

"And this is for *her*." Instead of running, I reached for the well of energy that resided just on the other end of our shimmering bond—*rais, nox, zar*, and the gods-given force of our newly mated dragons. The Tetrum Cordis surged like a second pulse.

Power exploded through me, so intense it nearly dropped me to my knees.

Tenebris felt it. Everyone on the gods' damned field must have.

His narrowed eyes gleamed. "So. It's true, then. Elian wasn't exaggerating." He stepped forward, runes flaring at his cuffs, voice dropping low and sharp like a blade sliding from its sheath. "Now, let's see what the new bond can really do."

One of the Royal Guardians stepped forward, freeing him of the gilded manacles.

My body seized. Like invisible chains wrapping around my spine. My father hadn't spoken a word yet, and already, I could feel it coming. The blood vow sparked to life, its hold over me tightening.

"Reign of Umbra," he hissed, "by the blood that binds you to me, by the vow you swore in shadow and in flesh, I command you—"

My knees buckled.

The blood vow slammed into me with the force of a thousand storms, and the world spun sideways. My breath was torn from my chest. My hands curled into fists, knuckles cracking. Shadows lashed out, wild and erratic, trying to obey.

"—to destroy the child of twilight."

No. No. NO.

I roared, staggering back, clutching at my head.

Aelia cried out, and somehow, her voice cut through the haze and found me. "Reign, fight! I know you can do this."

"To kill your mate!" His words pounded through my skull, powerful, all-consuming.

But I wouldn't concede. I could never hurt Aelia. I felt her through the cuorem. Her light. Her fire. The threads of her *rais* curled around my soul, not like a noose, but like a lifeline.

Phantom's voice thundered across my mind like a battle drum. *Do not yield.*

Solanthus followed, his roar so loud it cracked the sky. *You are not his. You are* ours, *Reign of Umbra. Do you hear me?*

I gasped. And then I reached deeper. Past the blood, past the pain, past the vow carved into my marrow.

I love you, Reign. You are icy Shadow, endless Night, my beginning and my end, and most importantly, you are stronger than hatred and vengeance.

I reached for *her.* Aelia, my starlight. My mate, my *cuoré*, my everything.

Her love. Her belief in me. Her kiss in the ruins. Her rage at injustice. Her laughter beneath moonlight. Her arms around me in the dark when I thought I didn't deserve to be held.

And there, with her, I found my anchor.

Power unlike anything I'd ever known ripped through me. It was shadow and flame, storm and starlight—not one force, but four. Not one heart, but ours.

The blood vow clamped tighter, a vice on my soul, crushing bone and spirit alike. My vision blurred. My breath hitched. I felt it wrench into me, demanding obedience, demanding death.

My knees hit the earth. My hands shook with the effort not to turn them into weapons. Not to become *his.* Pain blistered through every nerve, tearing me open from the inside out. My name didn't feel like mine anymore. My will was slipping. Oh, gods, I only hoped Aelia couldn't feel it through our bond. It was excruciating.

But then I heard her.

Aelia's voice. I felt it through the mystical strands, through the light that refused to let go of me. *Reign. Come back to me.*

I reached beyond the pain, beyond the ancient chains etched in blood and shadow to something even more ancient, even more powerful. I reached for her, and the moment I touched that flicker of love, of fire, of unwavering belief in me, I was home.

The blood vow that had tethered me to my father since before I could properly hold a sword snapped like brittle bone. I let out a strangled cry and buckled over. My vision swam. Shadows peeled from my body in great ragged waves.

Tenebris stumbled back, blinking. "Impossible." He mouthed the word, eyes like gaping, full moons.

I had resisted him. "I am not *yours*," I snarled, rising slowly to my feet. "Not anymore."

Behind me, Phantom shrieked, a triumphant sound that shook the ground, and Solanthus flared his wings wide, bathing the clearing in radiant firelight.

Tenebris's jaw clenched, his façade slipping for just a breath. A flicker of something unfamiliar crossed his face.

Fear.

I turned to Aelia. She was glowing, eyes like twin stars, hands wreathed in silver and midnight fire. Her lips parted, her breath catching. "You broke it... Without the Shard."

"I did," I whispered hoarsely. "Because of you."

Her hands flew to her mouth, eyes brimming with tears.

And then I faced my father again.

"You taught me to kill," I growled, my voice hollow but growing in conviction with each word I forced past my lips. "You taught me to destroy. But *she* taught me how to fight for something. And that's why you'll lose."

Tenebris said nothing. The monster who had raised me simply stood there gaping for an endless moment before a storm of shadows erupted around him, swallowing him, Elian and his gilded warriors into the void.

Chapter Sixty-Three

A *elia*

Moonlight spilled through the windows like a whisper, soft and silver as it traced the edge of Reign's jaw. He lay beside me, one arm folded behind his head, eyes half-lidded but restless. His shadows pulsed gently along the sheets, reacting to every flicker of thought he refused to speak aloud.

But I could hear every single one now. Much like I'd felt every ounce of agonizing pain he had endured to overcome his father's hold. It still echoed through my bones, sending a chill up my spine. Blinking quickly, I banished the dark memories, choosing to focus on the here and now instead.

I propped myself up on one elbow, dragging my fingers through the tousled strands of obsidian hair at Reign's temple. "You should be sleeping."

"I can't," he murmured, voice rough with fatigue. "Not yet."

"You should at least try. Ruhl's already gone to reinforce the border. The Kin are safe for now."

He turned toward me, brows pinched. "I can't stop thinking about it. Replaying it. How close I came to hurting—"

"But you didn't," I interjected. "That blood vow has ruled your life for years. And you broke it. Without the Shard. *You* did that." I traced the line of his collarbone, grounding him with my touch when words felt too overwhelming.

His throat worked around the lump I could practically feel there. "But it wasn't me. I didn't break it. You did."

I frowned. "Reign..."

"You, Phantom, Solanthus. Our bond. The dragons. All of it." His eyes flickered to mine, dark and endless and brimming with something I couldn't name. "I reached for power, and I found you."

A slow, aching smile curved my lips. "Then maybe we don't need the Moirai Shard anymore."

He huffed a dry laugh. "We're not just going to return it."

I raised a brow. "Why not?"

"It's too dangerous."

"Then smash it to bits. Feed it to Phantom. Drop it in a molten river." I shrugged, grinning.

"If it can sever blood vows, who knows what else it could do? It has the power to break bonds created by the gods, Aelia. It might be the only bargaining chip we have left." He glanced at me sidelong. "Or the only weapon."

"You always ruin my dramatic ideas with logic."

"I know. It's a curse."

I leaned in closer, my mouth brushing the edge of his. "Maybe you need a different kind of curse. The kind that erupts from your mouth when I'm—"

His eyes darkened. "Aelia..."

"Hmm?"

His hand slid to my waist, pulling me across the sheets until I was half draped over him. "You're dangerous when you're like this."

"Like what?"

"Teasing. Smirking. Wearing absolutely nothing but that smug look on your face."

"I'm not smirking," I replied, fully smirking.

He growled softly, the sound vibrating between us, and then his lips were on mine. Not soft. Not hesitant. But hungry, claiming, as if he needed to remind himself that I was real. That we were both still here, still breathing, and still alive.

I answered with equal fire, threading my fingers into his hair and pressing my body against the hard lines of his. His shadows flared, curling around us like smoke and silk. My *rais* sparked in response, a bright warmth kissing every place our skin met.

The bond between us hummed, hot and full of need. And I felt him, not just physically, but everywhere. In my blood. My breath. My soul.

His lips moved to my throat, teeth grazing skin that flushed at the mere promise of his mouth.

"I love you," I whispered into the darkness.

"I'd burn the world for you," he whispered back. "But right now, I just want to worship you."

"Well then, who am I to stop you?"

He was slow and thorough, as if time had paused just for us. His words echoed in my chest long after his mouth found mine again.

This would be our first time together since that soul-rending ritual. Everything between us had grown sharper, deeper, more consuming since then, and I was certain this would be no different. Reign moved slowly at first, as if relearning me. Mapping me with hands that were both reverent and rough, his touch trailed over my ribs, hips, thighs like I was made of something sacred. And maybe I was. Maybe we both were now. We'd been changed by dragonfire, bonded by starlight and shadow.

I arched into him, gasping when his mouth found the swell of my breast, teeth grazing, tongue soothing. The way his shadows moved with him made it impossible to tell where he ended and I began. They curled around my limbs, brushing over bare skin like velvet. My *rais* responded with golden heat, dancing along the curve of his spine, pulsing between us until the air shimmered with our power.

"I feel you," I whispered, breathless. "Everywhere."

"Good." His voice was gravel and sin. "Because I never want you to forget who you belong to."

"Then maybe you should remind me."

A slow, wicked smile tugged at the corner of his mouth. "With pleasure, love."

His fingers slipped between my thighs, and I cried out, the sound swallowed by his kiss as he slammed his lips to mine. I clung to him as his touch coaxed stars from my skin, the tension building like a crescendo in my veins. My back arched, hips rising, seeking more.

Moving his hand, he shifted above me. Bracing himself on his forearms, eyes locked on mine, he slid into me in one slow, devastating thrust.

The bond flared.

And gods, it was so much more than only physical. I *felt* him. Not just inside me but *through* me. His pain. His pleasure. His awe. All of it crashed into my senses like a tidal wave of raw, aching love.

He moved slowly at first, as if savoring each moment, each sound I made. But the pace built with every breath and every whispered name until we were chasing something wild and ancient together. The sheets tangled. Our powers surged, heat and dark, light and shadow, crashing and twining in waves until I was unraveling beneath him.

"Aelia," he rasped, voice barely a sound, but I heard it, felt it. "I'm yours. I'll always be yours."

We shattered together.

Energy bloomed around us, stars sparking across the ceiling and shadows curling like smoke caught in a breeze. His name tore from my lips as I came apart in his arms, the world narrowing to only him. He followed with a groan against my throat, collapsing against me. Our bodies were tangled and slick with sweat, our hearts beating in perfect rhythm.

For a long time, neither of us moved. Because we both knew that tomorrow, the war would come. But tonight, we were smoke and starlight. And nothing else existed.

The inner courtyard of the Shadow Fortress buzzed with motion, soldiers fitting on leathers and armor, their weapons clashing in practice strokes as the sun grew ever brighter across the river. Our dragons preened restlessly atop the outer cliffs, the same nervous energy zipping through all four of us. The air crackled with tension and anticipation, but also something else.

Resolve. Determination. As if we might actually win this. Word of the sacred bonding had already spread like wildfire across the fortress. And unlike the last time we faced the Night King, today we would fight together. The entire force of Light and Shadow.

Even with the battle on the horizon, something about this morning felt different. Lighter. Sharper. I had just cinched the last of my plated bracers at my wrist when Rue strolled over. My best friend was clad in gilded armor that shimmered faintly beneath the twinkling starlight. Her hair was braided down her back in a long, gleaming rope, and she wore a broadsword across her back.

"Well, don't you look terrifyingly regal," she said, bumping her shoulder into mine.

"Hardly," I huffed, adjusting the strap that kept sliding down my arm. "This thing was not designed for actual breathing."

"Beauty is pain, little Kin," Symon added as he approached, swinging his luminescent war hammer onto his shoulder with exaggerated flair. "And in your case, legendary beauty requires a bit of struggle."

I rolled my eyes. "You're ridiculous."

"Yes, but charming." He winked, then glanced toward

Reign, who stood across the courtyard speaking with General Arven. Still, every other moment, his gaze drifted toward me. "Besides, you've got the brooding death prince practically vibrating to get you out of that armor already. I don't blame him."

"Symon," Rue groaned. "Please. Some of us are trying to keep our breakfast down."

"As if you and Devin are any less obnoxious."

"We are not!" She rolled her eyes, but her cheeks rosied all the same. With everything going on, I'd barely had time to check on her relationship status, but from what little I'd heard, she and Devin were solid. Which made me beyond happy.

Symon bowed dramatically, tossing an apple at Windy who devoured it in one massive chomp. "Fine, fine. Let's all behave for now."

Before I could reply, a gentle voice floated across the courtyard.

"Aelia," Vaelora called, approaching beside Kaelith. Her stark white hair was braided and pinned into a crown, navy eyes glowing softly. Despite the armor covering her robes, she still moved with the grace of a goddess.

She paused beside me, then turned to Reign as he strode over. Her hand reached for his, gently cupping it between both of hers. "I wanted to wish you both luck today." Then her gaze settled on her grandson. "You have become something more than I ever dared hope for."

Reign blinked, clearly stunned, and tried to mask it with a half-smile. "You haven't seen me in battle yet."

"I've seen enough to know." Her voice trembled. "You carry the fire of your grandfather, and your mother's relentless spirit. But what truly sets you apart from the ruthless Night Fae, Reign, is your heart. Karnax would've been proud of you. "And one day" —she brushed her hand over his cheek—"you will be a great king."

Emotion flickered behind Reign's eyes. "Thank you, Vaelora."

She leaned forward and pressed a kiss to his forehead. "Return to us whole, both of you."

A thick silence descended across the courtyard, the weight of her words pressing into my mate and ricocheting through our bond.

She's right. I sent the thought across the shimmering strands that bound us.

You're both too kind.

A familiar voice rang out, drawing me from our mental conversation.

"Hope I'm not too late."

I turned, heart lurching as Heaton emerged from the lower hall with his staff slung across his back and a determined glint in his eyes. He moved toward us slowly, the pounds of muscle lost while he remained bedridden evident, but still he marched with purpose.

"Heaton, no." I crossed the courtyard in three long strides. "You're not ready—"

"I'm not staying behind again, Aelia." His jaw was set, stubborn in the way only he could be. "My family is out there, you and Rue and my team. Not to mention our brother Lawson, who is still fighting for the wrong monarch. I won't hide while everyone fights."

"You could get killed," Rue said softly, stepping beside me. "Or worse, captured again."

"So could any of us," he replied without hesitation. "And if today is my day to fall, then I'll fall protecting the people I love."

My throat tightened. "You're too brave for your own good."

He smiled faintly. "I learned from one of the best on my team."

I stepped forward, wrapping my arms around his shoulders and holding him tightly. "Just promise me you'll stay close to us."

He chuckled against my shoulder. "Now, that I can do."

Behind us, the horns sounded, deep and solemn, shaking the stones beneath our feet.

The time had come.

I turned, finding Reign already waiting for me, shadows curling at his feet. Phantom stood over him, wings pounding the earth and ready for flight. Solanthus loomed just behind her. His talons scraped the earth and plumes of smoke rose from his flared nostrils.

Reign reached for my hand and squeezed.

As we mounted our dragons and rose toward the clouds, I glanced down once more at the fortress below. And prayed the next time we returned, we'd still be whole.

Chapter Sixty-Four

R*eign*

An unnatural stillness cloaked our ranks as we soared above the war-scorched canopy of Feywood. Below, the forest bled. Blackened earth, twisted trunks, and the acrid stench of smoke and blood rose to meet us on the wind. Just ahead, I could already see the clash of forces where Ruhl and the Umbral Guard held the line against the advancing Night Fae.

Noxus, protect us. Protect her.

I risked a glance past Phantom's wing.

Aelia. My warrior queen. Forged in fire and shadow. Crowned in light. The unyielding heart of this war.

She rode Solanthus like a star descending to end the darkness, her presence defiant and blinding. And yet, a whisper of dread coiled low in my gut. My fingers found the inner pocket of my cloak, brushing the cold edge of the Moirai Shard.

It had called to me this morning from the old armoire, subtle but urgent. Not in words, but something darker... As if the gods themselves had placed it in my path for this moment. Perhaps it hadn't been meant to destroy the bonds of the blood vow, but for something else entirely.

I didn't know what it would demand. Or what it would cost.

But if it could grant her even a fraction of more time, one breath or one heartbeat, it would be worth it. Because by night-fall, Aelia would stand victorious. She would raise this broken realm from ash and shadow and carry us into the dawn. I felt the truth of it in the deepest marrow of my bones.

Even if it meant I would not rise beside her.

I love you. I sent the thought through our bond, and Aelia's gaze snapped to mine over the powerful flaps of our dragons' wings.

Don't you start that, professor. A hint of amusement laced her tone, but something darker lay just beneath.

Start what? I can't tell you how much I love you?

Not before we descend into battle... it sounds too much like a goodbye.

Never, starlight. I threw her a smirk, forcing a nonchalance I didn't quite feel. *The cuorem bond is forever, remember? You're stuck with me for all eternity.*

I wouldn't have it any other way.

Will you two stop chattering on and on? We have a war to win. Phantom's voice rushed through our bond.

Be nice, Phantom. Solanthus chimed in next, gently scolding his mate, although I definitely heard something akin to humor in his voice.

Yes, I thought you'd be in a better mood now that you've been mated, old girl.

My dragon snorted, angling her wings toward the earth. *I'll be in a better mood once this is all over.*

Well then, let's finish it now. Aelia's smile was fierce, determination surging through our connection.

Our skyriders dove in perfect unison with the rest of our aerial forces following suit. As not all of our warriors were blessed with winged-beasts, the rest of our troops would come by other means, traveling by light or shadows and forming the second wave.

The moment Phantom's claws touched the scorched earth, the world erupted into chaos. Ruhl was the first to greet us with blood streaking his temple, one sleeve torn and charred. His sword dripped with black ichor, his expression grim.

"You're late," he growled.

"We came as quickly as we could," I replied, vaulting off Phantom's back just as Solanthus landed beside us with a roar that shook the trees. The ground trembled under their combined weight, and several Night Fae faltered mid-charge.

Aelia slid down with grace that contradicted the oppressive weight of battle. "You held the line."

"Barely," Ruhl replied, wiping his umbral blade on his thigh. "We're being pressed hard. They came through the southern glade an hour ago and haven't stopped."

All around us, the forest howled with war cries. Trees snapped, fire crackled, and the shrieks of dying beasts split the air.

"Then let's end this," I growled, echoing my *cuore's* earlier words to our skyriders and drawing both my blades, one of pure shadow, the other steel. My shadows hissed and curled across my shoulders, anxious for the fight. Aelia stood beside me, peering across the smoky field. Reaching for her through our bond, I felt nothing but sheer determination as she hardened her gaze.

With a quick scan of our gathered forces, Flare Squad along with some of our closest friends, she lifted her dagger, the infernium blade catching the light of the mid-day sun. "For Aetheria," she cried out.

An answering roar echoed across the assembled warriors, Light and Shadow both fighting as one. As we should have been all along.

To my left, Rue, Symon and Devin charged forward with matching wild grins, each slightly wind-blown from the flight but filled with fiery defiance.

"I told you she'd bring us to the heart of the slaughter," Rue quipped, not even glancing at me as she loosed an arrow into a Night Fae's chest.

"And I told you I look excellent in battle smoke," Symon retorted as he buried his luminescent blade into the belly of a Demon male.

Heaton stumbled up next, his leathers slightly too big after all the weight he'd lost and a light spear clutched in his hands.

Aelia turned, alarm flashing in her eyes, and I felt the fear for her friend shoot down the bond. "Heaton! No. You're not—"

"I am," he interrupted, planting the spear into the dirt like a declaration. "You need every blade. And I already told you I'm not hiding in some tent while our world burns."

Aelia opened her mouth to protest, but I gently touched her arm. "Let him fight. He's made his choice."

Before she could respond, Belmore and Ariadne flanked our side, the male barking orders while Ariadne conjured sweeping gusts of ethereal light to knock back enemy archers from the tree line. I never thought either student would amount to much, but I'd been wrong. Happily, so.

Kaelith emerged from the fray moments later, cloak ripped at the hem, staff glowing with *zar* as he incinerated a cluster of advancing Night Fae with scorching hellfire. Just behind him, a familiar form took shape. Oh, gods, no. Gideon appeared, panting, his armor glinting beneath the moonlight. I couldn't remember the last time I'd seen him brandishing a weapon.

"Reign!" he called, waving with one hand while wielding a sword of writhing shadows in the other. "I'm here to help!"

I stared at him in horror. I loved my best friend, but he did not belong on the battlefield. The library was his domain. "Stay behind us," I growled, knowing full well I'd never be able to convince him to leave. "Don't move from Kaelith's side. If anything comes near you, run."

He nodded, gripping the hilt with both hands. "Give me a

little credit, my broody prince. I may have never been the warrior you are, but I can hold my own."

"Just be careful."

"Of course." With a mock salute, he raced behind Kaelith into the skirmish.

Aelia and I turned in unison to face the approaching wave. The Night Fae came with beasts stitched from smoke and sinew, eyes glowing red, limbs too long and twisted. Their riders bore obsidian blades, dripping with venomous *zar*. A shriek pierced the air, and the charge really began.

And so did ours.

We met them in a collision of fire and fury. Aelia moved beside me like liquid light, her blades singing with *rais*. I struck low, shadows curling from my wrists, pulling enemies into the dark where they didn't rise again.

Then, I felt it. Not just the cuorem, but something deeper. Older.

Power. Pure, living, breathing power coursed through the bond. I reached for Aelia through it and found no resistance, only welcome.

It was like nothing I'd ever felt before in battle. Or ever, really.

It wasn't only Phantom's power now. I could feel Solanthus, his fire smoldering in my chest and his fury fueling my limbs. I could feel Aelia's *rais*, as if the sun had slipped under my skin and was burning away every shred of hesitation. My *nox*, it responded like it never had before; it was sharper, hungrier, *alive*. And beneath it all, the murky *zar* surged, rippling through my blood like lightning in ink.

With a shout, I splayed out my fingers on instinct as potent energy rushed through my veins. A vortex of shadowfire laced with starflame and powered by Solanthus's roar exploded from my fingertips. It obliterated a creature in midair, scattering its remains into glittering ash.

Aelia spun at me, eyes wide. "Well, that's new."

"It certainly is."

Without another word, she turned back to the fight and arched her luminescent daggers, her blades blazing white-gold and violet, carving through armor and bone like silk. Her face was alight. She was a goddess, queen, warrior, all in one.

The Night Fae regarded her in horror. And rightfully so.

From above, Phantom shrieked a war cry, casting an umbral veil over half the field. Solanthus followed with a pillar of golden flame that set the sky ablaze. The beasts of smoke fell one by one. Even the resurrected Night Fae revenants succumbed to their fury.

We fought as one. Four hearts. One breath.

Ariadne screamed a warning. I spun, too slowly, and found a Night Fae blade coming within inches of my neck.

Only, it never landed.

Kaelith slammed the attacker with a blast of *zar* so violent it sent the Night Fae female hurtling against a tree, and with it came his dry smirk. "You're welcome."

I threw him a matching grin.

"Thank you," Aelia breathed beside me.

But then the lavender-haired female pushed herself off the ground and turned her matching lavender gaze on me, then Aelia.

Something twisted in my gut as I took the female in.

That face. Those eyes. They were different, yet familiar, somehow. Sharper. More angular. No longer masked in soft illusion. It was her, but not. A darker reflection. One that sent every instinct in me screaming.

Aelia's expression faltered, confusion rippling across her features. "Liora?"

Chapter Sixty-Five

R*eign*

The female smiled. But there was nothing kind about it, not like she'd presented it before, as she glared at Aelia. Now, it was razor-edged and filled with malice.

"You finally figured it out," Liora said, her voice somehow both honeyed and cold as ice. "Took you long enough, *cousin*."

Cousin?

My shadows flared instantly, coiling around my shoulders like vipers.

Aelia staggered back a step. "*What?* No. That's not possible."

"Oh, but it is. Our grandfather sired *many* females, Aelia. My mother's name was Sorynth, and she was half-sister to your mother, Sable."

A faint gasp parted Aelia's lips.

You can't trust anything she says, starlight. I sent the thought racing through our bond.

Why would she lie about this, Reign? Helroth could easily confirm or deny it. Her response was immediate.

It doesn't matter who she is. All that matters is that she betrayed you.

Liora rose fully now, and the illusion around her cracked, like glass shattering. She shimmered, then solidified into something wholly different.

Her skin darkened into an obsidian hue with veins of iridescent violet. Her eyes glowed like amethysts left too long in the void. Pure night unfolded behind her, jagged and sleek like the *zar* of the royal Night Fae.

Realms, she *was* a true princess of the Court of Infernal Night.

"So Helroth sent you," I muttered.

Liora's smile widened. "I was supposed to watch her. To guide her. To make sure her transition to power served our purpose. And it was going so well until *you* came along, Reign. I tried my best to distract you from her, but Zaroth, you were simply *obsessed.*"

Aelia's daggers were in her hands in a blink, both hilts glowing with *rais.* "You lied to me. All this time—"

"I *protected* you," Liora spat. "While you were flailing through your identity crisis, '*Am I a powerless Kin, Light Fae, Shadow Fae...*' I was reporting everything to Helroth. Everything. He knows your strengths, your weaknesses. Your love for Reign. Your pathetic obsession with mercy."

She lunged in a blur of shadows and rage.

Aelia met her mid-air, blades clashing in a blaze of violet and gold. Sparks flew. The forest around them trembled as *rais* and *zar* collided, the air splitting with the crack of the mystical discharge.

I surged forward, but Aelia's voice stopped me.

"No. She's *mine.*"

With a snarl of frustration, I dug my heels into the earth and watched—even if my every instinct screamed to do the opposite. I knew my mate could handle her.

Aelia fought like she had been born for this moment. Every motion was deliberate. Every strike forged from fury and betrayal. The two females moved like twin storms, dark and light, each strike dredging up another old memory, another wound.

"I trusted you," Aelia shouted between blows. "I should have listened to Rue. I never should've given you the benefit of the doubt."

"That's exactly your problem," Liora hissed back. "I pity you. You're *weak*."

Their powers tangled, then broke apart. Aelia's dagger slashed across Liora's side, and a streak of black blood splashed the charred ground. The Night Fae hissed out a curse.

Aelia stepped back, a gasp squeezing through her clenched teeth as she eyed the wound. Liora dropped to one knee. She was panting and wounded, but her eyes still gleamed with hatred.

Aelia stood over her cousin, blades raised. She could have ended her in that moment. But I knew my *cuoré*. She was too kind, too merciful, even with those who didn't deserve it. It was exactly what made me love her even more, while simultaneously driving me mad. She blew out a breath and lowered her daggers. "I won't kill you," she whispered, voice trembling. "You may have betrayed me to our grandfather, but you are still blood. And that means something to me."

Liora barked a cruel laugh as she reached for her sword. "You're still so pathetic." She jabbed it upward, but I was already moving. Because I was neither weak nor merciful. Shadows erupted from my body like a tidal wave, swallowing the space between us.

"You should've stayed dead in the Wilds," I hissed, just before my shadows pierced her heart.

Liora gasped, something like shock rippling through her.

Her mouth moved, forming one final word, "professor," but it never passed her lips.

Then, her body crumpled onto the blackened earth. Her lavender, vacant eyes lifted up to the sky on a final exhale.

Aelia fell to her knees beside her body, her expression unreadable. I dropped beside her, pulling her into my arms just as her blades clattered to the ground.

"She was my family," she whispered hollowly. "And she betrayed me. Gods, why do they always betray me?"

"She chose her side," I murmured into her hair. "And so did we." Tightening my arms around her, I held her for as long as she would allow. But soon, the fighting surged around us, ripping us from the quiet moment within the chaos.

Ruhl appeared, fighting like a demon unleashed, blood on his teeth and war in his bones. "Don't fall behind, big brother!" he called, slashing a beast nearly in half.

All around us, the tide was turning, but we hadn't won... yet. I scanned the masses, searching for the Night King as Aelia and I rose to our feet, but he was nowhere to be found.

From deep within the trees, leaves rustled and crackled as something massive moved. Then the earth trembled.

"Aelia," I said, breath catching.

"I feel it," she whispered, stepping into my side.

The Moirai Shard in my pocket pulsed, warm and cold, light and shadow. It was as if it was waiting for something. Something big.

A low rumble rolled through the trees, ominous and menacing. The hair on my nape rose. Then it came again. Not the stomp of feet or the beat of wings. It was something deeper, like the forest itself groaning under the weight of some terrible thing waking from slumber.

Silence swept the battlefield in its wake. Even the Night Fae froze.

I took a step back, pulling her with me, every instinct howling at me to move. "Aelia..."

The sky darkened. No, it was blotted out, inky darkness

sweeping in and blanketing corpses and scorched earth. From the shattered edge of the northern part of the glade, it emerged.

A beast of myth. Born not of bone and blood but woven from shadow and nightmares. Twice the size of our dragons.

Dozens of limbs, each one lashing through trees like blades. A crown of bones and thorns curled atop its head, where six glowing eyes bled black ichor down its face. Wings like broken sails dragged behind it, shredded but still powerful enough to stir a cyclone with a single beat.

Behind me, Phantom roared, and for the first time since we'd bonded all those years ago, I felt fear lance across her mind.

"Please tell me that's a cursed illusion," Symon spluttered. He, Rue, Devin and Heaton appeared beside us.

"Gods, I wish it were."

It's a Noctal Revenant. Phantom's whispered words slithered through my thoughts. *Something that should've died with the Night Fae at the end of the Two Hundred Years' War.*

"I thought they were extinct," Aelia breathed, echoing my own thoughts as she processed Phantom's words through our bond, awe and terror warring in her voice.

"They are," Kaelith said grimly from behind us. "Or, they were. Helroth must've reanimated it and brought it from the nightmare realm." His voice dropped, reverent and horrified all at once. "The Fae nicknamed it the Gravecaller."

"How perfectly accurate," Symon deadpanned.

The beast opened its maw and released a howl that turned the twilight sky to pitch and the ground to rot. The words of the scroll I'd found in Tenebris's empty cage all those weeks ago at the Castle of Ethereal Light flashed across my mind.

Either salvation or oblivion awaits, for when twilight reigns, the final hour begins.

This was it. The child of twilight, the prophecy, me... *twilight reigns*. My thoughts spun, but I shoved everything down, focusing on one thing only. Aelia. I didn't care if I shattered. I didn't care if this forest swallowed me and everyone else whole. As long as Aelia lived. That was the only victory I needed.

Ruhl cursed under his breath. "No sword will take that thing down."

"Then we find another way," Aelia said, reaching instinctively for her daggers. Infernium vein. She held them up and the crystals embedded in the hilts pulsed with light, flecks of the Moirai Shard. They vibrated with power, the echo pounding the surrounding air.

"Aelia." I turned to her, shadows already curling tighter around my wrists. "You can't."

She was pale. Glowing. Her *rais* pulsed like the last flame in a dying world. "I have to try."

Phantom and Solanthus landed beside us, the ground trembling with their fury. They roared in unison, the bond between us thrumming to life again, louder and wilder. The Tetrum Cordis pulsed with energy, begging for release.

"Then we do it together," I replied.

The Gravecaller surged forward, crushing trees beneath its talons, its eyes burning holes through the battlefield as it locked on to us.

To Aelia.

Symon gasped beside me, having noticed it too. "It's coming straight for her."

"No," I snarled. "Not today."

Shadows exploded from my fingertips, but they weren't alone. *Rais* flooded me with searing light. *Zar* twisted like liquid night down my spine. All three surged together—*nox*, *rais*, and *zar*—merging, writhing, and begging to be unleashed.

The Gravecaller reared, screaming a soundless wail that made the shadows bend and the Light Fae fall to their knees.

We charged.

Chapter Sixty-Six

A *elia*

The world narrowed to that single monstrous shape. The Gravecaller tore through the battlefield crushing Light, Shadow, and Night Fae alike. Its crown of bone sliced through the mist, six eyes burning with eternal rage. With every beat of its ruined wings, the sky trembled. Its screech warped the air itself, dark *zar* twisting every tree and soldier it passed.

Even the Night Fae scattered in its wake. It didn't fight only for Helroth. It fought for utter chaos.

And I could feel it now, something primal, something ancient stirring deep in my chest. It was as if my blood recognized the creature that had haunted Aetherian nightmares for centuries. The mythical beasts of the Wilds, the ones that lived in children's bedtime stories, had been reborn.

It's coming for you. Sol whispered in my mind, low and urgent.

Let it come.

Reign stood at my side, his shadows flaring like a cloak of smoke and vengeance. The Gravecaller shrieked again, and then he turned to me, eyes burning like obsidian stars.

Ready? His question streaked through the cuorem.

Always.

Phantom and Sol soared above us with wings stretched, preparing to strike from above. But the beast was nearly upon us. There would be no time for fire or skyborne assaults. This was ours to finish.

I drew my daggers, the twin blades of infernium vein pulsing with light and shadow. The tiny specks of the Moirai Shard buried deep within the crystals' hilts, once dormant, now burned like miniature stars. It was as if the bond we'd forged in Aekorith had awakened something more powerful within them as well.

Beneath my skin, *rais* surged like molten gold. Around my ankles, shadows danced like soldiers waiting for orders. And from the center of my chest, something even deeper stirred. *Zar*, heavy and deadly, and craving blood.

The Gravecaller struck, one massive limb crashing into the ground feet from where we stood, tearing apart rock and root. Its six eyes locked onto mine.

It saw me. It knew me. The child of twilight.

I moved first.

The battlefield disappeared. It was just me and the monster. Light flared from my hands as I hurled twin blades of pure *rais*. Reign's shadows joined mine mid-air, weaving around the light like ribbons of night. They struck the creature's flank, one blade embedding into its leathery hide. It shrieked, spinning toward us with impossible speed.

Reign launched forward, his *nox* crackling with raw fury. Phantom's essence surged through him. His movements were faster, more fluid, more savage. He leapt toward the beast, striking it with a spear of writhing *zar*. It exploded on contact, black ichor raining down.

But the Gravecaller didn't fall. No, it reared, roaring so loudly the very ground split at our feet. I cried out, stumbling, hands shooting out to steady myself. A second later, Reign was at my side catching me.

"Together," he growled, his breath hot against my cheek.

I nodded and lifted the daggers again, the hilts glowing brighter now. They were almost too bright to look at. The bond surged between us. Not just the cuorem, not even just the Tetrum Cordis. Something *more*.

Give it everything, I whispered through the mystical strands that connected us all.

And we did.

All four of us. Me. Reign. Sol. Phantom.

Rais, *nox*, and *zar* collided, woven together through the threads of our bond, pouring into the twin daggers in my hands. The crystals flared, absorbing it all, our power, our rage, our love. They vibrated once, twice, then exploded in light so bright the battlefield turned to day.

I screamed as I hurled both blades with every shred of power in my being. They flew like meteors, streaking toward the Gravecaller's center mass, aiming for the largest glowing eye at the center of its skull. The beast shrieked in fury and pain as the daggers hit, detonating in twin bursts of golden-black fire.

The creature bucked, limbs flailing, wings snapping through the air. The force of the blast threw Reign and me backward, slamming us into the charred earth. I rolled across the ground before I came to a stop, the wind knocked clean from my lungs.

An impossibly long moment of silence followed. Then, a thundering crack, like the sky itself was splitting open.

I pushed up onto one elbow, eyes locked on the Gravecaller. It stood for one endless heartbeat, its eyes wide and shining. Then, it shattered.

Light and shadow broke apart like glass, dissolving into ash, smoke, and the final scream of a nightmare ending at last.

The battlefield went still.

My chest heaved, my heart pounding in my ears as I looked

around. Phantom roared above us. Sol's golden fire flickered down like snow.

Raysa, we'd done it. The Gravecaller was dead.

Reign dropped to his knees beside me, pulling me into his arms, his shadows wrapping around us protectively. "You did it," he gasped, forehead pressed to mine.

"No," I whispered. "*We* did it."

We just sat there, holding each other for a long moment as the entire battlefield lay in stunned silence.

Ash drifted like snow, glowing faintly with dying embers. The Gravecaller was gone. Its monstrous form had dissolved into the soil like it had never existed, but the tremble in my hands said otherwise. The burn behind my eyes. The weight of what we'd done.

Reign helped me to my feet, his fingers tight on mine. Both of us were still breathless and unsteady, our bond humming with spent power. All around us, the army slowly gathered again. Rue and Symon stood shoulder to shoulder, bruised and bloodied but grinning like crazy. Heaton waved from farther back, leaning on Devin, while Kaelith barked orders to the warriors to regroup wasting no time on emotion.

The battle with that monster may have been won, but the war was far from over.

A slow, deliberate clap suddenly broke the silence, the sound cutting through the battlefield like a blade. More clapping. Measured. Mocking.

Every head turned toward the tree line beyond the battleground.

A tall figure emerged from the misted pines, flanked by glittering Royal Guardians. He walked as though the battle hadn't touched him. Not a speck of ash or soot mottled his pristine gold-and-white armor. A circlet of glittering platinum sat atop his golden head like a halo forged of lies.

King Elian.

The blood in my veins froze.

"Bravo," he called, his voice smooth and honeyed, echoing unnaturally far. "A stunning display. Truly. I haven't seen power like that in my lifetime. I'm not sure I've even read of anything like it in Aetherian history."

"Uncle," I spat the word like venom.

The earth rumbled beneath our feet as our dragons landed behind us. Reign stepped in front of me instinctively. Phantom growled low in her throat, her tail sweeping defensively. Sol's heat flared through my back like a warning. All our friends tightened the circle around us.

"What in all the realms is this?" Rue muttered beside me, not even bothering to disguise her shock.

Before I could respond, two figures bound in chains emerged.

Behind Elian, dragged forward by soldiers, were two males I thought I'd never see together. Especially not like this.

King Helroth, his sweeping silver hair tangled and his crown gone, wore a sneer of cold disdain. Even in shackles with one arm missing, he stood tall, like a predator waiting to find a faulty rod in its cage.

And beside him...

Reign's sharp inhale echoed through our bond. Then Ruhl cursed.

Tenebris.

Despite Reign having severed his father's blood vow, I could still feel the sliver of dread winding through my mate.

"Ah, both of my sons have come today. How fitting," Tenebris snarled. "Here for my crown, Ruhl?"

The Shadow Regent remained silent, mouth drawn into a curve, not giving his father anything.

Tenebris was bound and shackled in cuffs that glowed with ancient runes. His head was bowed, obsidian hair falling across his face. But those glowing star-bright eyes lifted to meet ours. He wasn't broken, and certainly not repentant.

He was just watching and waiting. Much like I imagine my grandsire was doing.

"Gods," I breathed. "How?"

"How did I manage to capture the Night King, dear niece?" His grin was cold and savage. "Simple. I offered him peace."

"And you betrayed him, too?"

His shoulders lifted nonchalantly. "War is war, Aelia. There is no price too high to ensure a win."

But it was the figure that appeared at Elian's side next that made my stomach truly plummet.

A male in dark Spellbinder robes, the same color as wet ash. His skin was like tarnished iron, coal black eyes and raven hair streaked with silver. His hands glowed faintly, one resting on a gnarled staff. I knew that face. Tharos Dren.

My breath caught.

The first time I'd seen him he was standing beside Helroth, when I'd been imprisoned at Helspire Keep. He was the one who had bound my powers at my parents' request all those years ago. And he was also the one who'd released them at my grandsire's command, cold and impassive as he watched me scream.

And now, he stood beside King Elian?

"Tharos?" I whispered, stunned. "Why...?"

The dark Spellbinder bowed his head slightly when our gazes met. "Princess."

"Don't call her that," Reign growled, stepping closer.

King Elian smiled faintly, as if he were hosting a court banquet rather than walking onto a battlefield smeared with death. "It's time to continue our conversation..."

Chapter Sixty-Seven

A^{elia}

"How dare you?" I hissed, my voice trembling with fury. "You brought Helroth and Tenebris to the heart of the war, after everything you've done, and expect a civil conversation now? After you set the Shadow King on *my* mate? To kill *me*?"

He waved a dismissive hand. "Who knew Reign had gotten powerful enough to defeat his own father?"

I knew. And he was about to find out the true extent of our combined powers.

"Helroth and Tenebris are no longer rulers," Elian continued smoothly. "They are weapons. Weapons I now control." He lifted a nonchalant shoulder. "I thought you'd be pleased, honestly."

Reign's shadows flared. "You think some measly shackles with celestial glyphs can hold my father? Or the Night King?"

Both Tenebris and Helroth stood a little straighter.

"Not shackles," Tharos interjected, his voice as calm as still water. "These are bindings of ancient consequence. There is no

461

power in this realm capable of breaking them, except perhaps the one that you all just awoke."

My stomach twisted. "You *were* watching," I rasped, realization hitting me like a blade.

"We all were," Elian replied, his smile faltering only slightly. "That dragon mating ritual, the Tetrum Cordis, it changed the balance of this realm. And now, I fear if I don't act right away, we'll be out of time. The prophecy will come to pass... with the wrong child of twilight."

"What in the realms are you talking about?" I growled.

A frigid smile crept across Elian's face, sharper than any blade.

"You truly thought it was you?" His voice was smooth and laced with derision. "That *you* deserved to be the child of twilight? Just because you were born of two courts, because you're a girl with pretty wings and a powerful bond?"

What in the realms? I took a step forward, fire igniting under my skin, but Reign's hand shot out to steady me. The dragons behind us growled low, thunder vibrating in their chests.

Elian's eyes flicked between us, calculating and cold. Then a flash of amusement sparked. "It was never about *you*, Aelia. Never about the dragons or the gods' little games. It's always been *me*. I was born after your father, the cursed second born, forced to live in the shadow of the great Alaric's glory. Until I took matters into my own hands. I refused to be overlooked for a moment longer. I should have been king from the start; I should have been the chosen one. I had the bloodline, the power, the right."

"What do you mean you took matters into your hands?" A prickle of unease raised the hair on my nape. "What did you do?"

He tsked. "What do you think, dear niece? Your father was wounded in battle, barely the shell of a man he once was. It was only the blasted mate bond with your mother that kept him alive..."

I gasped, all the air siphoning from my lungs. "*You* killed her?"

Elian shrugged, nonchalantly. "A cursed Night and Shadow

Fae of mixed dark blood never should've been anywhere near the Light Throne. Your father was weak, a lovesick fool."

A surge of rage, wild and powerful, built in my core. My *uncle*, my father's own *brother*, killed my parents, not Helroth or Tenebris. My own damned blood. Gods, I couldn't believe it. At least Helroth had been telling the truth about this all along.

He sneered. "First, I had to suffer your father, and then you... You stole what should've been mine. You and your abomination of a bond."

"You don't get to rewrite the prophecy," I snapped, voice trembling with restrained rage. "It is not for you to say who lives and who dies. You don't get to twist the fate of this world because you're desperate for power."

"No," he agreed. "I don't need to rewrite it." He raised one hand. "I'm going to *become* it, the true child of twilight."

Before either Reign or I could move, Tharos lifted his staff. With a guttural word in a language I didn't understand, the runes on his staff flared violet-black, blinding in their brilliance.

A pulse of *lys* rippled outward, the smoky scent clinging to my nostrils. Time slowed, then fractured completely.

Every warrior behind us, Ruhl, Kaelith, all of Flare Team, even Phantom and Solanthus froze mid-motion. Wings outstretched. Weapons half-drawn. Mouths parted in silent cries.

"No—!" I raced to our friends, to the Fae who had become my family, and reached for them but my fingers passed through Ruhl, then Rue and Symon as if they were carved from smoke.

Panic rushed my veins, icy and unrelenting.

Reign cursed under his breath. "What did you do?"

Tharos lowered the staff slowly, the hazy *lys* still clinging to its length like bleeding shadows.

"A temporal stasis spell," he said simply. "Only the chosen remain unaffected."

"And us," Reign growled. "Why not freeze us too?"

"Because you're going to watch," Elian said. "The fall of the kings, and the rise of a god."

The chains binding Helroth and Tenebris flared violently, pinning them in place. The moment the Night King tried to surge forward, the sigils around his cuff ignited, burning down his arm. He snarled in fury, teeth bared before a scream ripped through his clenched teeth.

"Run, Aelia," Helroth roared.

A tiny dead part of me flared with hope at my grandfather's words.

"Go, now," he gritted out, eyes meeting mine.

"It's too late for that." Elian's grin was pure evil.

"You're mad," Reign spat. "You'll destroy everything."

"I intend to rebuild," he replied coolly. Then he stepped forward, toward a blackened altar that Tharos had conjured from the ashes with a wave of his hand. Atop it rested a golden relic, pulsing with ancient power. The circular medallion was etched with the triskelion of the three Fae gods—Raysa, Noxus, and Zaroth—three interlocking spirals radiating from a common center. The air bent around it, wrong and heavy.

What in all the worlds is that? My question raced through our bond, now much quieter with the absence of our dragons.

I have no idea... likely some lost artifact of the gods.

"You can't do this—" I cried.

"I can," Elian snapped. "And I will."

Rais bloomed along my fingertips, *nox* surging to the surface of my skin. I would not let my uncle destroy everything after all we'd fought for. All we'd lost.

"Careful, princess." Elian tsked again, wagging a finger. "You wouldn't want something to happen to your dragons while they're completely helpless." He ticked his head over Reign's shoulder where a dozen Royal Guardians materialized, luminous swords poised at Sol's and Phantom's throats.

"No," I growled.

"If you draw even a drop of blood from either of our dragons," Reign snarled, "I'll rip you apart limb from limb then feed your mutilated carcass to each of them."

"There's no need for such savagery if you simply behave." He drew a long, curved cutlas from his hip, its edge glowing with divine light. Without flinching, he slashed the blade across his palm, blood spilling freely. "Don't worry, it will all be over soon."

Elian let it drip onto the medallion, then drew it over his head. Then, raising his other hand, he and Tharos began to chant.

Dark words. Old ones. The air cracked with thunder, the earth groaning beneath our feet. Storm clouds spiraled above, thick and roiling, blacking out the sun.

What do we do? Even I could hear the tremble in my tone.

The Moirai Shard... It could sever whatever divine bond Elian is trying to create. His voice was calm and deliberate, but I could feel the frenzied rush of emotions coursing through our connection. *As soon as it's complete, we make our move.*

Reign, you can't. What about the sacrifice?

I will pay it. Whatever it is. We cannot allow Elian to assume all that power.

Claws of fear raked across my heart, and I drew in a sharp breath. *I won't let you. I cannot lose you.*

Helroth and Tenebris suddenly screamed, drawing me back to the present as the runes on their cuffs blazed blinding white, then ripped open. Shadow and Night, *nox* and *zar*, bled from their bodies, pulled into a swirling vortex above the altar.

They buckled, knees hitting the dirt as their gods' given abilities were torn from them. Siphoned. Consumed.

No.

Their bodies withered in an instant, the terrible power devouring them from the inside out. When the light faded, nothing remained of Helroth or Tenebris but ash scattered on the wind. An unexpected sharp pang twisted in my chest. My grandsire, for all his cruelty, was still my blood. His end should have brought only relief, yet a sliver of sorrow coiled inside me all the same.

Through the bond I could feel the same feeling of loss curling through Reign. Despite everything Tenebris had put him through.

Elian's body convulsed as he drew in the power, eyes glowing, skin now seared with divine markings. The triskelion medallion floated from his hands and seared into his chest like a brand. The power of Night and Shadow poured into him like molten godsfire.

He threw his head back and roared, a sound that split the sky.

The energy lashed outward, and I was thrown off my feet, Reign crashing beside me. Pain seared through my veins, and I was certain somehow that our dragons felt it too, despite their frozen state.

Then silence, thick and oppressive.

When the dust finally cleared, Elian stood at the center of a black crater, cloaked in shadow and fire. His hair was a white flame, his eyes bottomless pits, one light and one dark.

He was no longer just Light. Not Shadow nor Night.

But all three. At once. A true abomination.

"I am reborn," he whispered, voice echoing with power that didn't belong to him. "The true child of twilight."

Chapter Sixty-Eight

A *elia*

Now, Aelia. We must use the Moirai Shard. It's our only chance.

I watched in sheer terror as Reign drew the shard of shimmering crystal from the folds of his cloak. Elian still stood in the crater, hellfire and shadows raging around him in a storm of power. His gaze was lifted to the heavens, lips flapping incoherently.

No... A tremor coursed through me, so violent my voice shook. *We don't even know if it will work.*

Reign tugged me into his arms, lips brushing a frantic kiss to my forehead. *But we must try.*

And if I lose you?

You could never lose me, starlight. I will be with you, always. He pressed his palm to my heart. *In here.*

I nearly shattered as he released me.

Reign's fingers curled around the Moirai Shard, and the

moment its crystalline edge caught the fractured moonlight across the battlefield, my heart stopped.

As if the gods themselves had sensed its presence, Elian's storm of stolen power faltered for the briefest breath.

A scream of primordial energy ripped through the air, deafening and divine. Light exploded from Reign's hand, something raw and furious. The Shard shimmered in a rainbow of essences of all the gods that ever were—golden for Raysa, obsidian for Noxus, violet for Zaroth, azure for Selraya, crimson for Avarnok. Then the triskelion of power that hung from Elian's chest spiraled outward in a vortex that blossomed across the night sky.

Elian's eyes widened. He turned, mouth open, hands flailing at Tharos. But before the dark Spellbinder could conjure something, some counterspell, maybe, Reign's mouth began to move.

He raised the Shard high and roared, *"Moirai incendiae."* Then louder. *"Moirai incendiae.* I sever this unnatural tether. Return what was stolen to the gods!"

The Shard responded like it had been waiting an eternity for this command.

A bolt of raw energy surged from the heavens, spearing directly into the Shard. The daggers at my sides vibrated, the tiny shards embedded in the hilts awakened by the force. Reign's entire body shuddered, his form aglow in radiant light. From the glowing prism, a pulse of divinity erupted, a tsunami of power that tore through the battlefield like a star being born. It hit Elian square in the chest, and his scream was like the tearing of reality itself.

"Reign!" I cried.

I'm okay, starlight. His voice wavered through the cuorem, but he held strong, bearing the fury of power.

The dark spell crumbled, ashes falling to the earth in a sooty haze. The bond between Elian and the gods snapped, a loud pop that vibrated the air.

The stolen powers, Helroth's twisted *zar*, Tenebris's venomous *nox*, even the corrupted light of Elian's *rais*, were ripped from his soul. Each one unfurled like silk threads rushing back toward the skies, into the great ether where they belonged.

Elian crumpled, gasping, his knees hitting the earth with a crack of bone. Steam curled from his mouth. A tangle of hellfire and radiant light licked across his form. His golden armor blackened and disintegrated to ash.

A sharp cry erupted from Tharos's gaping mouth as the spell dissolved to nothing, along with Elian himself. He scrambled backward, but Reign was already moving.

My *cuoré* stalked across the field like a living shadow, eyes glowing like twin stars. The Shard had altered him somehow. It had poured the strength of the gods through his veins, and for this moment, he was limitless.

Tharos raised a hand, invoking some incantation, but Reign's blade found his throat before the words could form.

"No more spells," Reign whispered, and his shadows devoured Tharos, body and soul. There was no scream, only silence, and then nothing but dust on the wind.

The storm suddenly died. The skies cleared and glittering sunlight parted the clouds. It was as if nothing had ever happened.

For a beautiful, perfect moment, everything was still. Then, just as suddenly, everything and everyone was back in motion. The grunts of wounded soldiers, the howls of pain, and the gasps of confusion echoed all around us.

I stood frozen, trembling, not from fear any longer but from the impossible weight of what had just happened. Gods, we did it.

Reign turned to me, eyes softening. The Shard had dimmed in his palm, now just a crystal husk completely spent. "We did it," he breathed, echoing my thoughts.

I launched myself at him, arms wrapping tight around his shoulders. "We did." He held me in his arms spinning me around as the battleground came alive once more. Then his lips crashed into mine, there in the center of the chaos with ash and starlight falling like snow around us. For a moment, a fleeting, wonderful moment, everything was right in the world.

Then Reign's knees buckled, and he slid from my arms. He crumpled onto the scorched earth as I watched horrified.

"Reign!" I dropped to the ground beside him, terror squeezing my lungs. "Reign!" I cradled his face, then drew him into my lap. His skin was ice. "No, no, no—stay with me."

I pressed my ear to his chest. Not a sound, not a heartbeat, not even a whisper of breath.

No! Reign? I searched deep within my core for the pulsing cuorem. It was still. The faint threads that connected us had gone silent. Completely silent. *Reign, please! Come back to me!*

A shape emerged through the mist, drawing my attention. The female was garbed in white and silver, eyes glowing with radiant wisdom and sorrow through a sheer veil. Her voice carried like a bell through the stillness.

"Greetings, child. I am a priestess of Selraya from the Lupherium. Your mate severed what none have dared to touch," she said, kneeling beside me. "In order to maintain balance in the world of the living, a thread must be cut so another can be spun."

"No, no... I do not accept this!" I cried, holding Reign tighter. "It's not fair. How can the gods demand such a sacrifice? He's my *cuoré*, chosen by the damned gods themselves to be with me. How can they steal him away?"

"It is for the Moirai to choose, child. Not us."

She placed a gentle hand over his heart. "He carries the burden of gods now. And gods do not slumber easily."

"No," I snarled again.

"Noxus's nuts, what happened?" Symon moved to my side, blinking the haze from his eyes. Then Rue, Devin, Heaton... all my friends surrounded me.

"Oh, gods, Reign. What did he do?" Ruhl slid to the dirt beside me, bloodied and covered in ash. His mouth twisted, darkness settling over his expression as he scanned his brother's still form.

"He... he used the Moirai Shard to defeat Elian..." My throat was raw, agony bloating my insides as I cradled Reign's head in my lap and rocked gently. A sob built in my chest, a torrent of emotions threatening to burst.

A rumble shook the earth beneath my feet and Sol's warm breath wafted across my shoulders. Then Phantom's agonized roar split across the sun-drenched sky.

He can't be gone. I will not allow it. I pushed the thought through our four—no, three-way connection.

Then fix it before it's too late for all of us. Phantom's voice was pure misery drenched in torment. *You are the child of twilight, blessed by the gods themselves. You have the power. Now* use *it.* Her words echoed in my skull like a drumbeat of fury and grief. Her anguish was my own. Sol's sorrow rolled through our bond like smoke and fire.

How?

Use your power, damn it, Aelia. Phantom's dark timbre only intensified. *All three of them.*

I looked down at Reign's lifeless face, his dark lashes still against pale cheeks, his lips tinged blue. My chest heaved, the world pressing in from all sides. A faint tremor vibrated the daggers at my sides, but I was too consumed with grief to focus.

No. Not like this. I refused to allow the gods to steal him from me. Not after how hard we fought to be together. Not ever.

My fingers curled tighter around him. "Do you hear me, Noxus?" I screamed into the sky. "You gave him to me. I will not allow you to steal him away!" I pressed my forehead to his. "I will tear the veil apart myself if I have to."

And then, I felt it. A flicker of power. Not from Reign... but from *me.* From *us.*

Not just the *rais* burning in my veins, or the *nox* I'd trained so hard to wield. Not even the insidious *zar* that hummed low and dangerous beneath the surface. This was something new.

It was wild and boundless, a streak of energy unfurling deep in my core. My heart pulsed in time with Solanthus's wrath and Phantom's sorrow. With their power behind mine, I reached deeper still, tapping into the trinity of energies within me. *Rais*—light. *Nox*—shadow. *Zar*—night.

Then it came to me. The one Night Fae ability I'd dreaded to master. Necromancy. Phantom was right. I *could* bring him back. But would the soul that returned still be my Reign?

The ancient Night Fae art whispered in my bones like a seductive promise. I had seen Helroth wield it, pervert it, turn it cruel. But I was not Helroth.

I was his antithesis. A daughter of Light.

"Help me," I whispered to the earth, to the gods, to whatever forces were still listening. Calling on my healing *rais*, the dark necromancy of *zar* and the cool shadows of *nox*, everything I needed to save Reign, I turned my focus inward. With Reign's hand in mine, I reached for my dagger and raised it toward the heavens. "Raysa, Goddess of Light, Noxus, God of Death, and Zaroth, Keeper of Night, hear me now. Grant me passage. Allow me to cross the Veil and bring him home."

The air thickened, charged with raw energy. The crystals in my daggers flared, flickers of the Moirai Shard spinning to life.

My body began to rise, hovering just inches above the battlefield. Below, Reign lay still beneath me. Golden light poured from my core, weaving with my shadows and threading with violet *zar*.

I closed my eyes and shadowtraveled. Not across the lands of Aetheria, but through realms. Through a veil of smoke and silence and starlight.

I fell into a cold place, gray and endless. The in-between. Spirits drifted like phantoms, whispers caught in endless wind. I screamed his name, again and again.

"Reign! Reign, where are you?"

Nothing.

Tears streamed down my cheeks as I searched the endless space. "Reign, *please*. You swore you'd be with me for eternity."

Time stretched on. Endless.

"You spoke the words, Reign." My voice faltered as memories consumed me. *"I will always come back to you. Even if I have to crawl through every realm of shadow to do it.* So do it now. I need you."

Then... a flicker. A curl of shadow and night, then a spark of *rais.*

I turned, and a sob broke free.

Reign. He stood in the void, bare-chested, shadows and night coiling at his feet, light gleaming from beneath his skin as if he was carved from moonlight itself.

But his eyes were pools of infinite darkness.

"Reign," I sobbed, running to him. "Please, come back. It's me."

He didn't move.

My knees hit the infinite space beneath. "Do you remember me, my love? Our bond. You're my *cuoré.* You are the other half of my soul, and without you, I will never be whole again." My voice cracked. "Remember the night in the cave. Our dragons. The first time you kissed me then stole my memories of it." I faltered, each word more of a struggle with the grief tearing me apart. "When you came for me at the cottage and saved me from that dark Fae lord."

His head tilted slightly. A flicker. A tremor. Like something inside him stirred.

I reached up and pressed my palm to his heart. "You promised we were forever," I whispered. "Now, I'm calling in your vow."

I poured everything I had into him. The healing Light, the icy Shadow, the thrilling Night. Fire from Sol. Grief from Phantom. Even the whisper of necromancy I'd pulled from the depths of the dark *zar.* The crystals in my daggers vibrated with power.

The wind howled in a whirlwind of energy. The Veil screamed as if the very fabric of existence were being torn apart. And then, Reign gasped.

His hand closed over mine as his once vacant gaze focused on my wild one. "Aelia," he breathed, voice cracked but real. "You came for me."

Another sob tore from my throat. "Always."

My soul reached out to his, enveloping it in a glittering mist. Then I pulled him into my arms and shadowtraveled hard, ripping us back through the Veil of death with nothing but sheer will and the fury of our bond.

We landed on the blood-soaked battlefield with a crack of light that split the dark clouds that had formed when my love fell.

I collapsed over him, heaving, and every part of me shaking. With my ear pressed to his chest, I heard it. It was faint at first...his heartbeat. Slow but steady. But it was there.

Reign's lids fluttered as I held my breath. "Starlight," he rasped, and I inched back to look at him when he blinked up at me. His voice was rough, deep and glorious. "That was one heart stopping kiss."

Laughter burst from me through the tears, messy, wild and alive.

We survived. We were together. And gods' help me, we would never be torn apart again.

Chapter Sixty-Nine

R^{eign}

Breath returned to me like breaking through the surface of a dark, endless sea. It was sudden and agonizing. For a moment, all had been quiet. Peaceful.

Now, the world was too bright. Too loud. Too alive.

But *she* was there. My Aelia. My *cuoré*.

Her face hovered above mine, streaked with soot and tears, radiant even in the chaos of battle. Her hands cupped my face like she was afraid I might vanish.

"You came for me," I whispered again, voice hoarse, like I'd swallowed smoke and ash.

She nodded, a sob catching in her throat. "Of course I did, professor. You think you get to die, not only breaking your promise but also leaving me to deal with all of this?"

I managed a raspy chuckle, lifting a shaking hand to brush a strand of hair from her face. "You could have handled it without me."

"Reign—" Her voice cracked. "Don't you ever do that again."

"I promise," I murmured. "No more dying."

Her lips crashed into mine with wild desperation, and I kissed her back like I was still fighting for my life. Because maybe I was. Because she *was* my life.

And somehow, against every rule of death and gods and fate, we'd won.

When we finally pulled apart, I let my head drop back against the scorched earth with a groan. "Okay, I might need a minute to recover before the next battle."

She let out a shaky laugh. "You just severed a binding power of the gods and died. I think you've earned a rest. We both have."

A shadow passed over us, and then I heard a familiar voice.

"Oh, thank the goddess you're back," Symon murmured. "I never could have borne the burden of consoling your grief-stricken *cuoré* if you'd died."

Aelia rolled her eyes without looking up. "Really, Sy? You're going to make this about you?"

Rue chimed in next. "Professor, I told him you were much too stubborn to ever stay dead."

"You're not wrong," I muttered.

Symon released a dramatic sigh. "Next time, can we maybe *not* die in the middle of a war? It's bad for morale."

A chorus of groans and chuckles rose around us.

I cracked one eye open to see the rest of Flare Team, along with Ruhl, Gideon, and Kaelith gathering around. Every single one of them was bloodied, bruised, and exhausted, but alive. And now they were smiling. Even Kaelith looked pleased. Or, at least, less angry and brooding than usual.

And beyond our circle, the fighting had stopped.

"You lot are a mess," I rasped, pushing myself into a sitting position. "I see I need to double your training efforts."

Ruhl stepped forward, expression tight. But his voice was gruff with something more than relief as he squeezed my shoulder. "Don't ever do that again, Reign."

"I wasn't exactly *trying* to die, brother."

He crossed his arms, but I could see the crack in his usual armor. "Well, next time, try harder not to. With Father gone, you can't leave me before the Ritual of the Shadow Throne begins."

I reached up, and he grasped my forearm in a warrior's grip, hauling me off the ground. The rare softness in his eyes said more than words.

Then Phantom landed with a bone-shaking thud behind me, Solanthus following close behind. Their eyes locked on mine, relieved, furious and overjoyed all at once.

You scared me. Phantom snapped through our bond.

Welcome back, Night Prince. Sol dipped his head. *I'm pleased you did not die. For Aelia's sake, of course.*

"I missed you both too," I muttered aloud, grinning like a fool.

Aelia tugged my hand, pulling it to her heart. "We're finally going to be okay now. We won."

I looked around at our ragtag family, then at the ashes of kings and broken chains of power. Then at our dragons, the soldiers, Light, Shadow and Night, and their torn banners waving in the wind. Some Night Fae fled, others were too wounded to move, but the ones that were able to, turned their weary gazes to Aelia and dropped to their knees in a wave. A ripple of gasps vibrated the air from the Light and Shadow lines.

"Princess Aelia of Inferna! Princess Aelia! Long live the future queen!"

The chants grew louder with each iteration as the Night Fae bowed down before her.

It was really over. I drew in a steadying breath before replying to Aelia. "I think, princess, for the first time in a long time, we just might be more than okay."

The great gilded gates of the Hall of Glory creaked open with a sigh, like the very alabaster stones of the academy exhaled at our return.

Dust swirled through the shafts of late afternoon light that spilled from stained glass windows. The Conservatory was silent, eerily so. No bells, no laughter, no clattering footsteps on marble floors. Just quiet and still.

Aelia's fingers still curled around mine as we stepped into the main hall, crossing through the Veil of Judgement, our footsteps echoing throughout the hallowed space. It was hard to believe this place had once been filled with life, with *rais*, with memory. With her.

"It feels smaller now, somehow," she whispered.

I glanced around at the sweeping arches, the vaulted ceilings. "Or maybe we've just grown bigger."

She smiled faintly at that, but her grip tightened. "It doesn't feel quite like home anymore."

I understood what she meant. The war had stripped so much from us, our innocence, certainty, peace, but this place held ghosts of who we were before all of it.

"Come on," she said suddenly, tugging me toward the east wing.

"Where are we going?"

"My dormitory of course," she answered over her shoulder, a mischievous lilt in her voice.

That made me blink. "Do you think I still have access?"

"Only one way to find out." She flashed a grin. "Either way, I'm sure the wards are too exhausted to stop us."

The corridors narrowed. I knew this hallway well. I'd stalked it too many times in the early days, broken and sullen, trying to avoid the powerless little Kin with starlight in her eyes and a spark in her smile.

Aelia stopped in front of a familiar door and pushed it open.

Her room was just as I remembered it: soft light filtering in through gauzy curtains, the faint scent of lavender clinging to the air, vines curling around her bed in the corner.

We stood there for a moment, not speaking.

Then I broke the silence, my thoughts spinning with all there was for us to do in the coming weeks. "The thrones are empty. Three courts with no rulers. There will be questions. Power vacuums. We'll need to—"

She turned and pressed her lips to mine. They were soft and certain but mostly silencing.

When she pulled back, her voice was quiet. "Not tonight. Please."

"Aelia..."

"Just for tonight," she said, taking my face in her hands. "Can we pretend it's the beginning again? That I'm just your powerless new student and you're the brooding professor who keeps finding excuses to arrange private training lessons?"

A grin curled my lips, my heart pumping faster.

She stepped in closer, fingers curling into the collar of my tunic. "Pretend that I snuck you in for a forbidden rendezvous. That this is all a scandal waiting to be uncovered. That nothing else exists outside this room but you and me."

I let out a shaky breath, resting my forehead against hers. "I can do that."

"Good." Her voice was a whisper now. "Because I don't want to think about thrones or crowns or what comes next right now. I just want this. Us."

I kissed her again. Slow, deep, and unhurried this time.

"Then let's pretend, starlight," I murmured against her lips. "For as long as you want."

And in that quiet dorm room, tucked away at the edge of the academy, I let the world fade. Let the weight of war, of gods, and of sacrifice fall away. Just a professor and his star-streaked student, tangled in something forbidden and beautiful.

For one night, it was enough.

Epilogue

R *eign*
Three Months Later

The ceremonial tunic itched. Which, considering it had been hand-stitched by the most revered Light Fae tailors in the realm with actual threads of moonlight and shadowflame, felt like some sort of celestial joke.

I tugged at the collar again as I stared at my reflection in the looking glass. My shadows buzzed across the fine fabric, as desperate to be free of it as I was.

"Touch that thing one more time," Ruhl muttered, "and I'm going to personally punch the new King of Night in the throat."

I shot him a glare through the mirror's reflection. "You'd hit a crowned ruler of Aetheria?"

"I'd hit my fool of a brother, and the crown can watch."

Despite everything, I smiled as I faced Ruhl. "You'd have to catch me first."

"You forget," he said, folding his arms and leaning against the carved stone wall, "I'm faster than you. Always have been."

I rolled my eyes and turned back to the mirror, attempting to adjust the high collar once more before giving up. My shoulders sagged, along with my shadows.

It was happening. This wasn't a vision or a fever dream. In less than an hour, I'd be crowned the King of Night. Beside the Queen of Light.

Me... Tenebris's bastard. I was never destined for the throne, but it had been thrust onto my shoulders all the same.

Gods help us all.

"Are you okay?" Ruhl's voice had dropped to something quieter, gentler.

I nodded slowly. "It's just... strange. I always thought you'd be the first to be crowned. The next Shadow King."

He snorted. "I still might be. Eventually. Though I suppose I've got a few things left to prove."

I glanced over at him. "The Ritual of the Shadow Throne?"

He hesitated for a beat before nodding. "It's custom, as you know. Shadow Fae heirs have to pass the trial before they can rule. With everything that's changing, I thought it right to maintain this one time-honored tradition. You're lucky you got out of it. On account of saving the entire realm and becoming a bonded god-child of the Tetrum Cordis or whatever."

I grinned faintly. "Surprisingly, the Night Fae have no such barbaric traditions."

"Mmm, shocking, indeed, given their blood-thirsty nature."

My grin widened. Gods, how I'd longed for this when we were young. The easy banter of brothers. Who knew we would find it all these years later after setting the entire realm ablaze?

Ruhl's smirk faltered. "Do you ever wonder," he said slowly, "if the throne will actually accept me?"

I blinked, giving him my full attention. "What?"

"In the vision I saw in the trials..." He trailed off, rubbing a hand over the back of his neck. "It said I would never take the throne."

I stilled. "That doesn't mean what you think it does," I said carefully. "Visions are just glimpses. They're never the full story."

"I know," he muttered. "But still. What if I'm not worthy? What if the throne refuses me?"

"You held Feywood during the battle with the Night Fae," I said. "You saved Kin. You never gave up, even when the gods themselves seemed to. You offered to walk away from it all, to assume my blood vow for the good of Aetheria. For my *cuoré*. That throne will recognize what you are. Shadowborn. Loyal. Stronger than anyone knows."

His jaw ticked, but something in his shoulders loosened. "You're certain?"

I crossed the room and clasped his shoulder. "Yes, there is no doubt in my mind. And anyway, you've got me now. We rule together. You're my blood, Ruhl. You're the only reason I survived half of this madness. The court wouldn't just be lucky to have you, they'd be fools not to follow you."

He swallowed hard, blinking fast. "You're really getting sappy in your old age, brother."

"I'm thirty."

"Ancient," he deadpanned.

I shoved him, and he punched me lightly in the arm.

"Besides," I added, quieter now. "Everything turned out exactly as it should. Maybe not as we expected. But exactly right."

He nodded, his voice rough. "Yes. Perhaps, it did."

A knock sounded at the door. One of the guards peeked in. "Highness, your Queen is ready."

I turned back to Ruhl. "Wish me luck?"

He smirked. "You don't need luck. You've got her."

I exhaled slowly, the weight of what was coming finally settling over me. Not just the looming crown. But the life we were building. Together.

With one last nod to my brother, I stepped out of the chamber.

Toward her.
Toward forever.

Aelia

Sunlight spilled through the grand arched windows of my chamber, casting ribbons of gold across the marble floor and the trailing hem of my elaborate gown. Outside, bells rang in the valley below the Castle of Ethereal Light, their song rising like a prayer to the gods.

Three months had passed since the war. Three months since we defeated my traitorous uncle, Elian. Since we banished the last of the twisted kings and watched the light return to Aetheria.

And now, somehow, I was here. Coronation day.

"Stop fidgeting," Rue scolded behind me, hands busy in my curls, pinning tiny golden stars into the waves. "You're going to ruin the braids. Do you want to look like a feral Wolvryn for your coronation?"

"Is that not the aesthetic?" I asked dryly, tilting my head to catch her eye in the mirror. "Queen of Light and Shadows with a dash of feral woodland chaos?"

Rue grinned. "Honestly? It wouldn't be that farfetched."

I laughed, but my stomach twisted with nerves. Lifting my hand, I stared at the sparkling gem that now adorned my ring finger. Reign had crafted it from a shard of the crystals etched into the hilts of my daggers. Like my new fiancé, its presence steadied me, anchored me against the gathering storm.

"It's beautiful," Rue crooned.

"I know." I couldn't help the smile from splitting my lips.

It had been less than a month since Reign dropped to one knee in front of the old cottage Aidan had raised me in Feywood and asked me to be his wife. It almost felt redundant, as if what we had was already much grander. After all, we were infinite. Forever.

Still, I'd squealed with joy and thrown myself into his awaiting arms.

Folding my hands in my lap, I focused on the shimmering threads of my magnificent gown. It was spun of white and silver silk, threaded with glittering strands of *rais* and was impossibly heavy. The pressure of what today meant settled on my shoulders like a second crown.

Today, I would become the Queen of Ethereal Light.

And Reign, my *cuoré*, my future husband, and the prince born of darkness and wrath, would be crowned King of Infernal Night beside me.

Two thrones. One court. United.

The thought alone made me want to both cry and throw up at the same time.

"Hey." Rue crouched beside me, mischief softening into something gentler. "You've already done the hard part, you know."

"Which part?" I asked. "Surviving Helroth? Killing a monster made of nightmares? Bargaining with ancient gods? Bringing Reign back from beyond the Veil?"

She shrugged. "All of it. You've proven you deserve the crown a thousand times over. And the Fae know it. Today is just the formality."

"And the pomp and circumstance," I added, glancing down at the intricate embroidery at my waist. "Gods, who knew court seamstresses could be this extravagant?"

Rue straightened with a dramatic toss of her braid. "It's your moment. Let them be extra. Besides—" her grin turned sly, "—this gown is only for part one."

I blinked. "'Part one'? What do you mean?"

Before she could elaborate, there was a knock at the chamber door. A Royal Guardian entered, bowing low. "Your Majesty, His Highness requests your presence in the Glass Garden."

Rue clapped her hands once. "Perfect! I'll finish your hair outside. Come on."

I frowned. "What's Reign doing in the garden before the coronation?"

Rue offered an exaggeratedly innocent shrug. "Maybe he's nervous, too."

But something tugged at my instincts, telling me it was more than that. Still, I followed.

The halls of the castle were awash in golden light, the banners of both courts, sunburst and obsidian hellfire, hanging side by side. Guards bowed as I passed.

The garden bloomed ahead, sunlight dancing across the reflective crystal tiles and blooming moonflowers, Reign's favorite. Phantom and Solanthus lounged lazily near the reflecting pool, both cleaned up and awaiting their grand entrance for the ceremony itself.

It seemed only right to include them as they were as much a part of me as Reign was.

Then I saw him.

Reign stood at the far end of the garden, dressed in obsidian and silver with violet stitching lining his collar. A crown rested in his hands. Mine.

But it wasn't the crown that stole my breath. It was the expression on his face. Wonder. Love. Nerves.

I stepped forward, heart thundering. "I thought I wouldn't see you until the coronation."

"I couldn't wait." His voice was rough with emotion as he took me in. "But... there's something else. I mean, it's not the only reason I'm here."

I narrowed my eyes. "Reign..."

"I'll see you in a little bit." Rue slipped away behind me, humming under her breath. Suspiciously smug.

"Three months ago," Reign said softly, "I thought I would never get another moment with you. And now, we have lifetimes stretched ahead of us. A thousand sunrises. A thousand shadows."

He stepped forward and took my hands. "I didn't want to wait anymore. For courts. For politics. For gods. I want to be yours, now. Today. Not just as King of Night, but as your husband."

My breath caught. "Wait... Reign—what are you saying?"

"I'm saying," he said, reaching into his cloak and revealing a pair of thin, woven rings, one of infernium veined with shadow-steel, the other braided light and silver, "that this isn't just a coronation."

He dropped to one knee. "This is our wedding."

My heart nearly stopped.

I looked down at the male who had begun as my captor, then my professor, my shadow, my shield, my protector, and finally, my love.

"Will you marry me today, in front of our friends, our family and both of our courts?"

I drew in a breath, all the oxygen suddenly evaporating from my lungs. "Yes," I whispered. "A thousand times yes."

He rose, placing the rings between our pressed palms.

Then, beneath the glowing moonflowers and beside the dragons who were our soulmates, Reign's lips found mine. This kiss was sweet and reverent and filled with so much hope my heart grew wings.

Our kingdoms would rise, and the empty thrones would be filled once again.

But in that moment, it was just us.

Light and shadow.

Starlight and storm.

King and Queen.

Forever.

Saying goodbye to Reign and Aelia was sooo hard! I've absolutely loved writing these two and this moment is so bittersweet. Sometimes it's hard to find the perfect ending to really do the characters justice. With these two, I felt like I could keep writing and their story would truly never end. But alas... it must.

I did however, write a spicy wedding night scene if anyone wanted a little more ;) Please note, it's more explicit than my normal writing so read at your own risk. Join my FB group, GK DeRosa's Realm of Readers or grab it here -> https://shorturl.at/AinWL. You're welcome.

And if you couldn't get enough of Ruhl and want to see his happy ending, I'm doing something a little different for him, it's called The Shadow Throne Chronicles. Check that out at www.mystricrosepress.com

I'm already working on the next story which will take place in the same world of Crescentia, *King of Fangs and Frost*. It'll be here in May 2026 and you can preorder it now! (Or maybe not, unfortunately I heard the link may not be working so make sure you're following me!) You've already gotten a sneak peek at Lunaris and the savage Wolvryn, and there will be more to come soon so make sure you're in my FB group or you're receiving my VIP newsletters for some sneak peeks. I can't wait for you all to read the next story I have planned :)

Here's just a little taste:

A wolfless outcast offered as a peace bride.

A savage Wolvryn King who hunts with winter in his veins.

A five-night Blood Hunt that could crown a queen or doom a kingdom.

Perfect for readers who love:

Enemies-to-lovers, arranged marriage, deadly moonlit trials, possessive wolf kings, and heroines who bite back.

Until then...
~GK

Guide to the Courts of
Aetheria

Court of Ethereal Light

King Elian of Ether

Light fae, beings associated with illumination and radiant energy, possess a variety of magical powers aligned with the forces of light and positive energy through *rais*.

Light Fae Abilities

1. Photokinesis:

The ability to manipulate and control light.

2. Healing Light:

The power to harness light energy for healing purposes.

3. Luminous Wings:

Only extremely powerful Light Fae can sprout ethereal, radiant wings that allow them to fly gracefully through the air.

4. Illumination Sight:

The ability to see beyond the visible spectrum, allowing Light Fae to perceive things such as auras, energy patterns, or hidden magical forces.

5. Solar Empowerment:

Drawing strength from sunlight, Light Fae experience enhanced abilities, increased vitality, and heightened magical powers when exposed to sunlight.

6. Prismatic Manipulation:

The power to control and manipulate prisms and rainbows.

7. Radiant Shields:

The ability to create protective barriers or shields made of radiant light.

8. Solar Flare Burst:

Unleashing bursts of intense solar energy, powerful Light Fae could create blinding flashes or focused beams to repel adversaries.

9. Light Infusion:

Infusing objects or individuals with radiant energy.

10. Harmony Induction:

The ability to radiate an aura of peace and tranquility.

11. Illuminate Knowledge:

The power to gain insights, visions, or access to hidden knowledge through the illumination of light.

Court of Umbral Shadows

King Tenebris and Queen Vespera of Umbra

Shadow fae, beings associated with darkness and shadows, possess a range of magical powers aligned with the forces of shadow and concealment through *nox*.

Shadow Fae Abilities

1. Umbrakinesis:
The ability to control and manipulate shadows.

2. Shadow Travel:
The power to traverse through shadows, allowing mature Shadow Fae to move swiftly from one shadow to another.

3. Cloak of Invisibility:
The ability to wrap themselves in shadows, becoming invisible to the naked eye.

4. Umbral Constructs:
The power to shape shadows into solid, tangible forms.

5. Fear Induction:
The ability to manipulate the fears and anxieties of others.

6. Eclipse Manipulation:
Control over celestial events, particularly eclipses.

7. Shadowmeld:
The power to merge seamlessly with shadows, becoming one with the darkness.

8. Umbral Blades:
Conjuring weapons made of solid shadow.

9. Whispering Shadows:
The ability to communicate through shadows.

10. Nightmare Weaving:
Crafting illusions and dreams that induce nightmares.

11. Corruptive Touch:

The power to taint or corrupt objects with shadows, extremely rare.

Court of Infernal Night

King Helroth of Inferna

Night Fae, or demon Fae, are beings associated with dark and malevolent powers aligned with the forces of night and demonic creatures through zar.

Night Fae Abilities

1. Infernal Manipulation:

Control over hellfire, allowing them to conjure and manipulate flames with demonic properties.

2. Soul Draining:

The ability to extract and consume the life force or essence of living beings, leaving them weakened or lifeless.

3. Cursed Illusions:

Creation of illusions that induce fear, despair, or madness in those who witness them.

4. Necromancy:

Command over the dead, allowing them to raise undead minions or manipulate the forces of death.

5. Pact Making:

The ability to forge binding contracts or pacts with mortals, exchanging power for a steep price.

6. Cursed Enchantments:

Creation of cursed artifacts or objects that bring misfortune, chaos, or corruption to those who possess them.

7. Blood Magic:

Utilization of dark rituals involving the sacrifice or manipulation of blood to achieve magical effects.

8. Astral Possession:

The ability to temporarily possess the bodies of others, manipulating them to serve the demon court's goals.

9. Nightmare Realms:

Creation of pocket dimensions or realms that reflect the twisted and nightmarish nature of the demon court.

Acknowledgments

A huge and wholehearted thank you to my dedicated readers! I could not do this without you. I love hearing from you and your enthusiasm for the characters and story. You are the best!

A special thank you to my loving and supportive husband who always understood my need for escaping into a good book (or TV show!). He inspires me to try harder and push further every day. And of course my mother who is the guiding force behind everything I do and made me everything I am today. Without her, I literally could not write—because she's also my part-time babysitter! To my father who will always live on in my dreams. And finally, my little hellions, Alexander and Stella, who bring an unimaginable amount of joy, adventure and craziness to my life everyday.

A big thank you to Stefanie from Seventhstar Designs, for creating a beautiful book cover, to Samaiya Beaumont for the lovely header designs, character art and all the swag. I could never come up with all the ideas that you do! Thank you to my editor Rachel for not only questioning all the things but also getting a laugh out of me every time. And a special thank you to my dedicated beta reader and best VA ever, Sarah. You've been my sounding board on everything from cover ideas, blurbs, and story details. Not to mention doing everything behind the scenes. And to my ARC readers who caught spelling errors, and were all around amazing.

Thank you to all my family and friends, author and blogger friends who let me bounce ideas off of them and listened to my struggles as an author and self-publisher. I appreciate it more than you all will ever know.

    ~ G.K.

USA Today Bestselling Author, G.K. De Rosa has always had a passion for all things fantasy and romance. Growing up, she loved to read, devouring books in a single sitting. She attended Catholic school where reading and writing were an intense part of the curriculum, and she credits her amazing teachers for instilling in her a love of storytelling. As an adult, her favorite books were always young adult novels, and she remains a self-proclaimed fifteen year-old at heart. When she's not reading, writing or watching way too many TV shows, she's traveling and eating around the world with her family. G.K. DeRosa currently lives in

South Florida with her real life Prince Charming and their little royals.

www.gkderosa.com